image comics presents

THE WALKING DEAD™

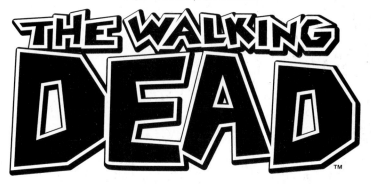

ROBERT KIRKMAN
CREATOR, WRITER

CHARLIE ADLARD
PENCILER, INKER

CLIFF RATHBURN
GRAY TONES

RUS WOOTON
LETTERER

CHARLIE ADLARD
&
CLIFF RATHBURN
COVER

For SKYBOUND ENTERTAINMENT

Robert Kirkman - CEO
J.J. Didde - President
Sina Grace - Editorial Director
Shawn Kirkham - Director of Business Development
Tim Daniel - Digital Content Manager
Chad Manion - Assistant to Mr. Grace
Sydney Pennington - Assistant to Mr. Kirkham
Feldman Public Relations LA - Public Relations

FOR INTERNATIONAL RIGHTS INQUIRIES,
PLEASE CONTACT FOREIGN@SKYBOUND.COM

WWW.SKYBOUND.COM

IMAGE COMICS, INC.
Robert Kirkman - chief operating officer
Erik Larsen - chief financial officer
Todd McFarlane - president
Marc Silvestri - chief executive officer
Jim Valentino - vice-president

Eric Stephenson - publisher
Todd Martinez - sales & licensing coordinator
Jennifer de Guzman - pr & marketing director
Branwyn Bigglestone - accounts manager
Emily Miller - administrative assistant
Jamie Parreno - marketing assistant
Sarah deLaine - events coordinator
Kevin Yuen - digital rights coordinator
Tyler Shainline - production manager
Drew Gill - art director
Jonathan Chan - design director
Monica Garcia - production artist
Vincent Kukua - production artist
Jana Cook - production artist

www.imagecomics.com

THE WALKING DEAD, VOL. 9: HERE WE REMAIN. Third Printing. Published by Image Comics, Inc. Office of publication: 2134 Allston Way, 2nd Floor, Berkeley, California 94704.

PRINTED IN THE USA

ISBN: 978-1-60706-022-2

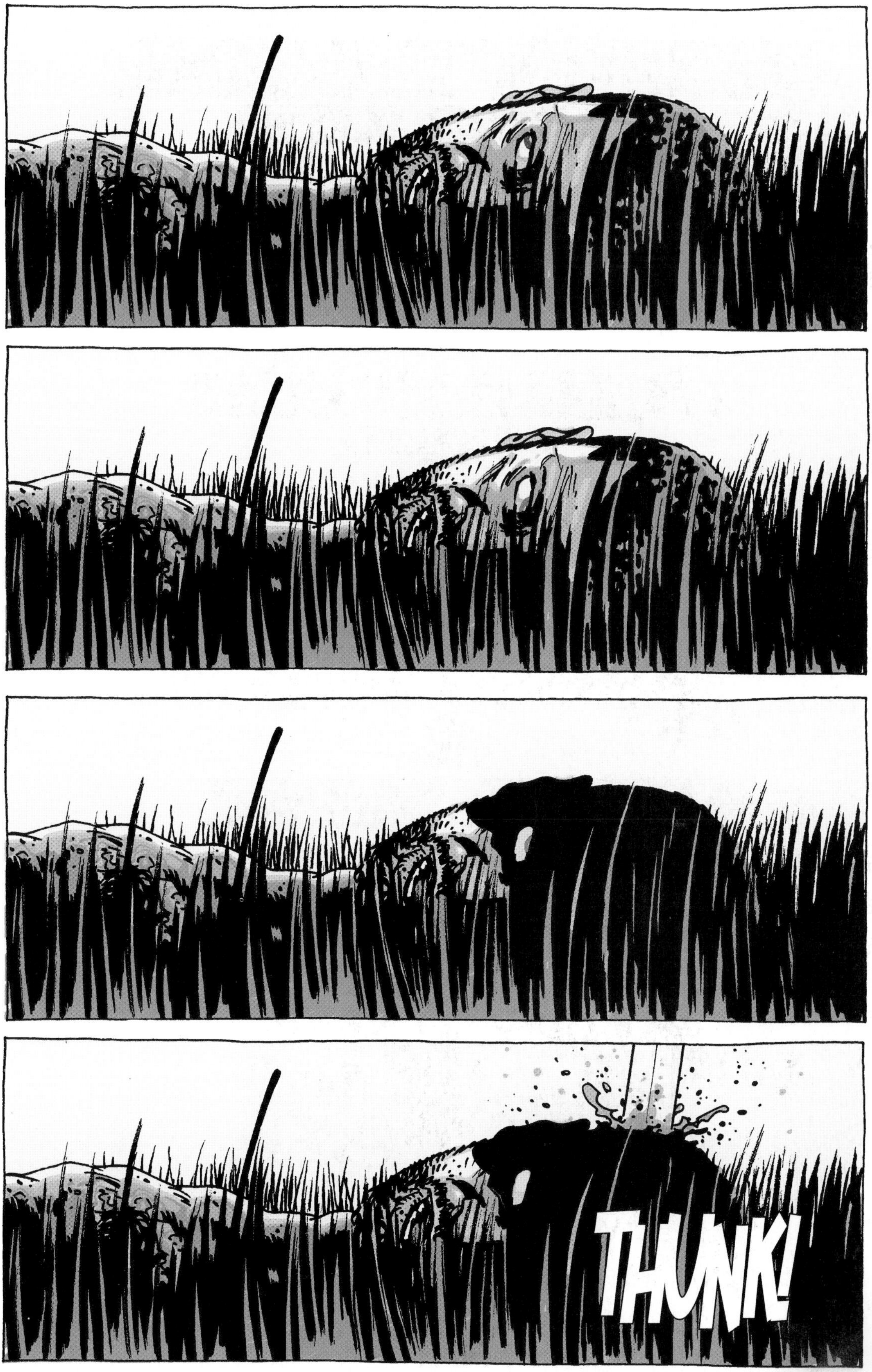
THUNK!

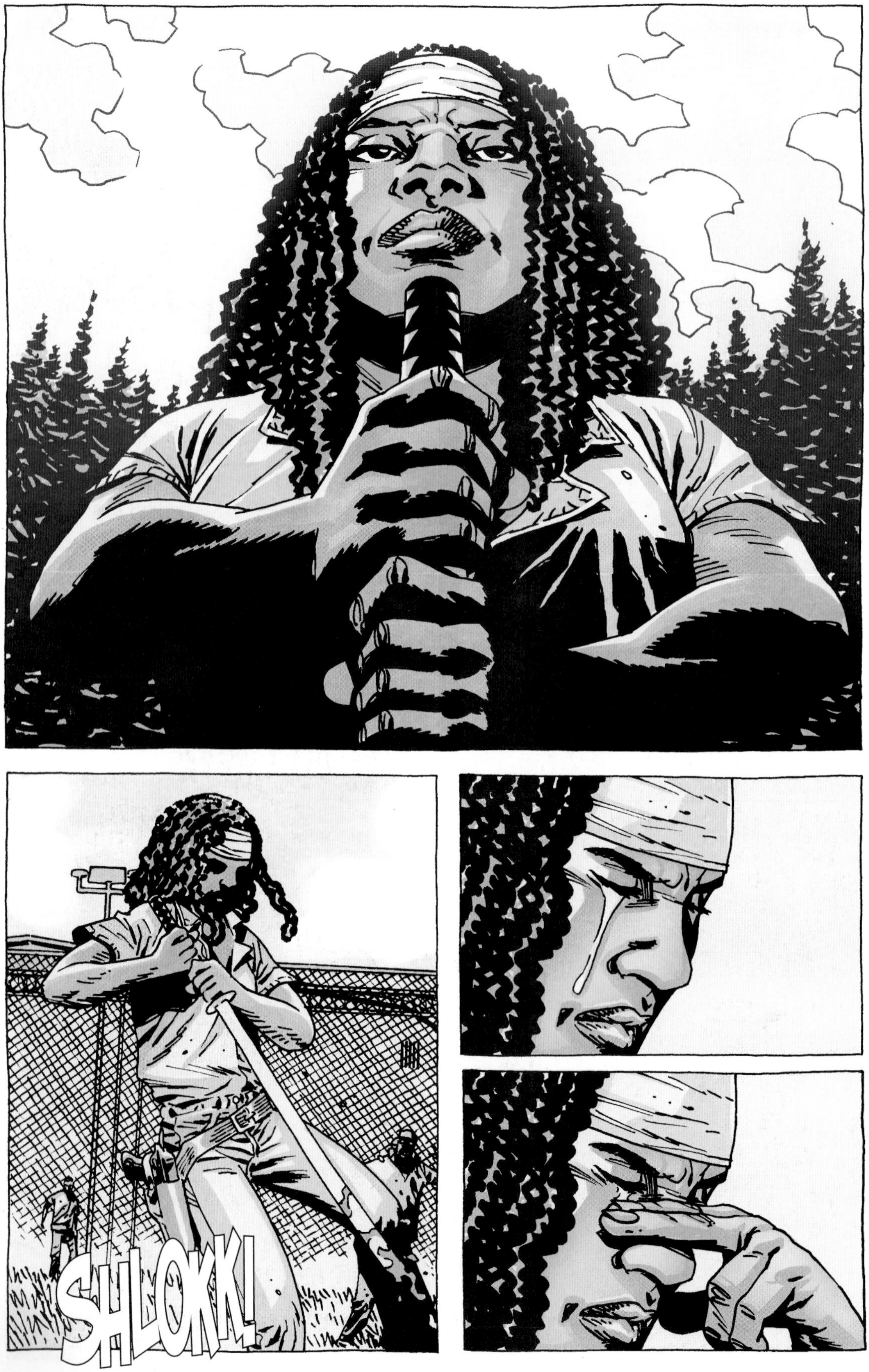
SHLOKK!

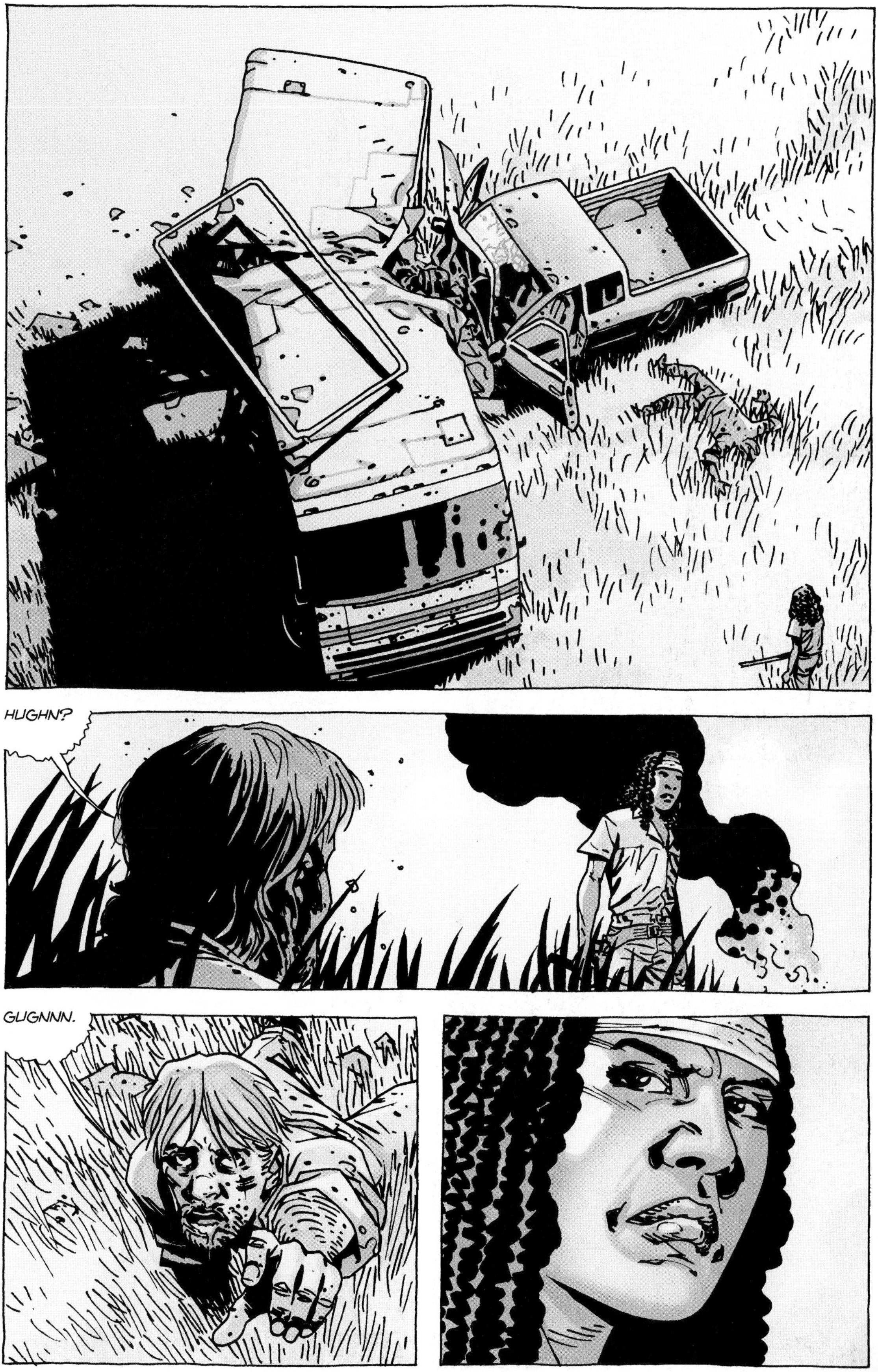
HUGHN?
GUGNNN.

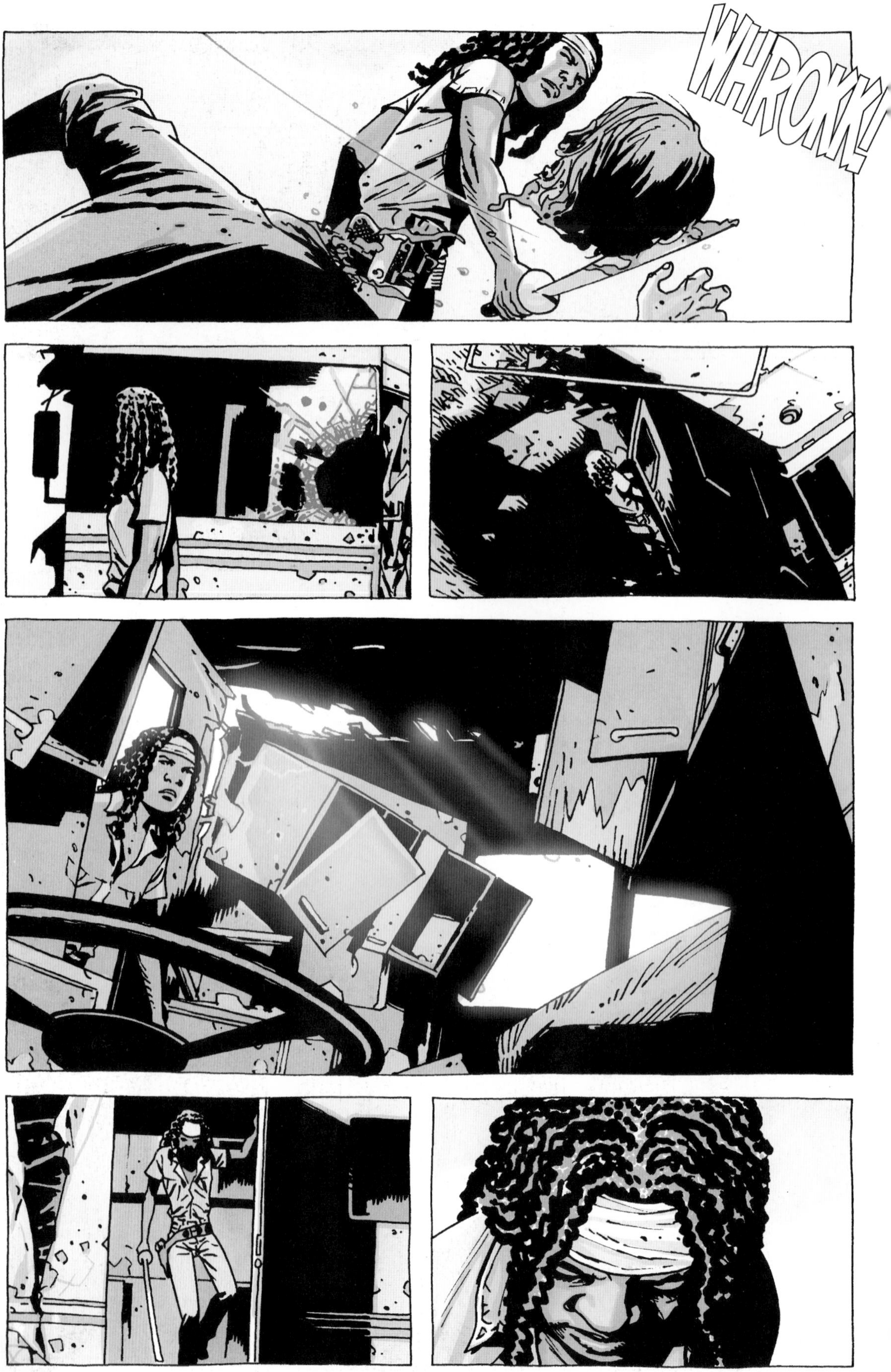
WHROKK!

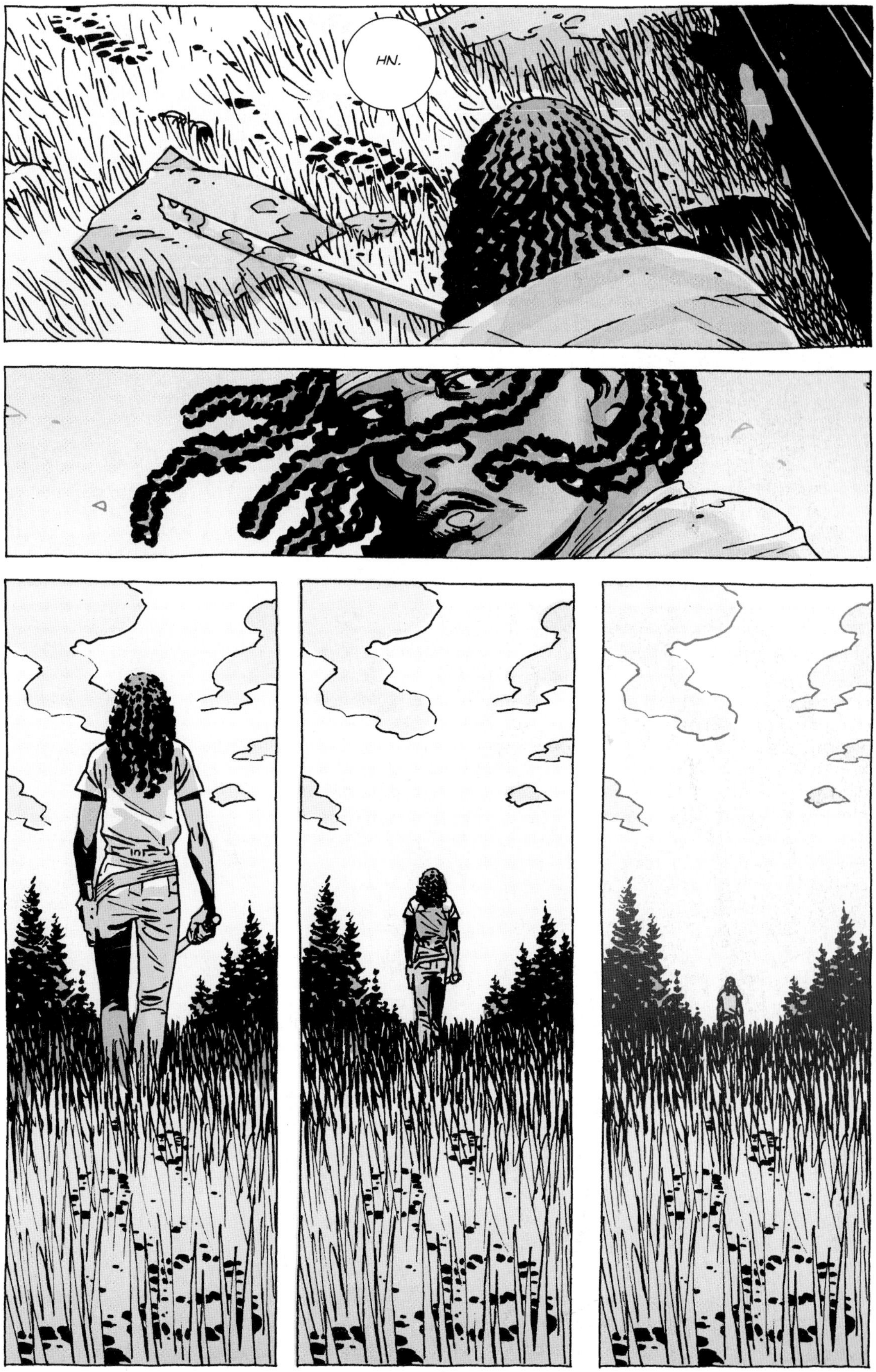
HN.

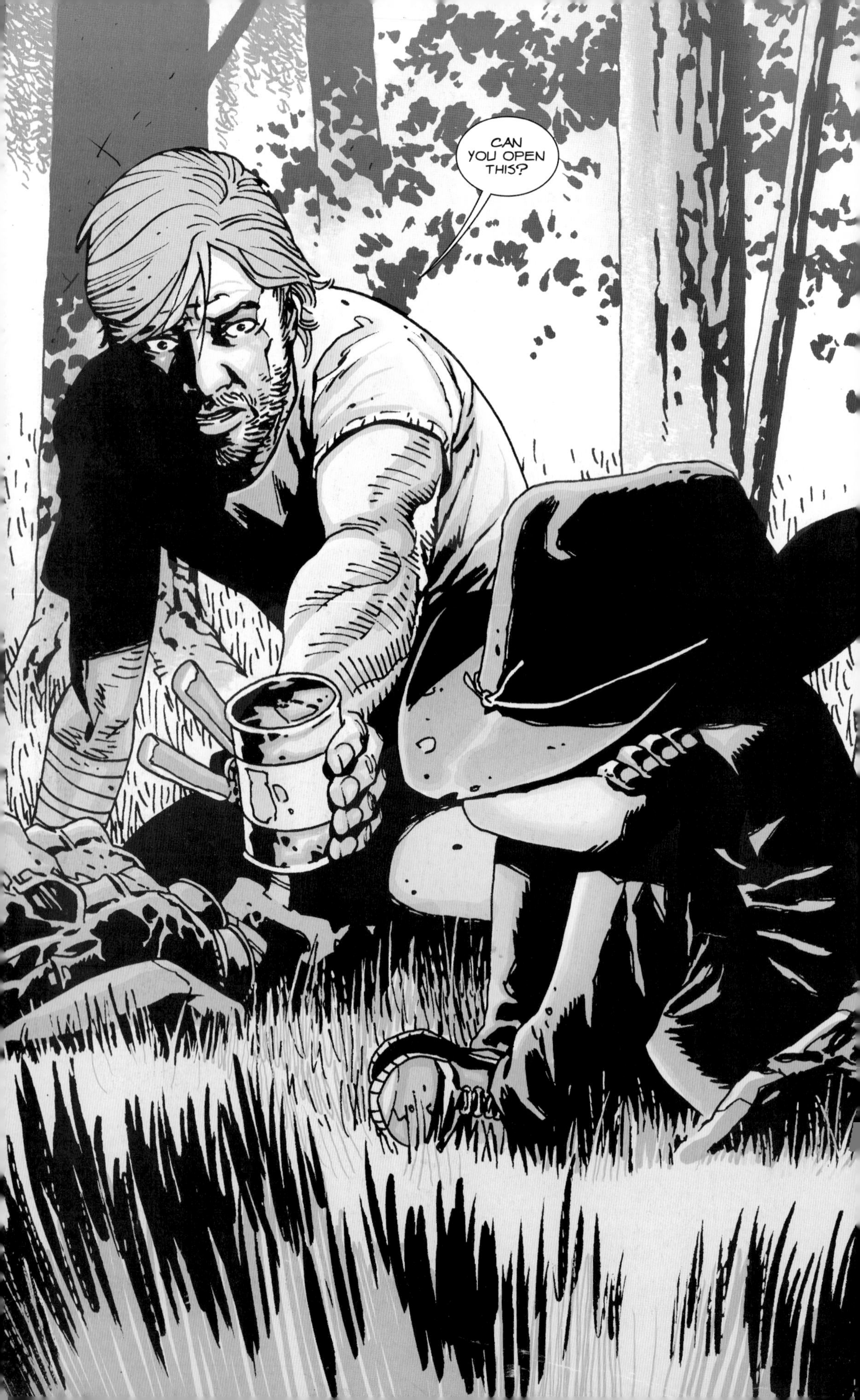
CAN YOU OPEN THIS?

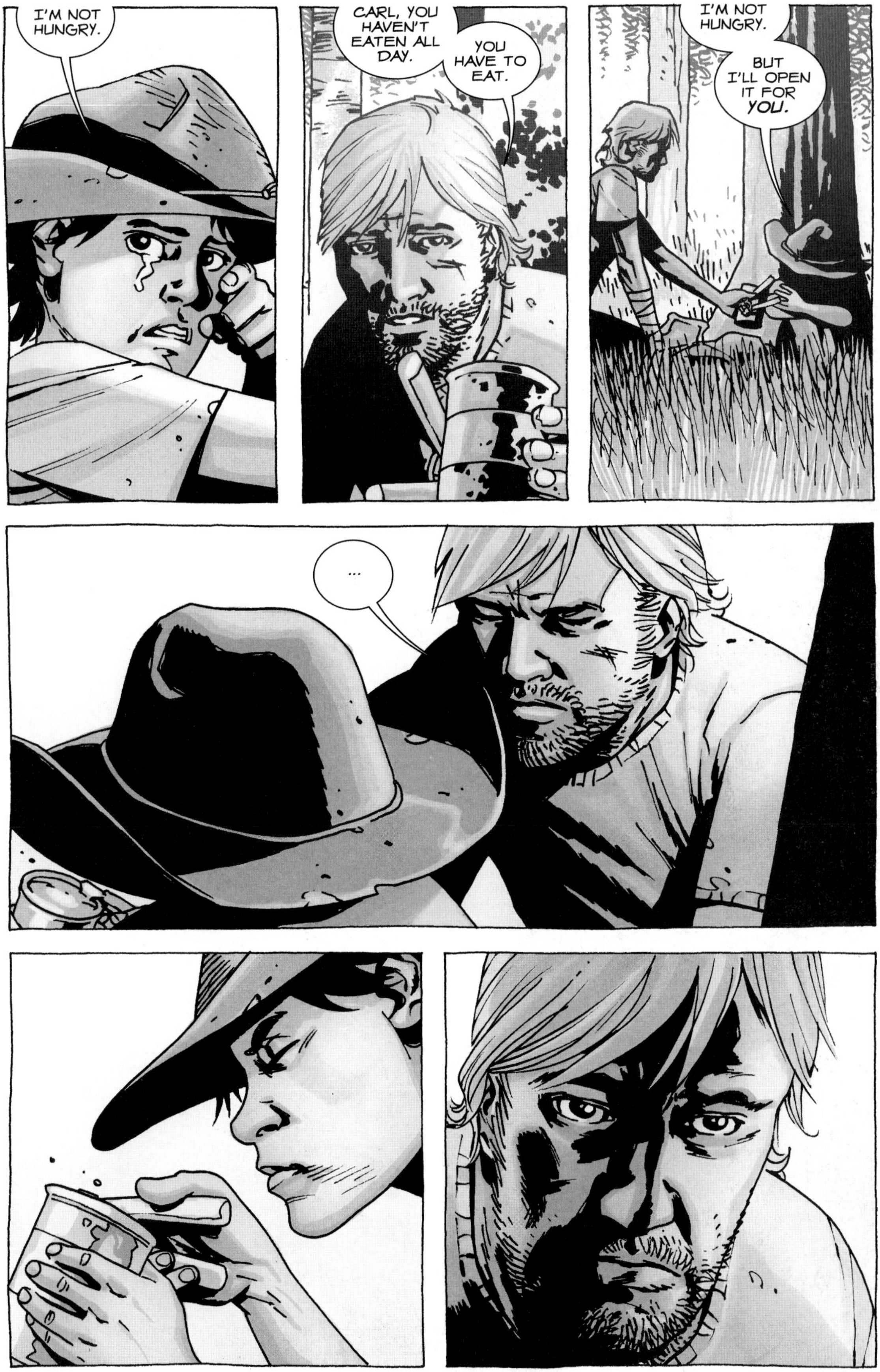
I'M NOT HUNGRY.
CARL, YOU HAVEN'T EATEN ALL DAY.
YOU HAVE TO EAT.
I'M NOT HUNGRY.
BUT I'LL OPEN IT FOR *YOU*.
...

THANKS.

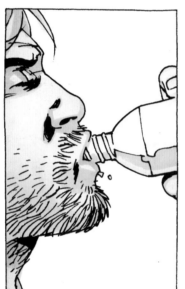

NO THANKS.

OKAY.

WE SHOULD PROBABLY GET MOVING ANYWAY-- FIND SOME SHELTER FOR THE NIGHT.

YOU GET HUNGRY, YOU LET ME KNOW. OKAY?

WE'LL STOP AGAIN-- WHENEVER YOU GET HUNGRY.

OKAY.

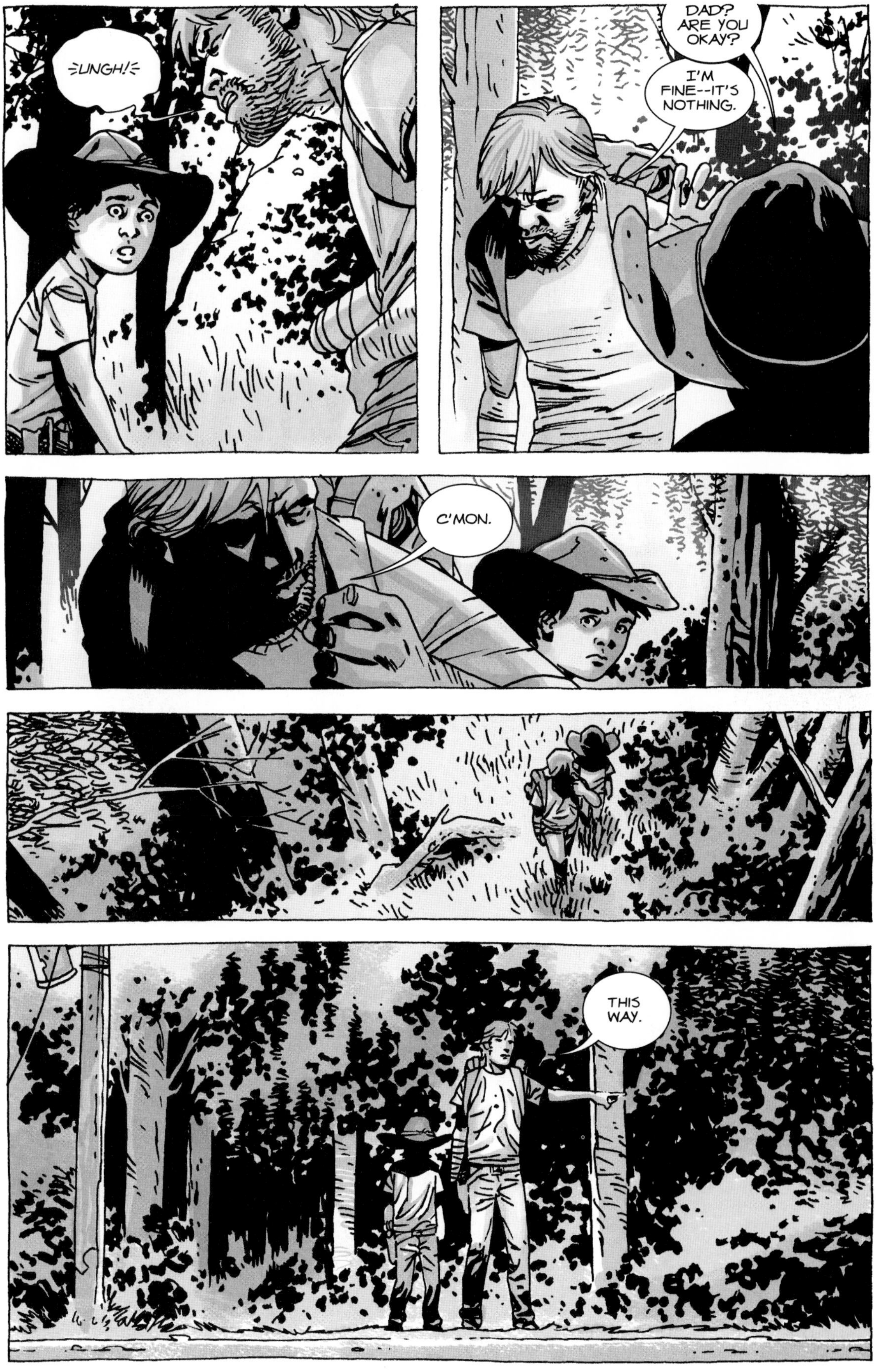
UNGH!
DAD? ARE YOU OKAY?
I'M FINE--IT'S NOTHING.
C'MON.
THIS WAY.

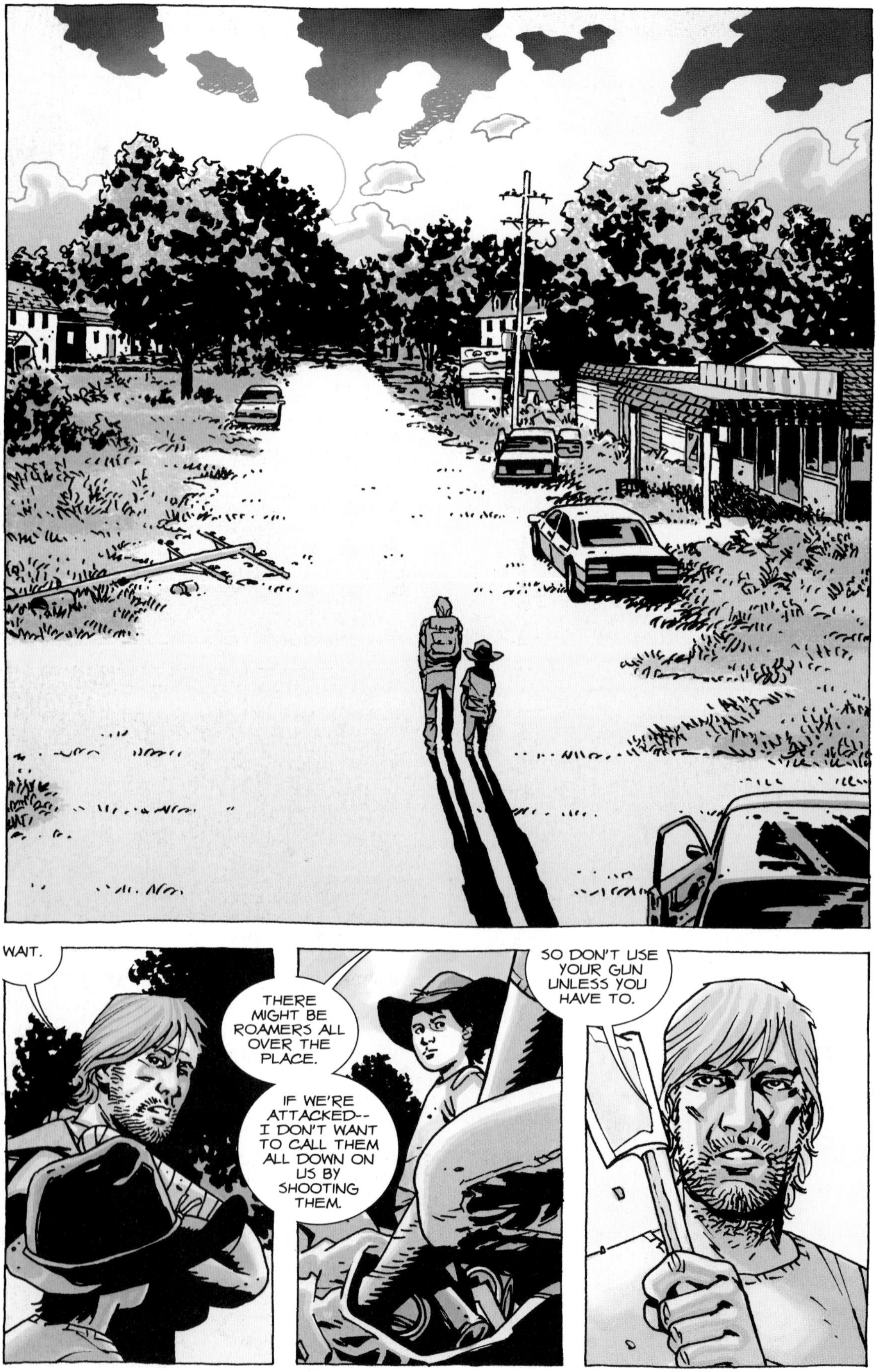
WAIT.
THERE MIGHT BE ROAMERS ALL OVER THE PLACE.
IF WE'RE ATTACKED-- I DON'T WANT TO CALL THEM ALL DOWN ON US BY SHOOTING THEM.
SO DON'T USE YOUR GUN UNLESS YOU HAVE TO.

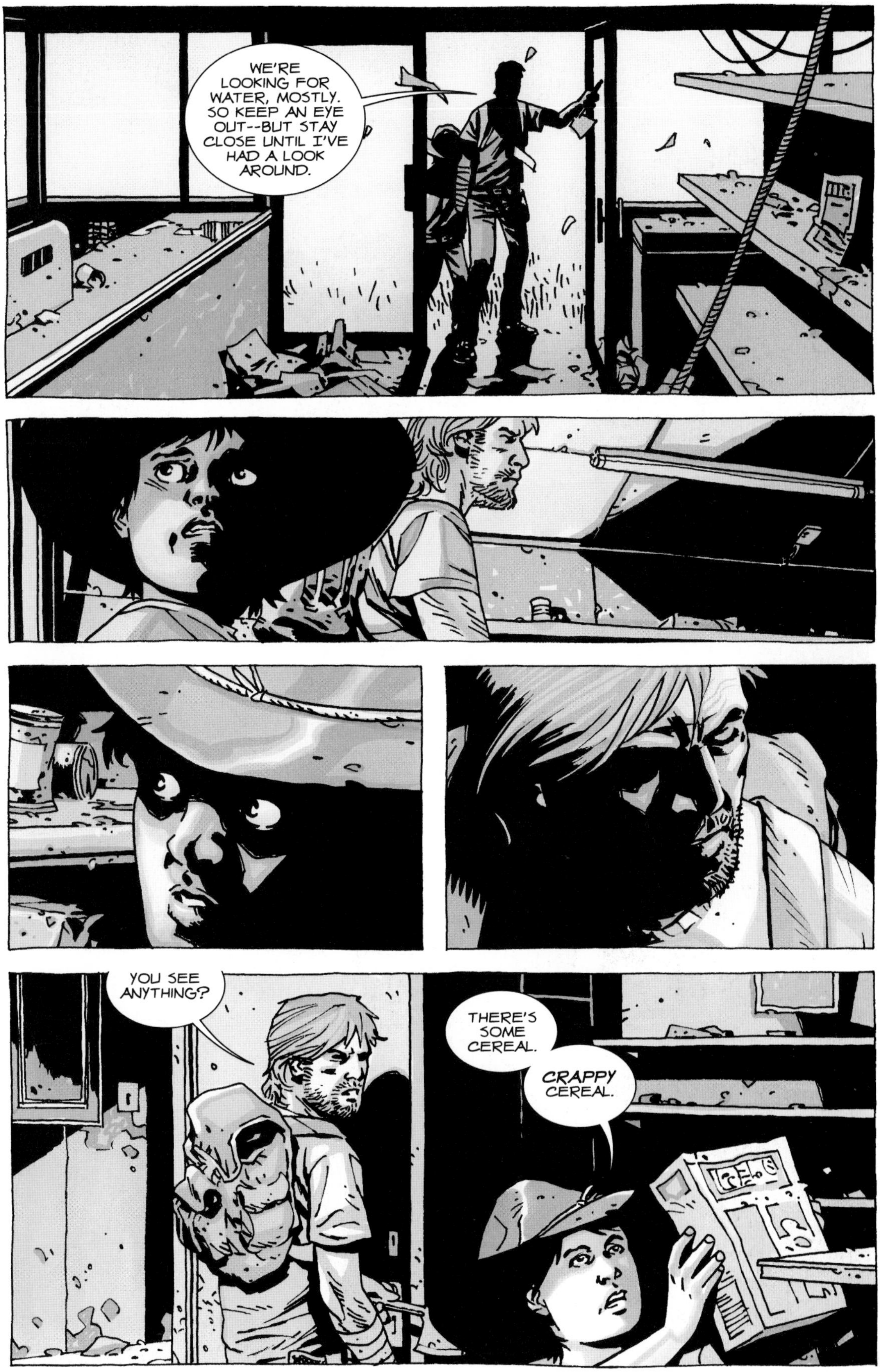
WE'RE LOOKING FOR WATER, MOSTLY. SO KEEP AN EYE OUT--BUT STAY CLOSE UNTIL I'VE HAD A LOOK AROUND.
YOU SEE ANYTHING?
THERE'S SOME CEREAL.
CRAPPY CEREAL.

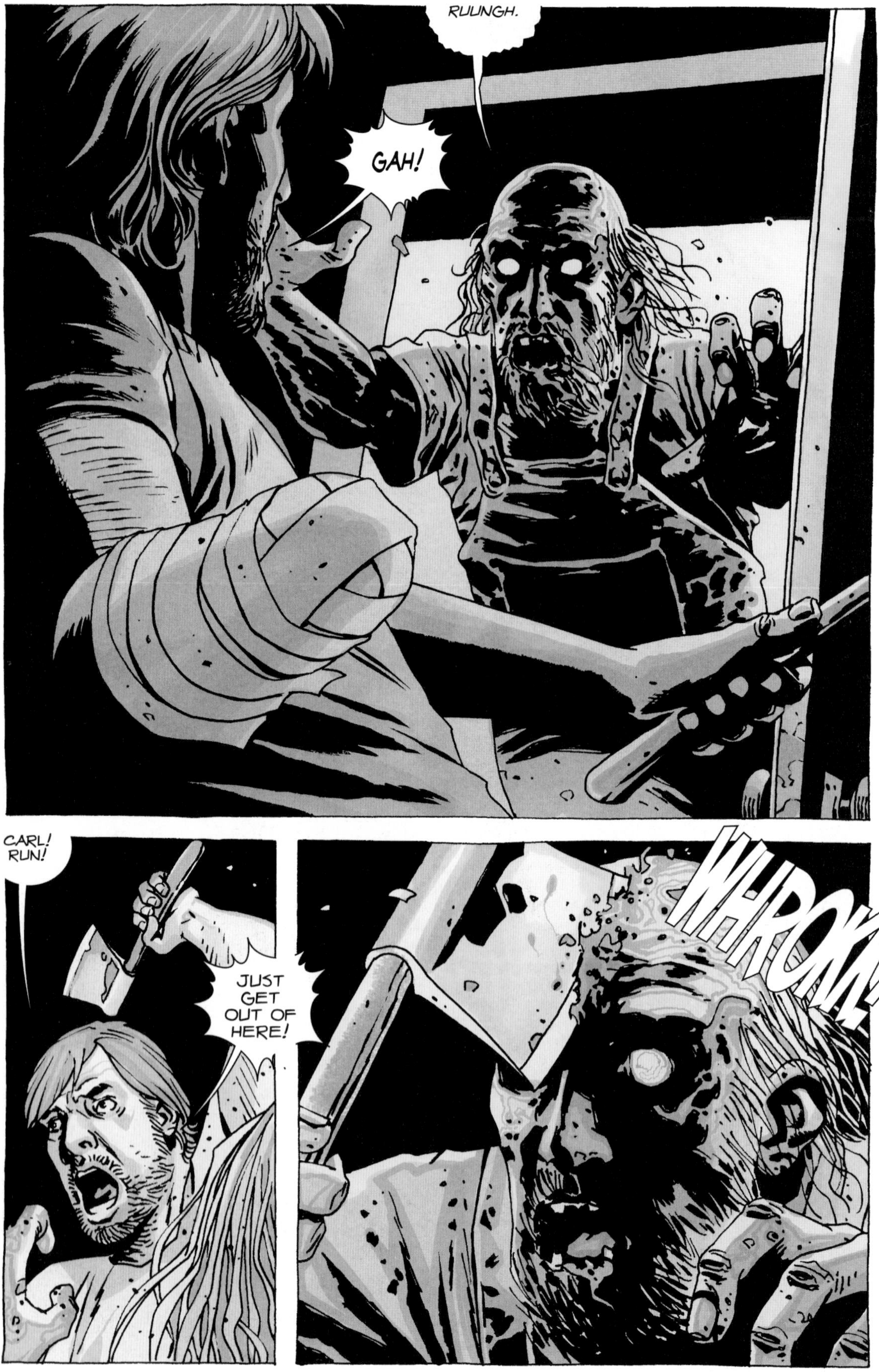
RUUNGH.
GAH!
CARL! RUN!
JUST GET OUT OF HERE!
WHROKK!

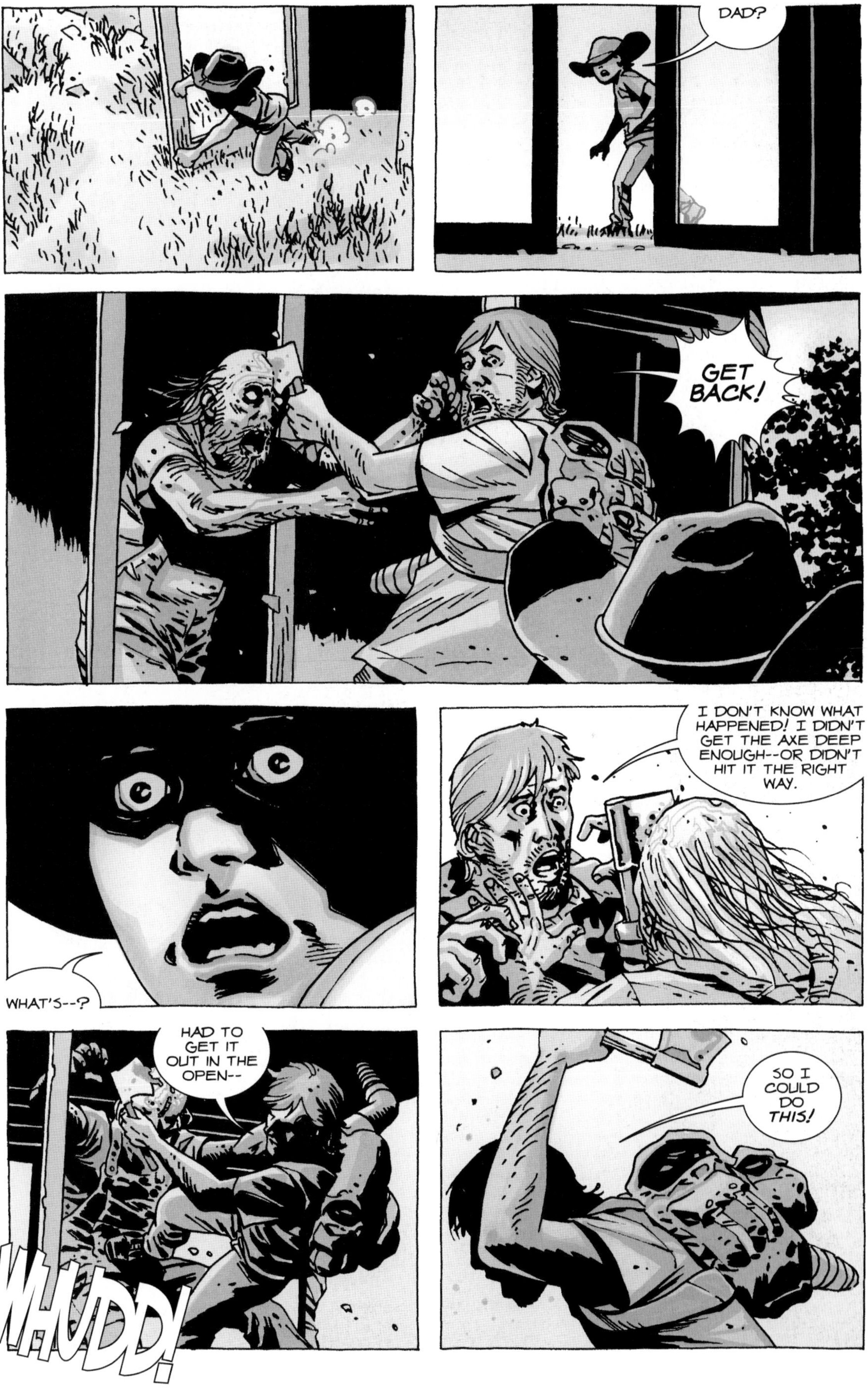
DAD?
GET BACK!
WHAT'S--?
I DON'T KNOW WHAT HAPPENED! I DIDN'T GET THE AXE DEEP ENOUGH--OR DIDN'T HIT IT THE RIGHT WAY.
HAD TO GET IT OUT IN THE OPEN--
WHUDD!
SO I COULD DO THIS!

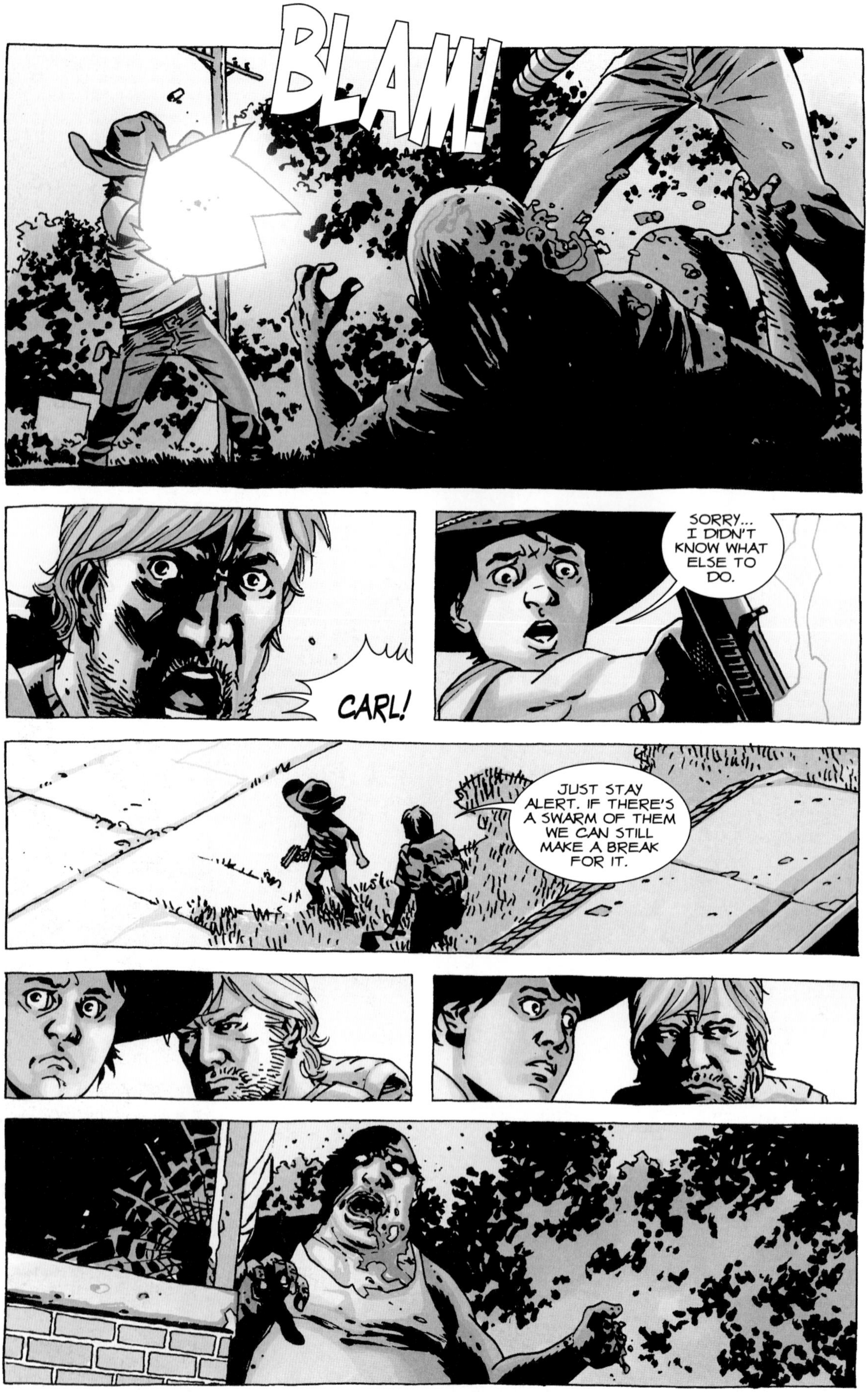
BLAM!
CARL!
SORRY... I DIDN'T KNOW WHAT ELSE TO DO.
JUST STAY ALERT. IF THERE'S A SWARM OF THEM WE CAN STILL MAKE A BREAK FOR IT.

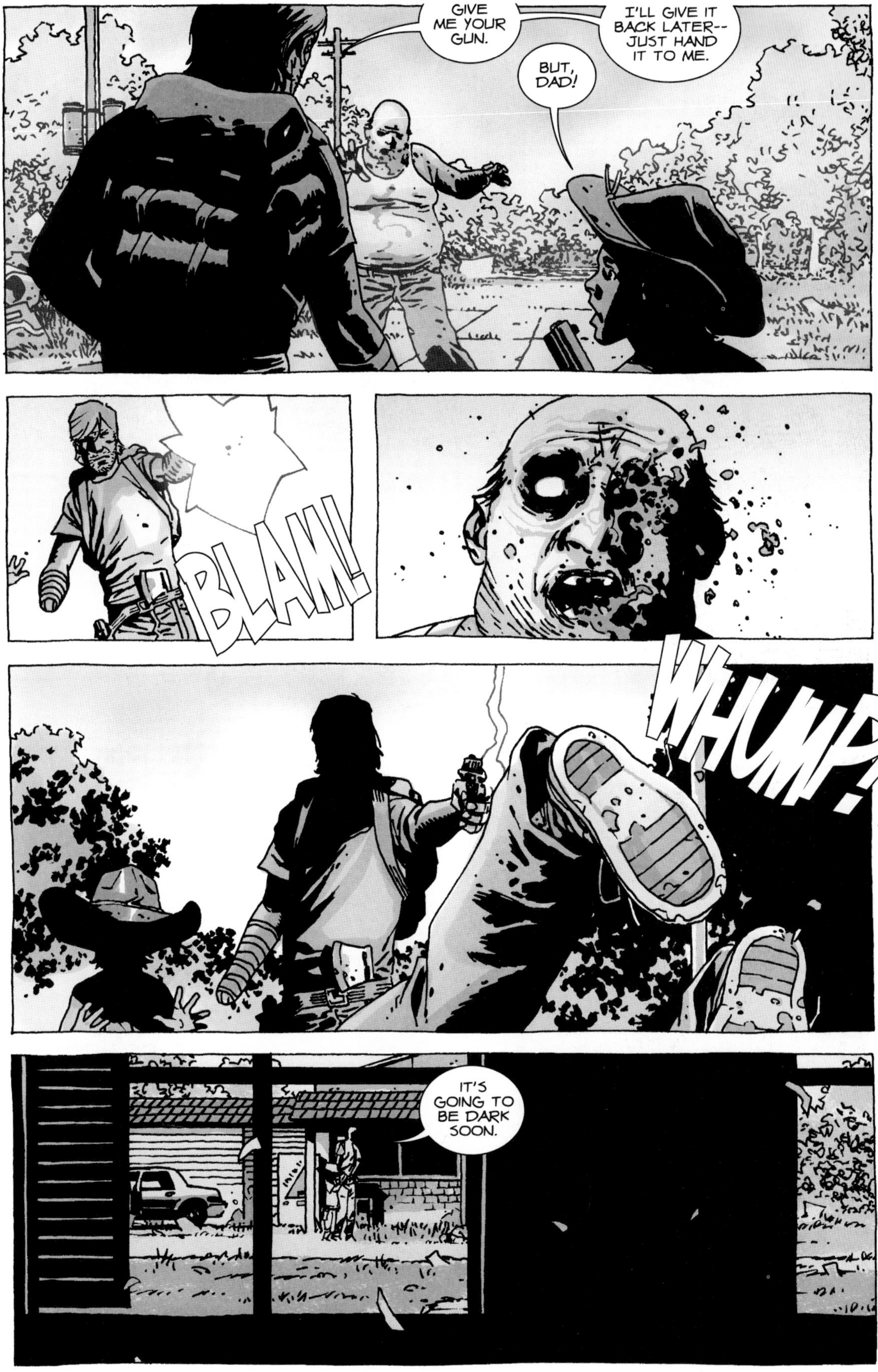
GIVE ME YOUR GUN.
I'LL GIVE IT BACK LATER-- JUST HAND IT TO ME.
BUT, DAD!
BLAM!
WHUMP!
IT'S GOING TO BE DARK SOON.

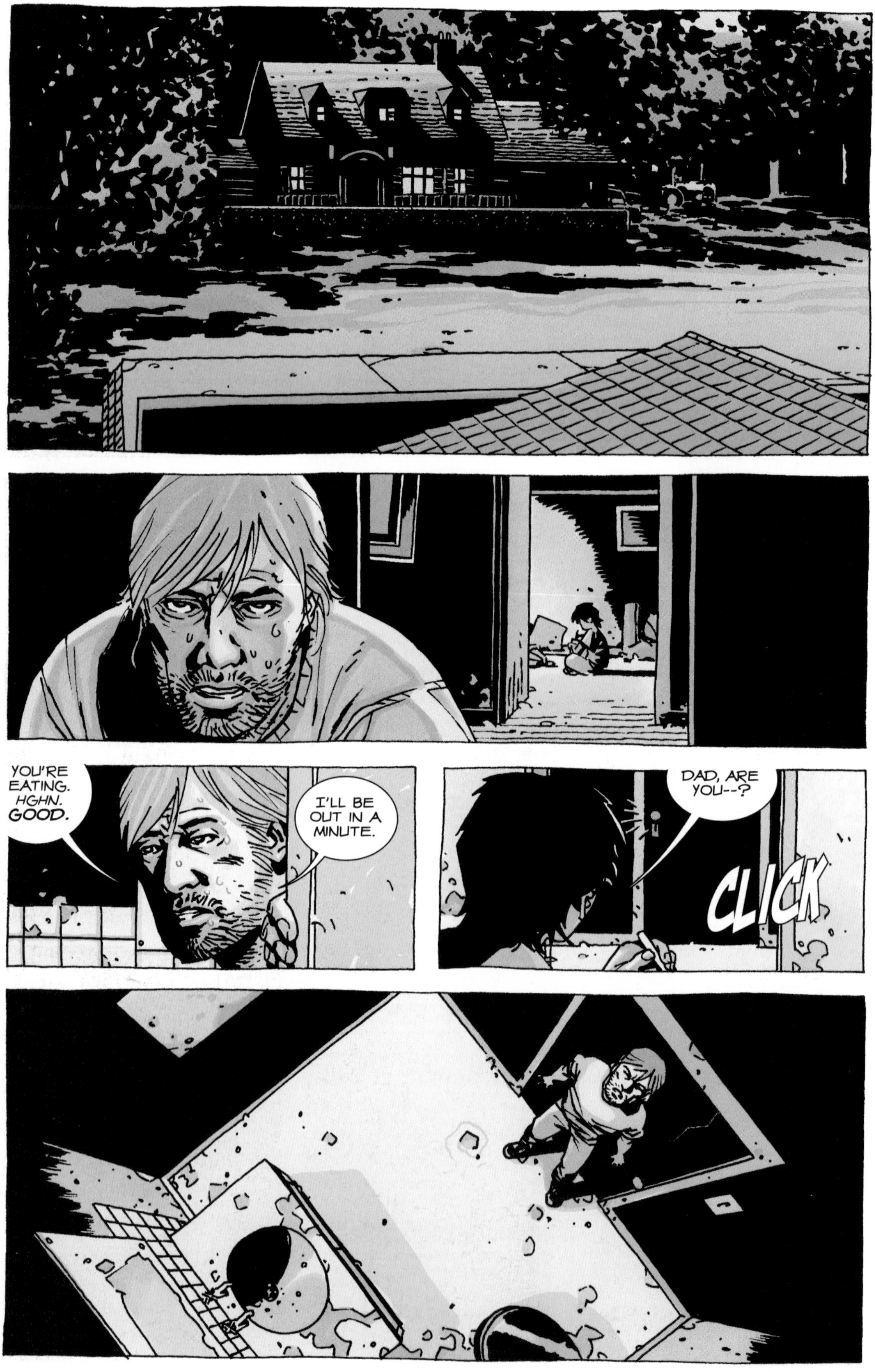
YOU'RE EATING. HGHN. GOOD.
I'LL BE OUT IN A MINUTE.
DAD, ARE YOU--?
CLICK

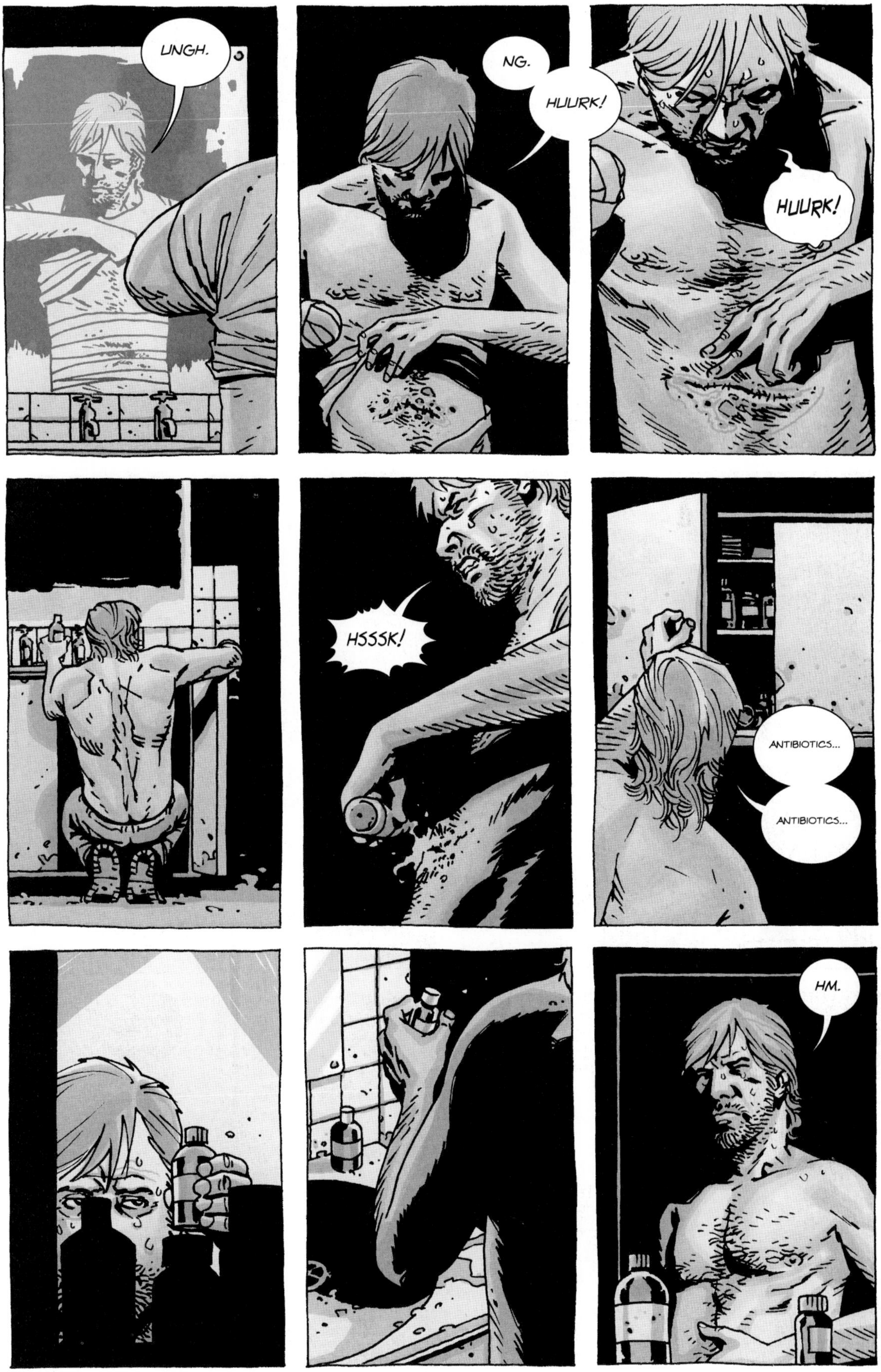
UNGH.
NG.
HUURK!
HUURK!
HSSSK!
ANTIBIOTICS...
ANTIBIOTICS...
HM.

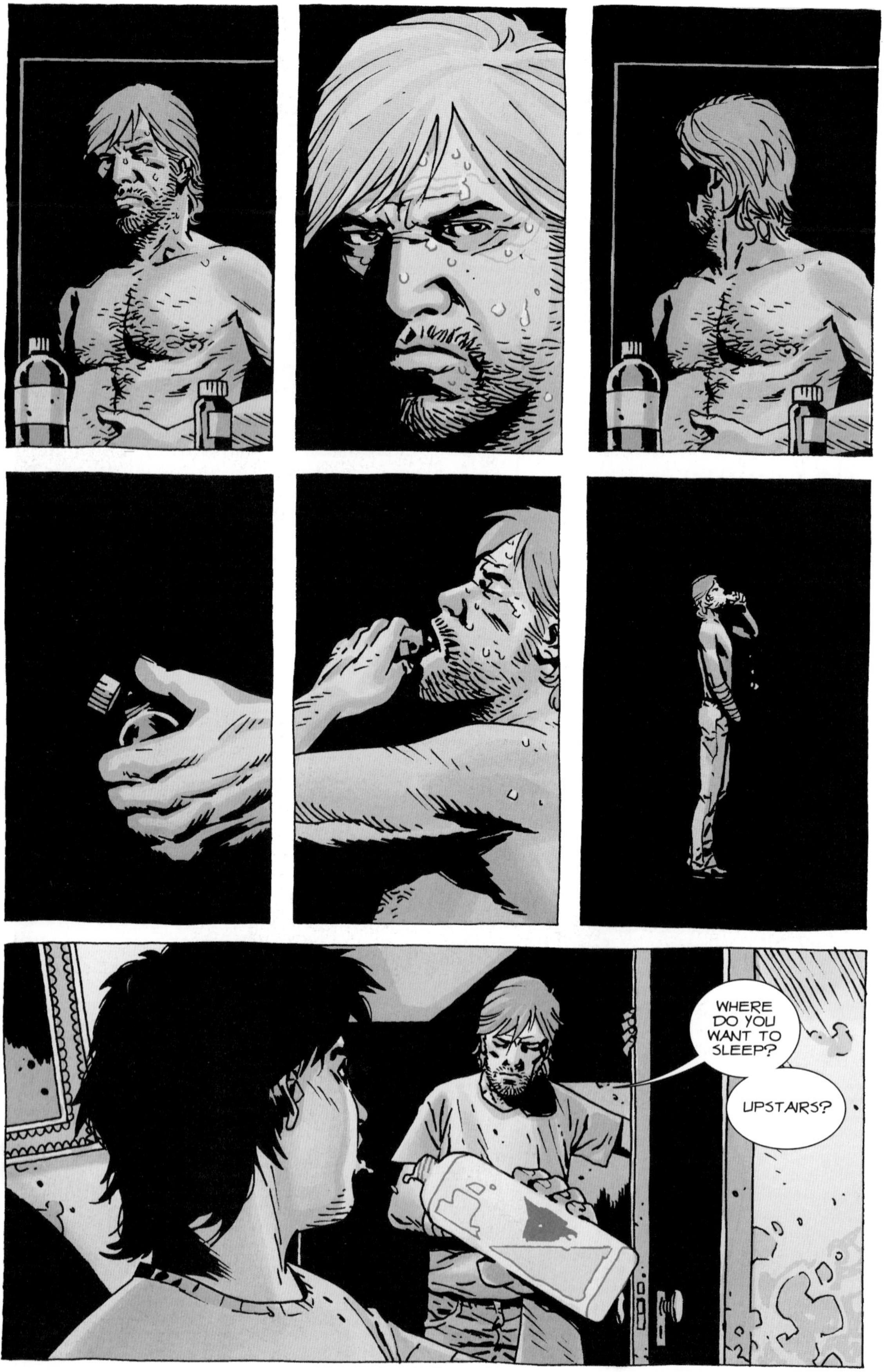
WHERE DO YOU WANT TO SLEEP?
UPSTAIRS?

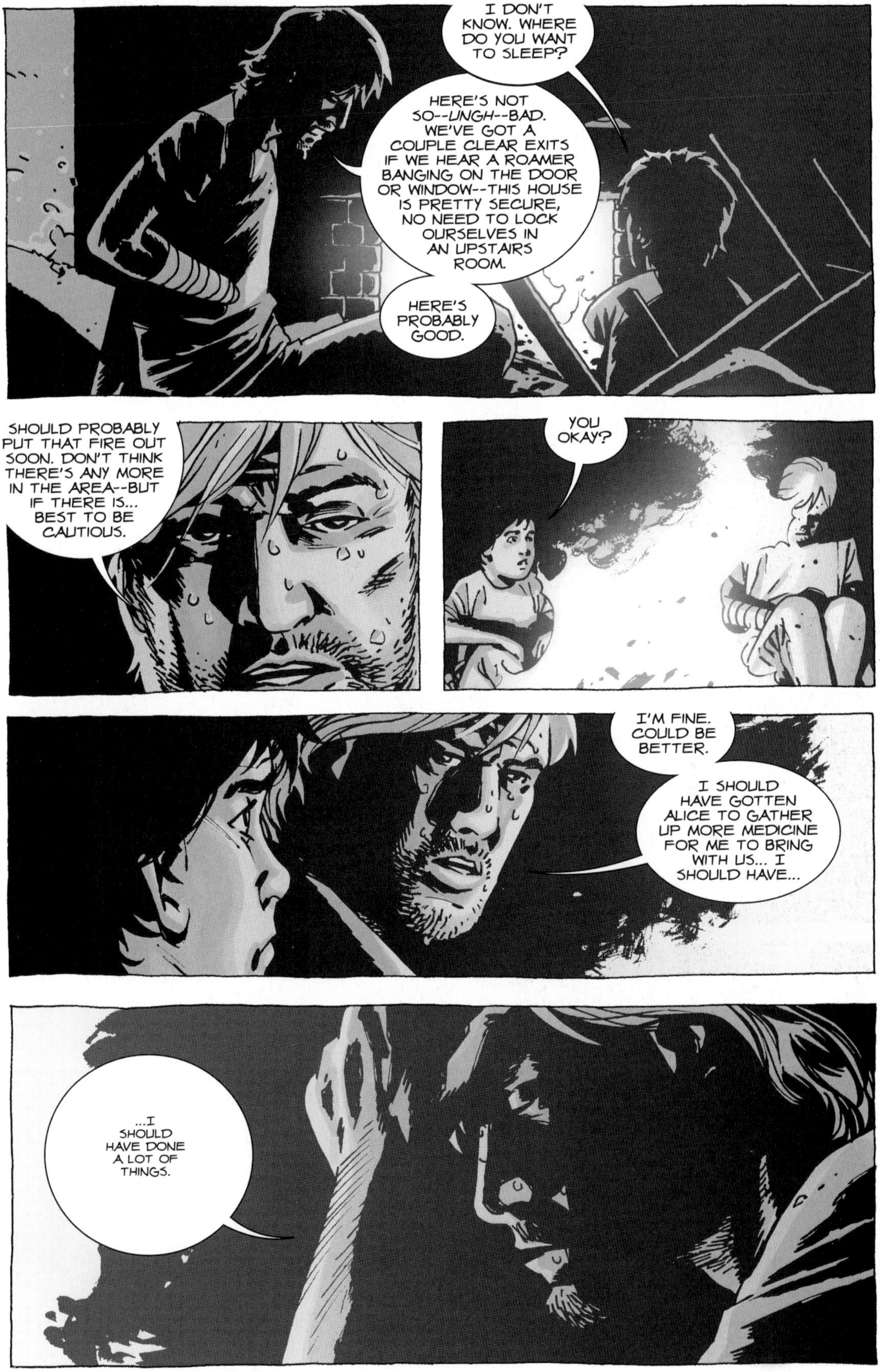
I DON'T KNOW. WHERE DO YOU WANT TO SLEEP?
HERE'S NOT SO--UNGH--BAD. WE'VE GOT A COUPLE CLEAR EXITS IF WE HEAR A ROAMER BANGING ON THE DOOR OR WINDOW--THIS HOUSE IS PRETTY SECURE, NO NEED TO LOCK OURSELVES IN AN UPSTAIRS ROOM.
HERE'S PROBABLY GOOD.
SHOULD PROBABLY PUT THAT FIRE OUT SOON. DON'T THINK THERE'S ANY MORE IN THE AREA--BUT IF THERE IS... BEST TO BE CAUTIOUS.
YOU OKAY?
I'M FINE. COULD BE BETTER.
I SHOULD HAVE GOTTEN ALICE TO GATHER UP MORE MEDICINE FOR ME TO BRING WITH US... I SHOULD HAVE...
...I SHOULD HAVE DONE A LOT OF THINGS.

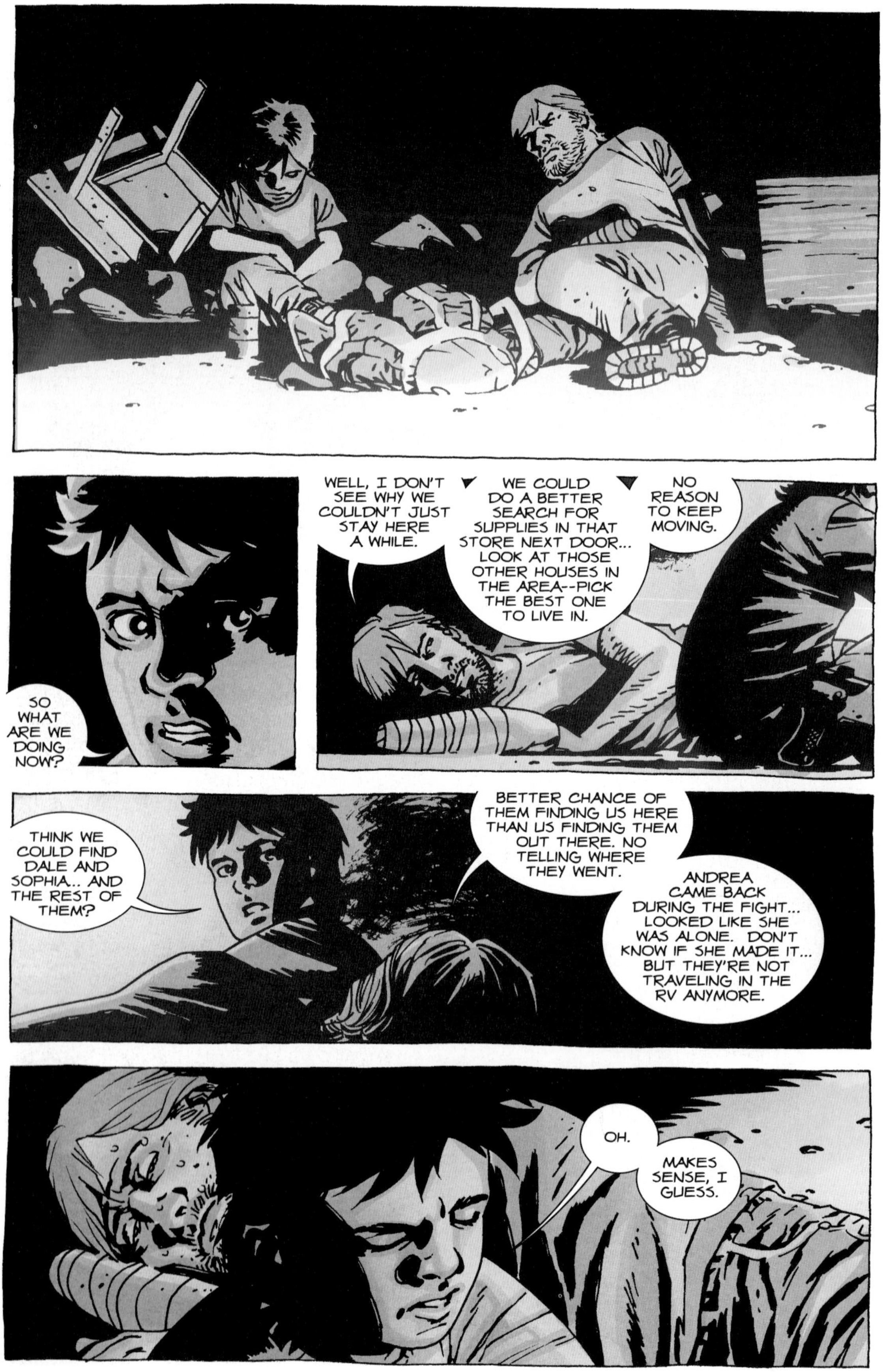
SO WHAT ARE WE DOING NOW?
WELL, I DON'T SEE WHY WE COULDN'T JUST STAY HERE A WHILE.
WE COULD DO A BETTER SEARCH FOR SUPPLIES IN THAT STORE NEXT DOOR... LOOK AT THOSE OTHER HOUSES IN THE AREA--PICK THE BEST ONE TO LIVE IN.
NO REASON TO KEEP MOVING.
THINK WE COULD FIND DALE AND SOPHIA... AND THE REST OF THEM?
BETTER CHANCE OF THEM FINDING US HERE THAN US FINDING THEM OUT THERE. NO TELLING WHERE THEY WENT.
ANDREA CAME BACK DURING THE FIGHT... LOOKED LIKE SHE WAS ALONE. DON'T KNOW IF SHE MADE IT... BUT THEY'RE NOT TRAVELING IN THE RV ANYMORE.
OH.
MAKES SENSE, I GUESS.

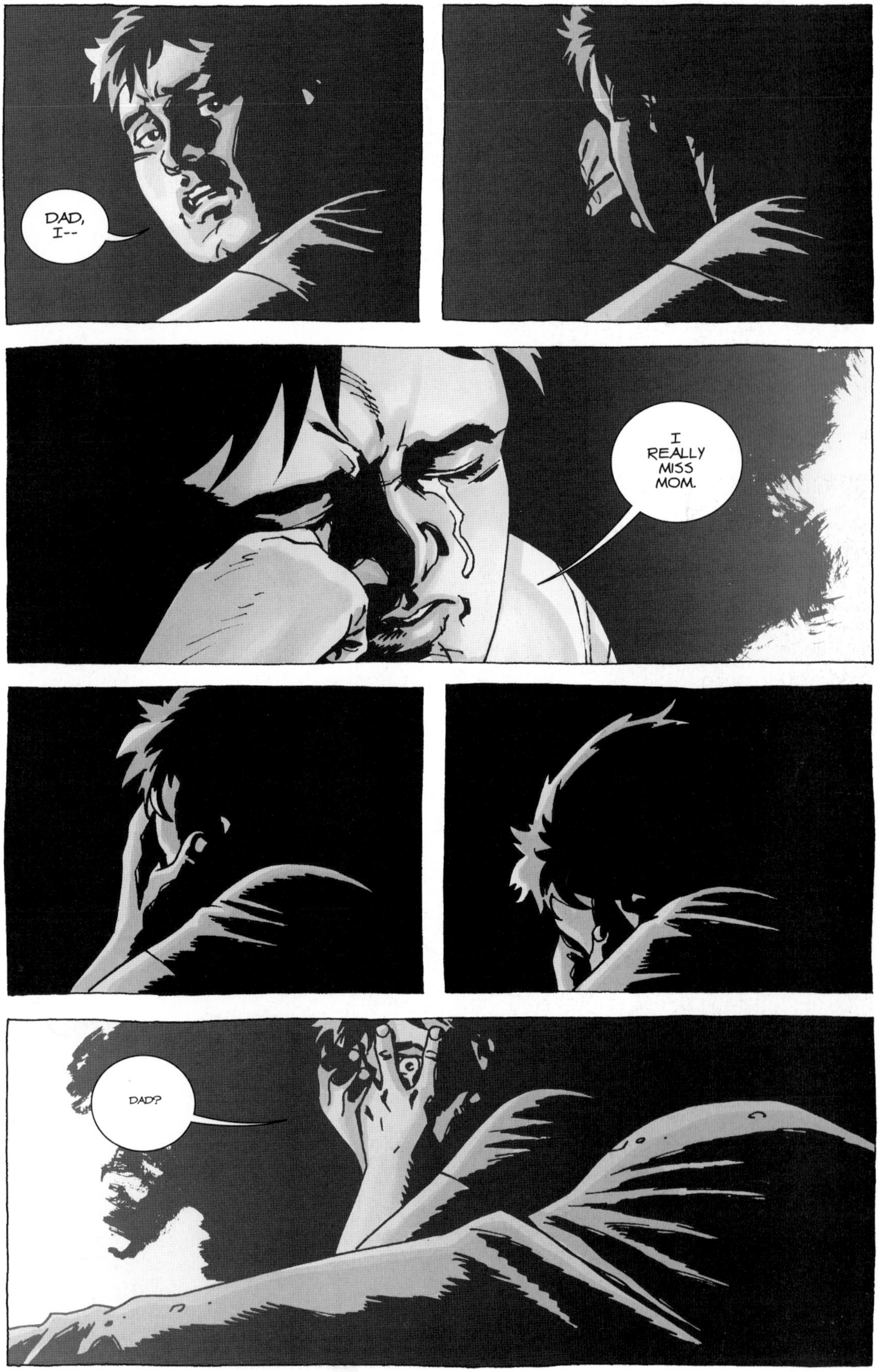
DAD, I--
I REALLY MISS MOM.
DAD?

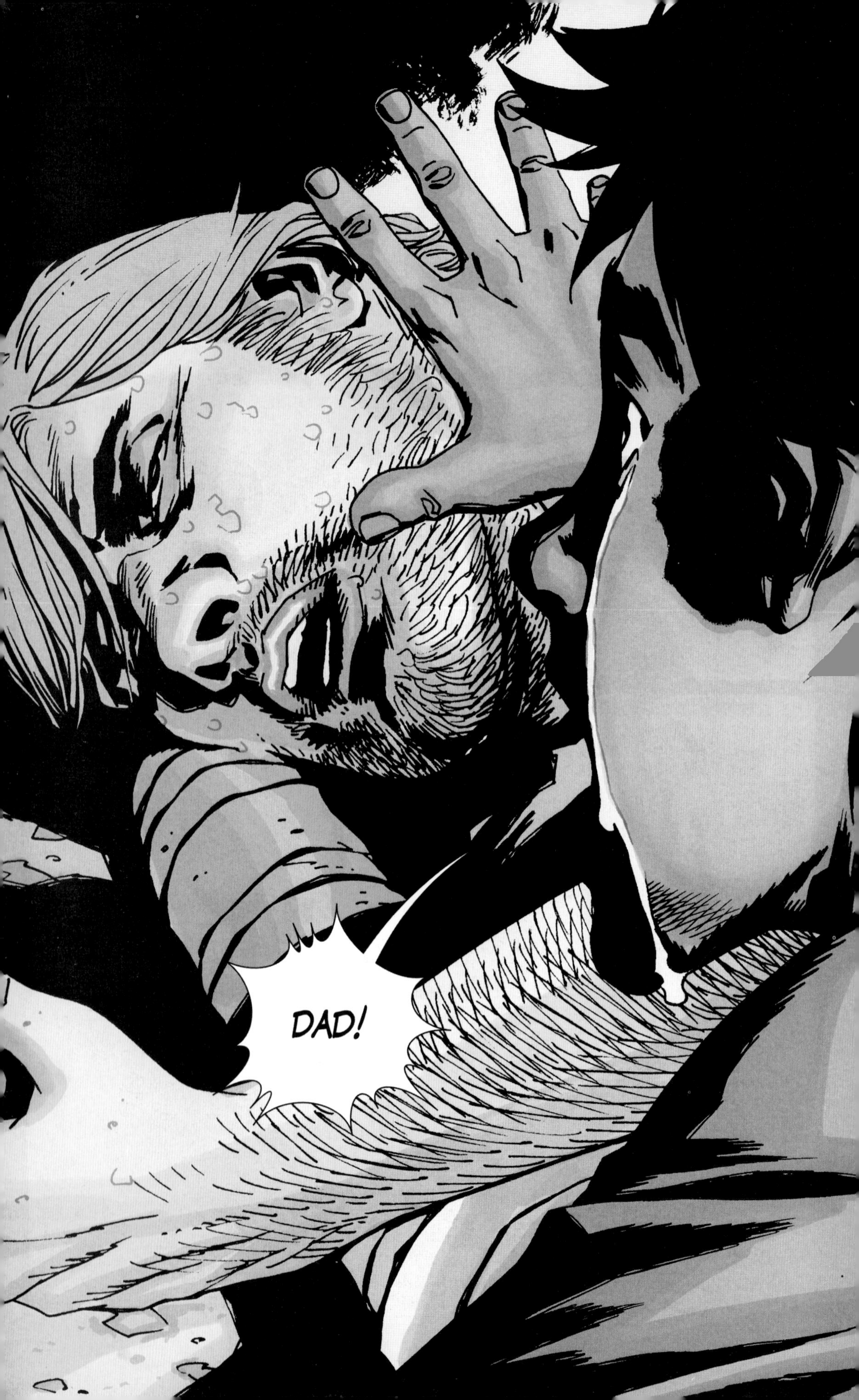
DAD!

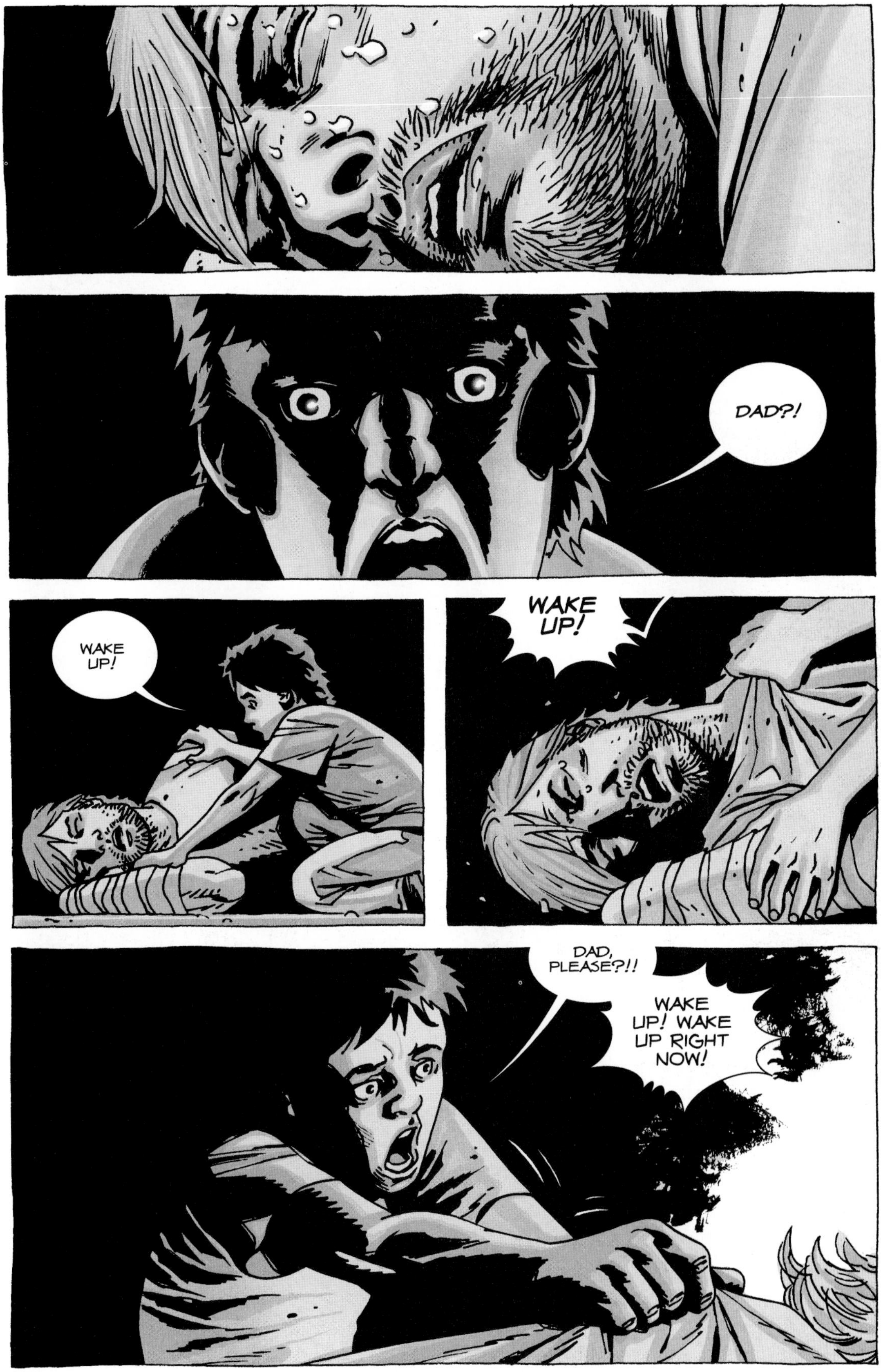
DAD?!
WAKE UP!
WAKE UP!
DAD, PLEASE?!!
WAKE UP! WAKE UP RIGHT NOW!

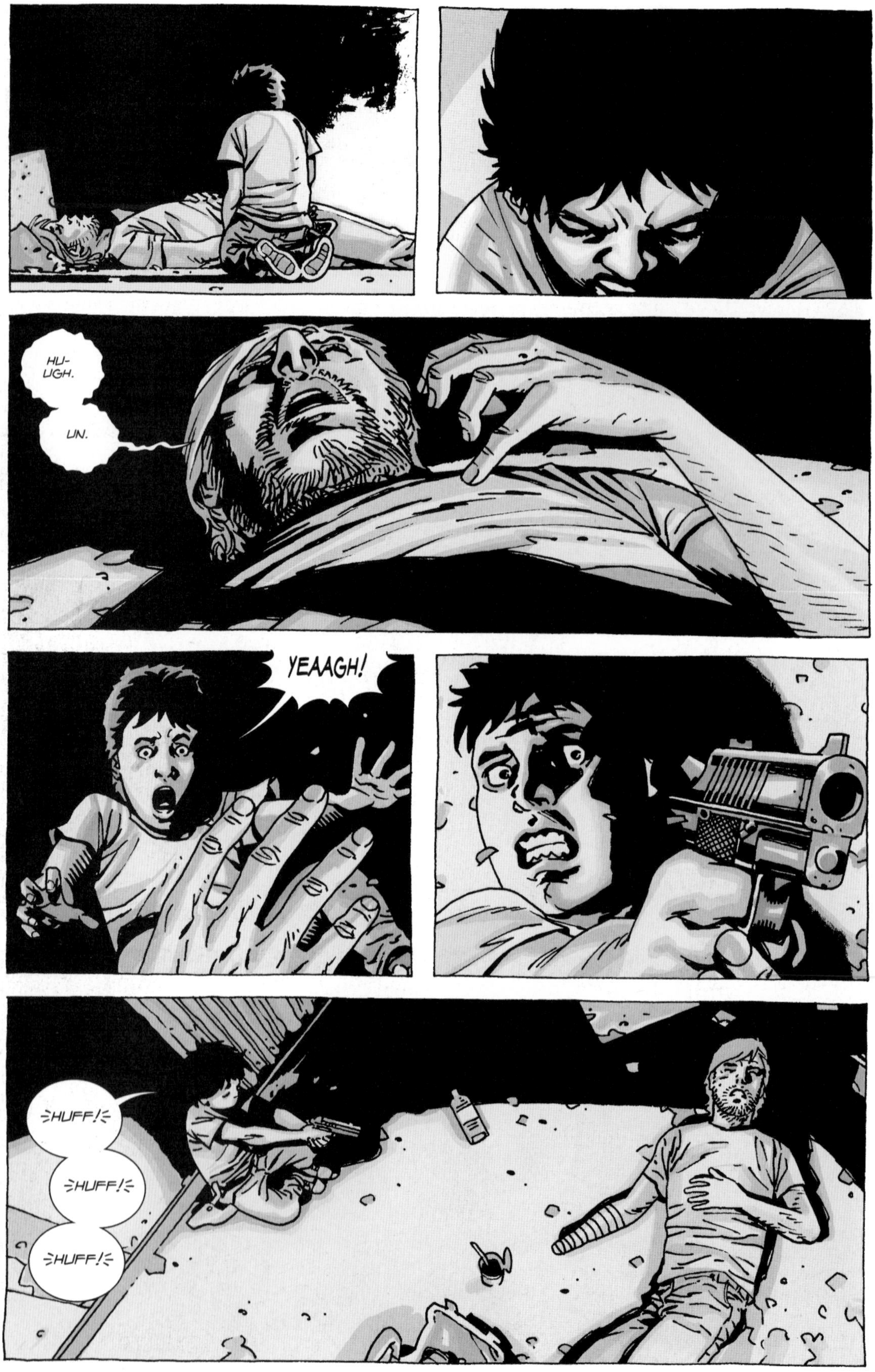
HU-UGH.
UN.
YEAAGH!
HUFF!
HUFF!
HUFF!

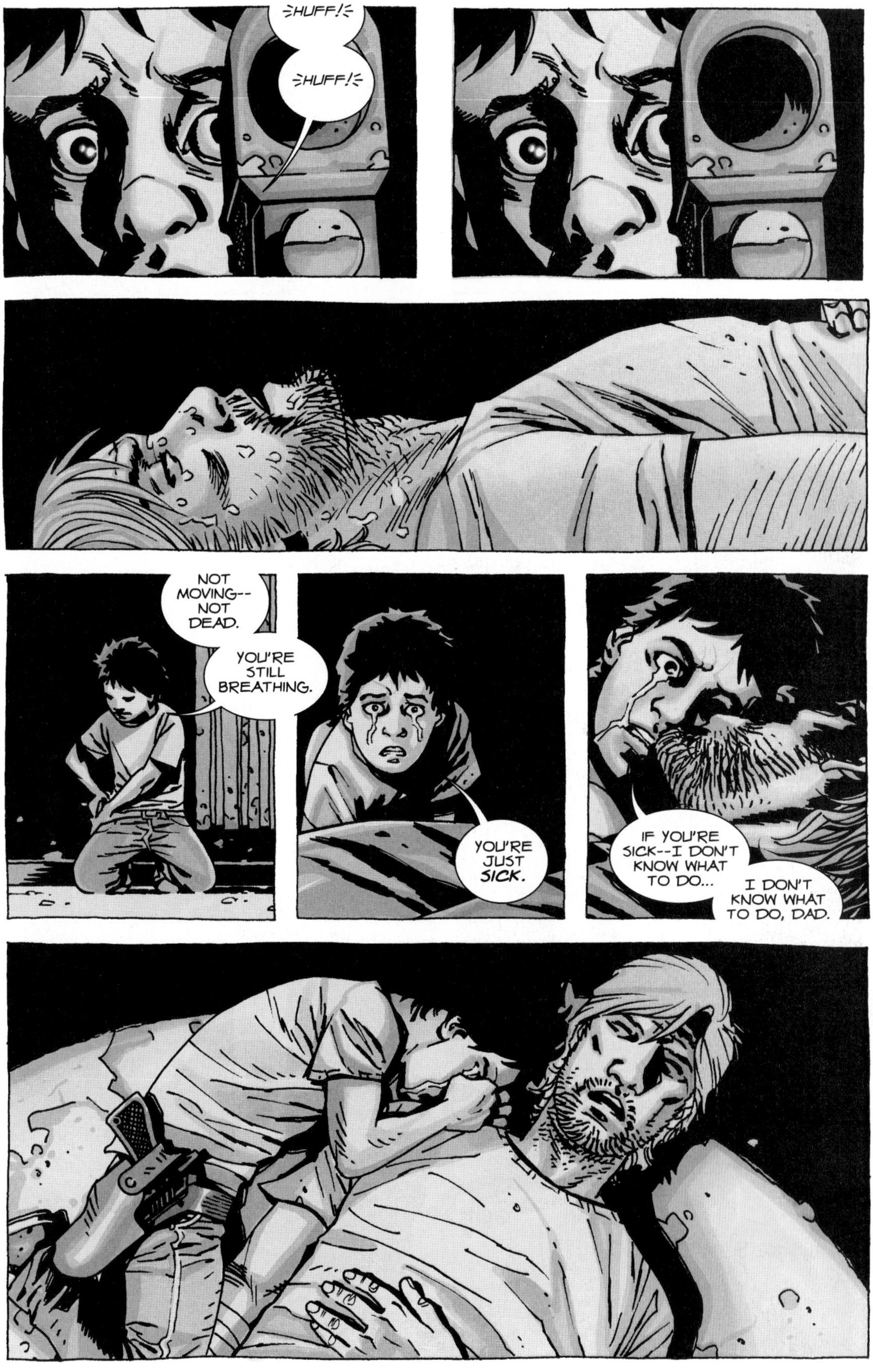
HUFF!
HUFF!
NOT MOVING-- NOT DEAD.
YOU'RE STILL BREATHING.
YOU'RE JUST SICK.
IF YOU'RE SICK--I DON'T KNOW WHAT TO DO...
I DON'T KNOW WHAT TO DO, DAD.

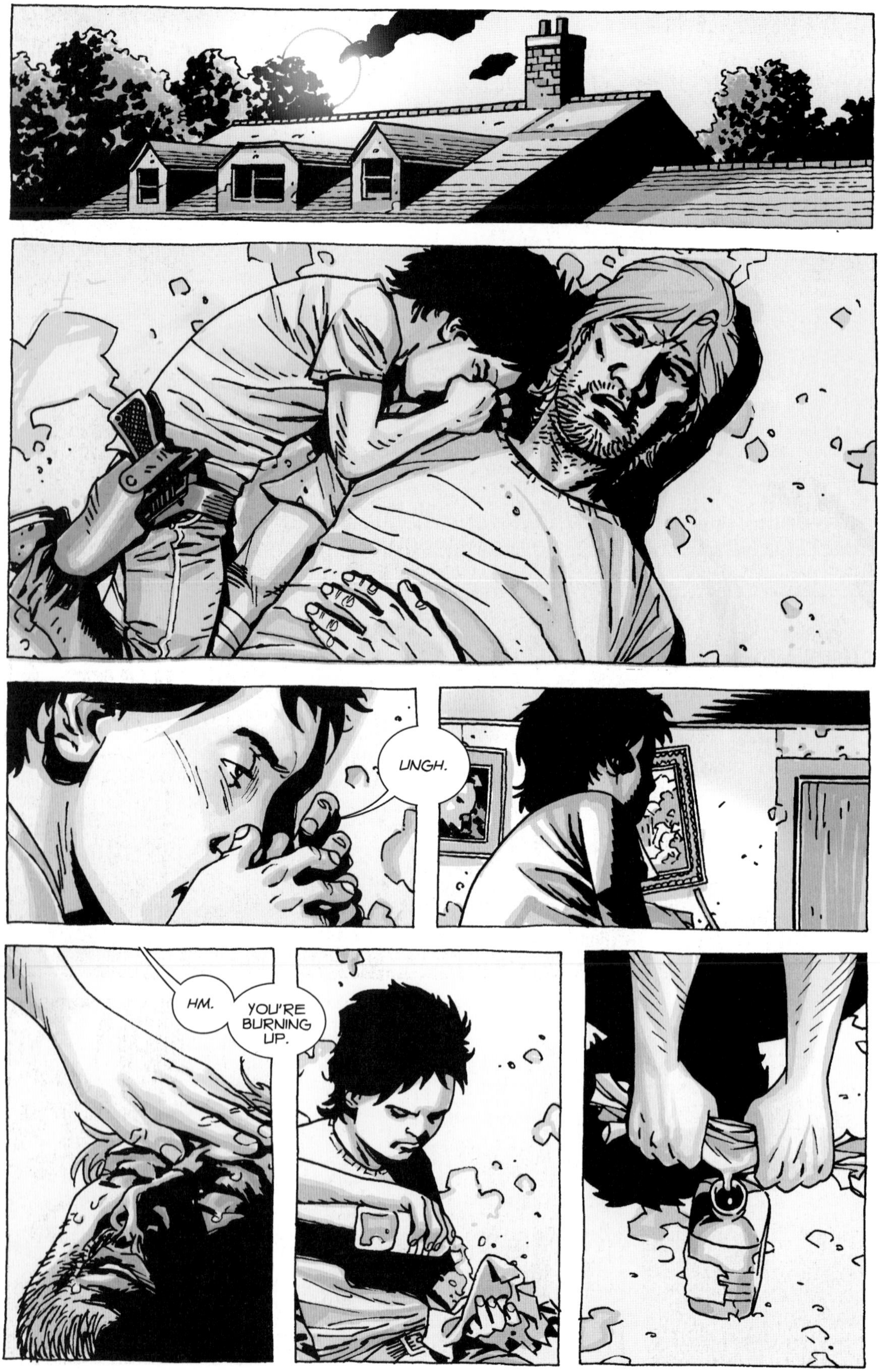
UNGH.
HM.
YOU'RE BURNING UP.

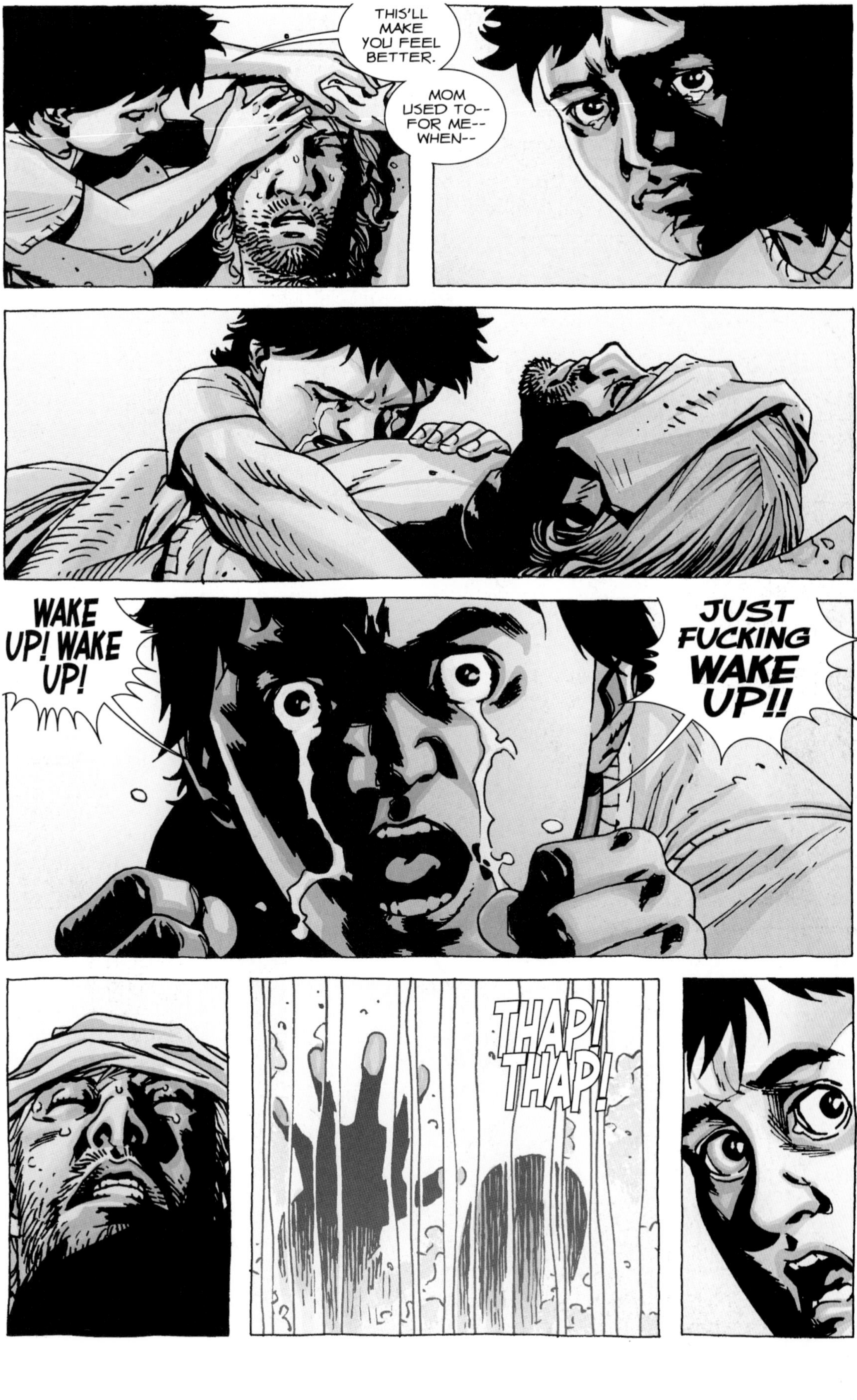
THIS'LL MAKE YOU FEEL BETTER.
MOM USED TO-- FOR ME-- WHEN--
WAKE UP! WAKE UP!
JUST FUCKING WAKE UP!!
THAP! THAP!

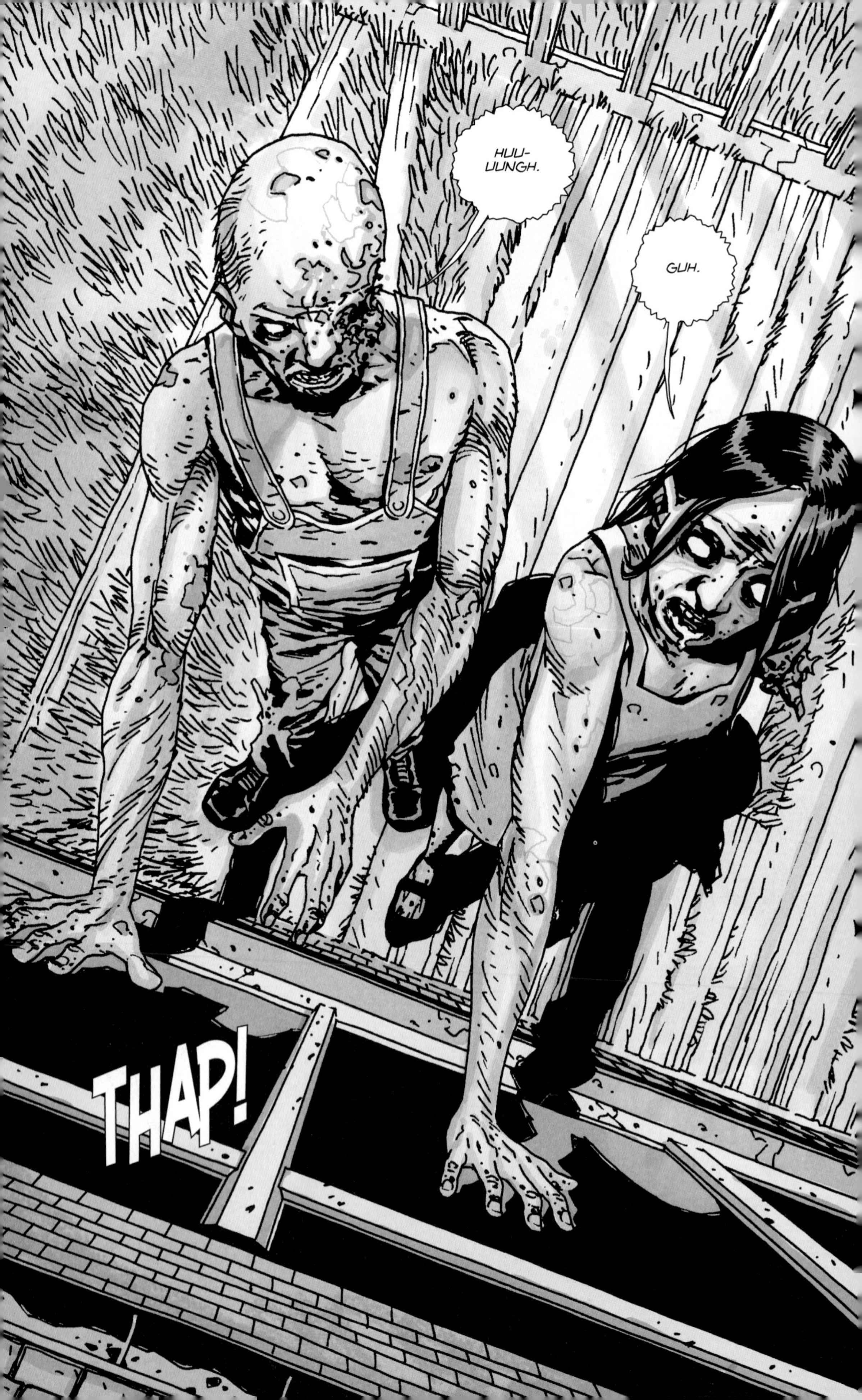
HUU-
UUNGH.
GUH.
THAP!

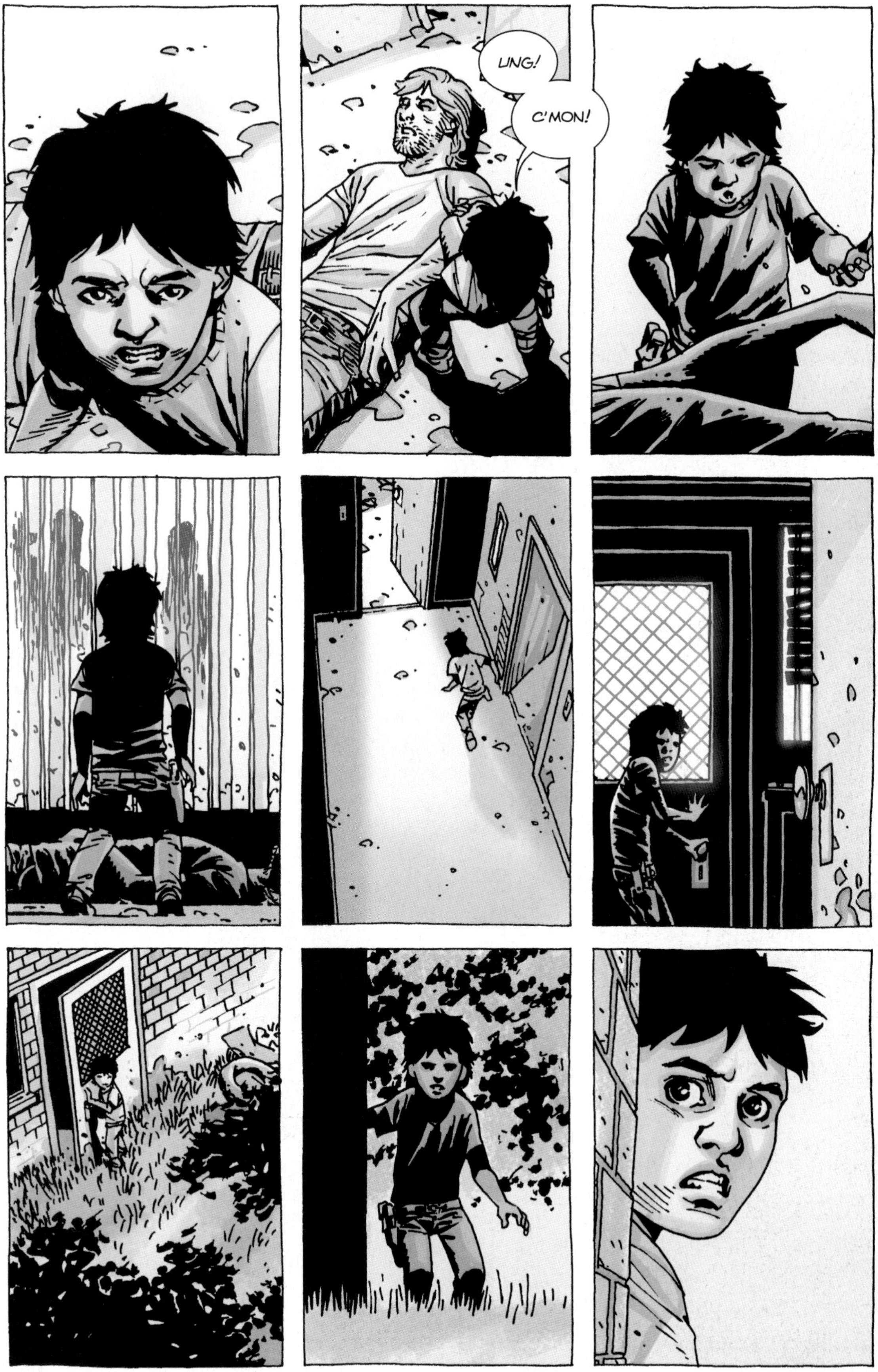
UNG!
C'MON!

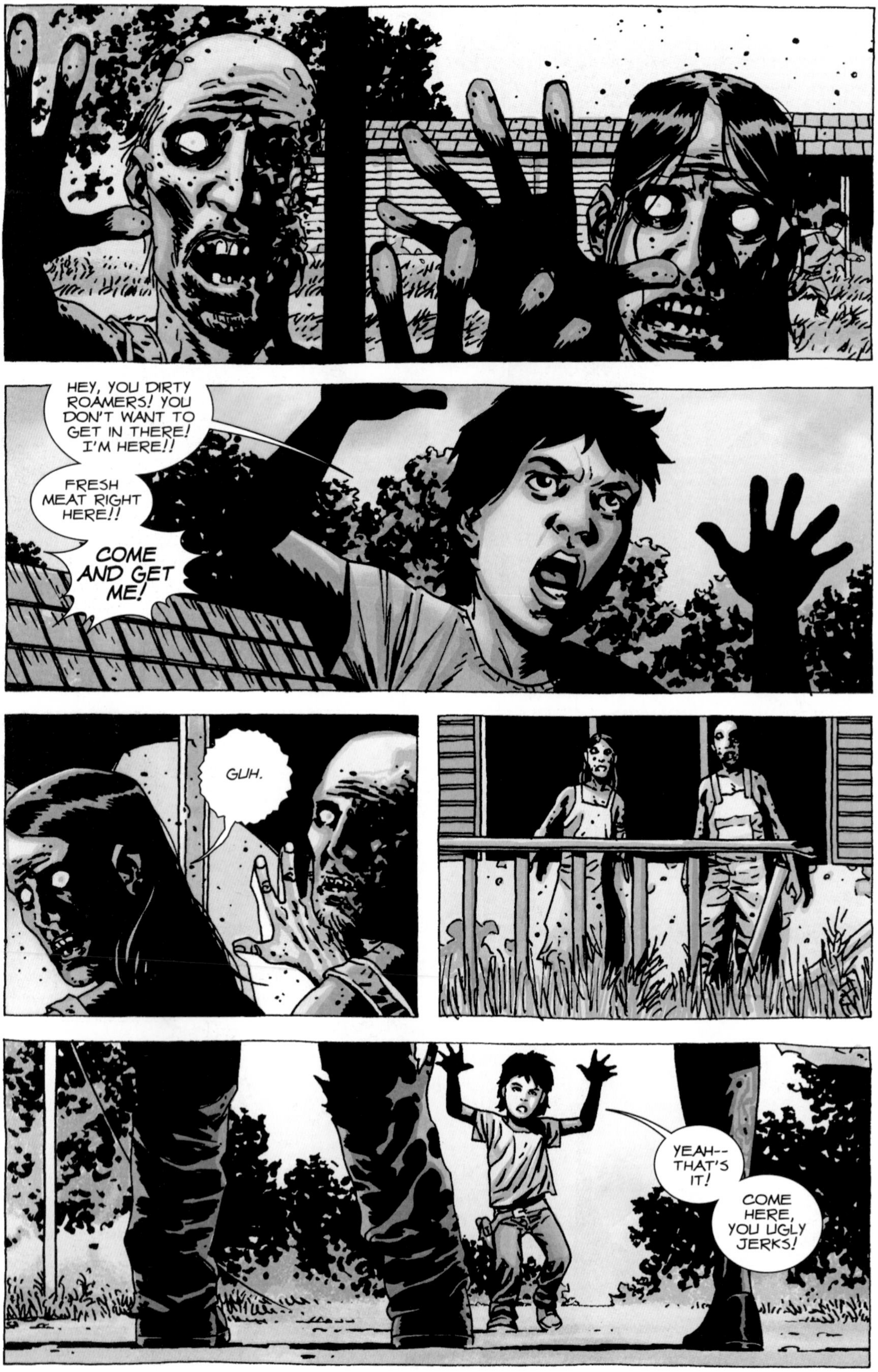
HEY, YOU DIRTY ROAMERS! YOU DON'T WANT TO GET IN THERE! I'M HERE!!
FRESH MEAT RIGHT HERE!!
COME AND GET ME!
GUH.
YEAH-- THAT'S IT!
COME HERE, YOU UGLY JERKS!

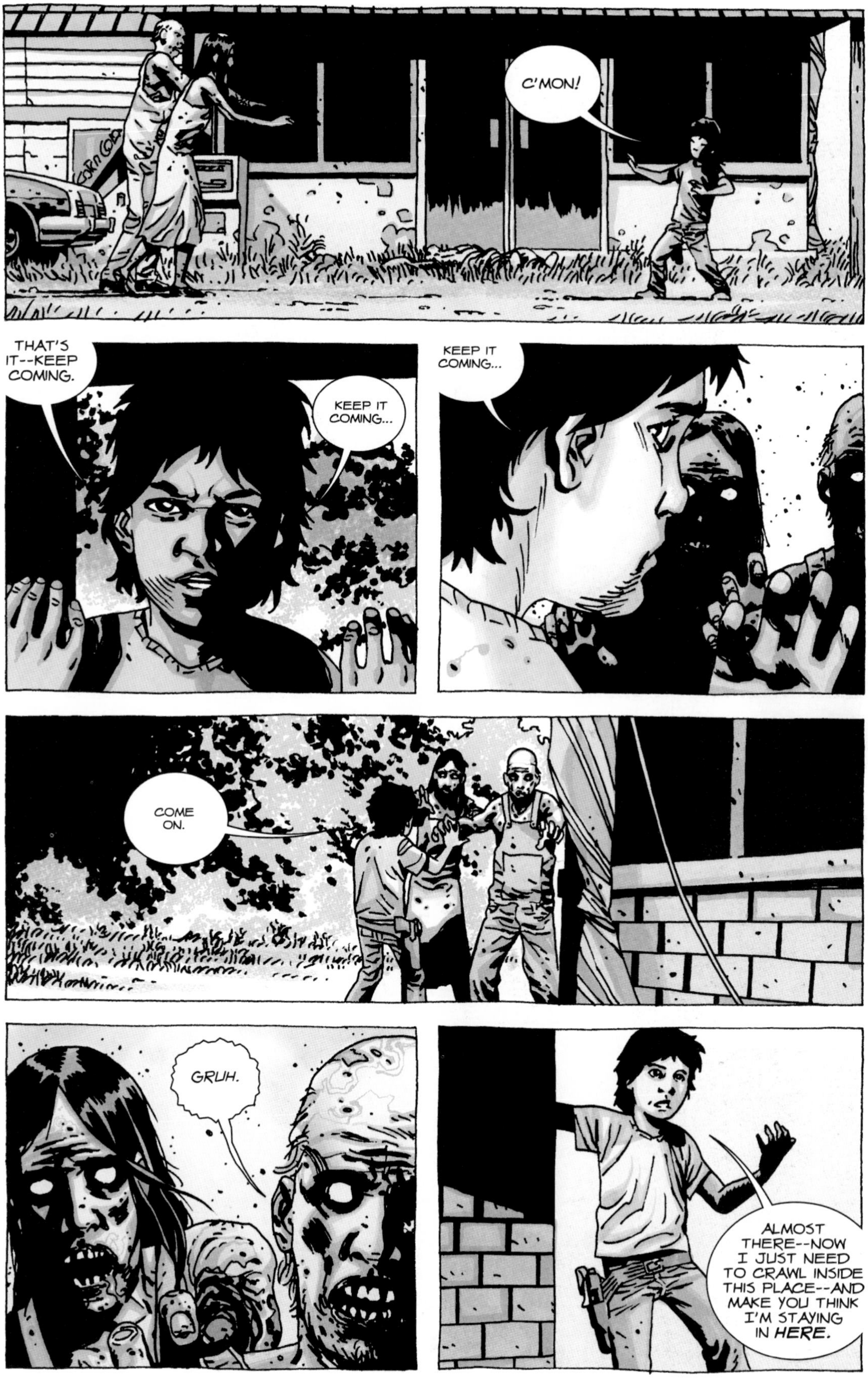
C'MON!
THAT'S IT--KEEP COMING.
KEEP IT COMING...
KEEP IT COMING...
COME ON.
GRUH.
ALMOST THERE--NOW I JUST NEED TO CRAWL INSIDE THIS PLACE--AND MAKE YOU THINK I'M STAYING IN *HERE.*

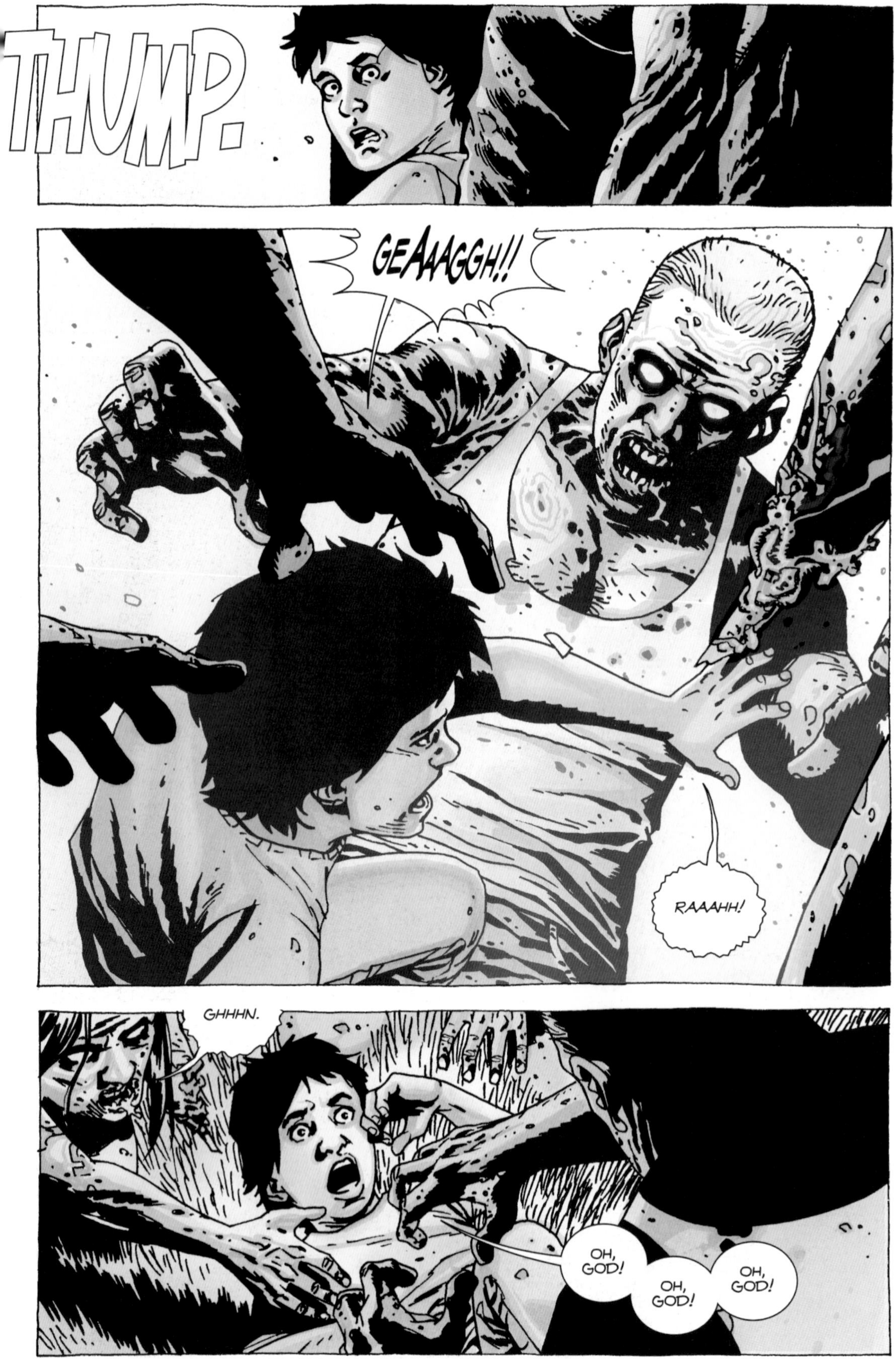
THUMP.
GEAAAGGH!!
RAAAHH!
GHHHN.
OH, GOD!
OH, GOD!
OH, GOD!

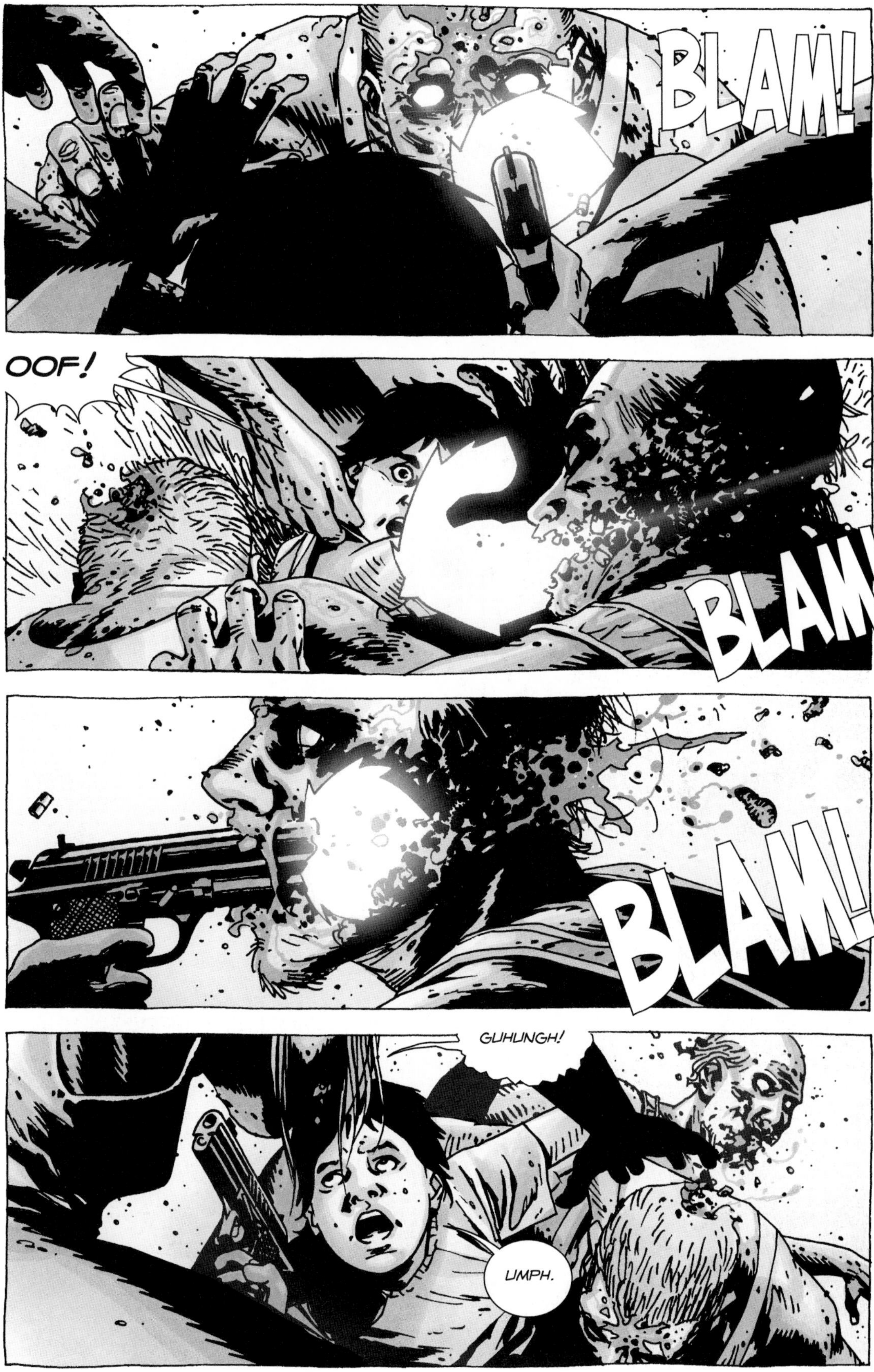
BLAM!
OOF!
BLAM!
BLAM!
GUHUNGH!
UMPH.

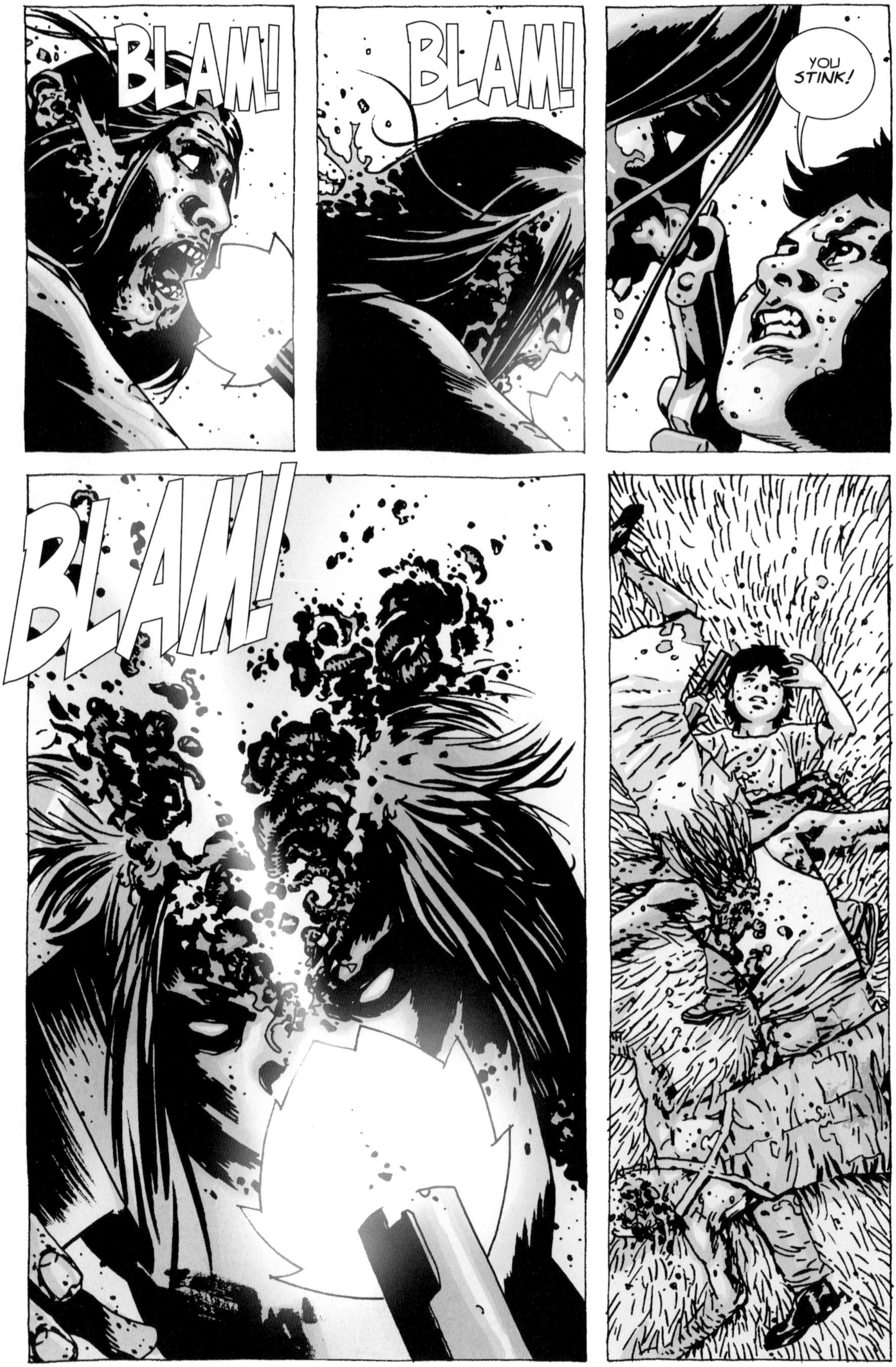
BLAM!
BLAM!
YOU STINK!
BLAM!

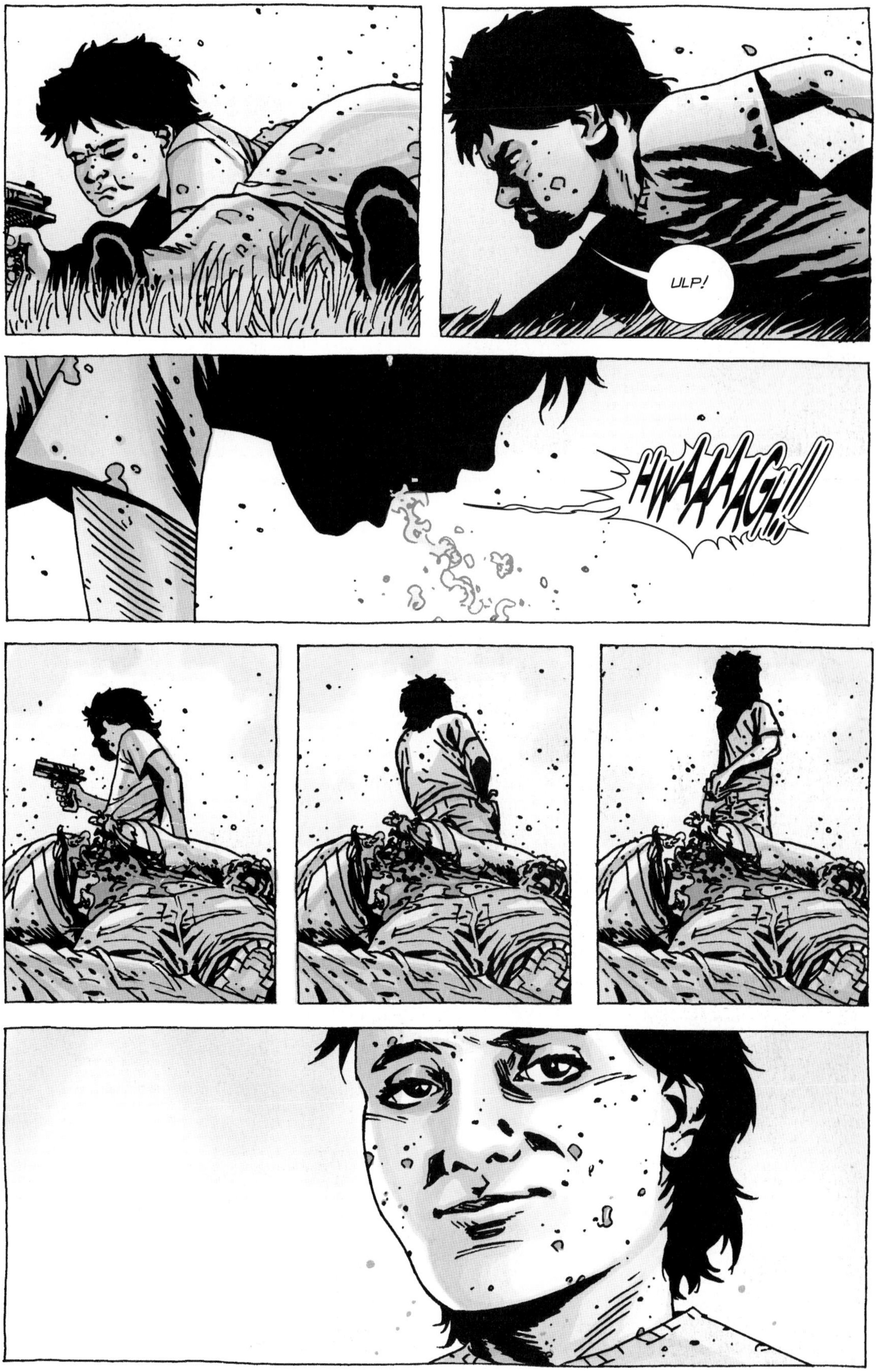
ULP!
HWAAAAGH!!

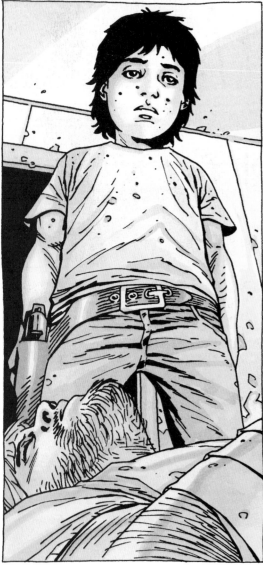

I JUST KILLED THREE ROAMERS, DAD.

THREE.

I KILLED THEM ALL BY MYSELF.

IT WAS JUST ME.

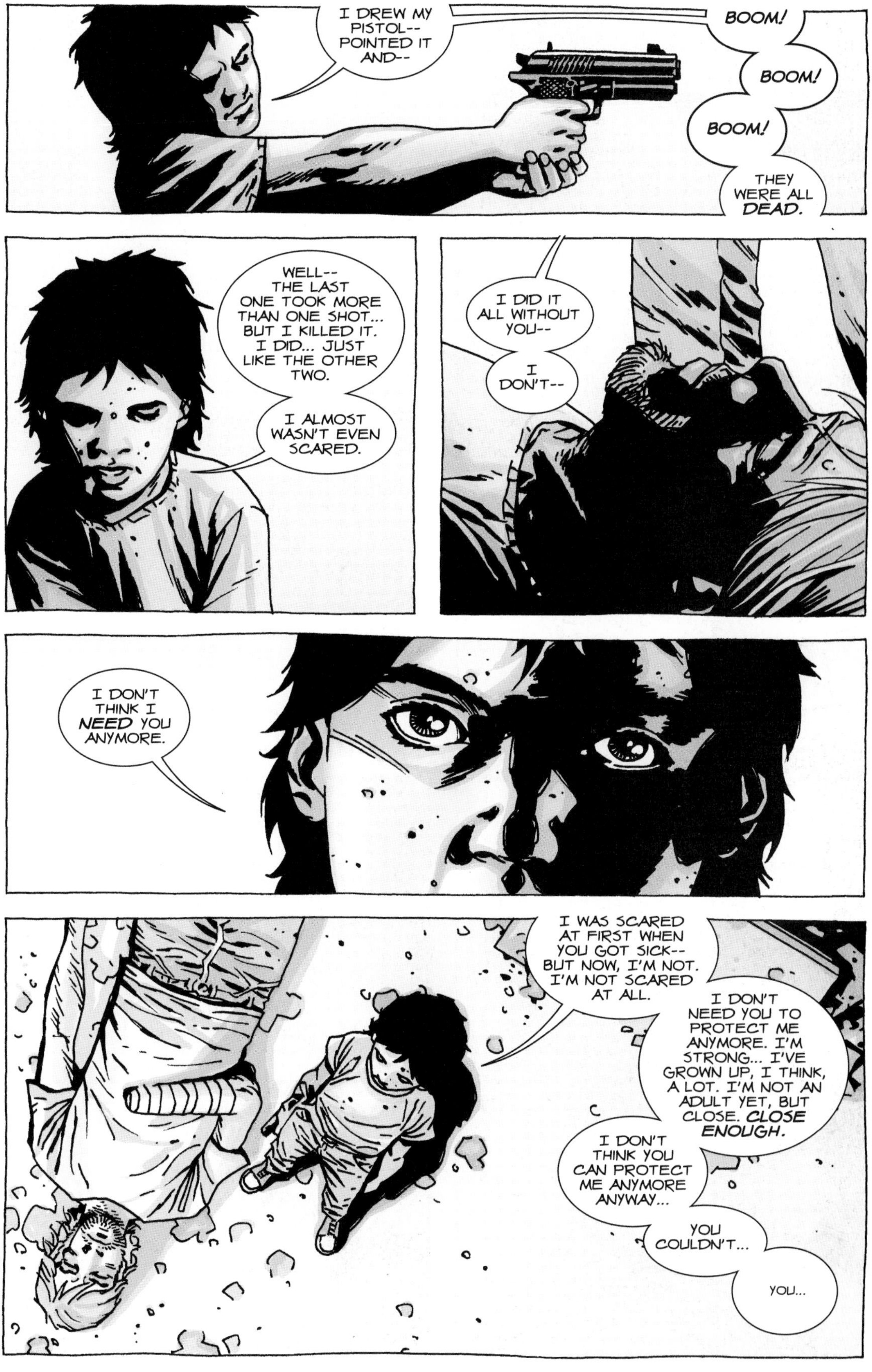
I DREW MY PISTOL-- POINTED IT AND--
BOOM!
BOOM!
BOOM!
THEY WERE ALL **DEAD.**
WELL-- THE LAST ONE TOOK MORE THAN ONE SHOT... BUT I KILLED IT. I DID... JUST LIKE THE OTHER TWO.
I ALMOST WASN'T EVEN SCARED.
I DID IT ALL WITHOUT YOU--
I DON'T--
I DON'T THINK I **NEED** YOU ANYMORE.
I WAS SCARED AT FIRST WHEN YOU GOT SICK-- BUT NOW, I'M NOT. I'M NOT SCARED AT ALL.
I DON'T NEED YOU TO PROTECT ME ANYMORE. I'M STRONG... I'VE GROWN UP, I THINK, A LOT. I'M NOT AN ADULT YET, BUT CLOSE. **CLOSE ENOUGH.**
I DON'T THINK YOU CAN PROTECT ME ANYMORE ANYWAY...
YOU COULDN'T...
YOU...

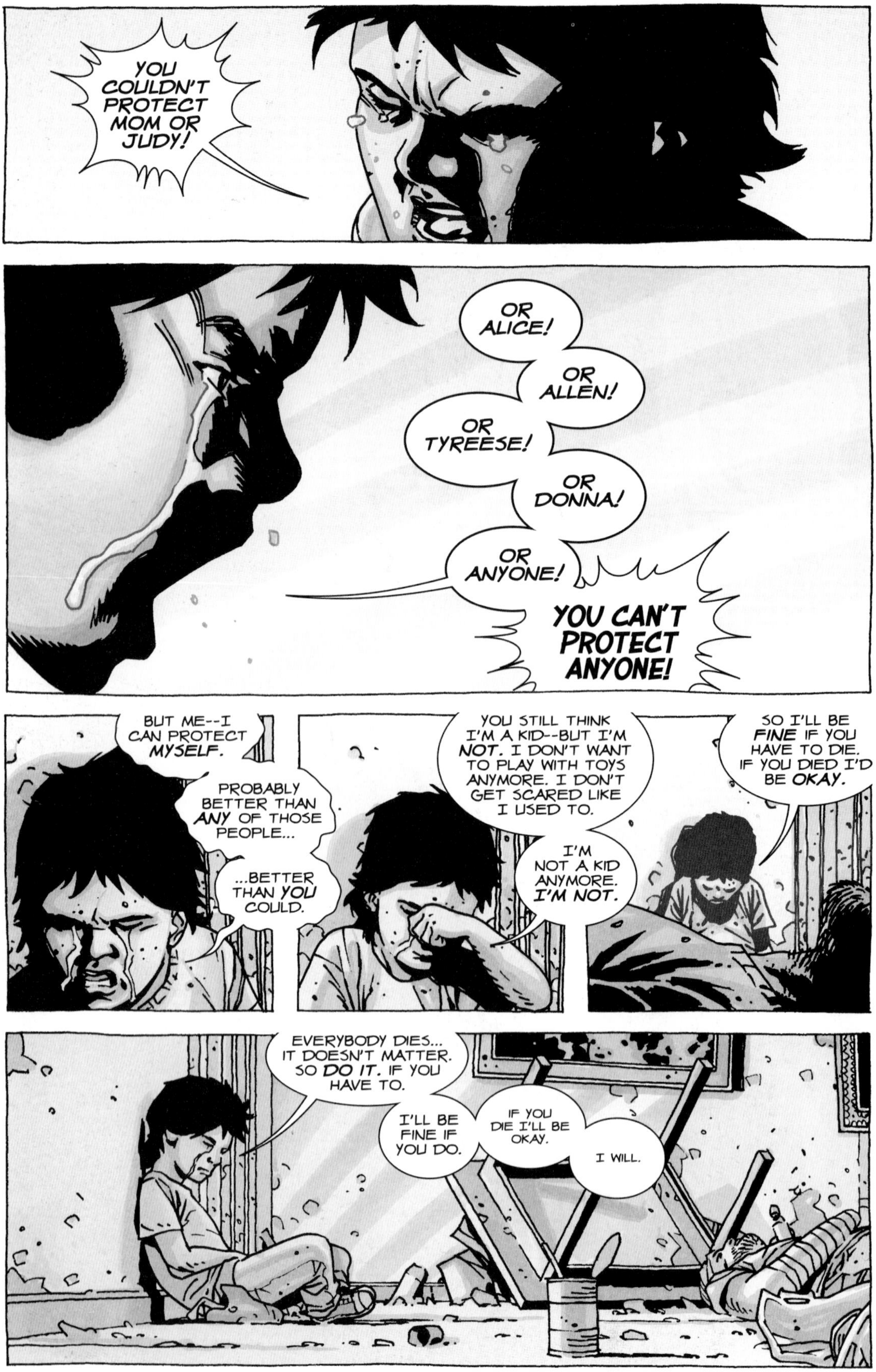
YOU COULDN'T PROTECT MOM OR JUDY!
OR ALICE!
OR ALLEN!
OR TYREESE!
OR DONNA!
OR ANYONE!
YOU CAN'T PROTECT ANYONE!
BUT ME--I CAN PROTECT MYSELF.
PROBABLY BETTER THAN ANY OF THOSE PEOPLE...
...BETTER THAN YOU COULD.
YOU STILL THINK I'M A KID--BUT I'M NOT. I DON'T WANT TO PLAY WITH TOYS ANYMORE. I DON'T GET SCARED LIKE I USED TO.
I'M NOT A KID ANYMORE. I'M NOT.
SO I'LL BE FINE IF YOU HAVE TO DIE. IF YOU DIED I'D BE OKAY.
EVERYBODY DIES... IT DOESN'T MATTER. SO DO IT. IF YOU HAVE TO.
I'LL BE FINE IF YOU DO.
IF YOU DIE I'LL BE OKAY.
I WILL.

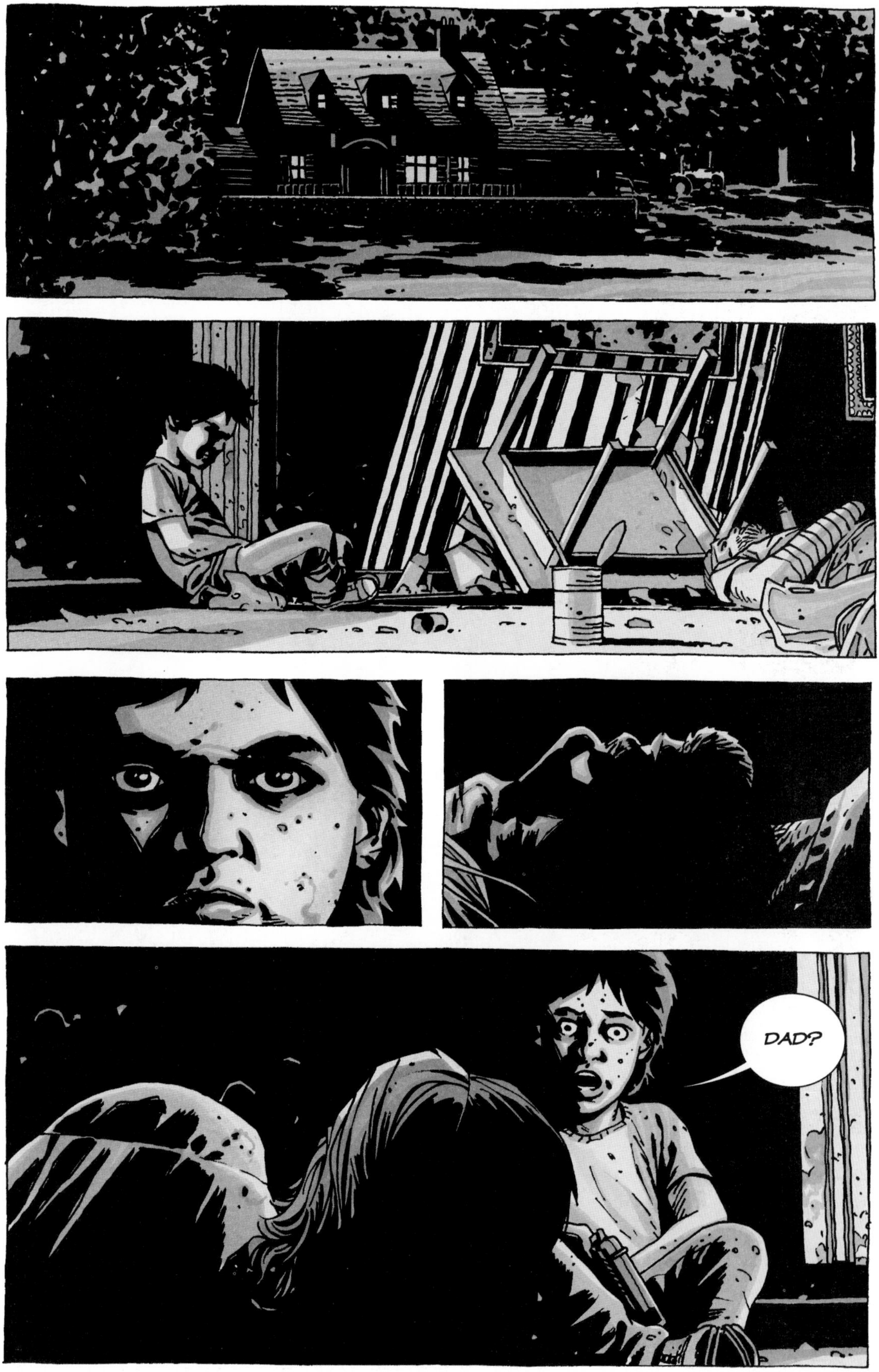
DAD?

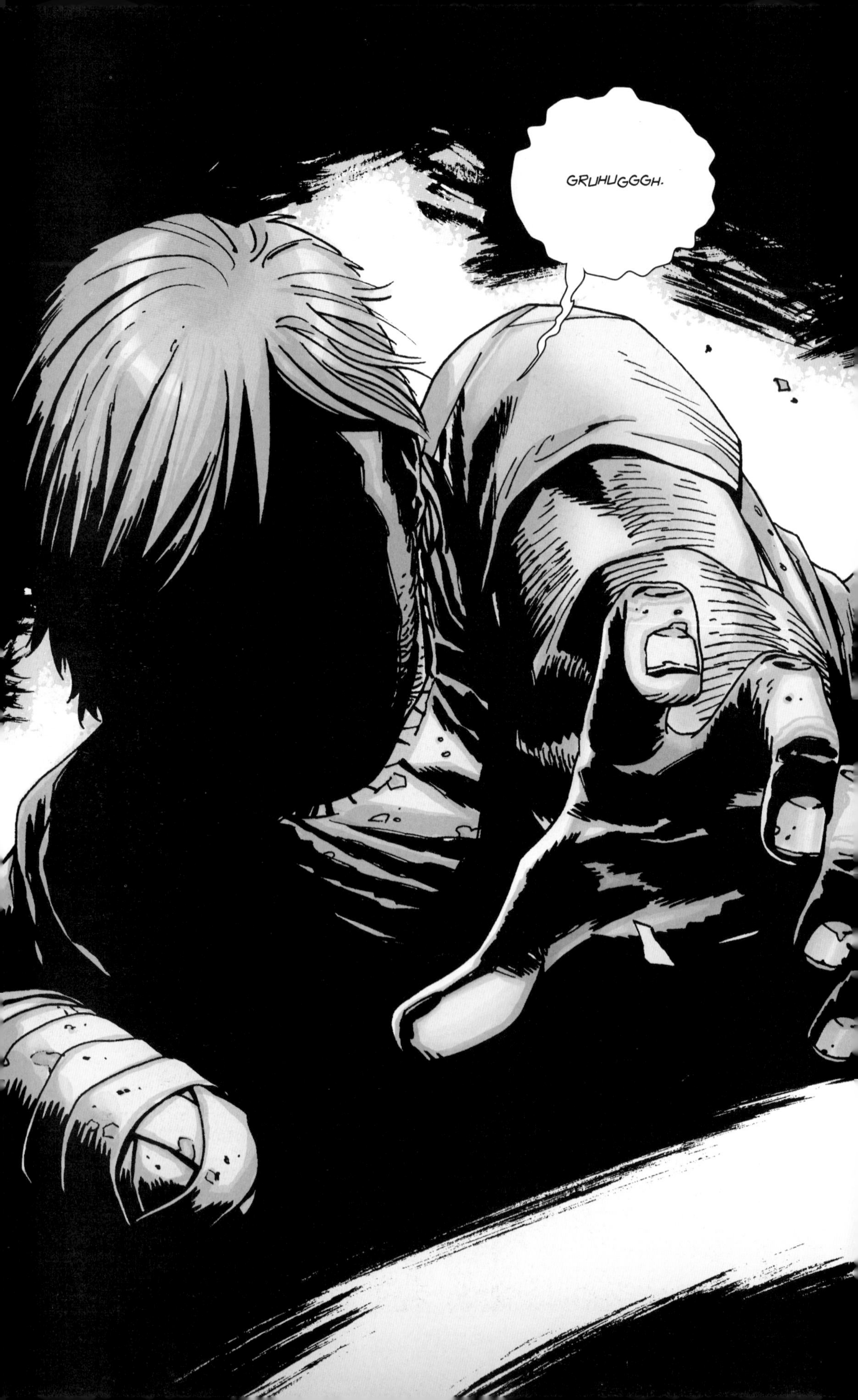
GRUHUGGGH.

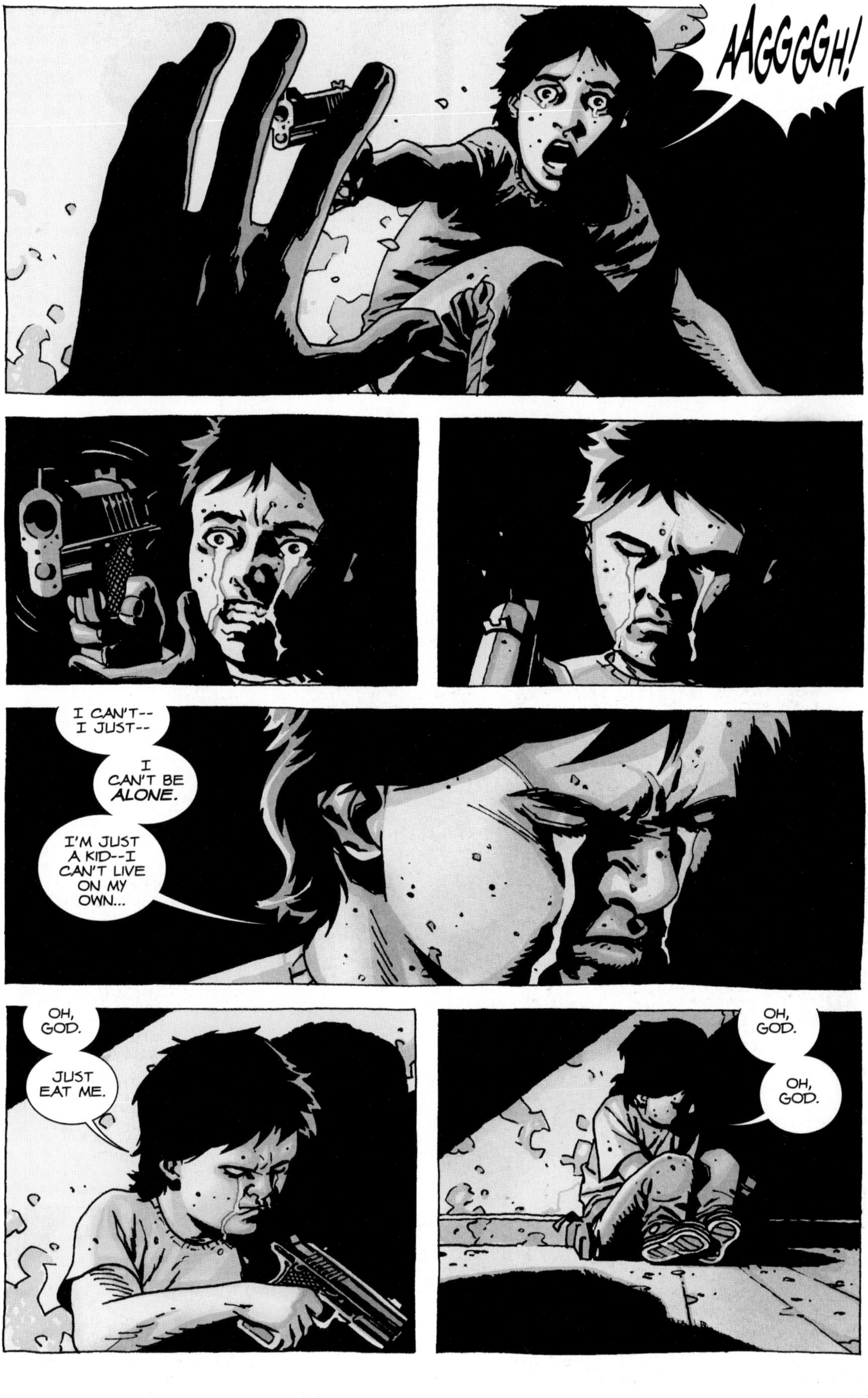
AAGGGGH!
I CAN'T-- I JUST--
I CAN'T BE ALONE.
I'M JUST A KID--I CAN'T LIVE ON MY OWN...
OH, GOD.
JUST EAT ME.
OH, GOD.
OH, GOD.

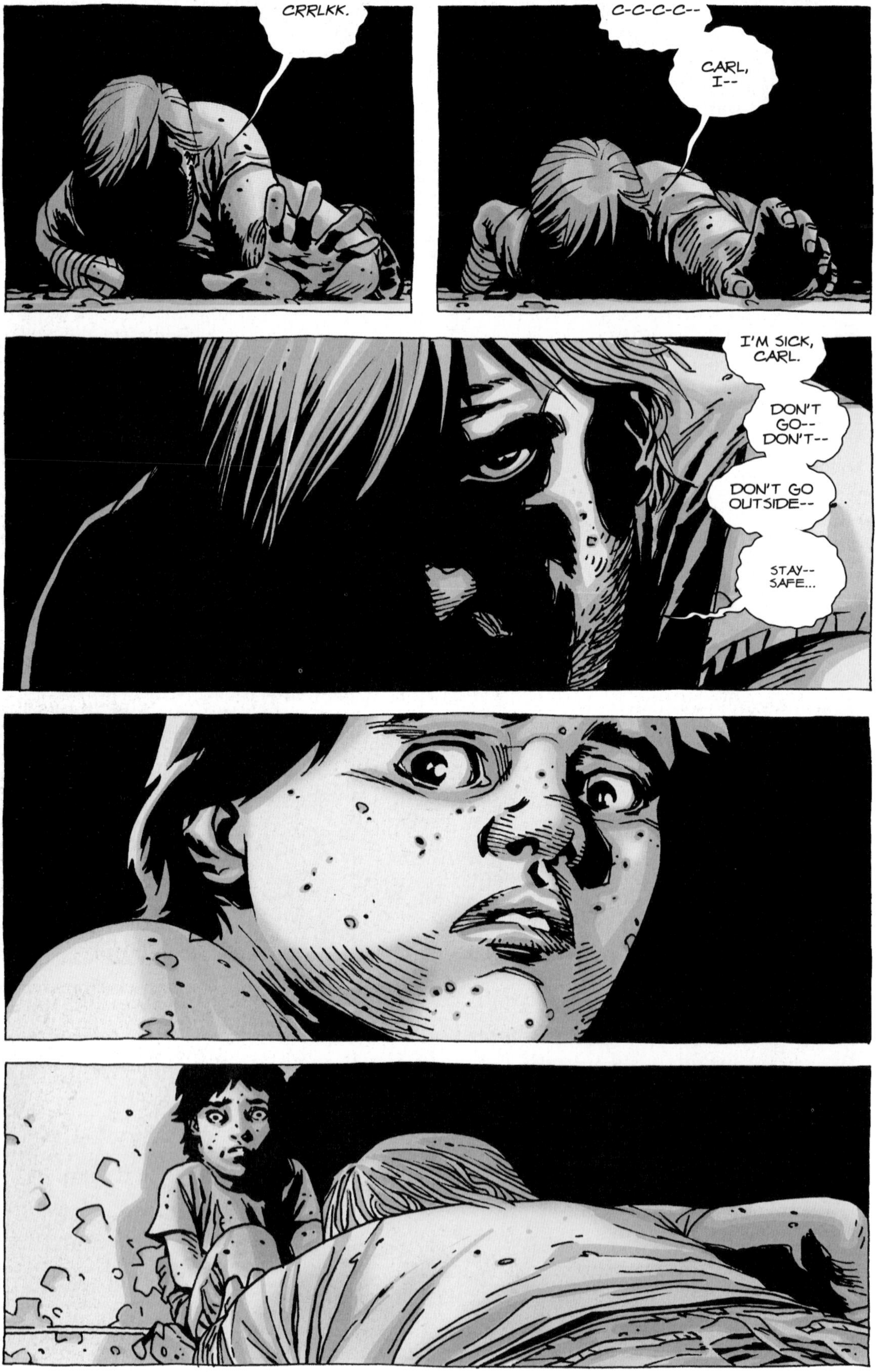
CRRLKK.
C-C-C-C--
CARL, I--
I'M SICK, CARL.
DON'T GO-- DON'T--
DON'T GO OUTSIDE--
STAY-- SAFE...

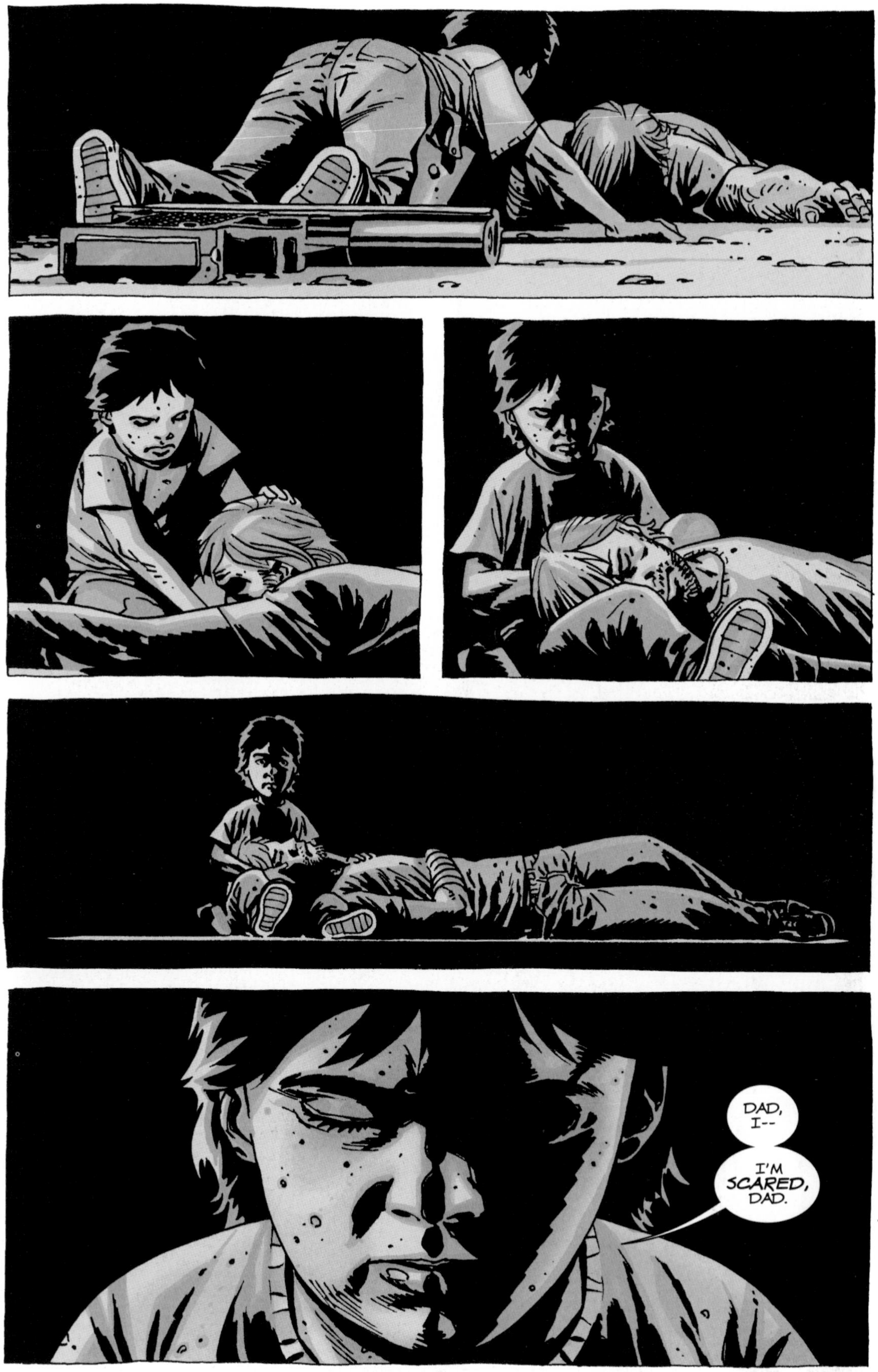
DAD, I--
I'M SCARED, DAD.

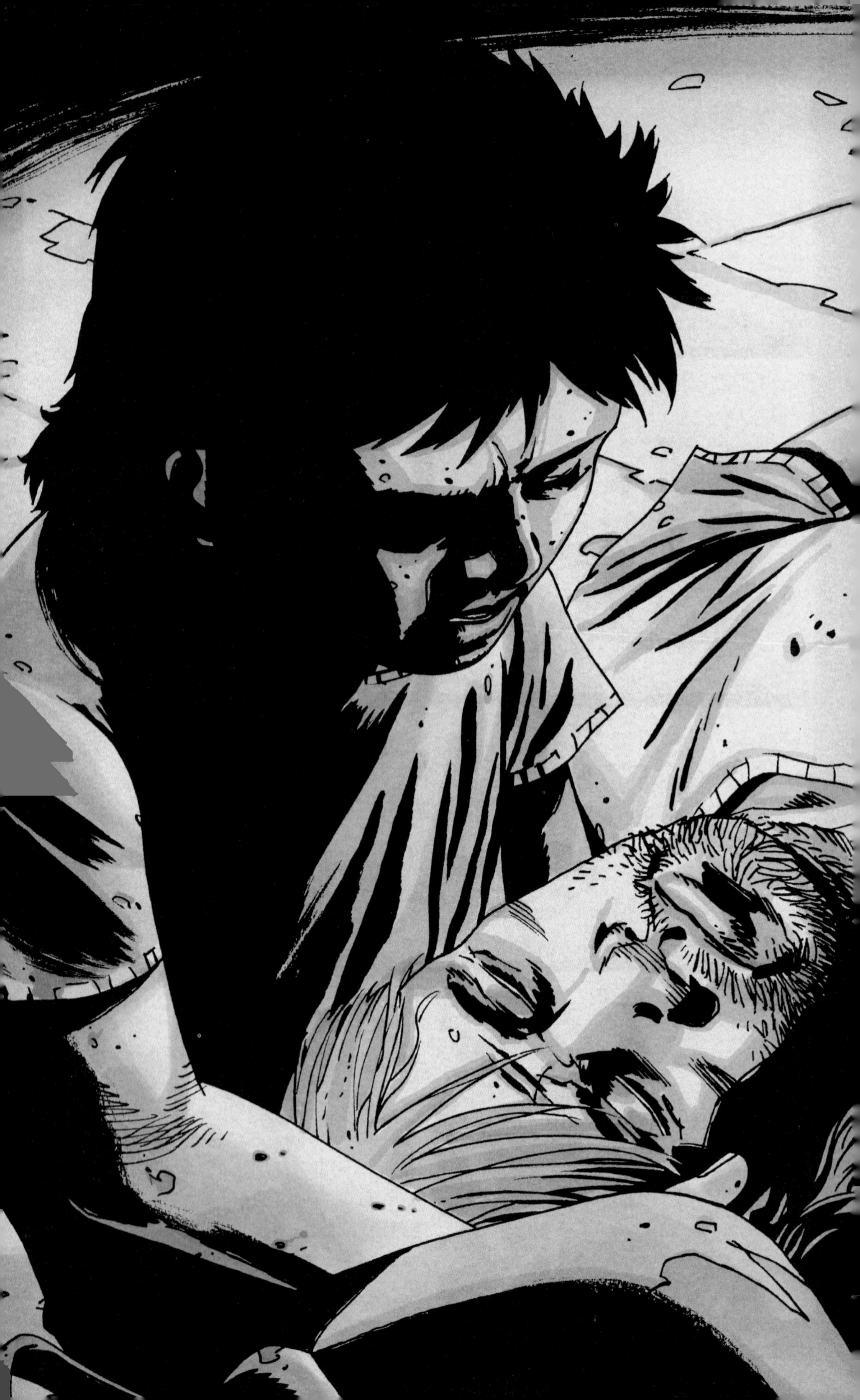

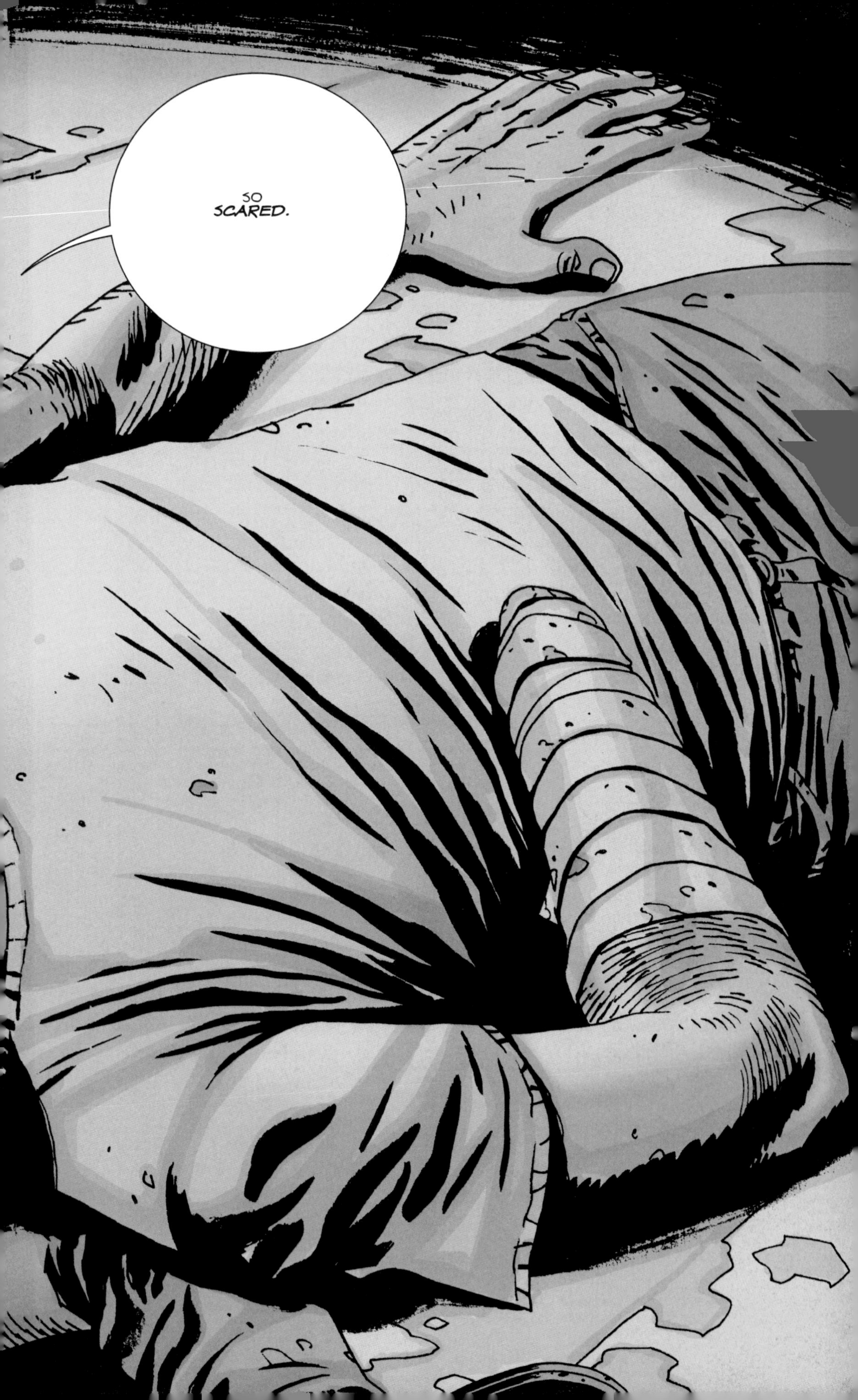
SO SCARED.

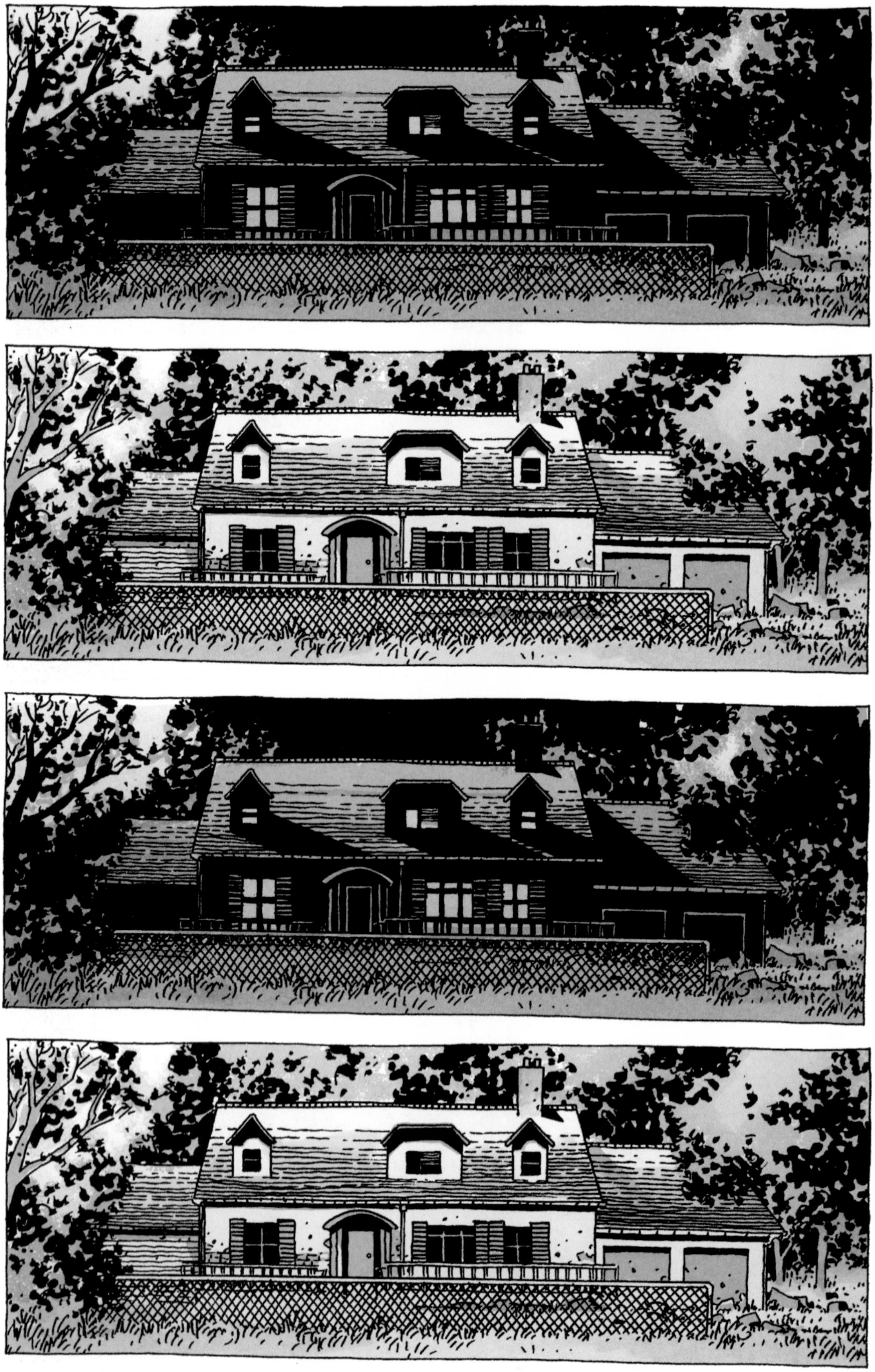

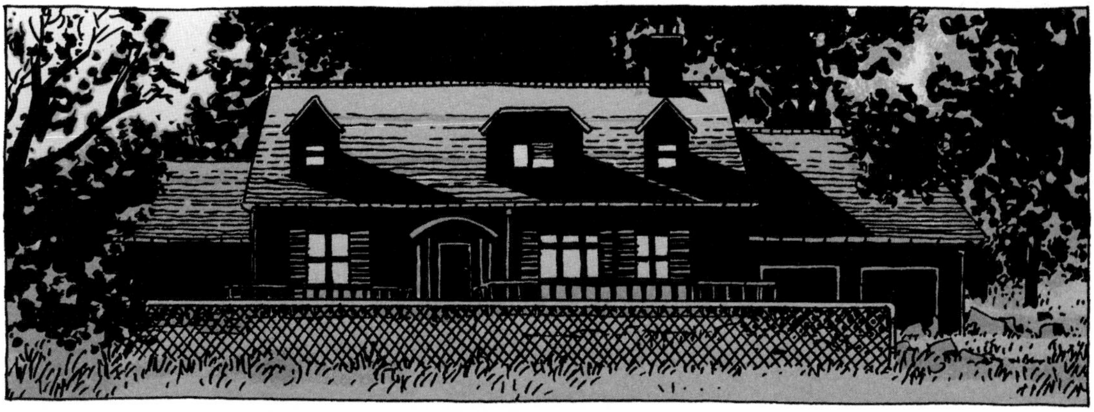
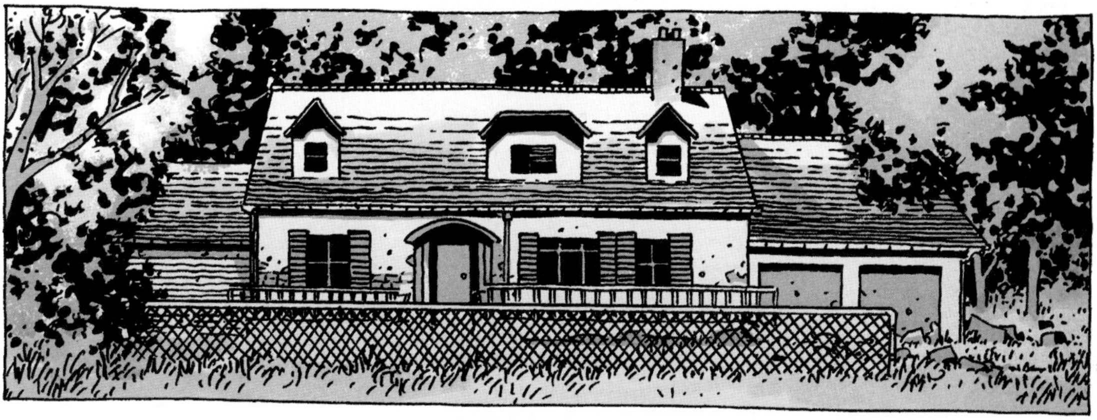
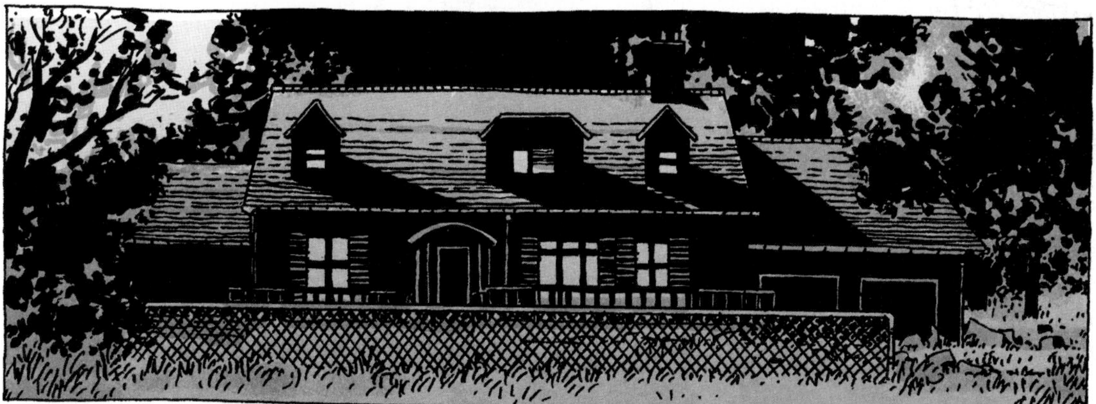
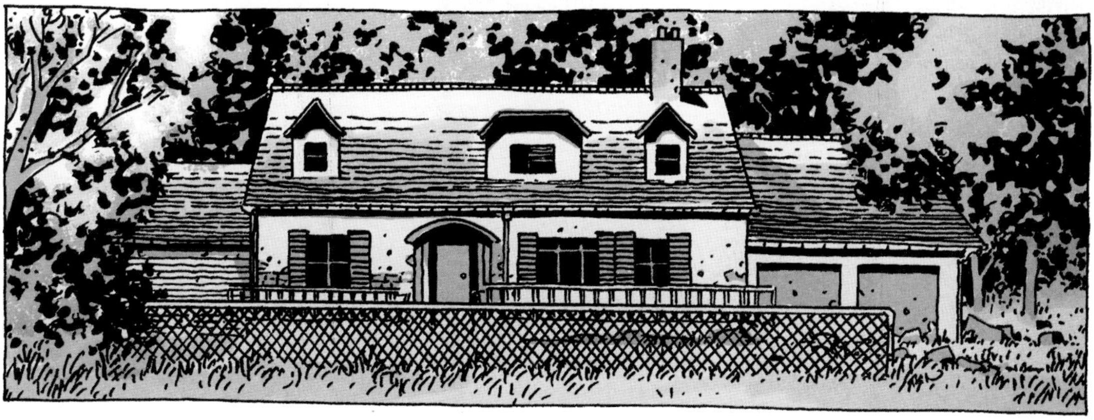

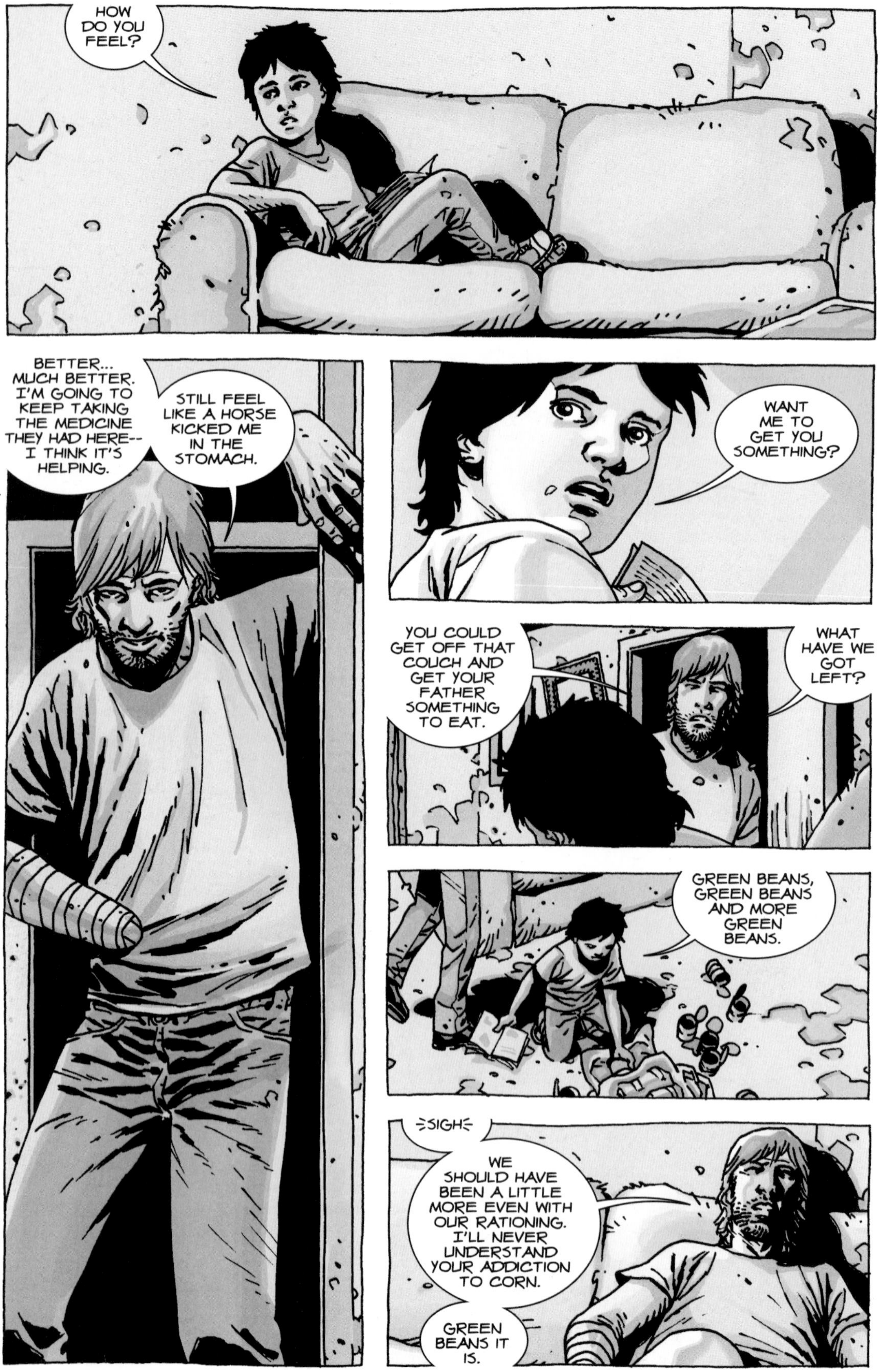
HOW DO YOU FEEL?
BETTER... MUCH BETTER. I'M GOING TO KEEP TAKING THE MEDICINE THEY HAD HERE-- I THINK IT'S HELPING.
STILL FEEL LIKE A HORSE KICKED ME IN THE STOMACH.
WANT ME TO GET YOU SOMETHING?
YOU COULD GET OFF THAT COUCH AND GET YOUR FATHER SOMETHING TO EAT.
WHAT HAVE WE GOT LEFT?
GREEN BEANS, GREEN BEANS AND MORE GREEN BEANS.
SIGH
WE SHOULD HAVE BEEN A LITTLE MORE EVEN WITH OUR RATIONING. I'LL NEVER UNDERSTAND YOUR ADDICTION TO CORN.
GREEN BEANS IT IS.

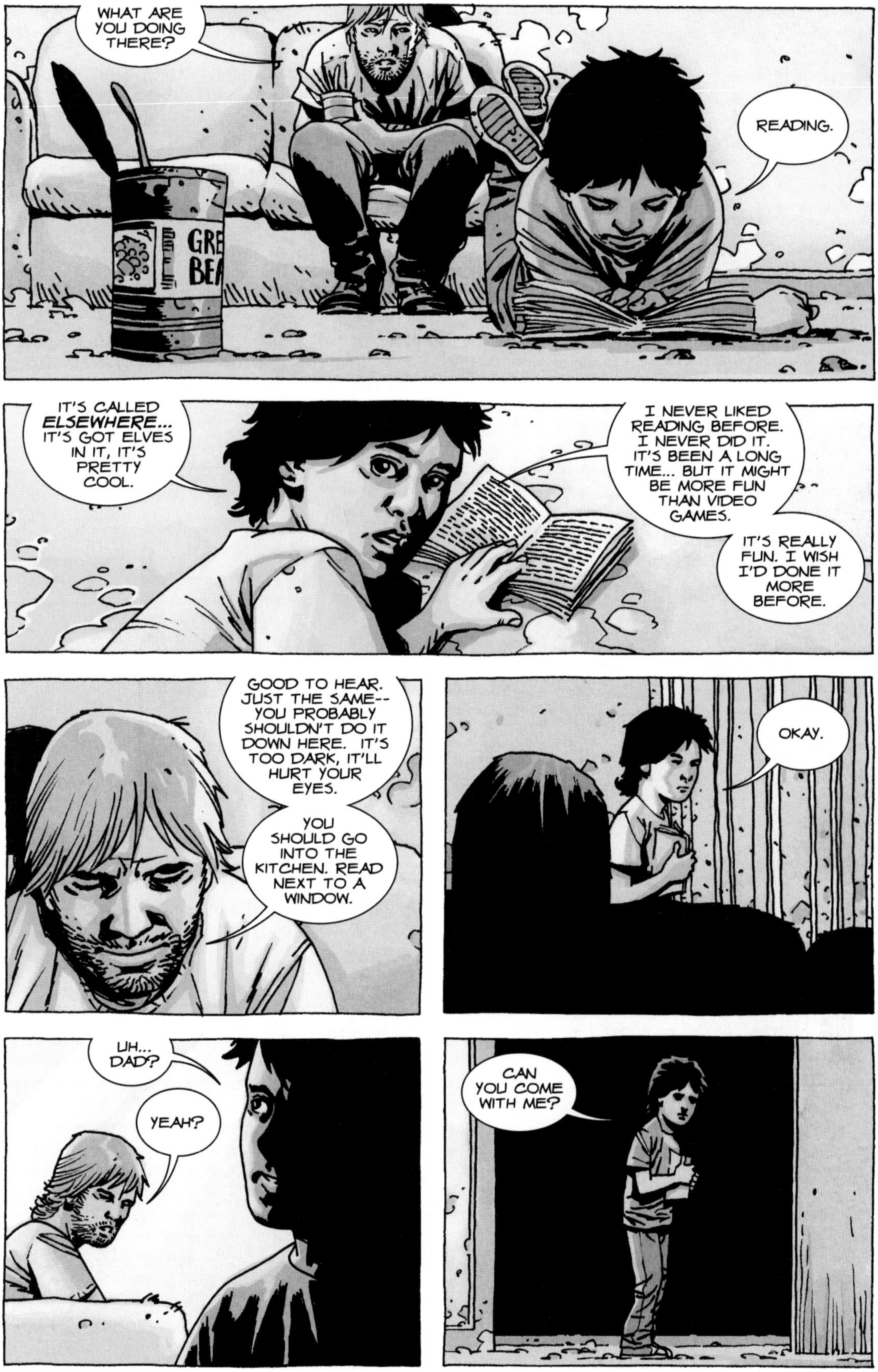
WHAT ARE YOU DOING THERE?
READING.
IT'S CALLED ELSEWHERE... IT'S GOT ELVES IN IT, IT'S PRETTY COOL.
I NEVER LIKED READING BEFORE. I NEVER DID IT. IT'S BEEN A LONG TIME... BUT IT MIGHT BE MORE FUN THAN VIDEO GAMES.
IT'S REALLY FUN. I WISH I'D DONE IT MORE BEFORE.
GOOD TO HEAR. JUST THE SAME-- YOU PROBABLY SHOULDN'T DO IT DOWN HERE. IT'S TOO DARK, IT'LL HURT YOUR EYES.
YOU SHOULD GO INTO THE KITCHEN. READ NEXT TO A WINDOW.
OKAY.
UH... DAD?
YEAH?
CAN YOU COME WITH ME?

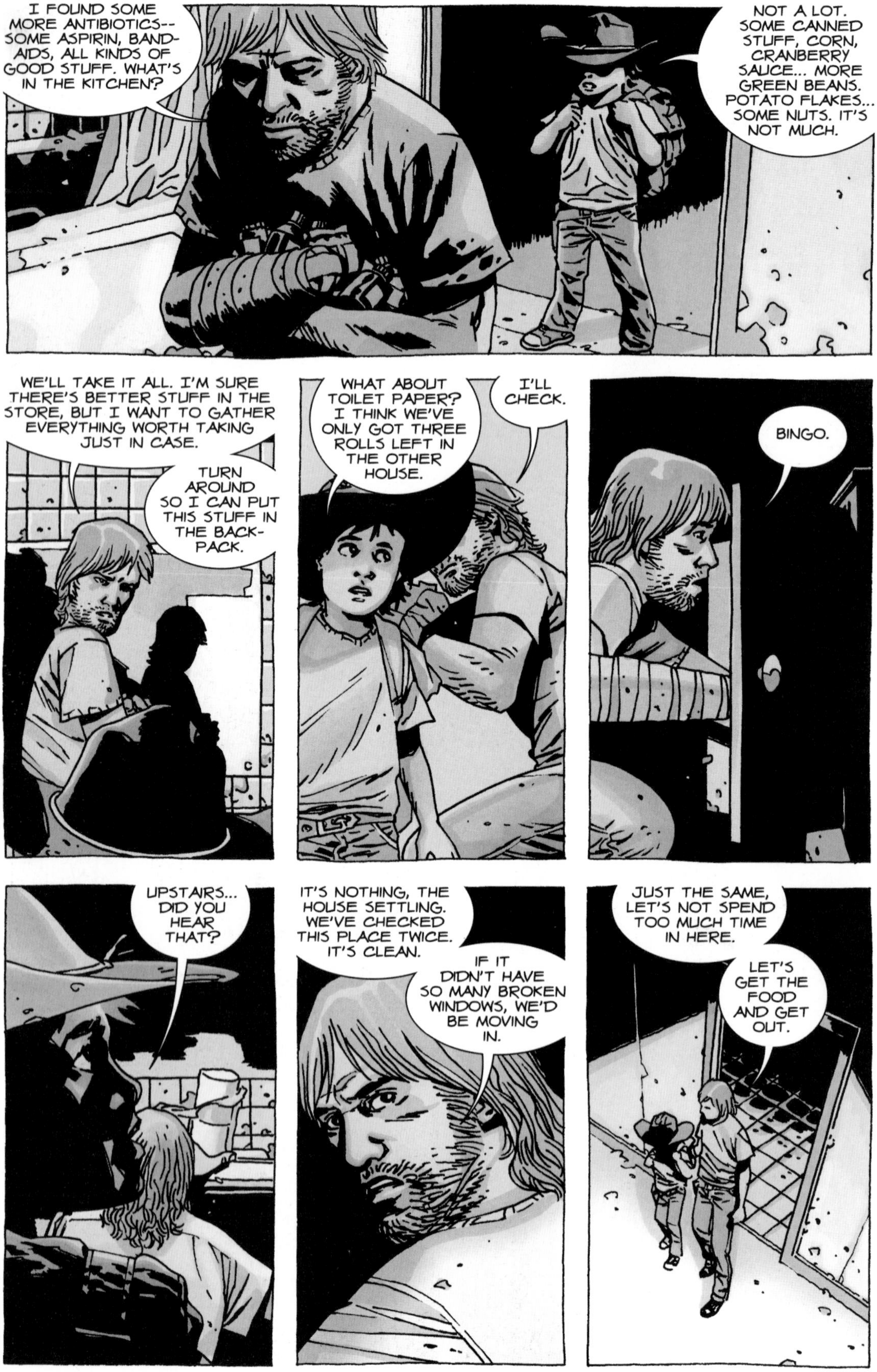
I FOUND SOME MORE ANTIBIOTICS-- SOME ASPIRIN, BAND-AIDS, ALL KINDS OF GOOD STUFF. WHAT'S IN THE KITCHEN?
NOT A LOT. SOME CANNED STUFF, CORN, CRANBERRY SAUCE... MORE GREEN BEANS. POTATO FLAKES... SOME NUTS. IT'S NOT MUCH.
WE'LL TAKE IT ALL. I'M SURE THERE'S BETTER STUFF IN THE STORE, BUT I WANT TO GATHER EVERYTHING WORTH TAKING JUST IN CASE.
TURN AROUND SO I CAN PUT THIS STUFF IN THE BACK-PACK.
WHAT ABOUT TOILET PAPER? I THINK WE'VE ONLY GOT THREE ROLLS LEFT IN THE OTHER HOUSE.
I'LL CHECK.
BINGO.
UPSTAIRS... DID YOU HEAR THAT?
IT'S NOTHING, THE HOUSE SETTLING. WE'VE CHECKED THIS PLACE TWICE. IT'S CLEAN.
IF IT DIDN'T HAVE SO MANY BROKEN WINDOWS, WE'D BE MOVING IN.
JUST THE SAME, LET'S NOT SPEND TOO MUCH TIME IN HERE.
LET'S GET THE FOOD AND GET OUT.

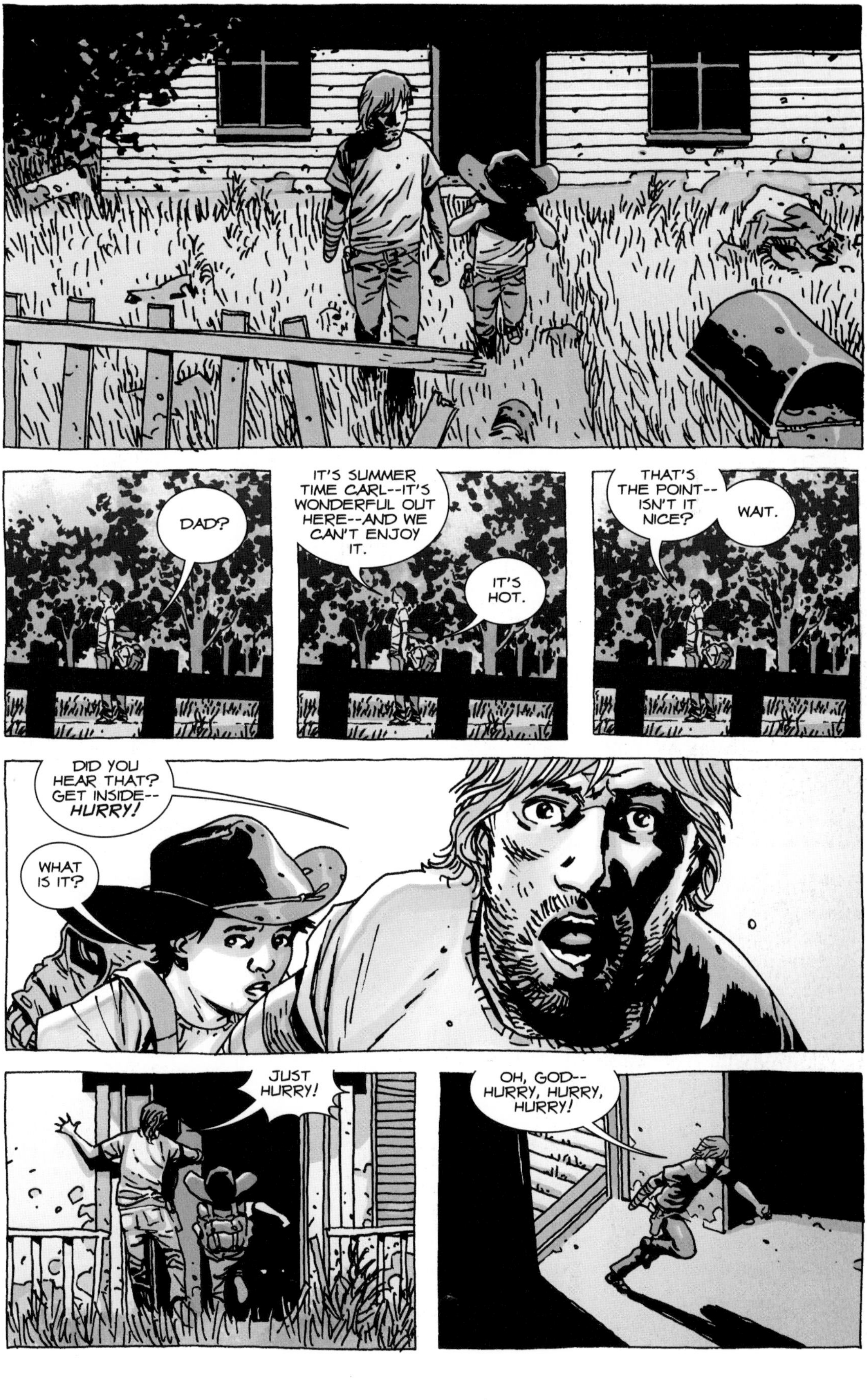
DAD?
IT'S SUMMER TIME CARL--IT'S WONDERFUL OUT HERE--AND WE CAN'T ENJOY IT.
IT'S HOT.
THAT'S THE POINT-- ISN'T IT NICE?
WAIT.
DID YOU HEAR THAT? GET INSIDE-- HURRY!
WHAT IS IT?
JUST HURRY!
OH, GOD-- HURRY, HURRY, HURRY!

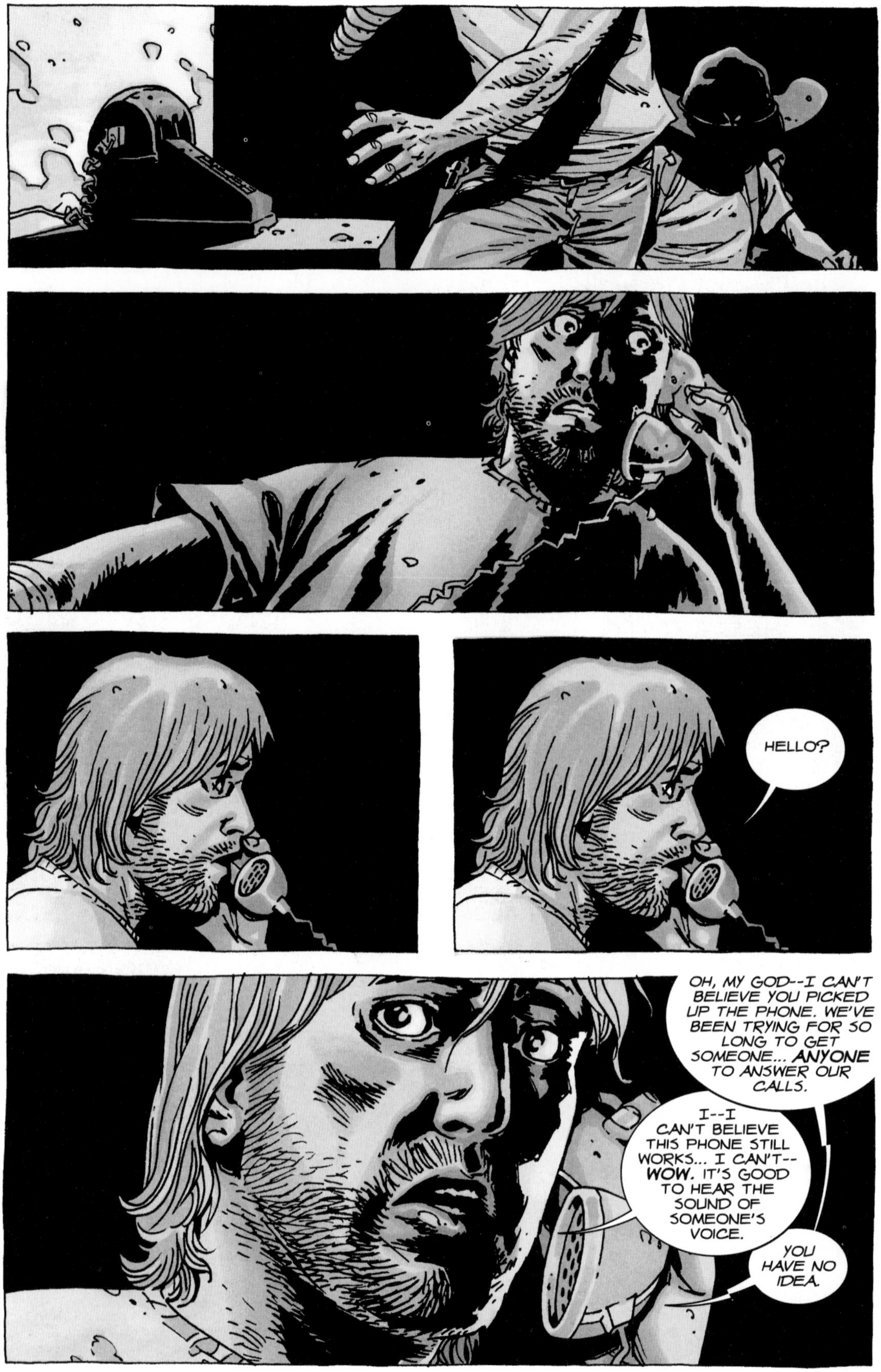
HELLO?
OH, MY GOD--I CAN'T BELIEVE YOU PICKED UP THE PHONE. WE'VE BEEN TRYING FOR SO LONG TO GET SOMEONE... ANYONE TO ANSWER OUR CALLS.
I--I CAN'T BELIEVE THIS PHONE STILL WORKS... I CAN'T-- WOW. IT'S GOOD TO HEAR THE SOUND OF SOMEONE'S VOICE.
YOU HAVE NO IDEA.

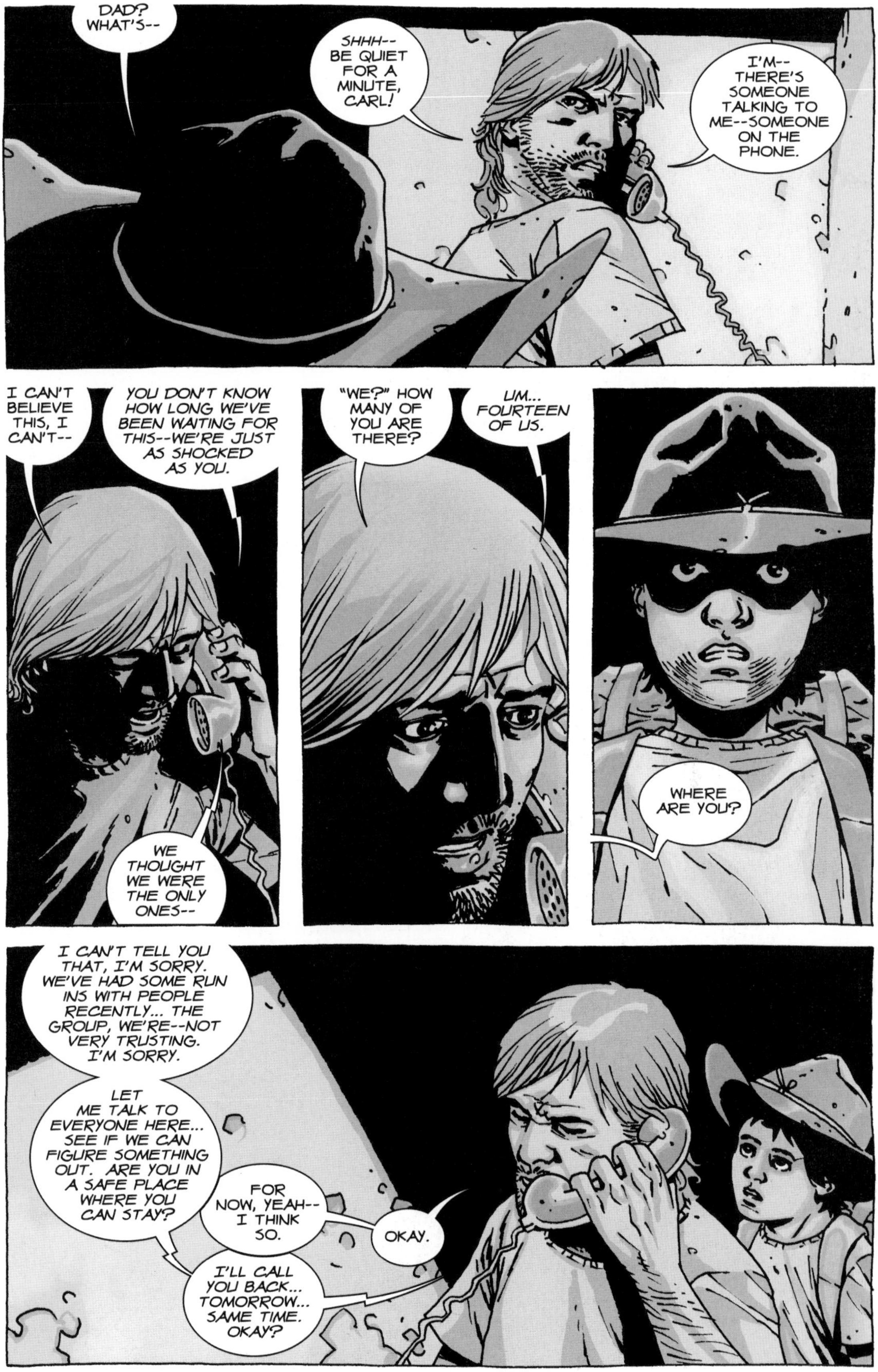
DAD? WHAT'S--
SHHH-- BE QUIET FOR A MINUTE, CARL!
I'M-- THERE'S SOMEONE TALKING TO ME--SOMEONE ON THE PHONE.
I CAN'T BELIEVE THIS, I CAN'T--
YOU DON'T KNOW HOW LONG WE'VE BEEN WAITING FOR THIS--WE'RE JUST AS SHOCKED AS YOU.
WE THOUGHT WE WERE THE ONLY ONES--
"WE?" HOW MANY OF YOU ARE THERE?
UM... FOURTEEN OF US.
WHERE ARE YOU?
I CAN'T TELL YOU THAT, I'M SORRY. WE'VE HAD SOME RUN INS WITH PEOPLE RECENTLY... THE GROUP, WE'RE--NOT VERY TRUSTING. I'M SORRY.
LET ME TALK TO EVERYONE HERE... SEE IF WE CAN FIGURE SOMETHING OUT. ARE YOU IN A SAFE PLACE WHERE YOU CAN STAY?
FOR NOW, YEAH-- I THINK SO.
OKAY.
I'LL CALL YOU BACK... TOMORROW... SAME TIME. OKAY?

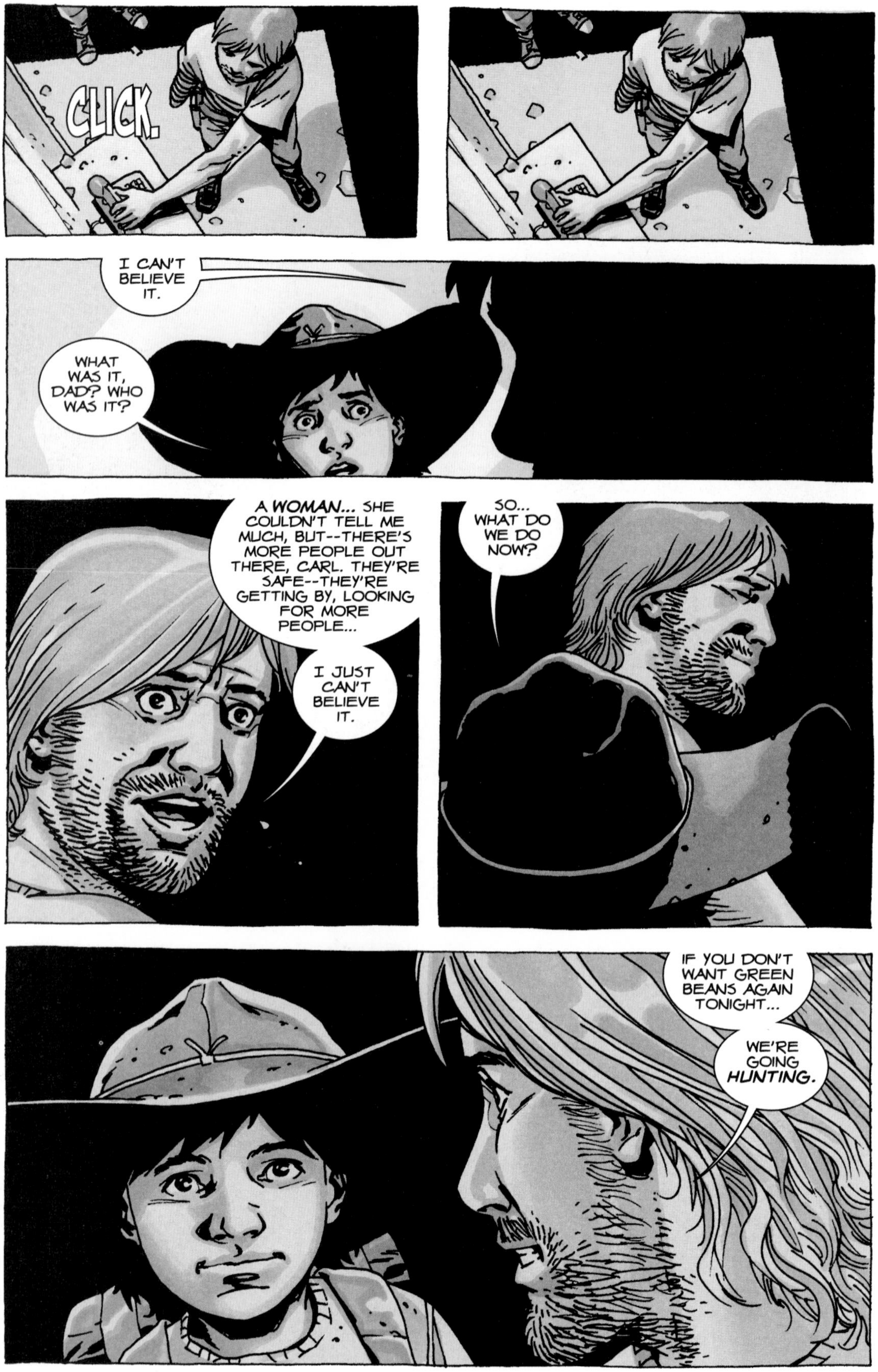
CLICK.
I CAN'T BELIEVE IT.
WHAT WAS IT, DAD? WHO WAS IT?
A *WOMAN...* SHE COULDN'T TELL ME MUCH, BUT--THERE'S MORE PEOPLE OUT THERE, CARL. THEY'RE SAFE--THEY'RE GETTING BY, LOOKING FOR MORE PEOPLE...
I JUST CAN'T BELIEVE IT.
SO... WHAT DO WE DO NOW?
IF YOU DON'T WANT GREEN BEANS AGAIN TONIGHT...
WE'RE GOING *HUNTING.*

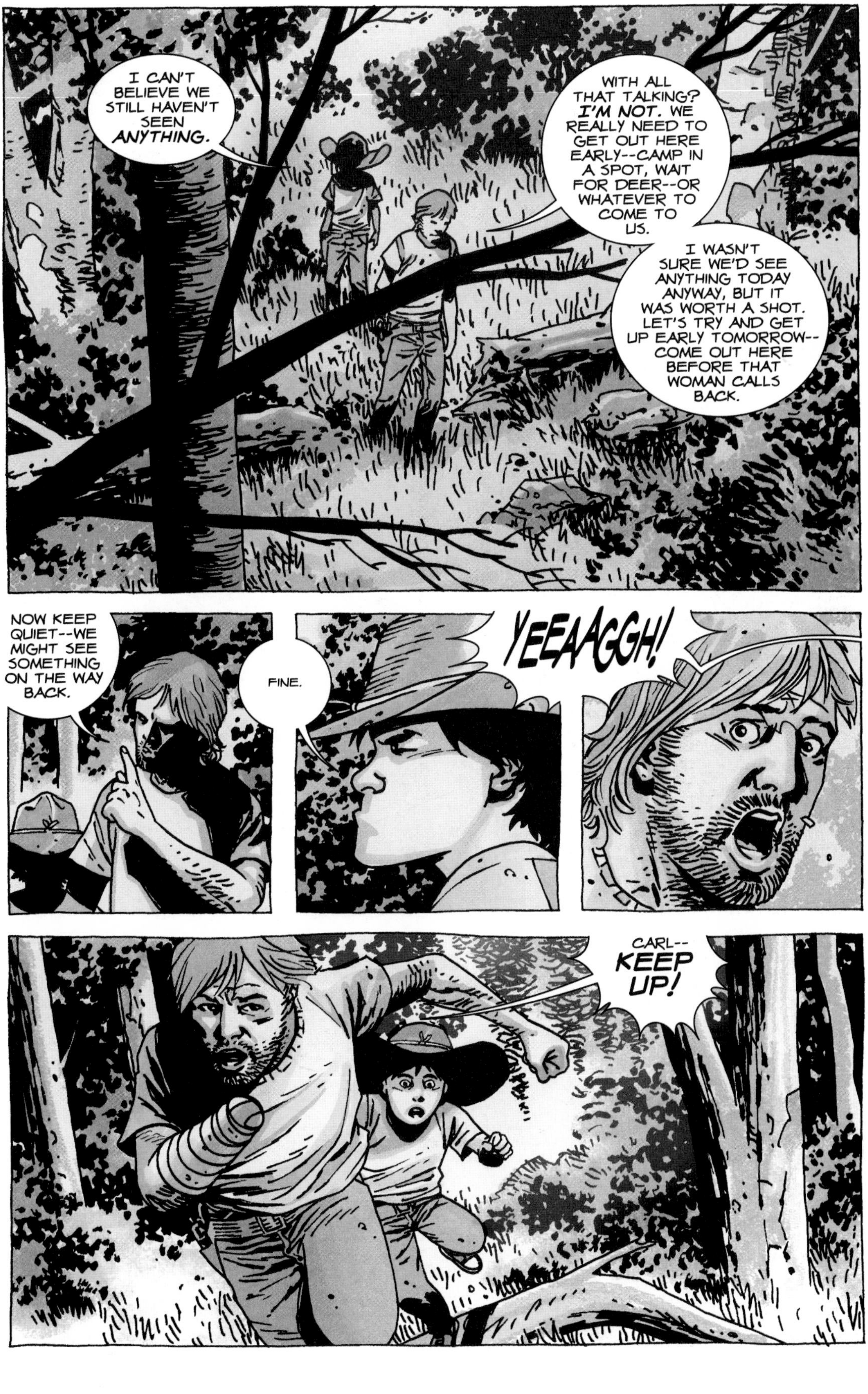
I CAN'T BELIEVE WE STILL HAVEN'T SEEN ANYTHING.
WITH ALL THAT TALKING? I'M NOT. WE REALLY NEED TO GET OUT HERE EARLY--CAMP IN A SPOT, WAIT FOR DEER--OR WHATEVER TO COME TO US.
I WASN'T SURE WE'D SEE ANYTHING TODAY ANYWAY, BUT IT WAS WORTH A SHOT. LET'S TRY AND GET UP EARLY TOMORROW-- COME OUT HERE BEFORE THAT WOMAN CALLS BACK.
NOW KEEP QUIET--WE MIGHT SEE SOMETHING ON THE WAY BACK.
FINE.
YEEAAGGH!
CARL-- KEEP UP!

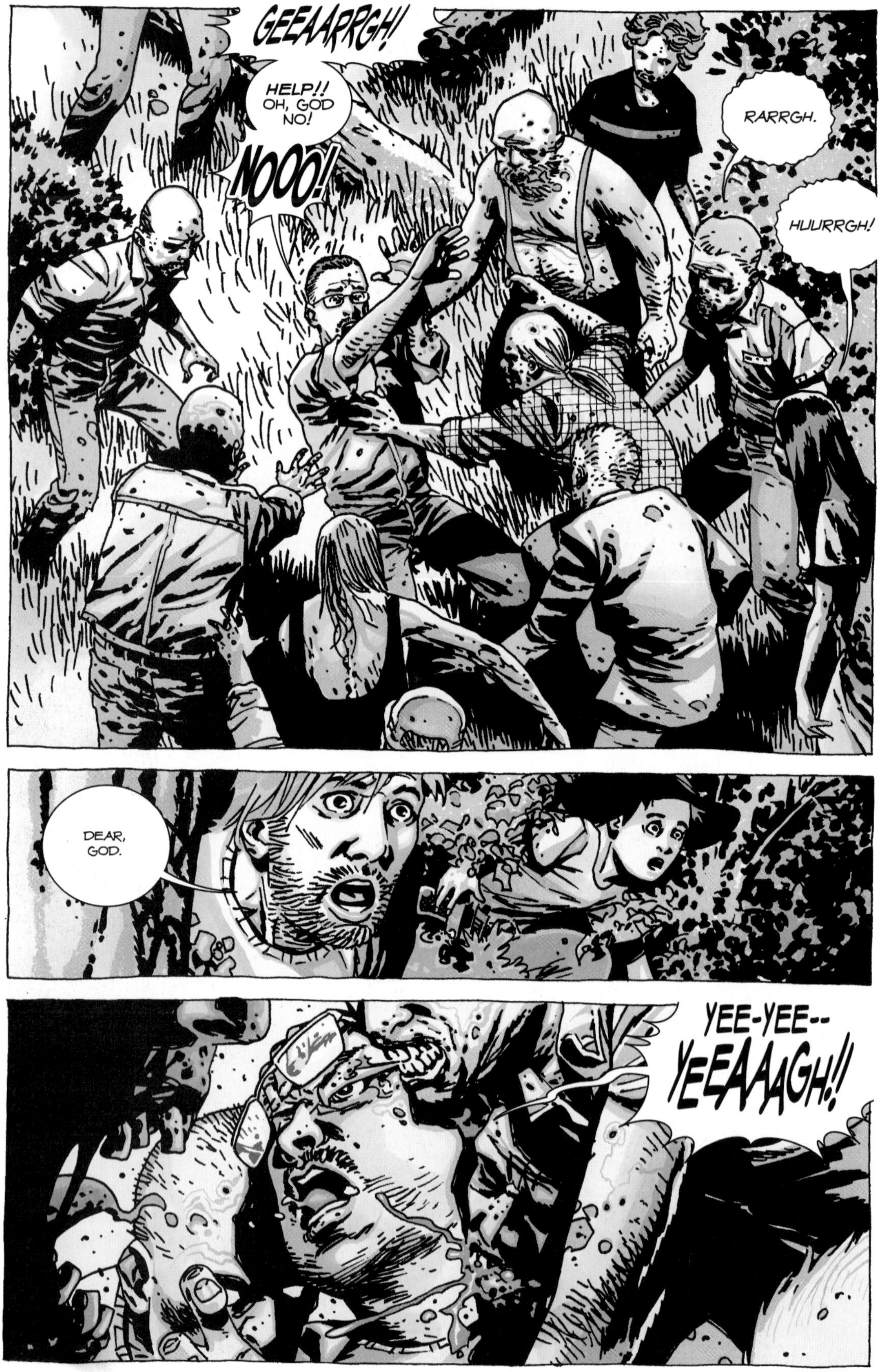
GEEAARRGH!
HELP!! OH, GOD NO!
NOOO!
RARRGH.
HUURRGH!
DEAR, GOD.
YEE-YEE--
YEEAAAGH!!

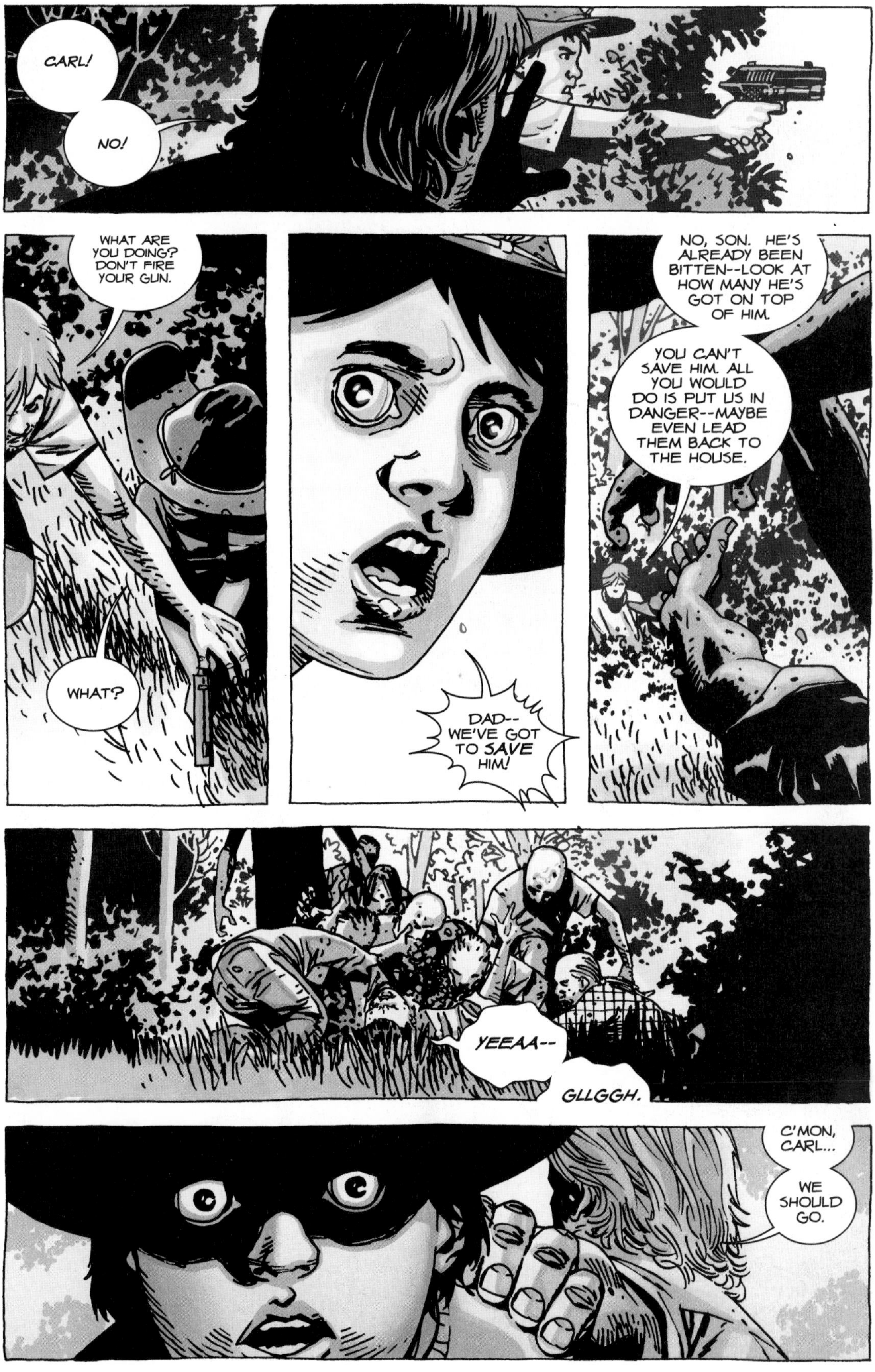
CARL!
NO!
WHAT ARE YOU DOING? DON'T FIRE YOUR GUN.
WHAT?
DAD-- WE'VE GOT TO SAVE HIM!
NO, SON. HE'S ALREADY BEEN BITTEN--LOOK AT HOW MANY HE'S GOT ON TOP OF HIM.
YOU CAN'T SAVE HIM. ALL YOU WOULD DO IS PUT US IN DANGER--MAYBE EVEN LEAD THEM BACK TO THE HOUSE.
YEEAA--
GLLGGH.
C'MON, CARL...
WE SHOULD GO.

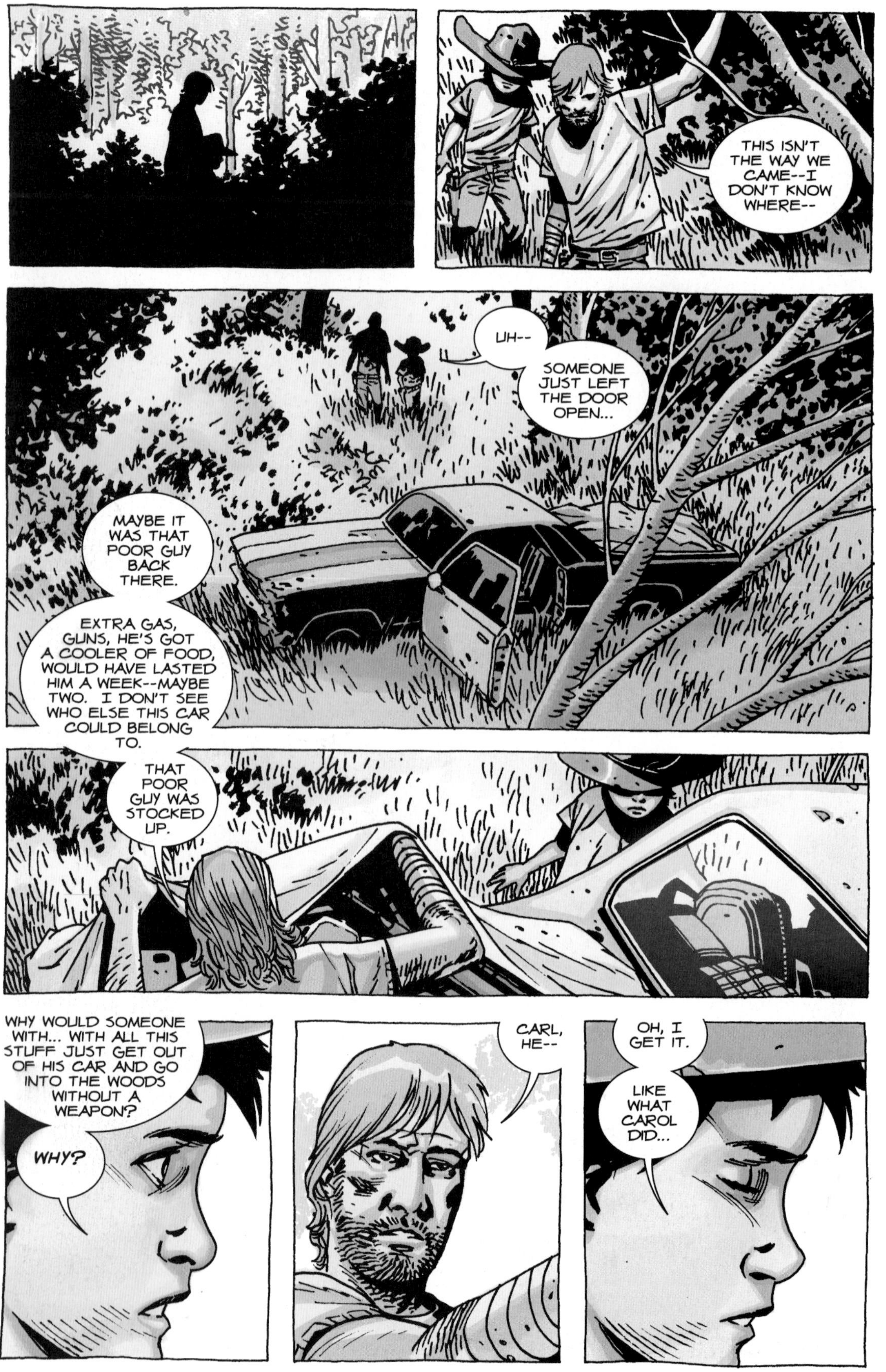
THIS ISN'T THE WAY WE CAME--I DON'T KNOW WHERE--
UH--
SOMEONE JUST LEFT THE DOOR OPEN...
MAYBE IT WAS THAT POOR GUY BACK THERE.
EXTRA GAS, GUNS, HE'S GOT A COOLER OF FOOD, WOULD HAVE LASTED HIM A WEEK--MAYBE TWO. I DON'T SEE WHO ELSE THIS CAR COULD BELONG TO.
THAT POOR GUY WAS STOCKED UP.
WHY WOULD SOMEONE WITH... WITH ALL THIS STUFF JUST GET OUT OF HIS CAR AND GO INTO THE WOODS WITHOUT A WEAPON?
WHY?
CARL, HE--
OH, I GET IT.
LIKE WHAT CAROL DID...

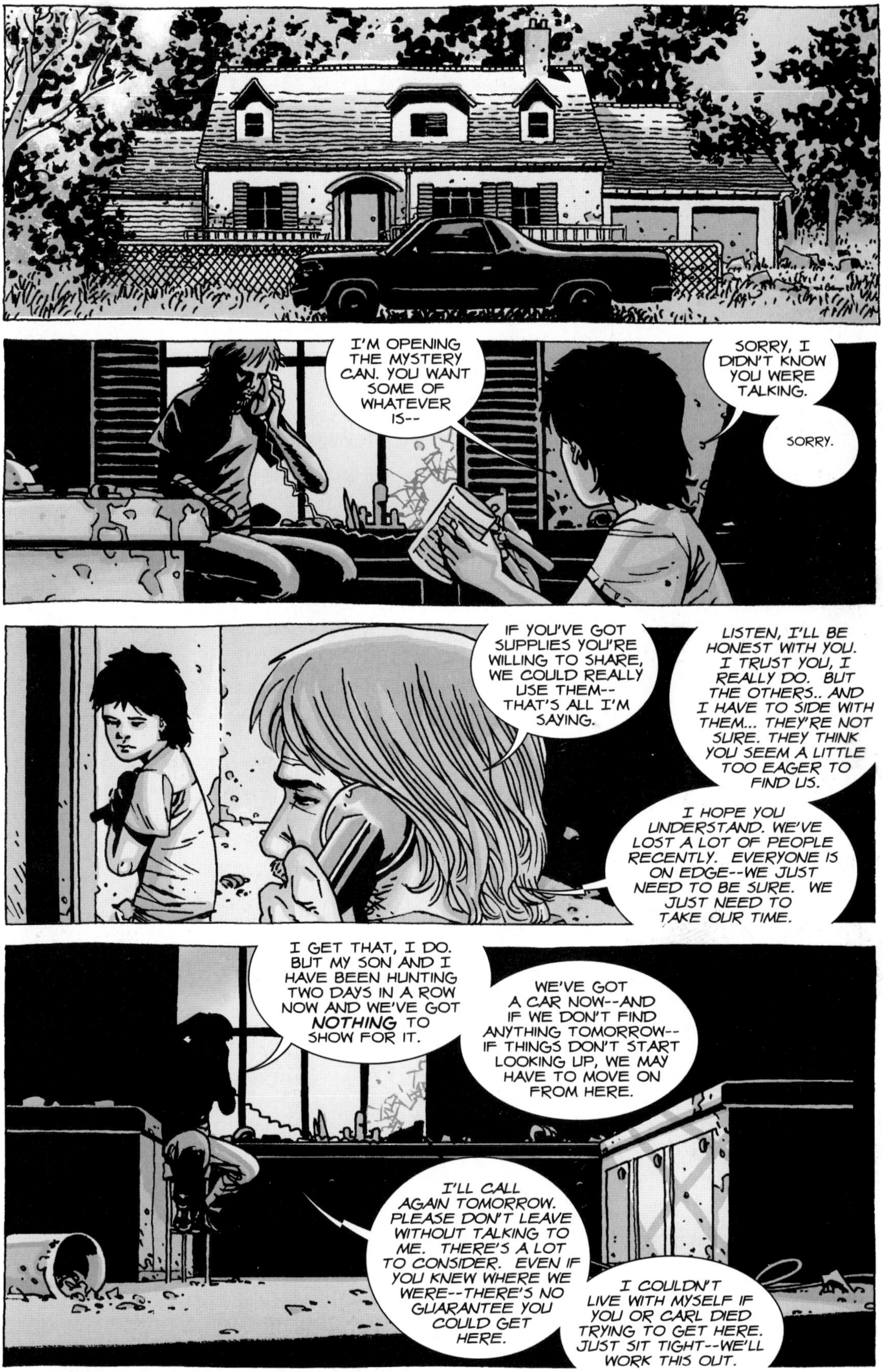
I'M OPENING THE MYSTERY CAN. YOU WANT SOME OF WHATEVER IS--
SORRY, I DIDN'T KNOW YOU WERE TALKING.
SORRY.
IF YOU'VE GOT SUPPLIES YOU'RE WILLING TO SHARE, WE COULD REALLY USE THEM-- THAT'S ALL I'M SAYING.
LISTEN, I'LL BE HONEST WITH YOU. I TRUST YOU, I REALLY DO. BUT THE OTHERS.. AND I HAVE TO SIDE WITH THEM... THEY'RE NOT SURE. THEY THINK YOU SEEM A LITTLE TOO EAGER TO FIND US.
I HOPE YOU UNDERSTAND. WE'VE LOST A LOT OF PEOPLE RECENTLY. EVERYONE IS ON EDGE--WE JUST NEED TO BE SURE. WE JUST NEED TO TAKE OUR TIME.
I GET THAT, I DO. BUT MY SON AND I HAVE BEEN HUNTING TWO DAYS IN A ROW NOW AND WE'VE GOT NOTHING TO SHOW FOR IT.
WE'VE GOT A CAR NOW--AND IF WE DON'T FIND ANYTHING TOMORROW-- IF THINGS DON'T START LOOKING UP, WE MAY HAVE TO MOVE ON FROM HERE.
I'LL CALL AGAIN TOMORROW. PLEASE DON'T LEAVE WITHOUT TALKING TO ME. THERE'S A LOT TO CONSIDER. EVEN IF YOU KNEW WHERE WE WERE--THERE'S NO GUARANTEE YOU COULD GET HERE.
I COULDN'T LIVE WITH MYSELF IF YOU OR CARL DIED TRYING TO GET HERE. JUST SIT TIGHT--WE'LL WORK THIS OUT.

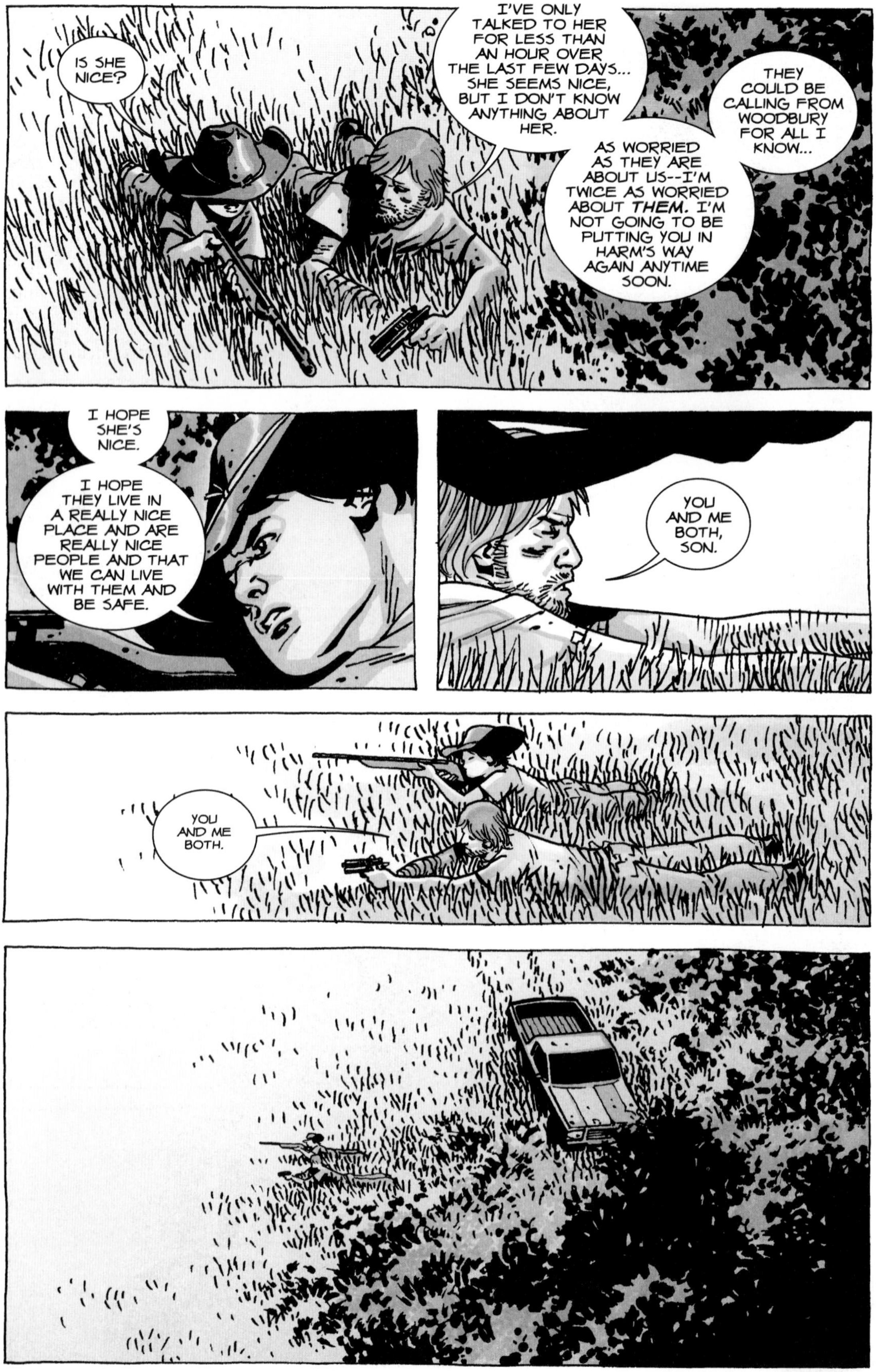
IS SHE NICE?
I'VE ONLY TALKED TO HER FOR LESS THAN AN HOUR OVER THE LAST FEW DAYS... SHE SEEMS NICE, BUT I DON'T KNOW ANYTHING ABOUT HER.
AS WORRIED AS THEY ARE ABOUT US--I'M TWICE AS WORRIED ABOUT THEM. I'M NOT GOING TO BE PUTTING YOU IN HARM'S WAY AGAIN ANYTIME SOON.
THEY COULD BE CALLING FROM WOODBURY FOR ALL I KNOW...
I HOPE SHE'S NICE.
I HOPE THEY LIVE IN A REALLY NICE PLACE AND ARE REALLY NICE PEOPLE AND THAT WE CAN LIVE WITH THEM AND BE SAFE.
YOU AND ME BOTH, SON.
YOU AND ME BOTH.

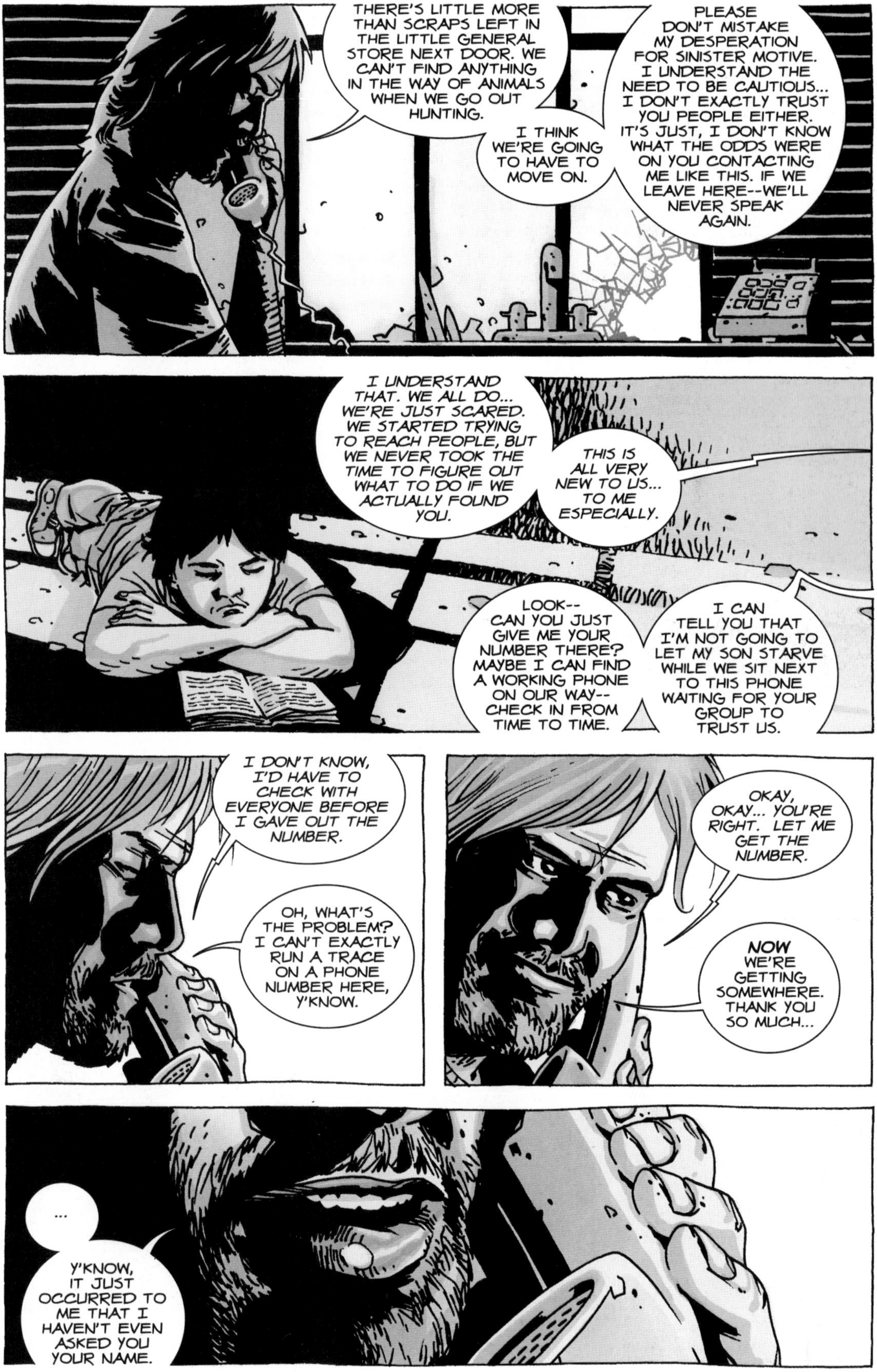
THERE'S LITTLE MORE THAN SCRAPS LEFT IN THE LITTLE GENERAL STORE NEXT DOOR. WE CAN'T FIND ANYTHING IN THE WAY OF ANIMALS WHEN WE GO OUT HUNTING.
I THINK WE'RE GOING TO HAVE TO MOVE ON.
PLEASE DON'T MISTAKE MY DESPERATION FOR SINISTER MOTIVE. I UNDERSTAND THE NEED TO BE CAUTIOUS... I DON'T EXACTLY TRUST YOU PEOPLE EITHER. IT'S JUST, I DON'T KNOW WHAT THE ODDS WERE ON YOU CONTACTING ME LIKE THIS. IF WE LEAVE HERE--WE'LL NEVER SPEAK AGAIN.
I UNDERSTAND THAT. WE ALL DO... WE'RE JUST SCARED. WE STARTED TRYING TO REACH PEOPLE, BUT WE NEVER TOOK THE TIME TO FIGURE OUT WHAT TO DO IF WE ACTUALLY FOUND YOU.
THIS IS ALL VERY NEW TO US... TO ME ESPECIALLY.
LOOK-- CAN YOU JUST GIVE ME YOUR NUMBER THERE? MAYBE I CAN FIND A WORKING PHONE ON OUR WAY-- CHECK IN FROM TIME TO TIME.
I CAN TELL YOU THAT I'M NOT GOING TO LET MY SON STARVE WHILE WE SIT NEXT TO THIS PHONE WAITING FOR YOUR GROUP TO TRUST US.
I DON'T KNOW, I'D HAVE TO CHECK WITH EVERYONE BEFORE I GAVE OUT THE NUMBER.
OH, WHAT'S THE PROBLEM? I CAN'T EXACTLY RUN A TRACE ON A PHONE NUMBER HERE, Y'KNOW.
OKAY, OKAY... YOU'RE RIGHT. LET ME GET THE NUMBER.
NOW WE'RE GETTING SOMEWHERE. THANK YOU SO MUCH...
...
Y'KNOW, IT JUST OCCURRED TO ME THAT I HAVEN'T EVEN ASKED YOU YOUR NAME.

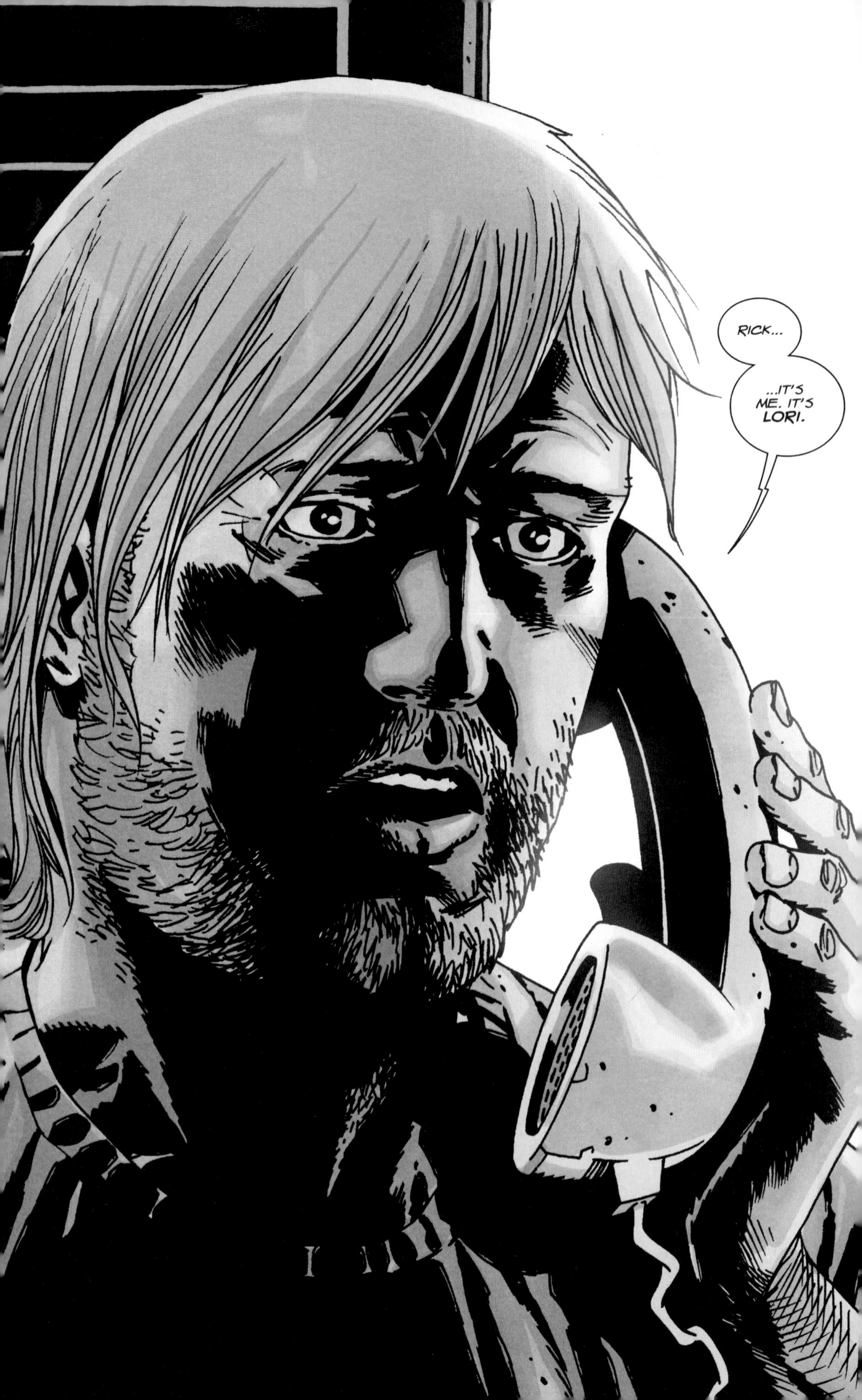
RICK...
...IT'S ME. IT'S LORI.

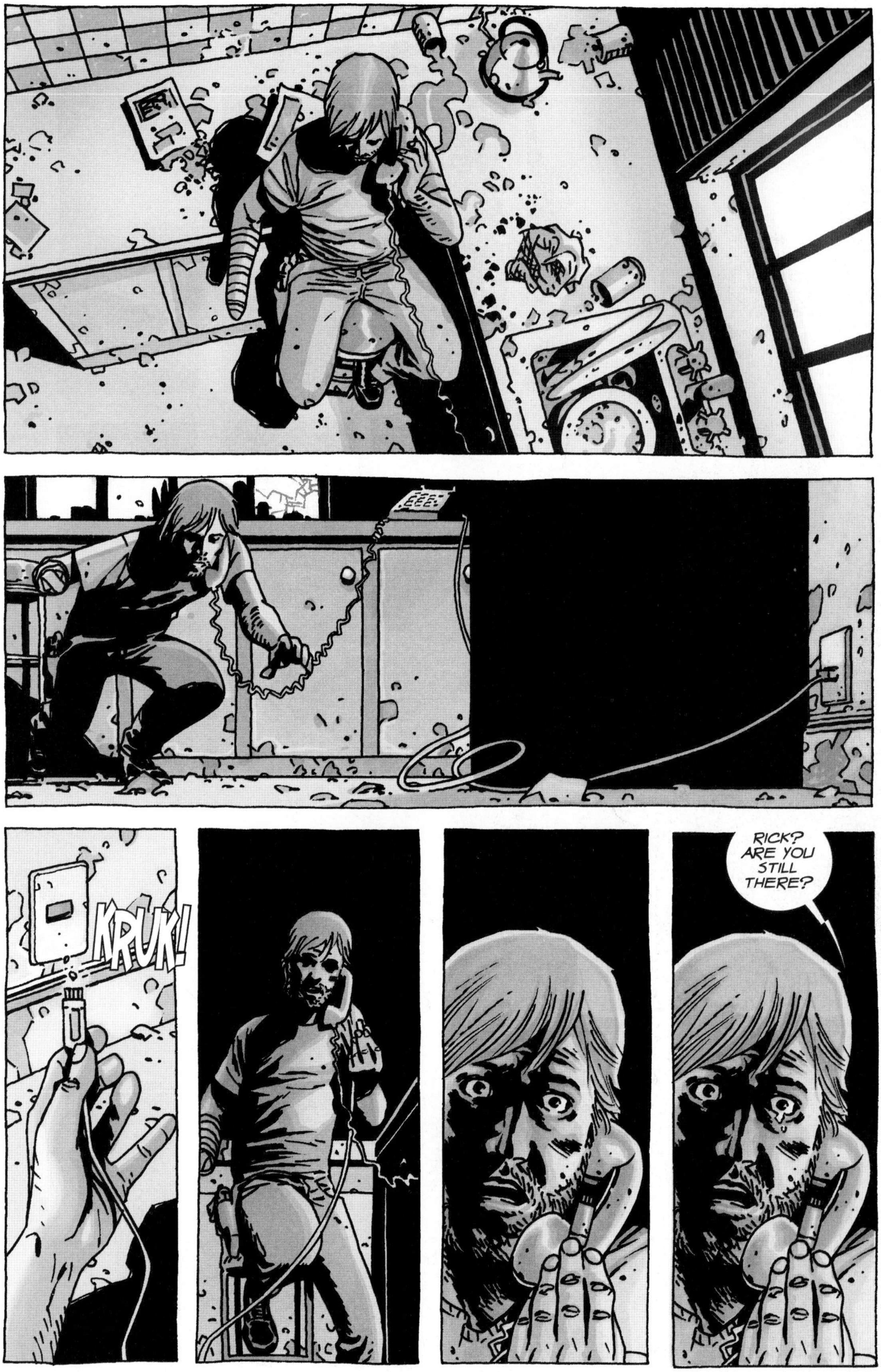
KRUK!
RICK? ARE YOU STILL THERE?

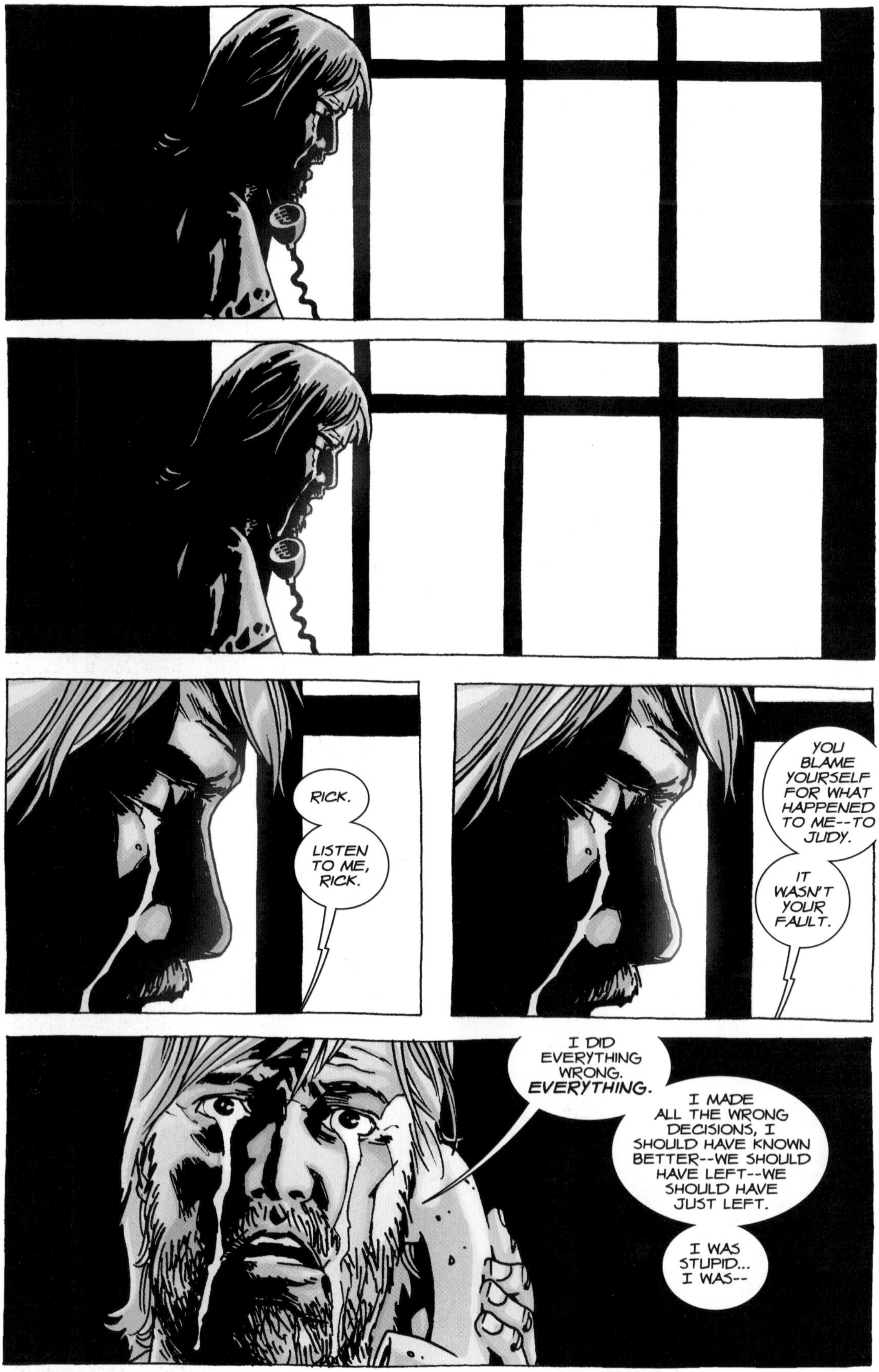
RICK.
LISTEN TO ME, RICK.
YOU BLAME YOURSELF FOR WHAT HAPPENED TO ME--TO JUDY.
IT WASN'T YOUR FAULT.
I DID EVERYTHING WRONG. EVERYTHING.
I MADE ALL THE WRONG DECISIONS, I SHOULD HAVE KNOWN BETTER--WE SHOULD HAVE LEFT--WE SHOULD HAVE JUST LEFT.
I WAS STUPID... I WAS--

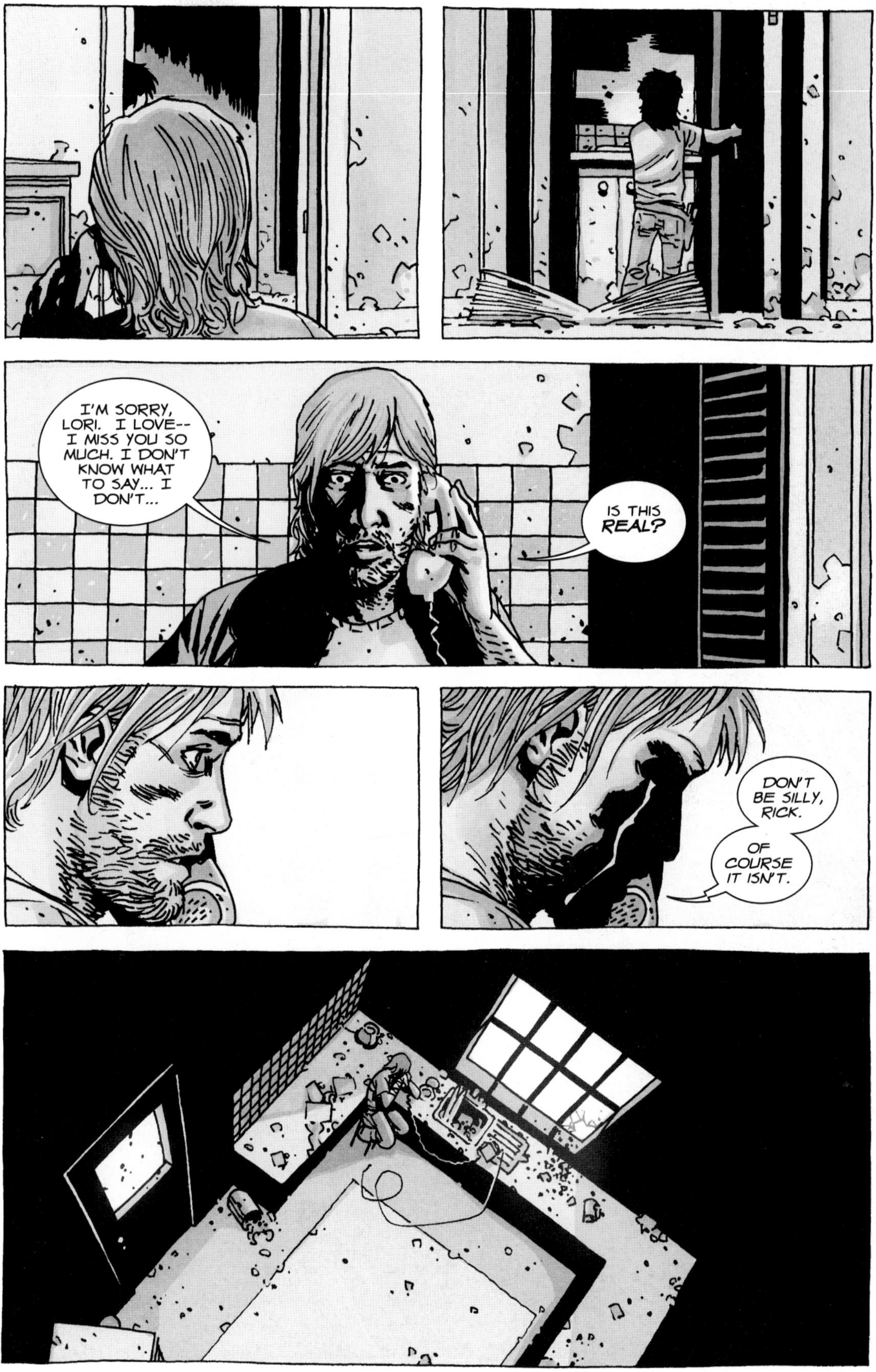

I'M SORRY, LORI. I LOVE-- I MISS YOU SO MUCH. I DON'T KNOW WHAT TO SAY... I DON'T...
IS THIS REAL?
DON'T BE SILLY, RICK.
OF COURSE IT ISN'T.

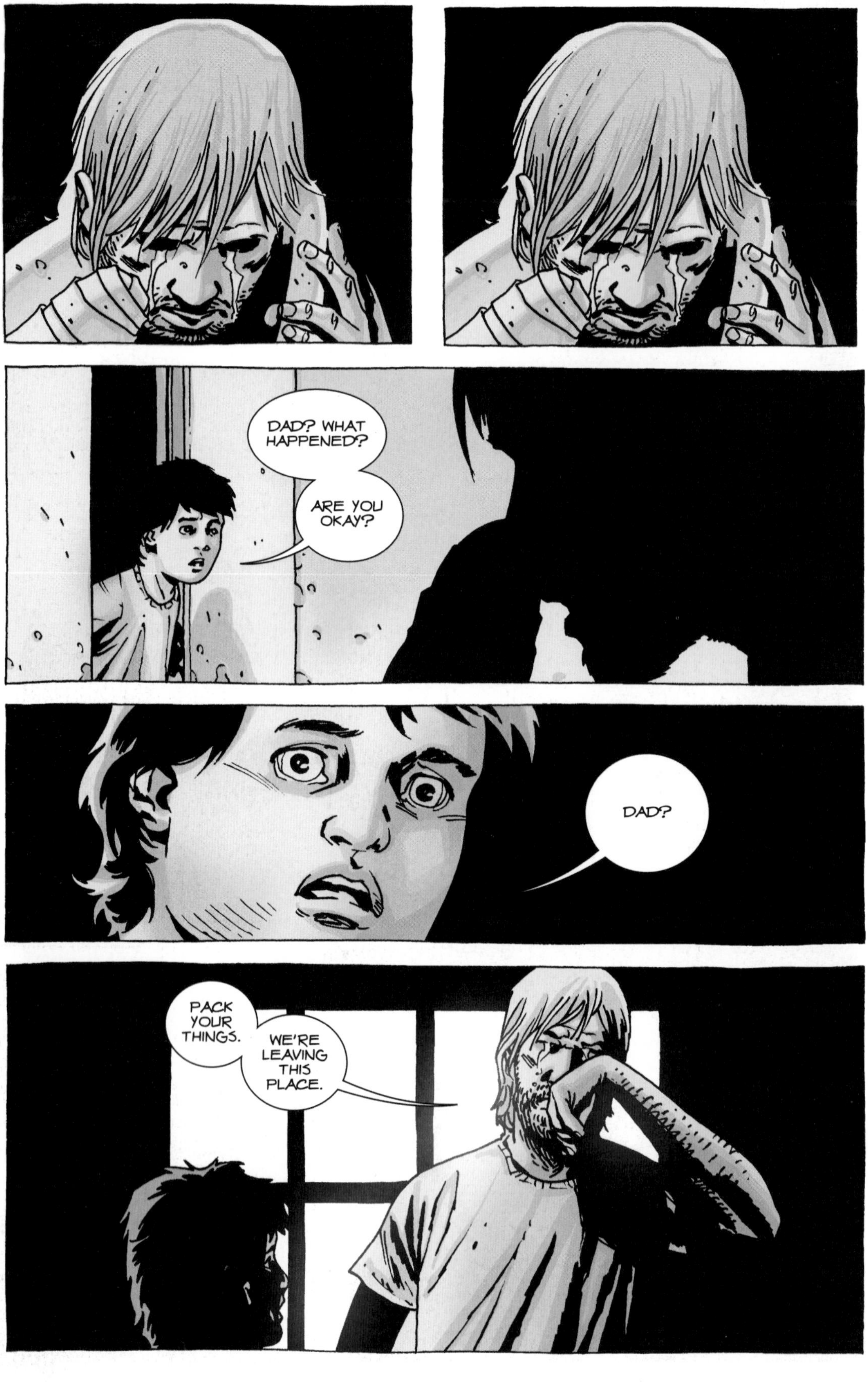
DAD? WHAT HAPPENED?
ARE YOU OKAY?
DAD?
PACK YOUR THINGS.
WE'RE LEAVING THIS PLACE.

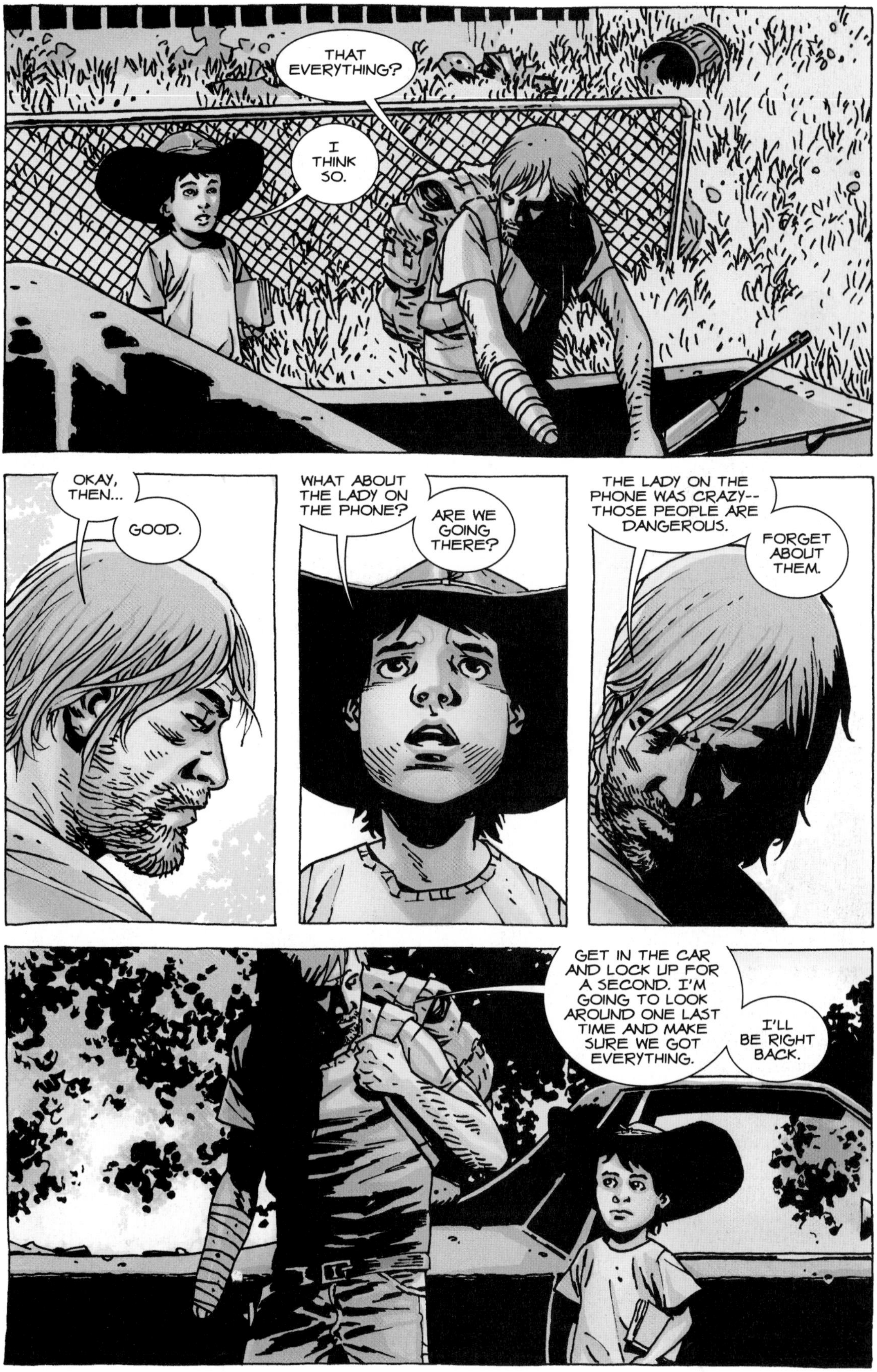
THAT EVERYTHING?
I THINK SO.
OKAY, THEN...
GOOD.
WHAT ABOUT THE LADY ON THE PHONE?
ARE WE GOING THERE?
THE LADY ON THE PHONE WAS CRAZY-- THOSE PEOPLE ARE DANGEROUS.
FORGET ABOUT THEM.
GET IN THE CAR AND LOCK UP FOR A SECOND. I'M GOING TO LOOK AROUND ONE LAST TIME AND MAKE SURE WE GOT EVERYTHING.
I'LL BE RIGHT BACK.

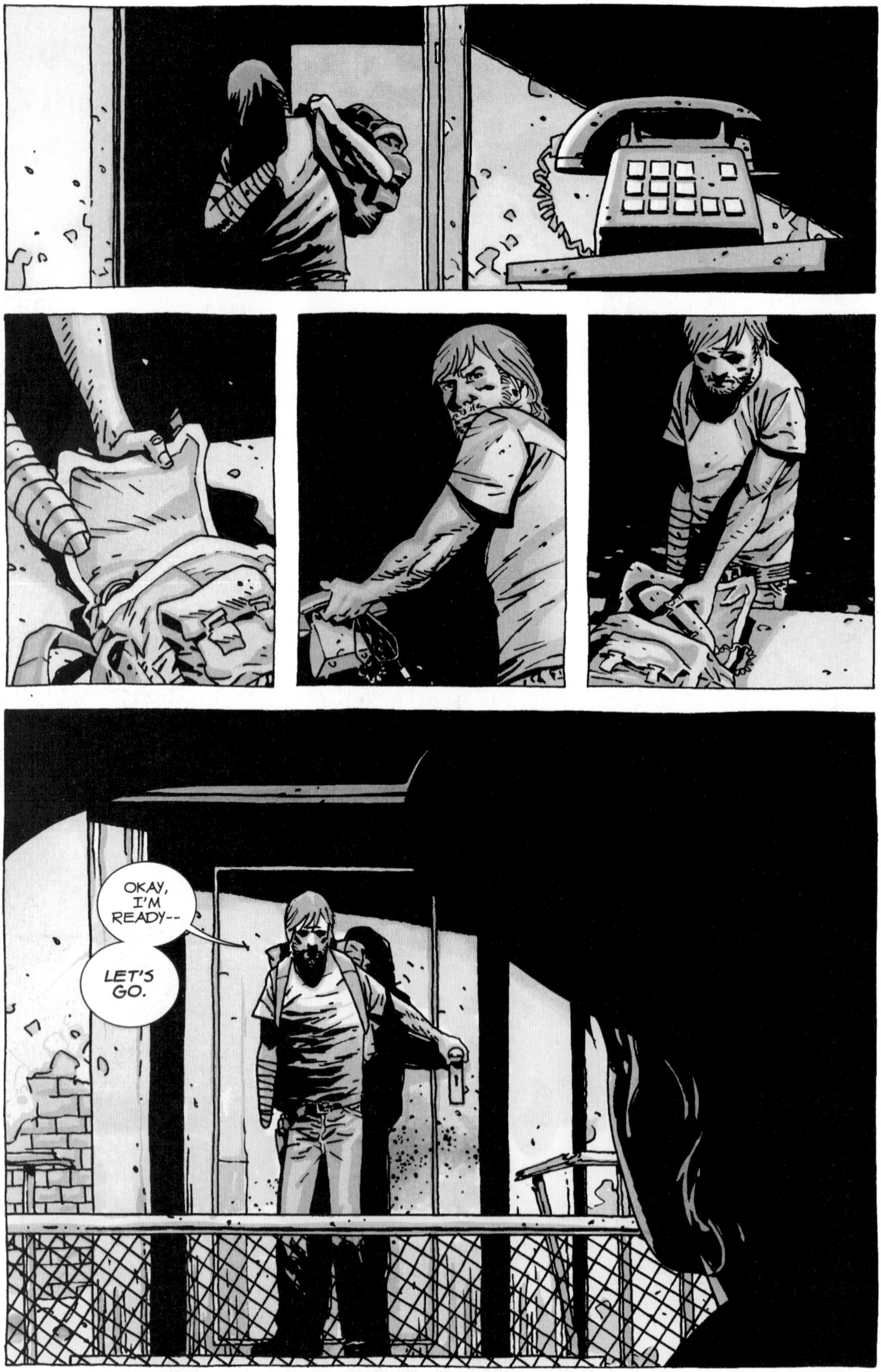
OKAY, I'M READY--
LET'S GO.

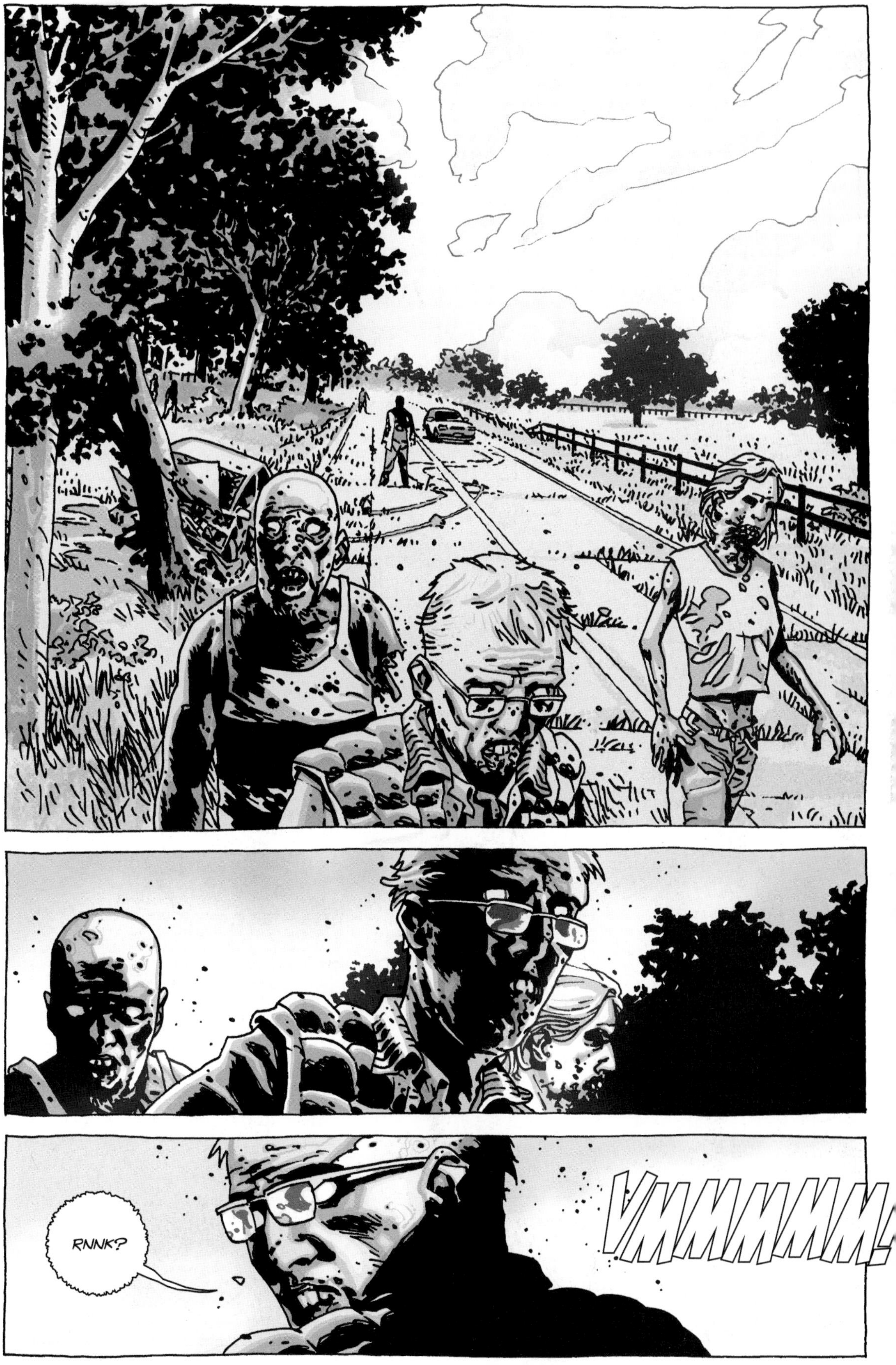
VMMMMMM!
RNNK?

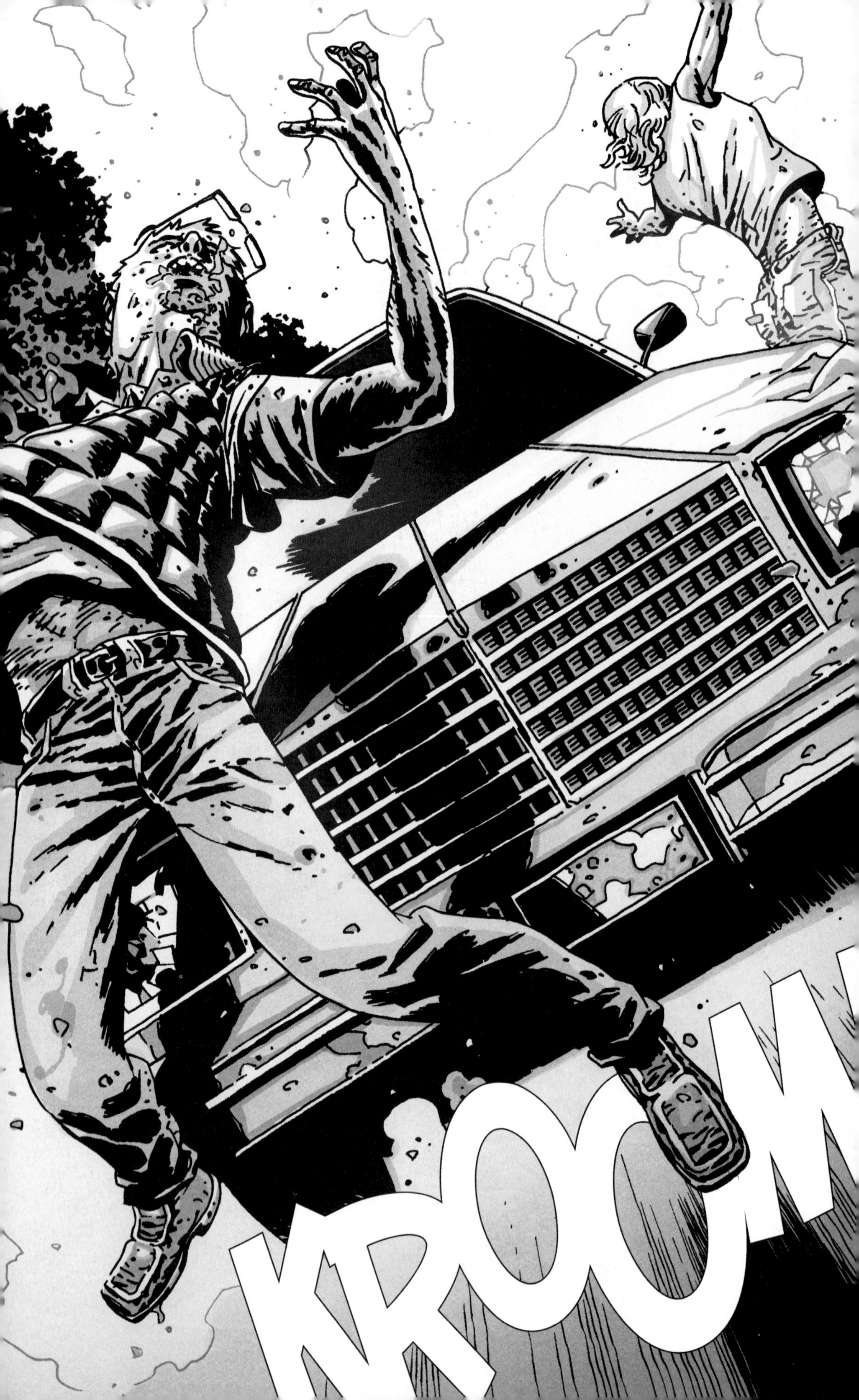
KROOM

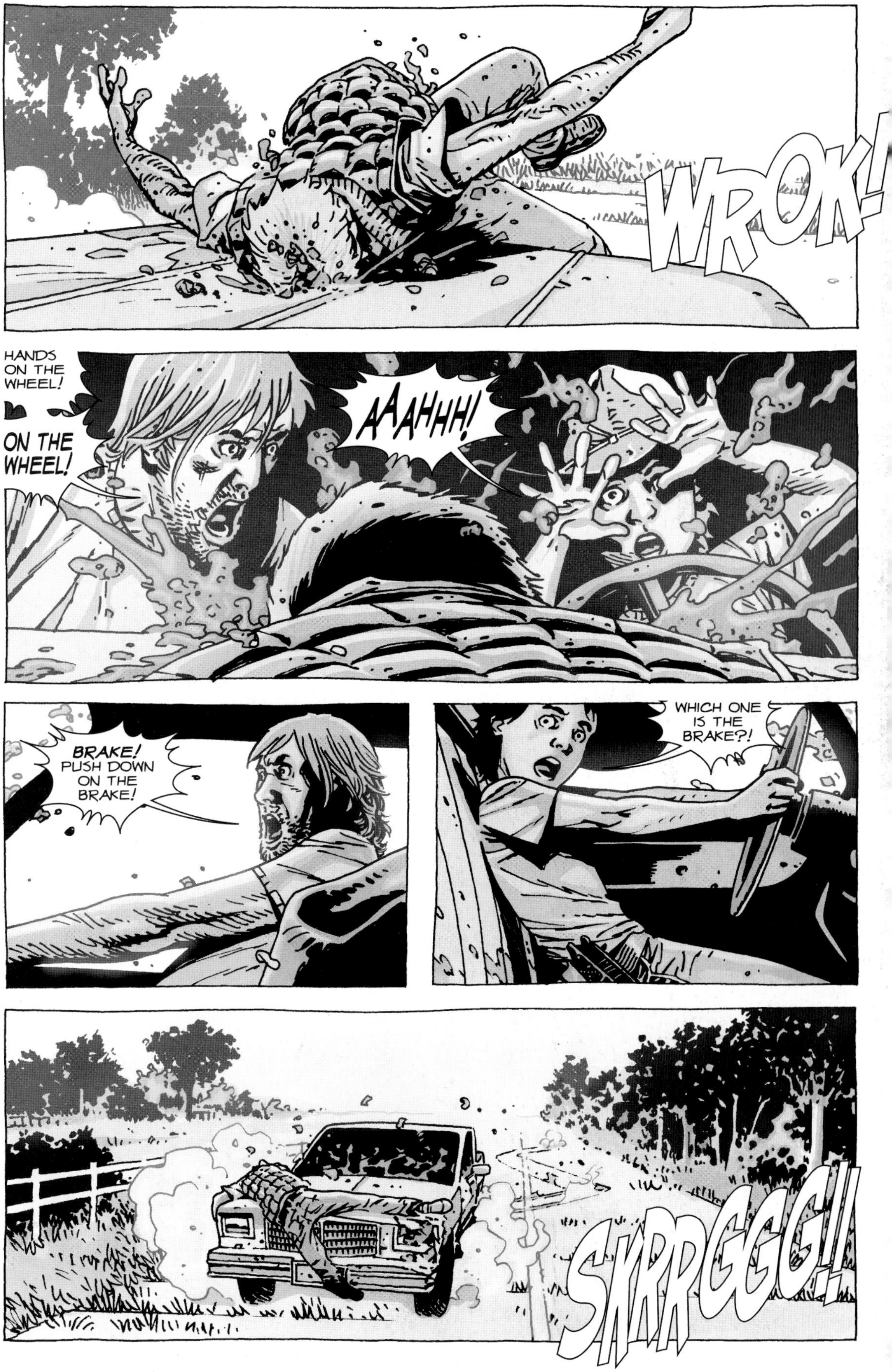
WROK!
HANDS ON THE WHEEL!
ON THE WHEEL!
AAAHHH!
BRAKE! PUSH DOWN ON THE BRAKE!
WHICH ONE IS THE BRAKE?!
SKRRGGG!!

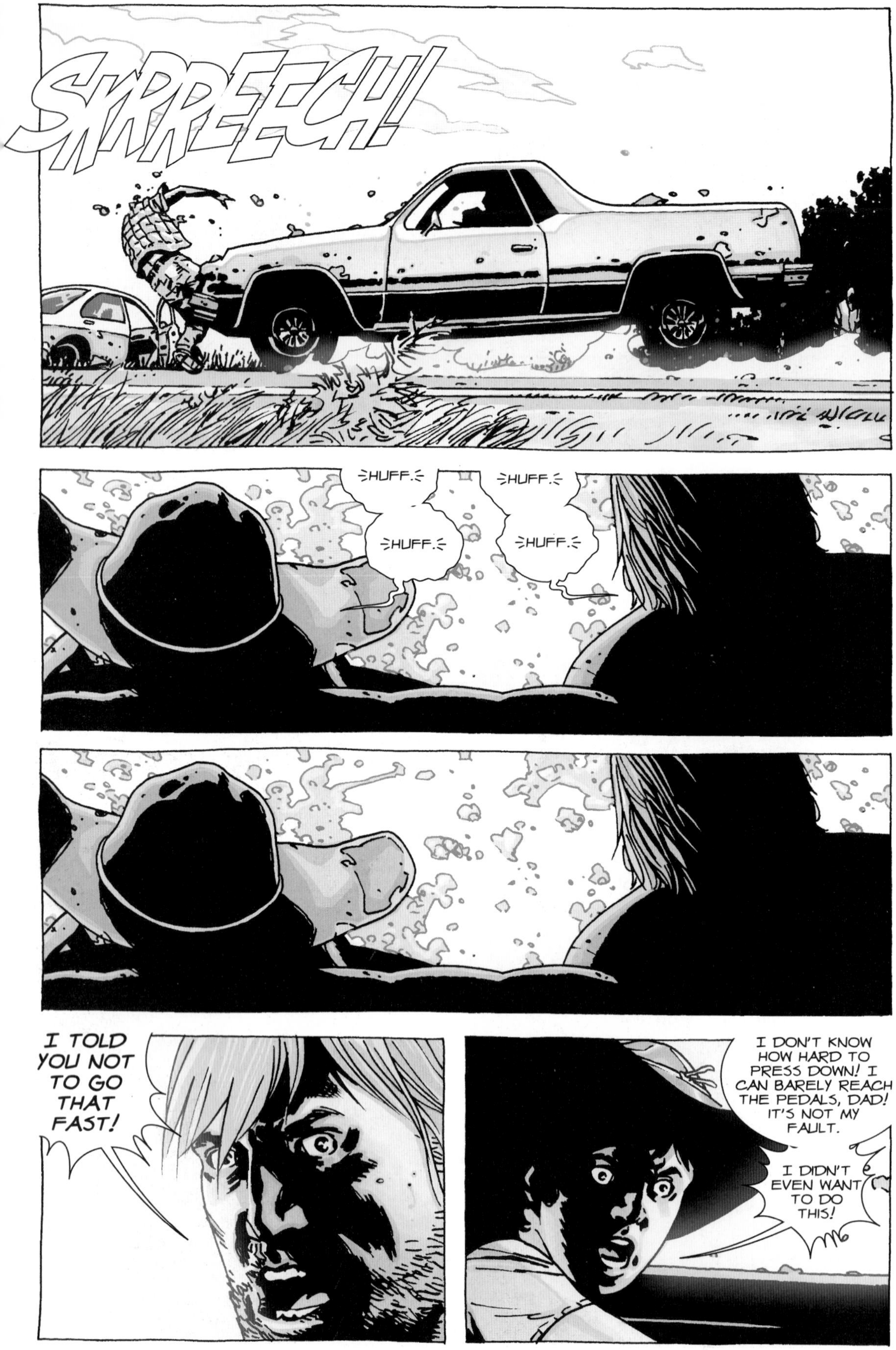
SKRREECH!
HUFF.
HUFF.
HUFF.
HUFF.
I TOLD YOU NOT TO GO THAT FAST!
I DON'T KNOW HOW HARD TO PRESS DOWN! I CAN BARELY REACH THE PEDALS, DAD! IT'S NOT MY FAULT.
I DIDN'T EVEN WANT TO DO THIS!

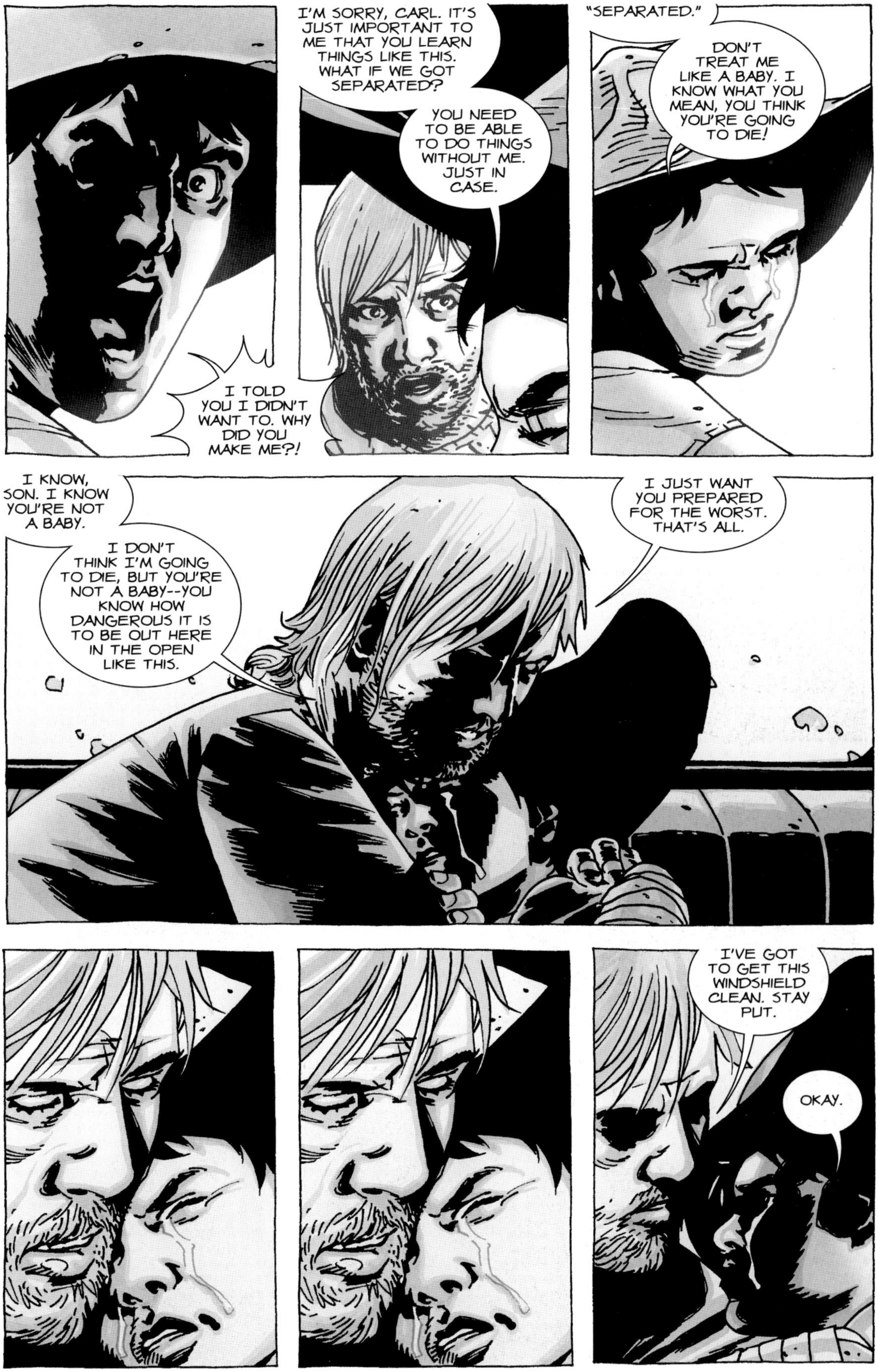
I TOLD YOU I DIDN'T WANT TO. WHY DID YOU MAKE ME?!
I'M SORRY, CARL. IT'S JUST IMPORTANT TO ME THAT YOU LEARN THINGS LIKE THIS. WHAT IF WE GOT SEPARATED?
YOU NEED TO BE ABLE TO DO THINGS WITHOUT ME. JUST IN CASE.
"SEPARATED."
DON'T TREAT ME LIKE A BABY. I KNOW WHAT YOU MEAN, YOU THINK YOU'RE GOING TO DIE!
I KNOW, SON. I KNOW YOU'RE NOT A BABY.
I DON'T THINK I'M GOING TO DIE, BUT YOU'RE NOT A BABY--YOU KNOW HOW DANGEROUS IT IS TO BE OUT HERE IN THE OPEN LIKE THIS.
I JUST WANT YOU PREPARED FOR THE WORST. THAT'S ALL.
I'VE GOT TO GET THIS WINDSHIELD CLEAN. STAY PUT.
OKAY.

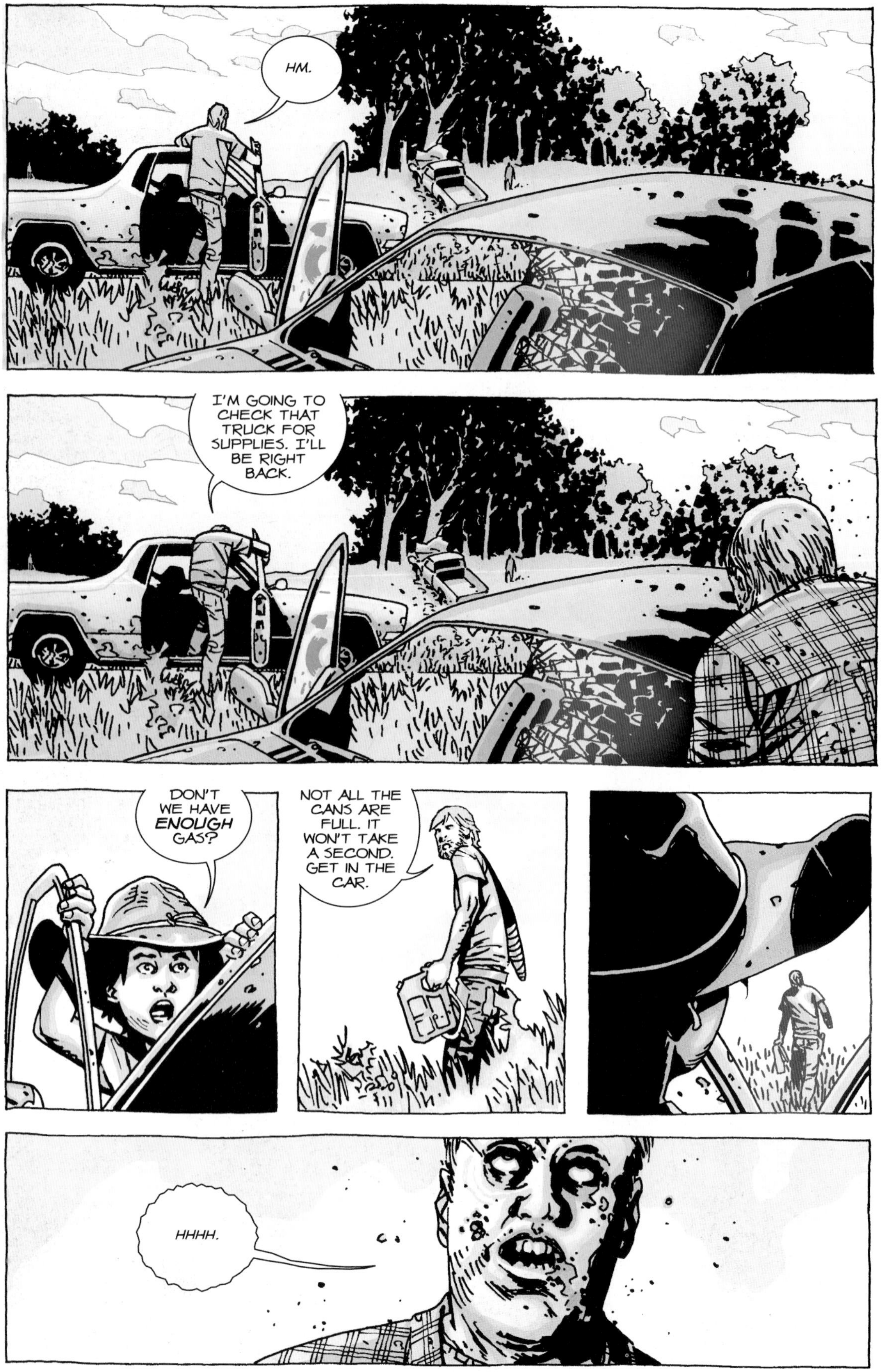
HM.
I'M GOING TO CHECK THAT TRUCK FOR SUPPLIES. I'LL BE RIGHT BACK.
DON'T WE HAVE **ENOUGH** GAS?
NOT ALL THE CANS ARE FULL. IT WON'T TAKE A SECOND. GET IN THE CAR.
HHHH.

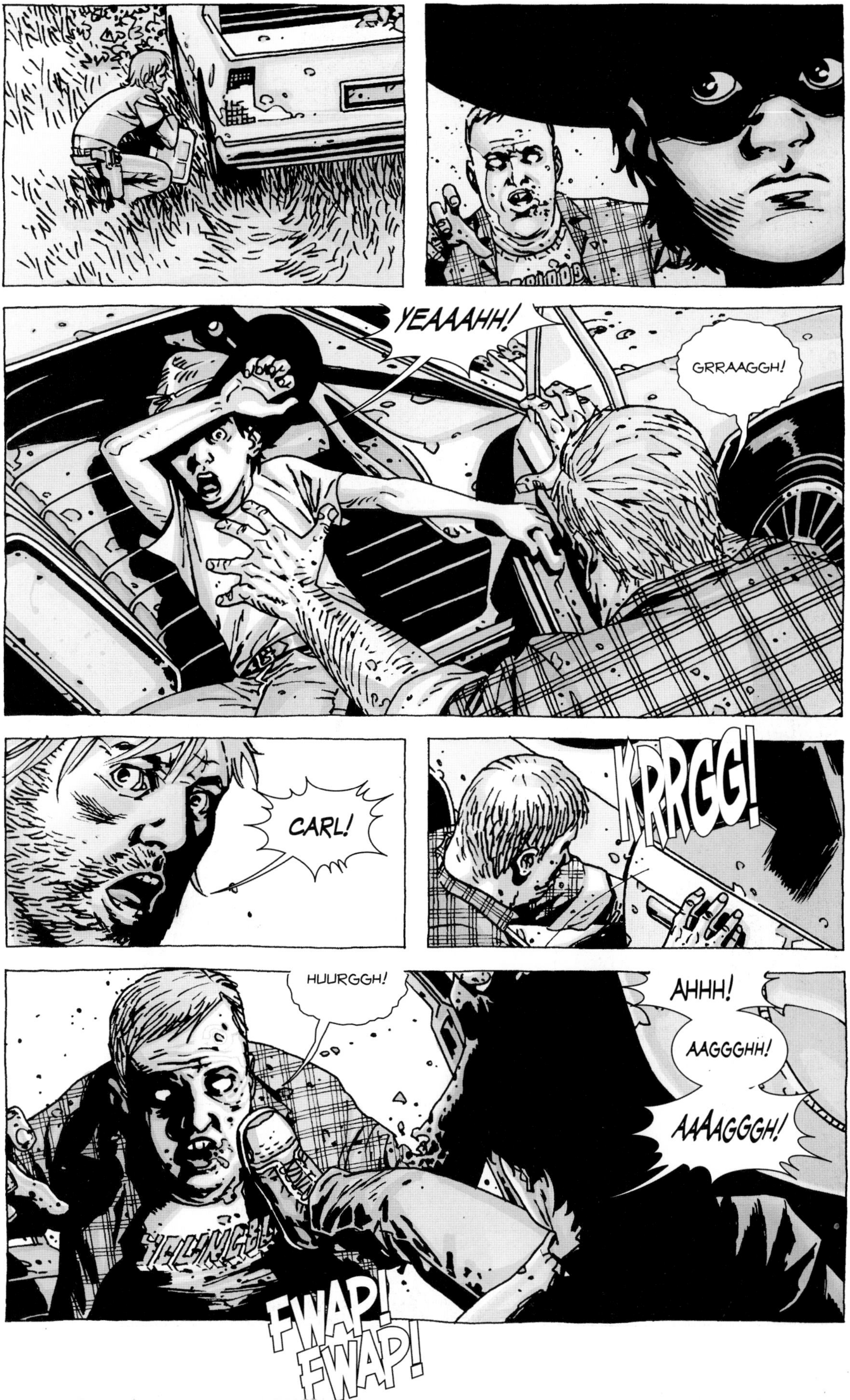
YEAAAHH!
GRRAAGGH!
CARL!
KRRGG!
HUURGGH!
AHHH!
AAGGGHH!
AAAAGGGH!
FWAP! FWAP!

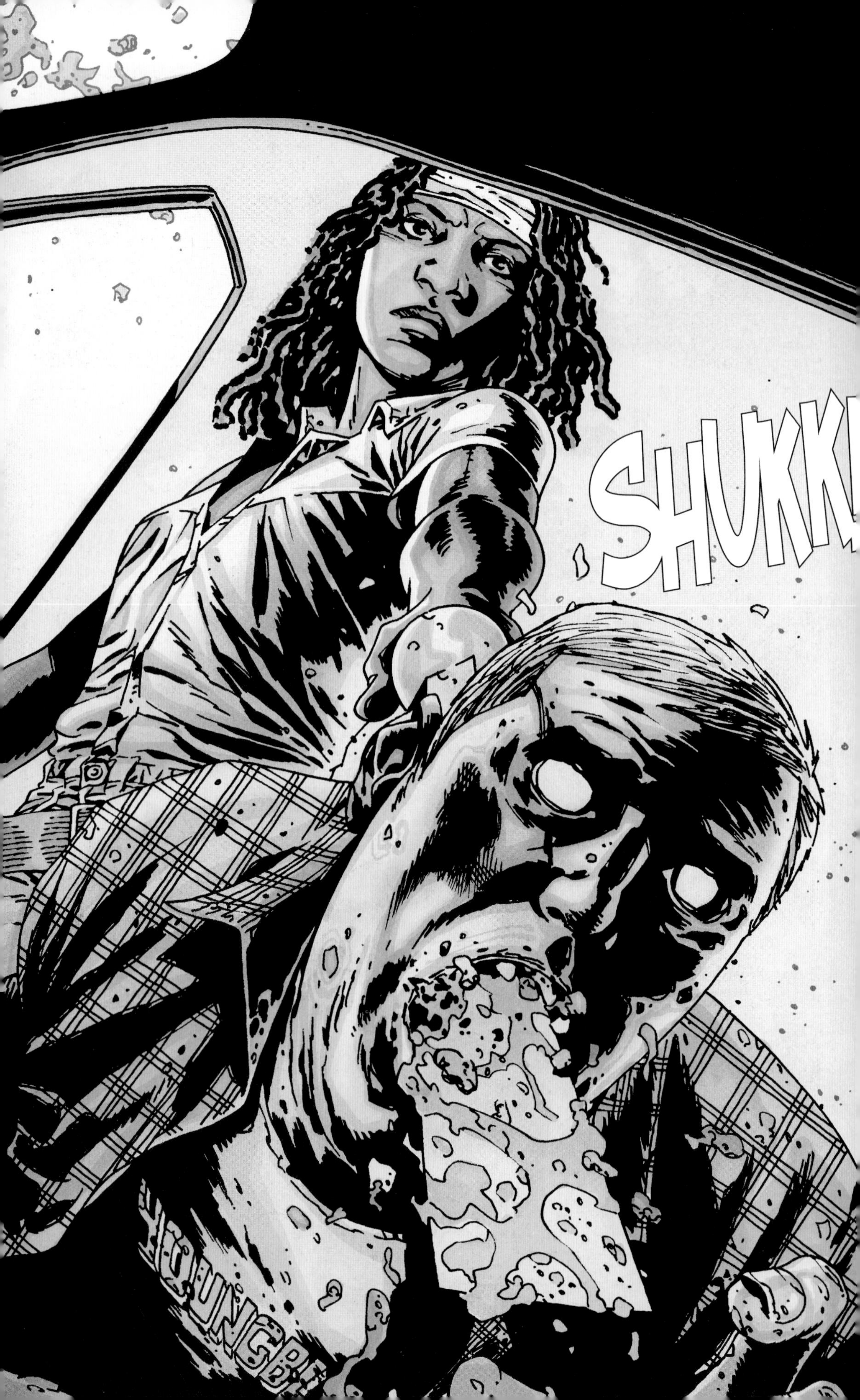
SHUKK

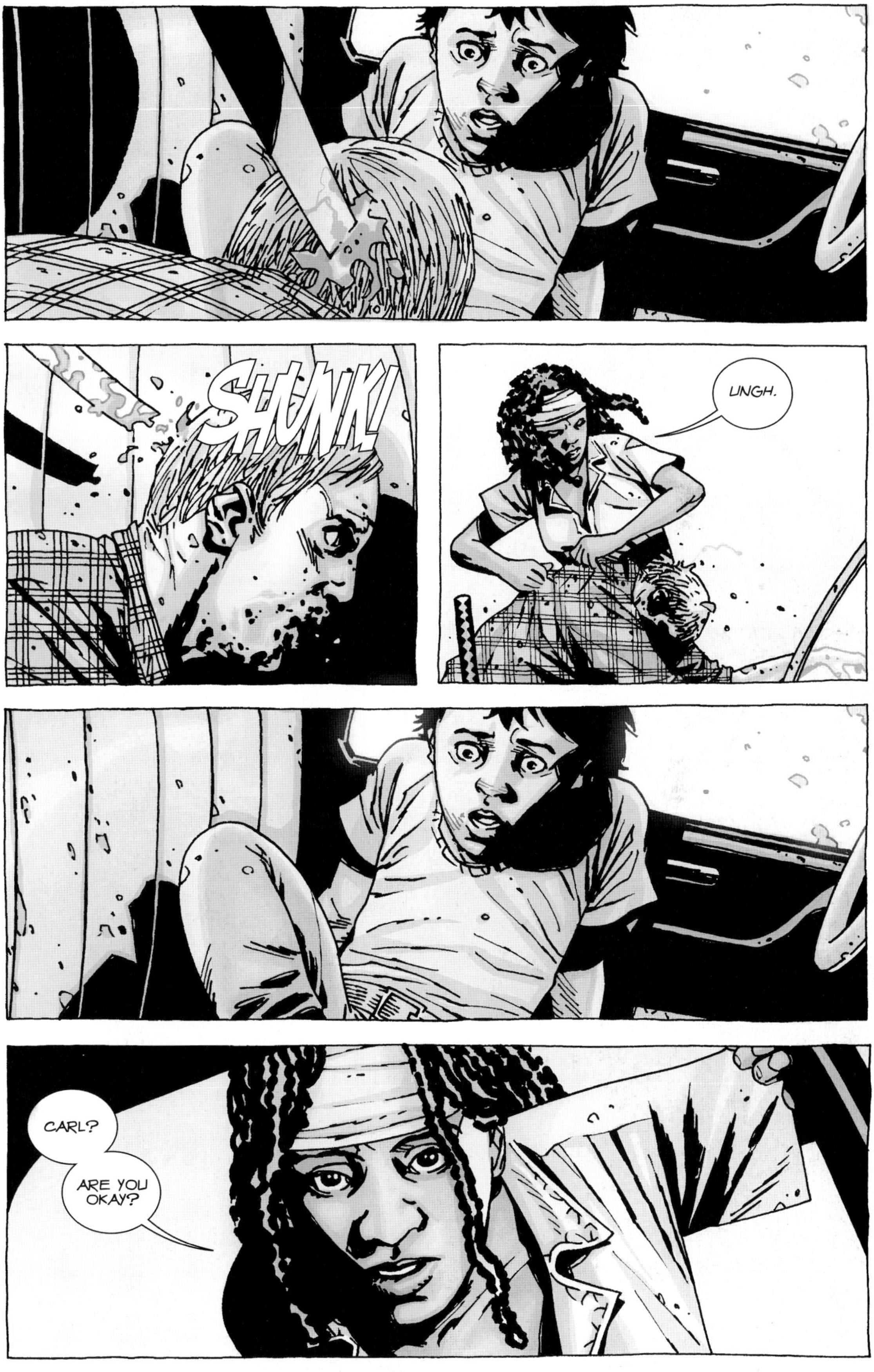
SHUNK!
UNGH.
CARL?
ARE YOU OKAY?

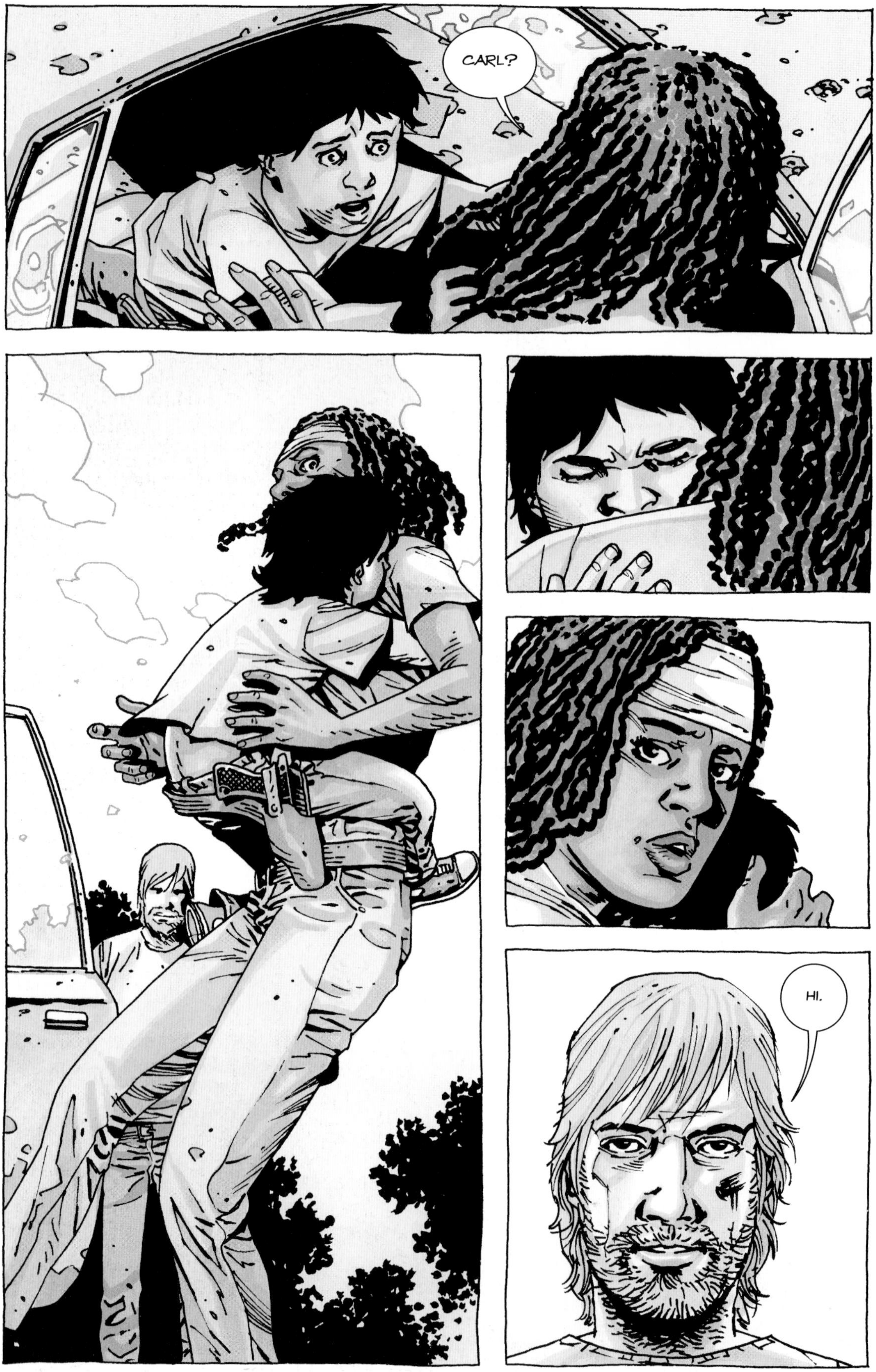
CARL?
HI.

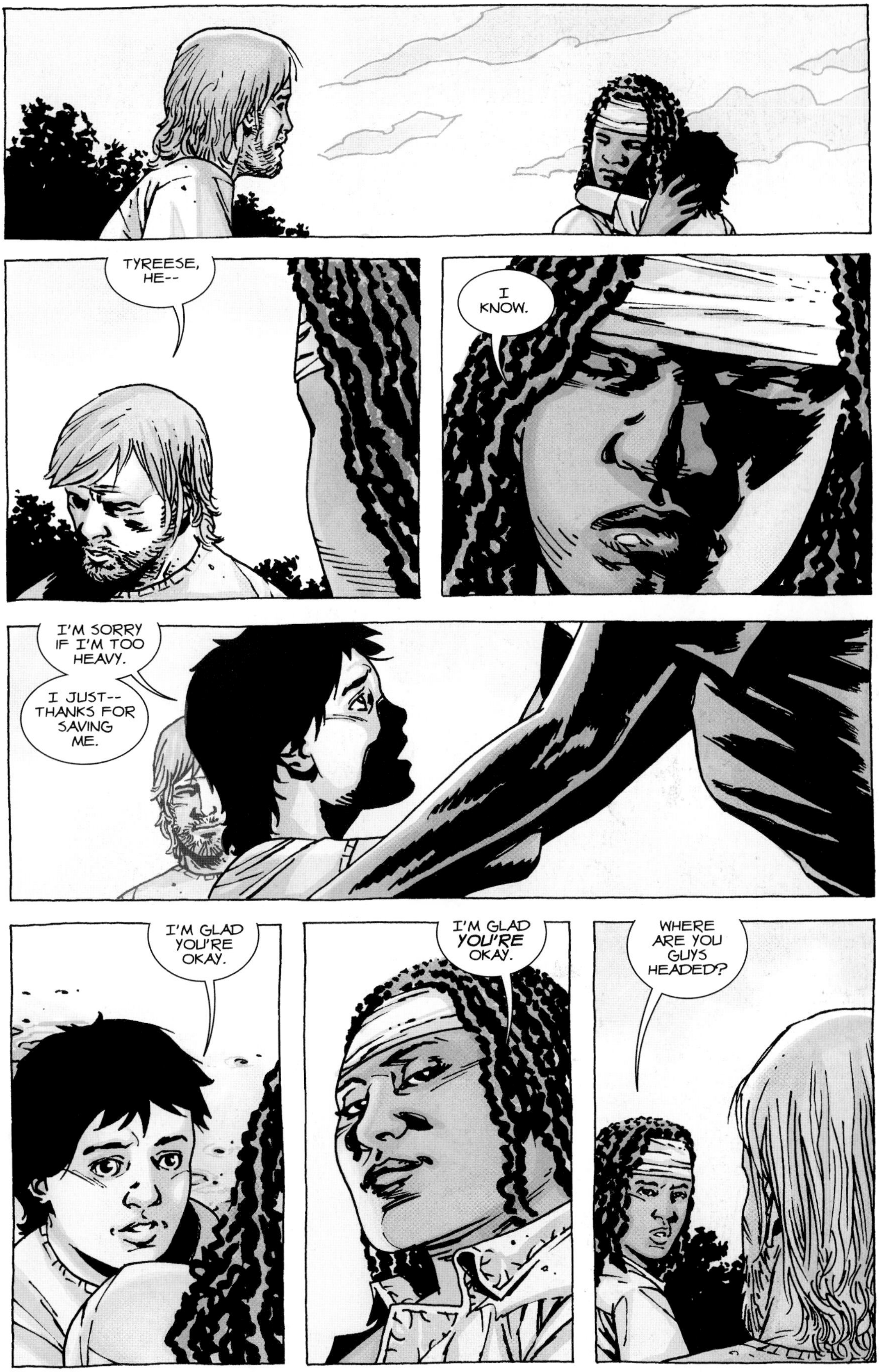
TYREESE, HE--
I KNOW.
I'M SORRY IF I'M TOO HEAVY.
I JUST-- THANKS FOR SAVING ME.
I'M GLAD YOU'RE OKAY.
I'M GLAD *YOU'RE* OKAY.
WHERE ARE YOU GUYS HEADED?

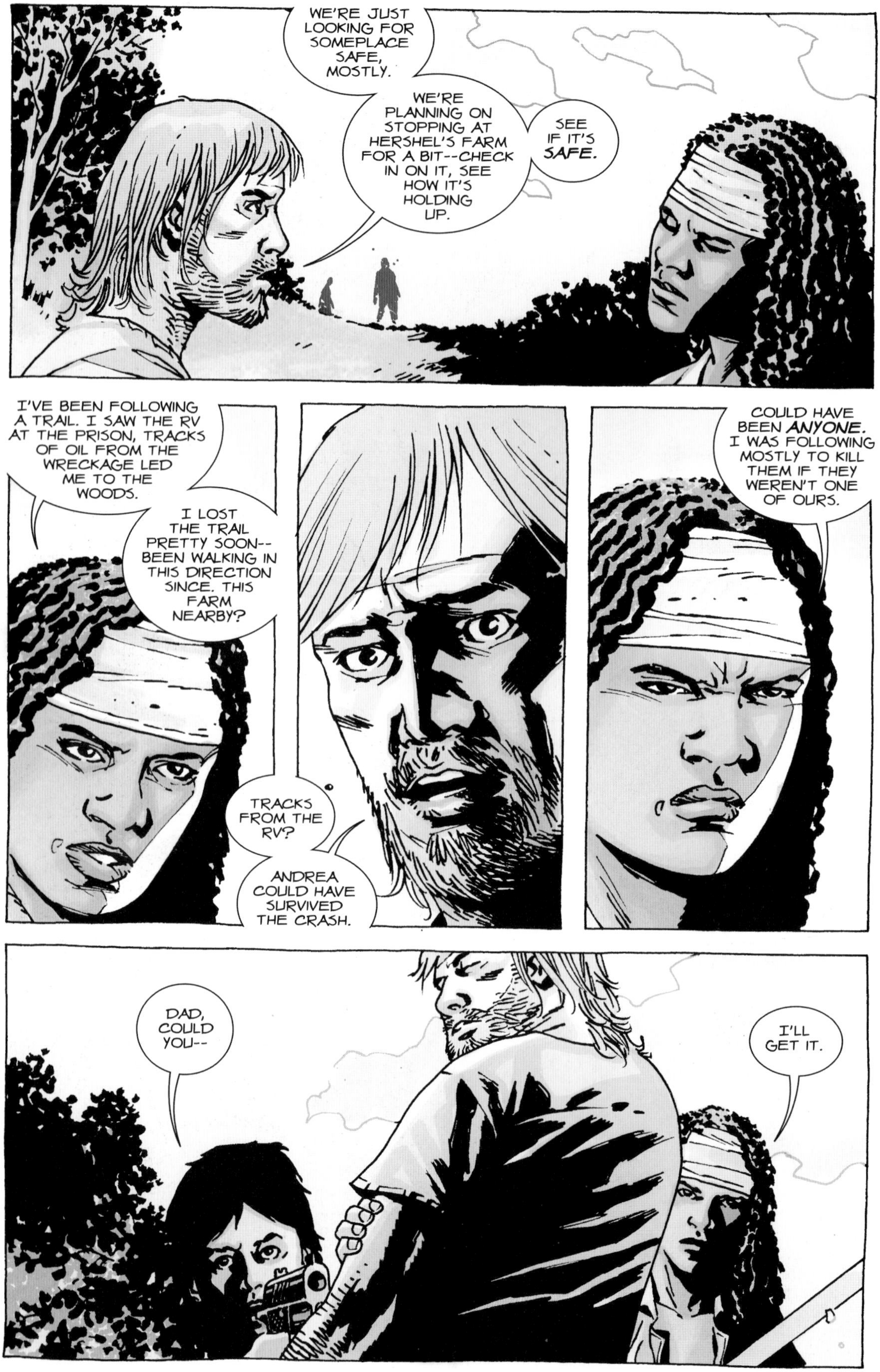
WE'RE JUST LOOKING FOR SOMEPLACE SAFE, MOSTLY.
WE'RE PLANNING ON STOPPING AT HERSHEL'S FARM FOR A BIT--CHECK IN ON IT, SEE HOW IT'S HOLDING UP.
SEE IF IT'S **SAFE.**
I'VE BEEN FOLLOWING A TRAIL. I SAW THE RV AT THE PRISON, TRACKS OF OIL FROM THE WRECKAGE LED ME TO THE WOODS.
I LOST THE TRAIL PRETTY SOON--BEEN WALKING IN THIS DIRECTION SINCE. THIS FARM NEARBY?
TRACKS FROM THE RV?
ANDREA COULD HAVE SURVIVED THE CRASH.
COULD HAVE BEEN **ANYONE.** I WAS FOLLOWING MOSTLY TO KILL THEM IF THEY WEREN'T ONE OF OURS.
DAD, COULD YOU--
I'LL GET IT.

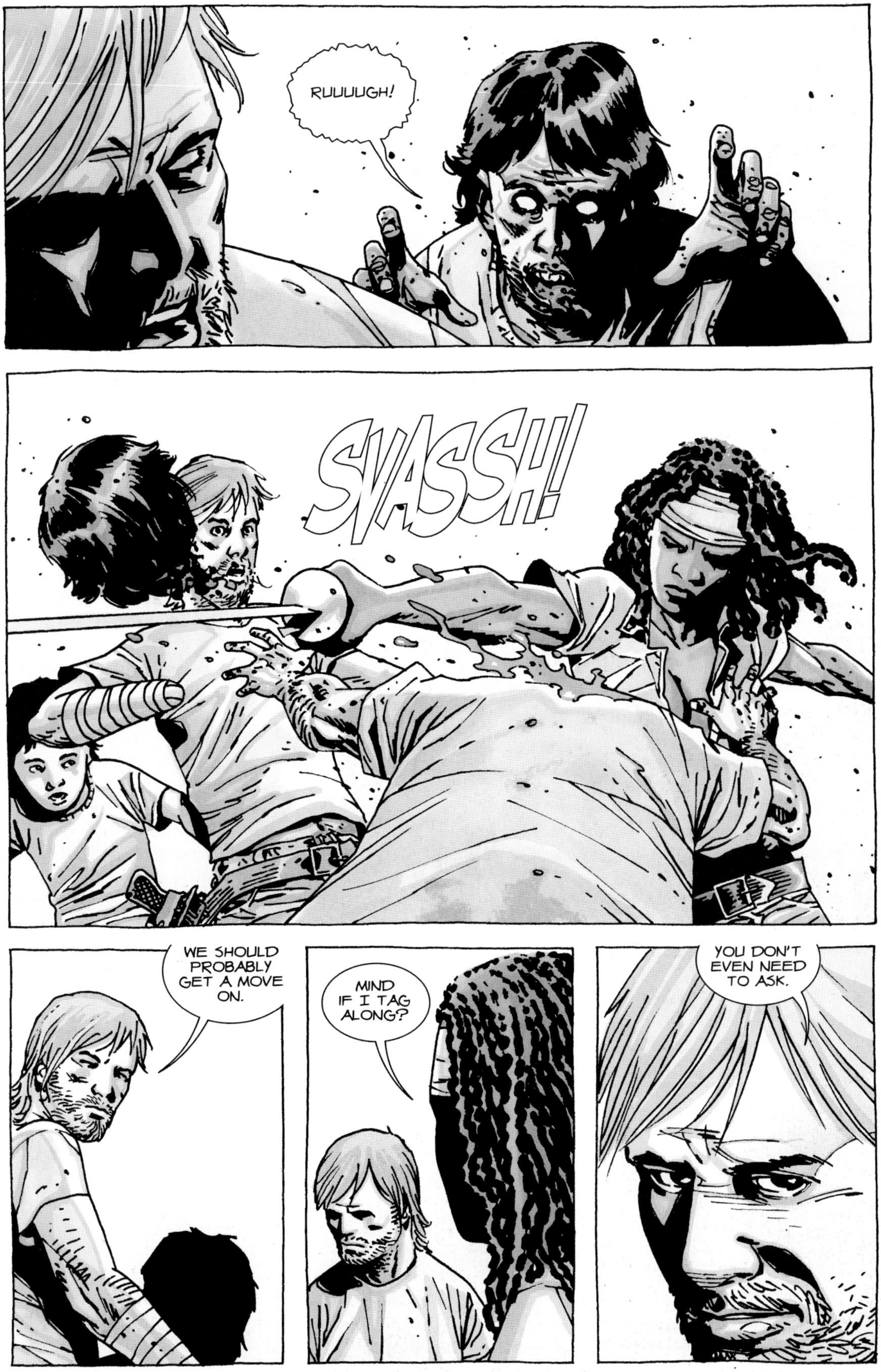
RUUUUGH!
SVASSH!
WE SHOULD PROBABLY GET A MOVE ON.
MIND IF I TAG ALONG?
YOU DON'T EVEN NEED TO ASK.

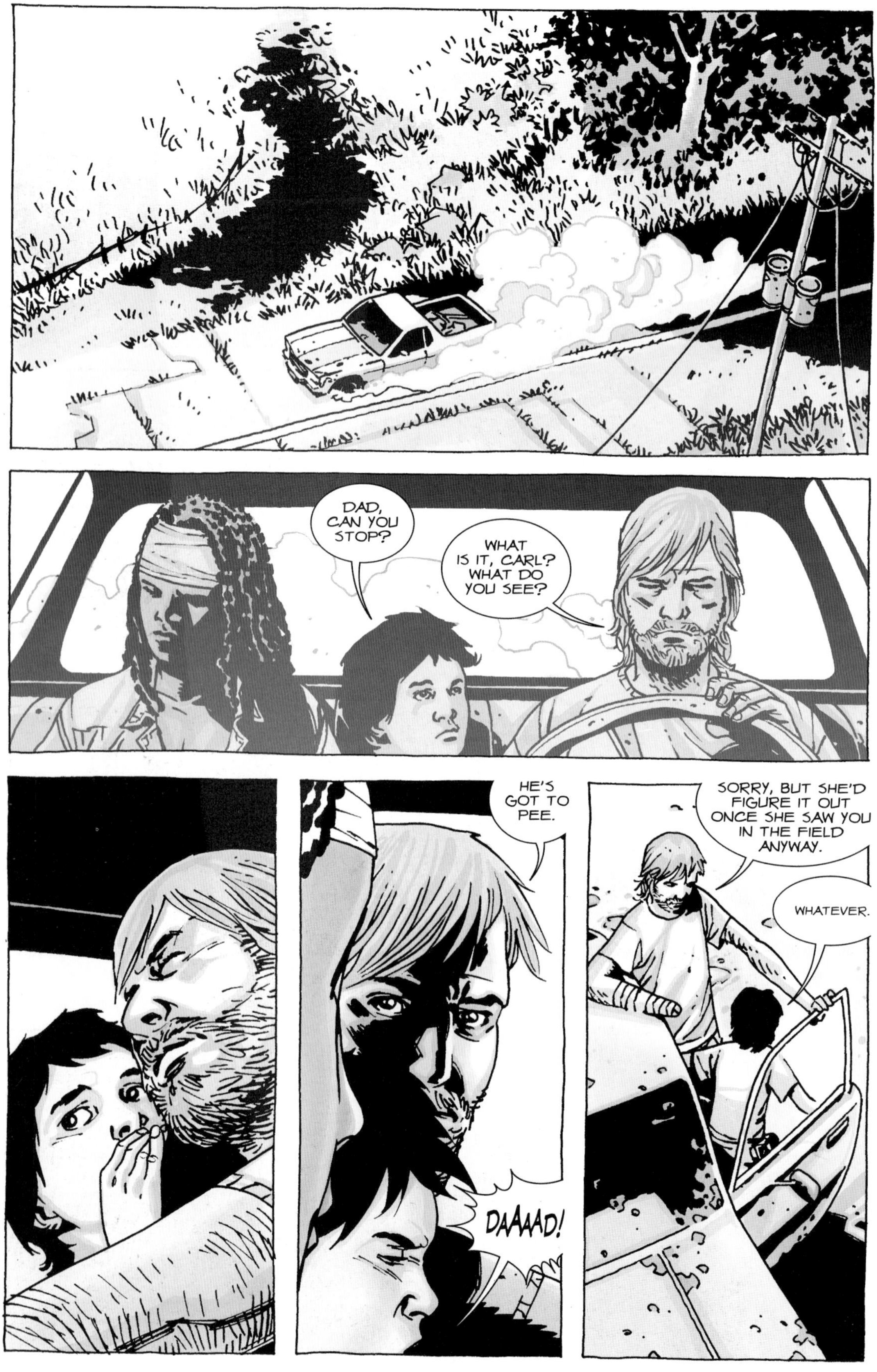
DAD, CAN YOU STOP?
WHAT IS IT, CARL? WHAT DO YOU SEE?
HE'S GOT TO PEE.
DAAAAD!
SORRY, BUT SHE'D FIGURE IT OUT ONCE SHE SAW YOU IN THE FIELD ANYWAY.
WHATEVER.

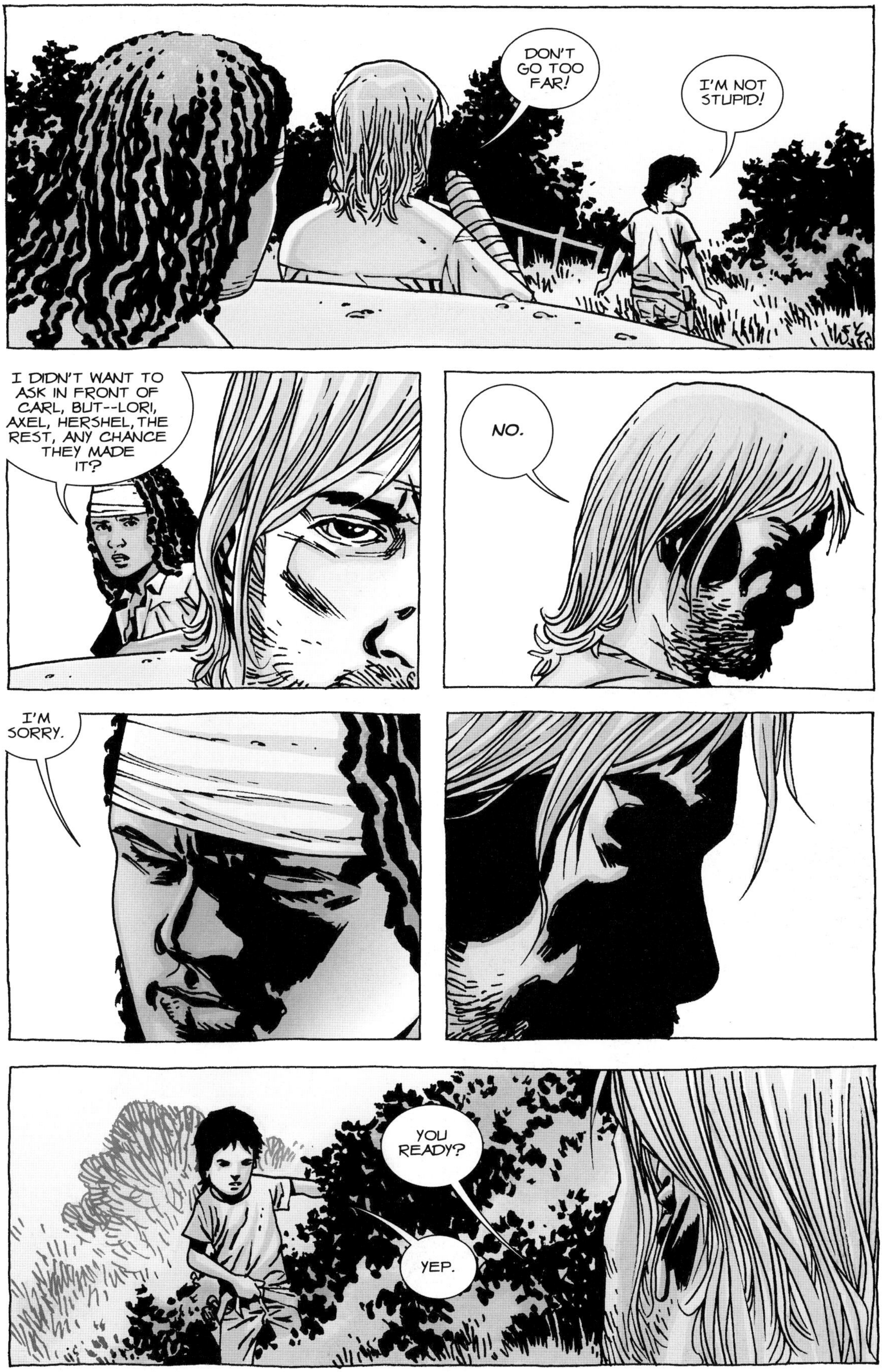
DON'T GO TOO FAR!
I'M NOT STUPID!
I DIDN'T WANT TO ASK IN FRONT OF CARL, BUT--LORI, AXEL, HERSHEL, THE REST, ANY CHANCE THEY MADE IT?
NO.
I'M SORRY.
YOU READY?
YEP.

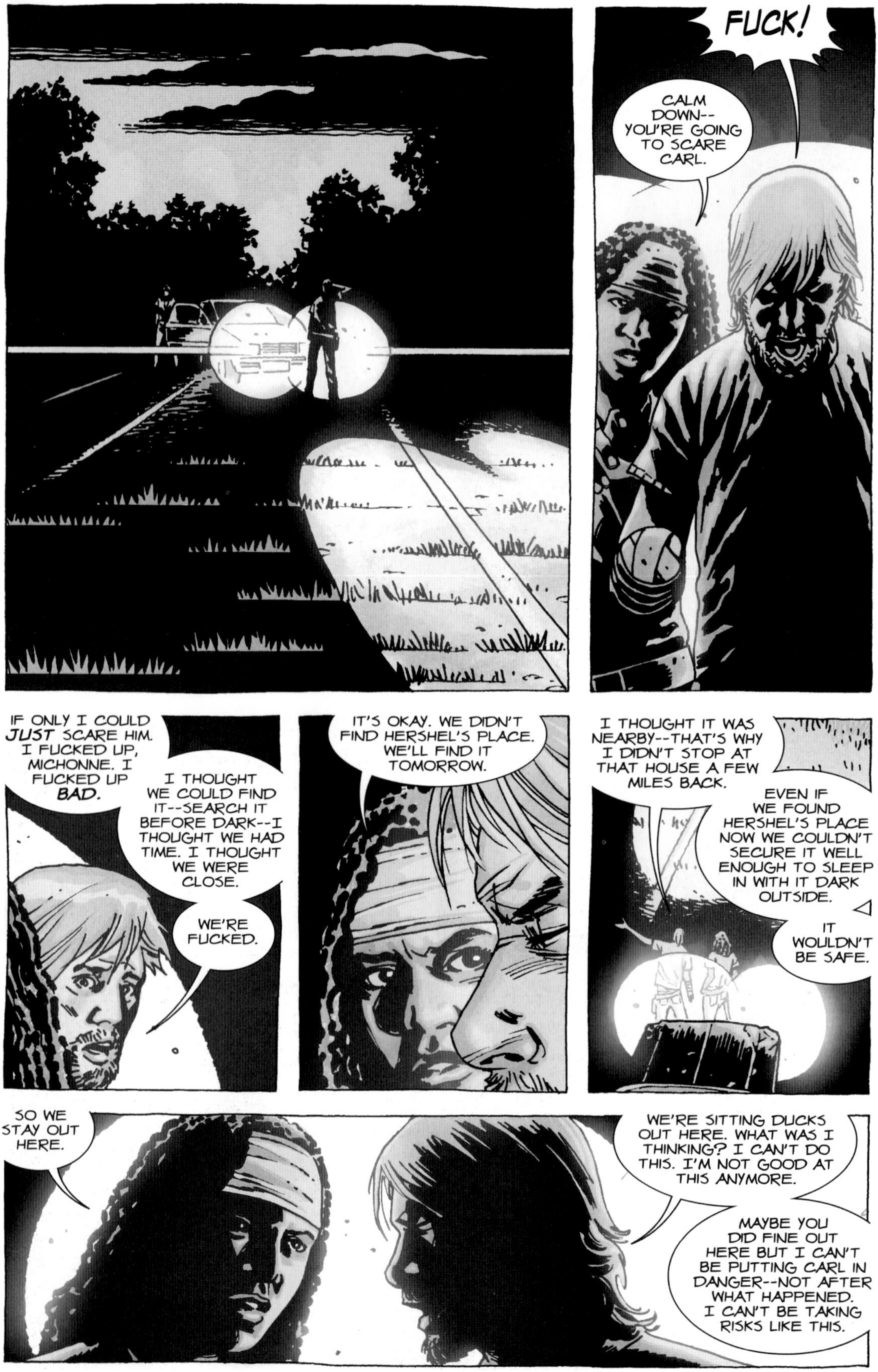
FUCK!
CALM DOWN-- YOU'RE GOING TO SCARE CARL.
IF ONLY I COULD JUST SCARE HIM. I FUCKED UP, MICHONNE. I FUCKED UP BAD.
I THOUGHT WE COULD FIND IT--SEARCH IT BEFORE DARK--I THOUGHT WE HAD TIME. I THOUGHT WE WERE CLOSE.
WE'RE FUCKED.
IT'S OKAY. WE DIDN'T FIND HERSHEL'S PLACE. WE'LL FIND IT TOMORROW.
I THOUGHT IT WAS NEARBY--THAT'S WHY I DIDN'T STOP AT THAT HOUSE A FEW MILES BACK.
EVEN IF WE FOUND HERSHEL'S PLACE NOW WE COULDN'T SECURE IT WELL ENOUGH TO SLEEP IN WITH IT DARK OUTSIDE.
IT WOULDN'T BE SAFE.
SO WE STAY OUT HERE.
WE'RE SITTING DUCKS OUT HERE. WHAT WAS I THINKING? I CAN'T DO THIS. I'M NOT GOOD AT THIS ANYMORE.
MAYBE YOU DID FINE OUT HERE BUT I CAN'T BE PUTTING CARL IN DANGER--NOT AFTER WHAT HAPPENED. I CAN'T BE TAKING RISKS LIKE THIS.

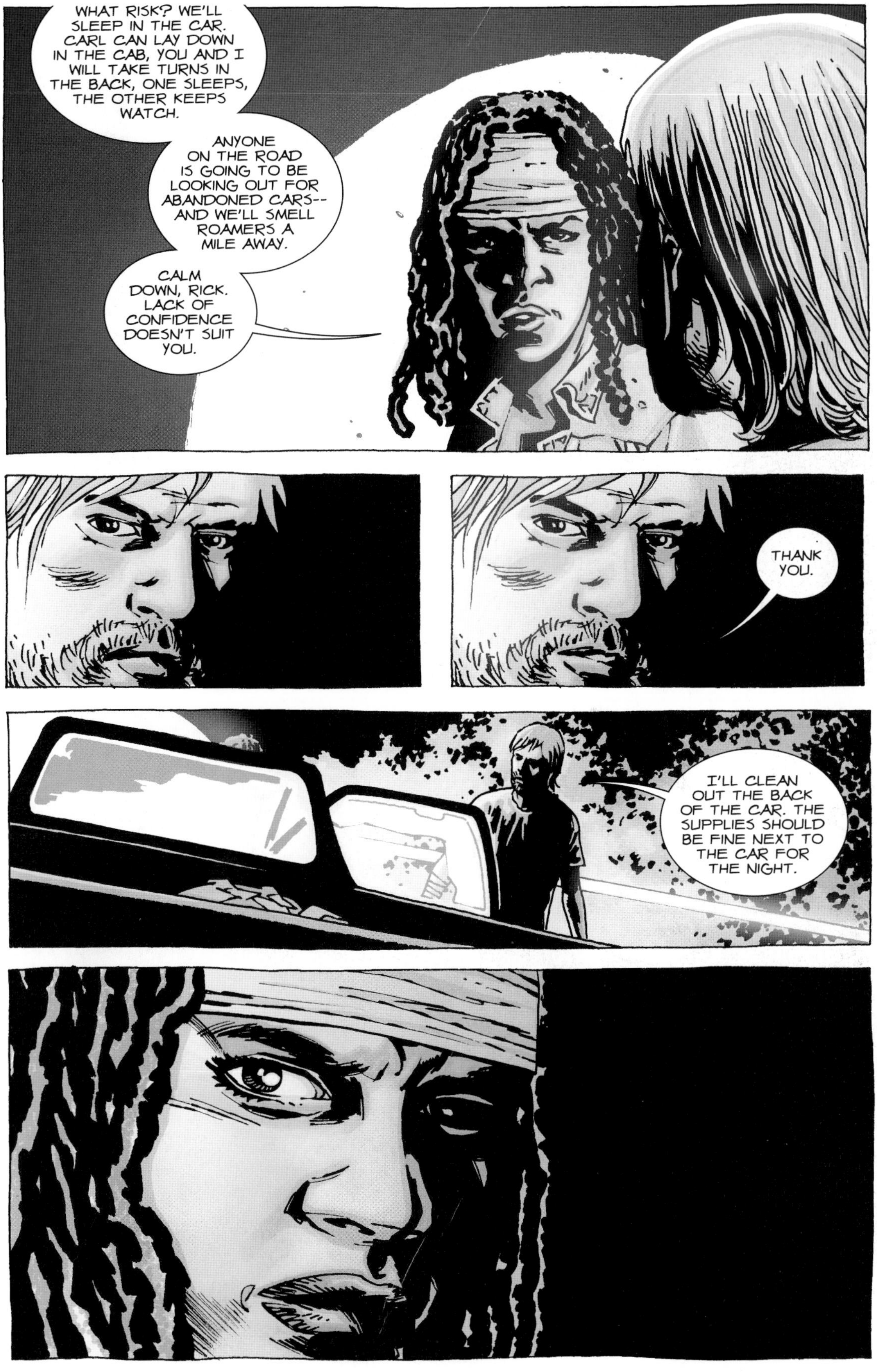
WHAT RISK? WE'LL SLEEP IN THE CAR. CARL CAN LAY DOWN IN THE CAB, YOU AND I WILL TAKE TURNS IN THE BACK, ONE SLEEPS, THE OTHER KEEPS WATCH.
ANYONE ON THE ROAD IS GOING TO BE LOOKING OUT FOR ABANDONED CARS-- AND WE'LL SMELL ROAMERS A MILE AWAY.
CALM DOWN, RICK. LACK OF CONFIDENCE DOESN'T SUIT YOU.
THANK YOU.
I'LL CLEAN OUT THE BACK OF THE CAR. THE SUPPLIES SHOULD BE FINE NEXT TO THE CAR FOR THE NIGHT.

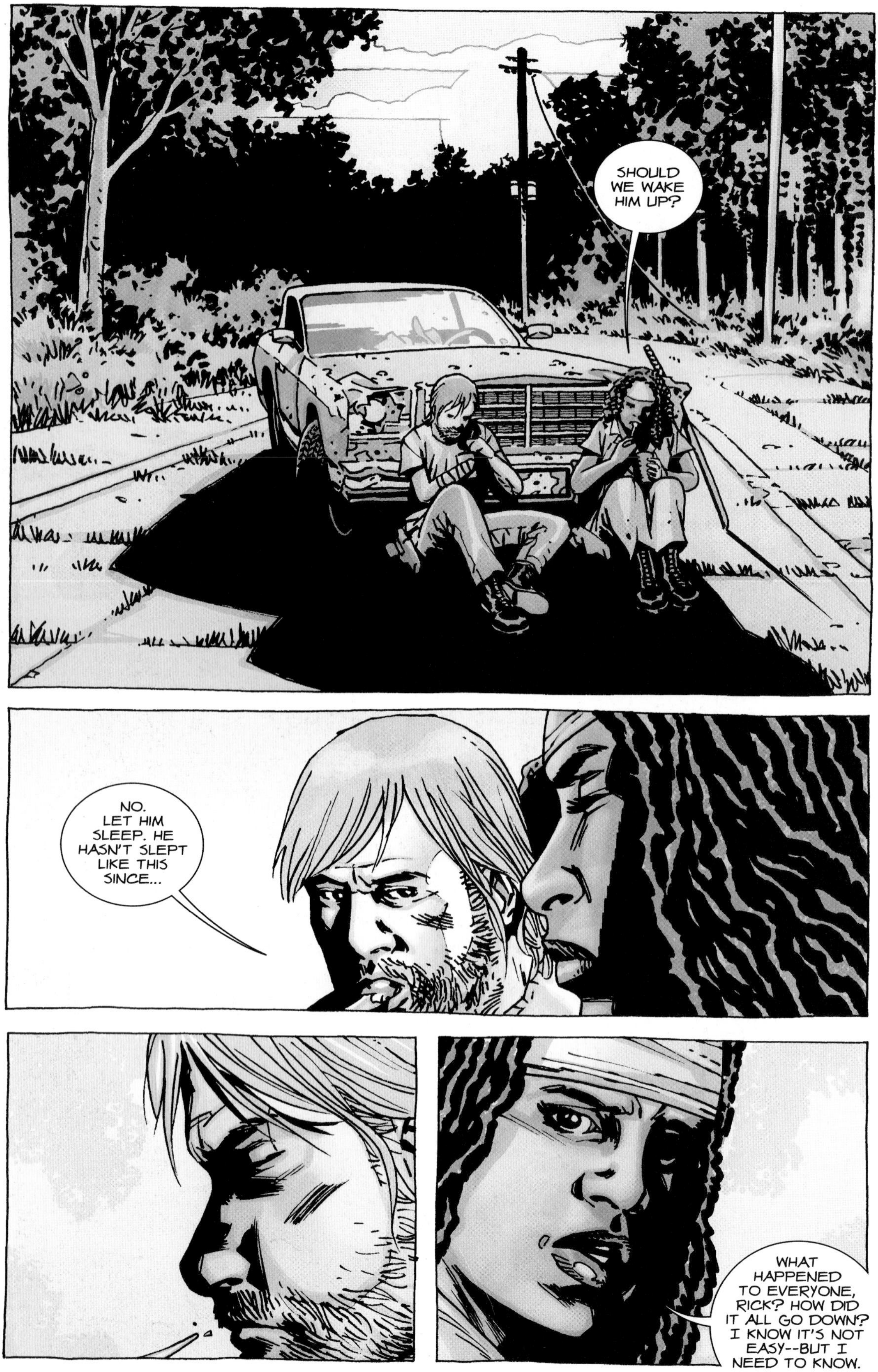
SHOULD WE WAKE HIM UP?
NO. LET HIM SLEEP. HE HASN'T SLEPT LIKE THIS SINCE...
WHAT HAPPENED TO EVERYONE, RICK? HOW DID IT ALL GO DOWN? I KNOW IT'S NOT EASY--BUT I NEED TO KNOW.

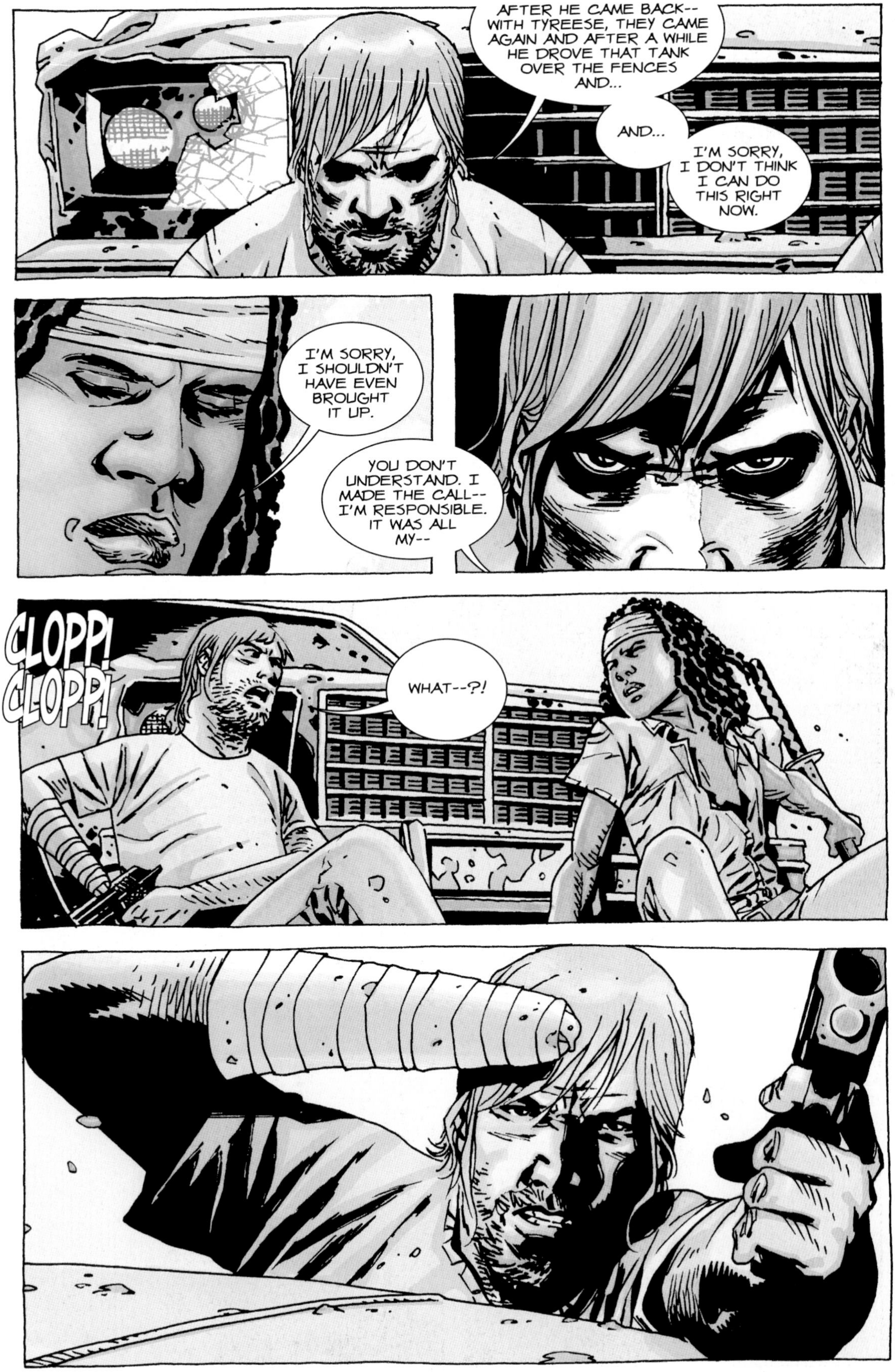
AFTER HE CAME BACK-- WITH TYREESE, THEY CAME AGAIN AND AFTER A WHILE HE DROVE THAT TANK OVER THE FENCES AND...
AND...
I'M SORRY, I DON'T THINK I CAN DO THIS RIGHT NOW.
I'M SORRY, I SHOULDN'T HAVE EVEN BROUGHT IT UP.
YOU DON'T UNDERSTAND. I MADE THE CALL-- I'M RESPONSIBLE. IT WAS ALL MY--
CLOPP! CLOPP!
WHAT--?!

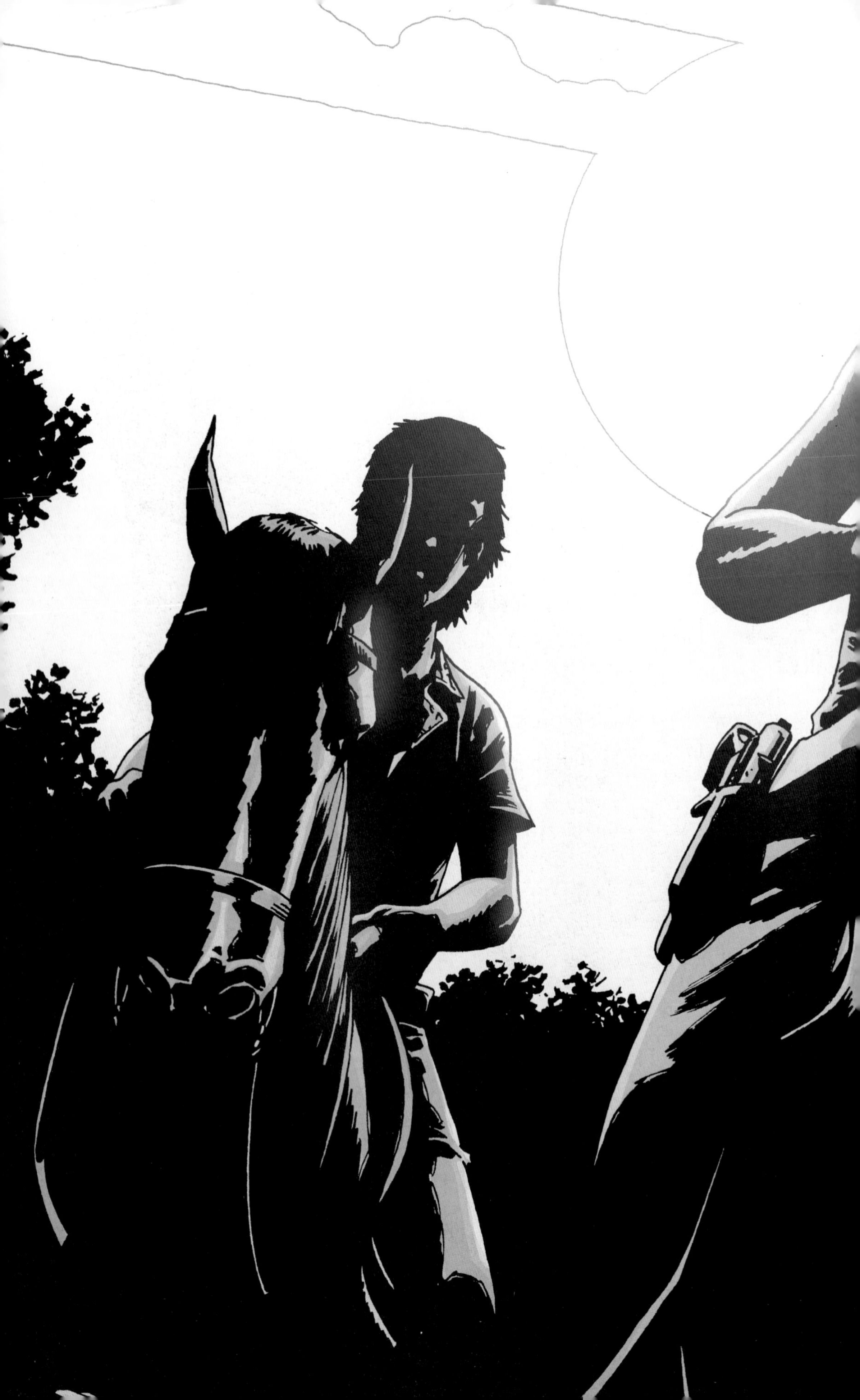

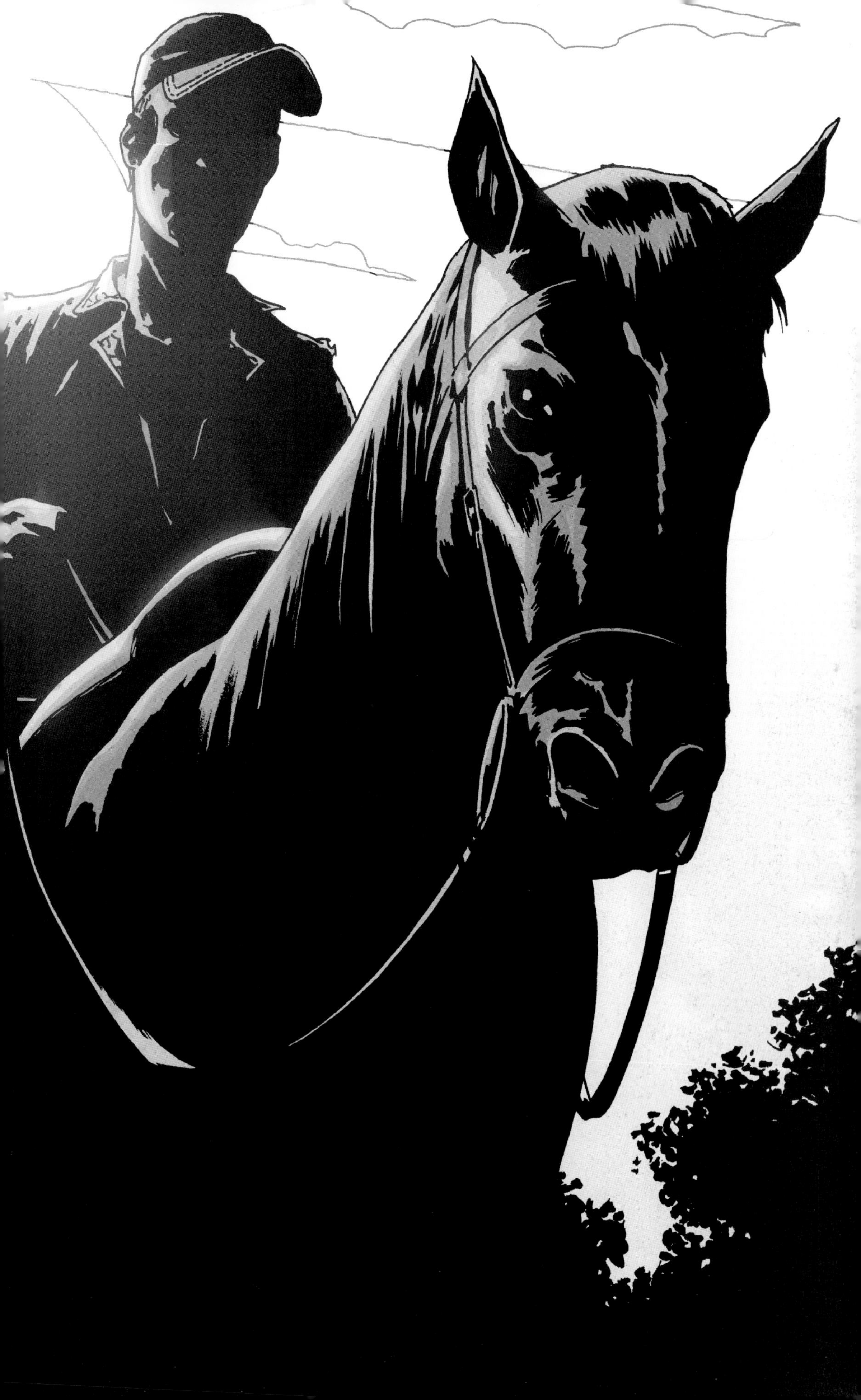

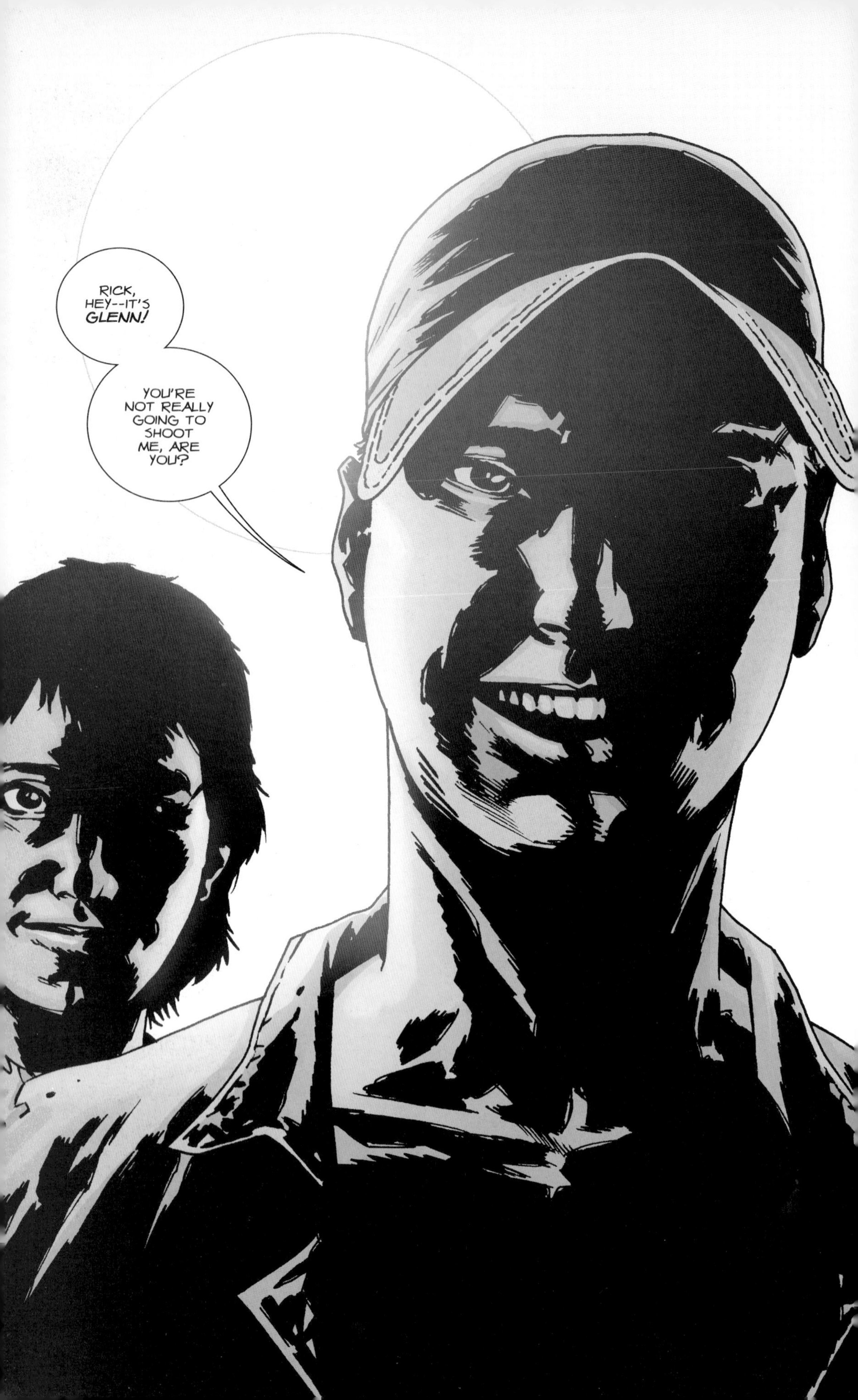
RICK, HEY--IT'S GLENN!
YOU'RE NOT REALLY GOING TO SHOOT ME, ARE YOU?

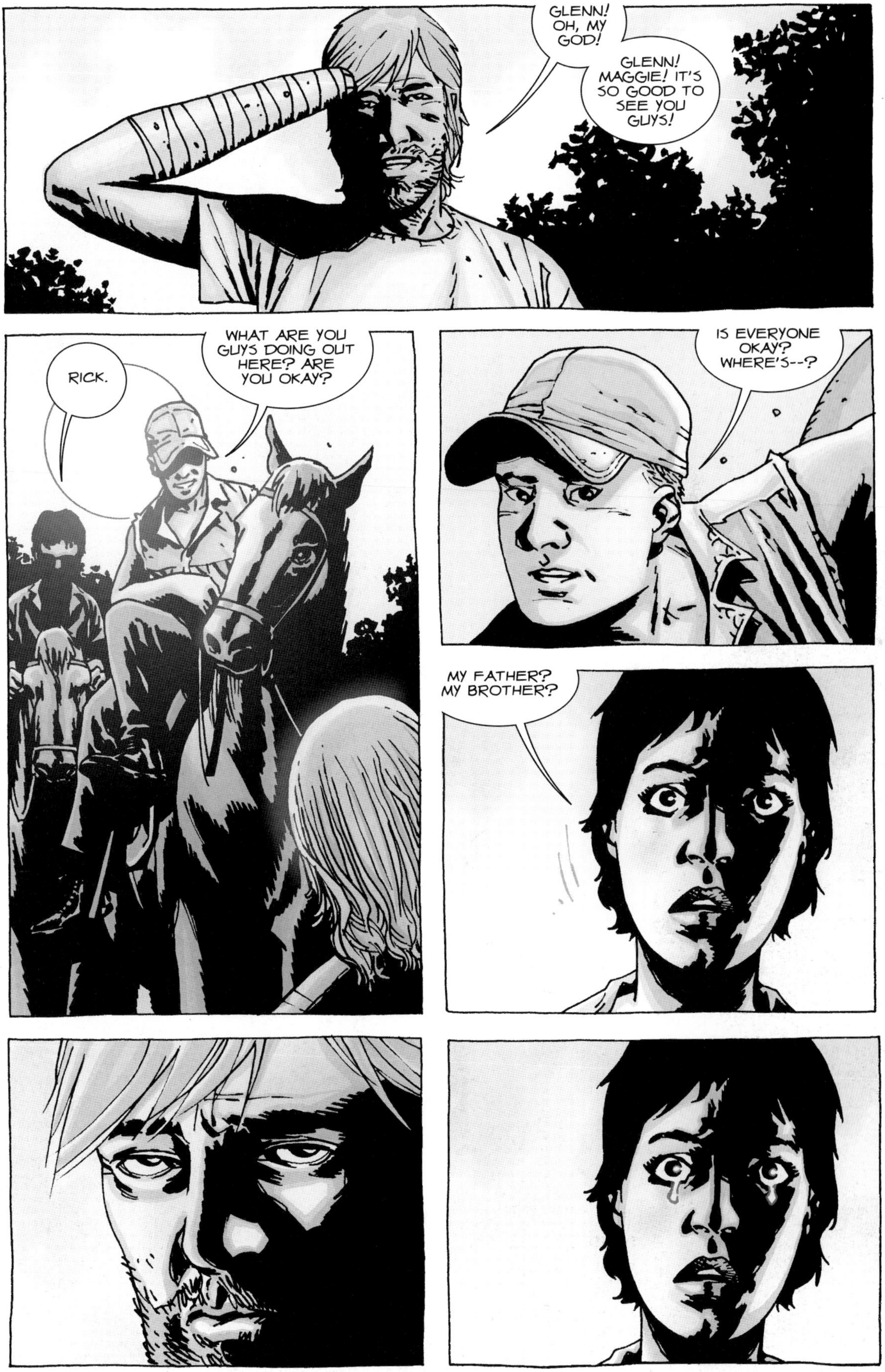
GLENN! OH, MY GOD!
GLENN! MAGGIE! IT'S SO GOOD TO SEE YOU GUYS!
RICK.
WHAT ARE YOU GUYS DOING OUT HERE? ARE YOU OKAY?
IS EVERYONE OKAY? WHERE'S--?
MY FATHER? MY BROTHER?

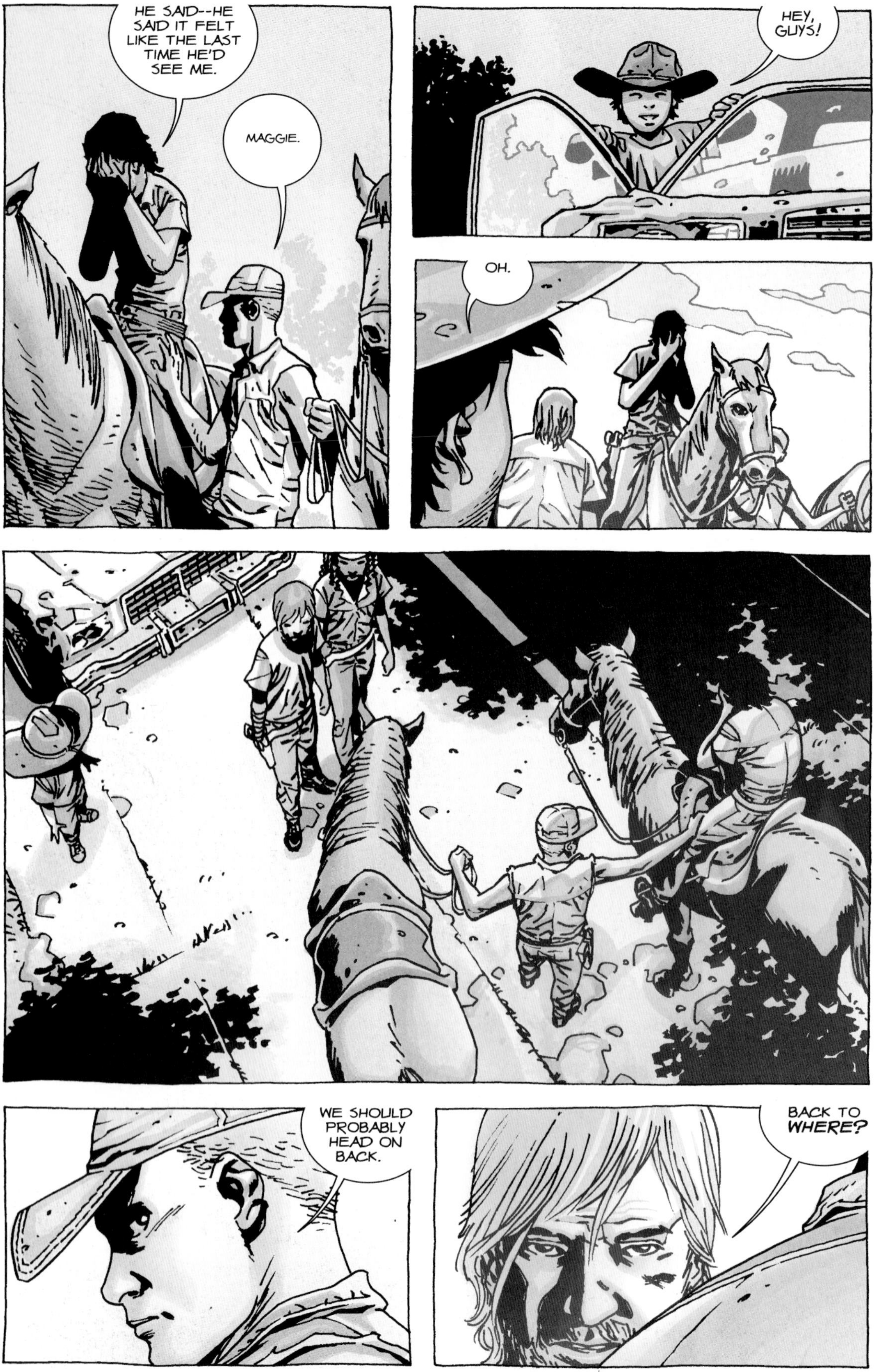
HE SAID--HE SAID IT FELT LIKE THE LAST TIME HE'D SEE ME.
MAGGIE.
HEY, GUYS!
OH.
WE SHOULD PROBABLY HEAD ON BACK.
BACK TO *WHERE?*

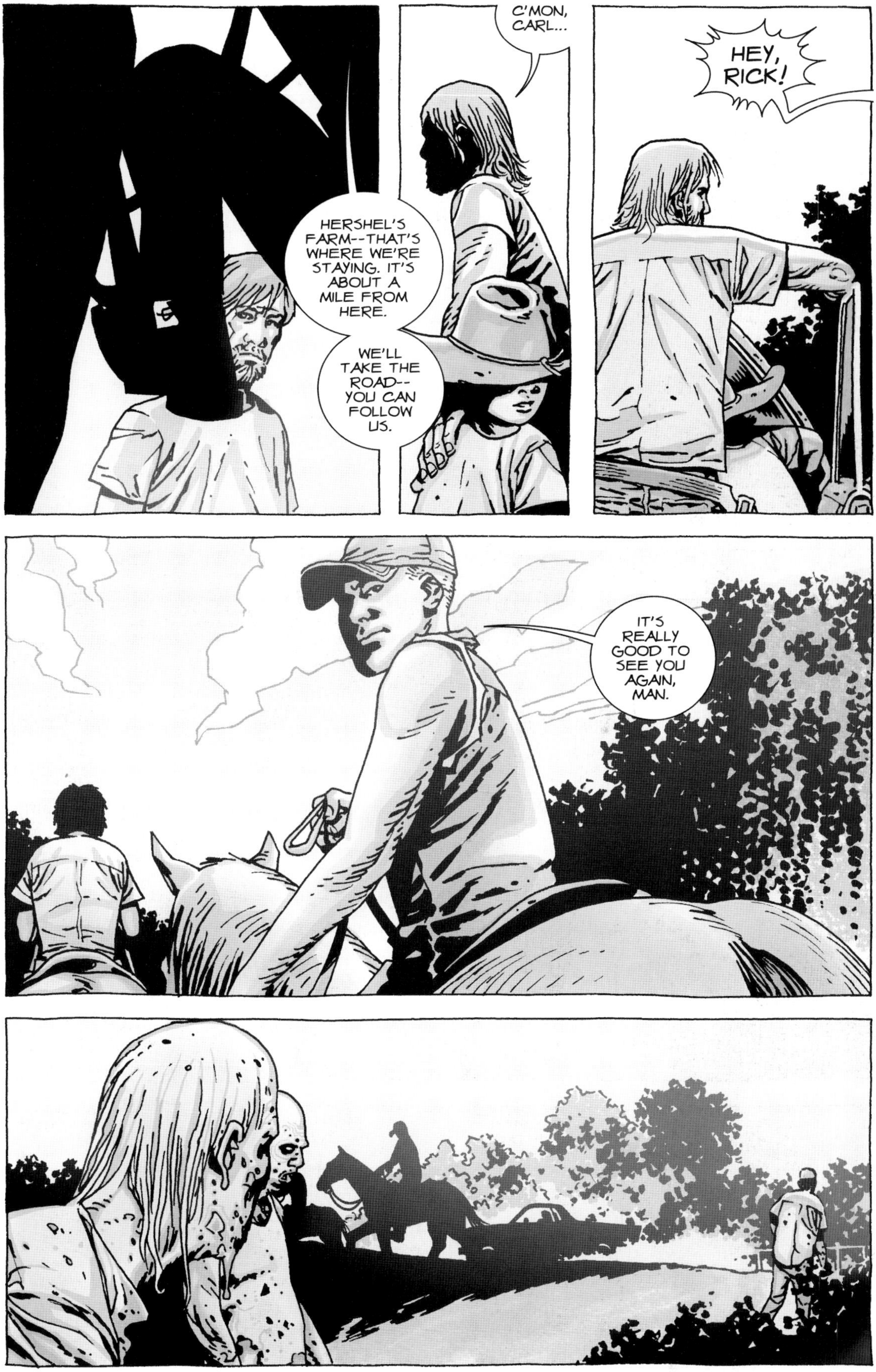
HERSHEL'S FARM--THAT'S WHERE WE'RE STAYING. IT'S ABOUT A MILE FROM HERE.
WE'LL TAKE THE ROAD-- YOU CAN FOLLOW US.
C'MON, CARL...
HEY, RICK!
IT'S REALLY GOOD TO SEE YOU AGAIN, MAN.

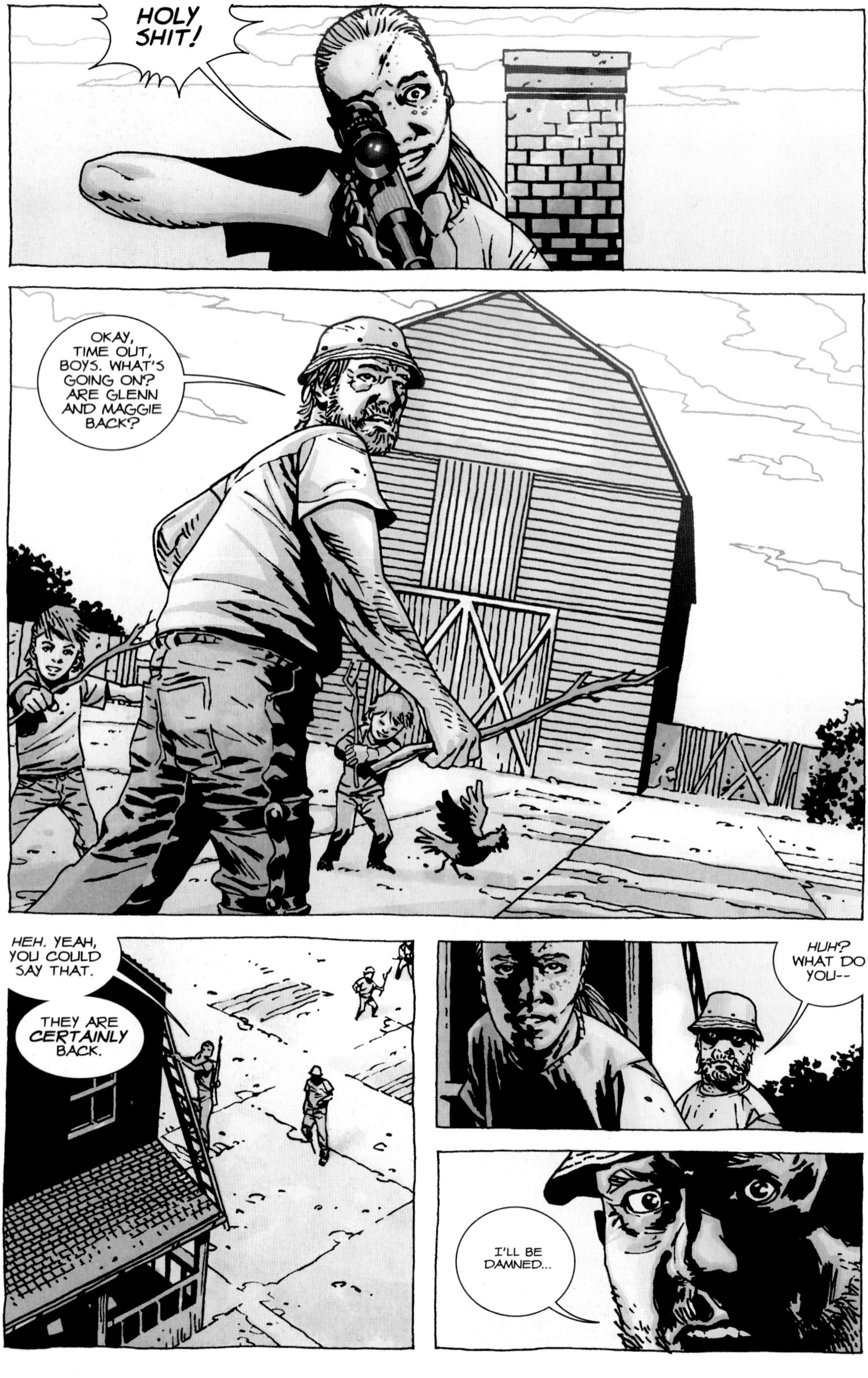
HOLY SHIT!
OKAY, TIME OUT, BOYS. WHAT'S GOING ON? ARE GLENN AND MAGGIE BACK?
HEH. YEAH, YOU COULD SAY THAT.
THEY ARE CERTAINLY BACK.
HUH? WHAT DO YOU--
I'LL BE DAMNED...

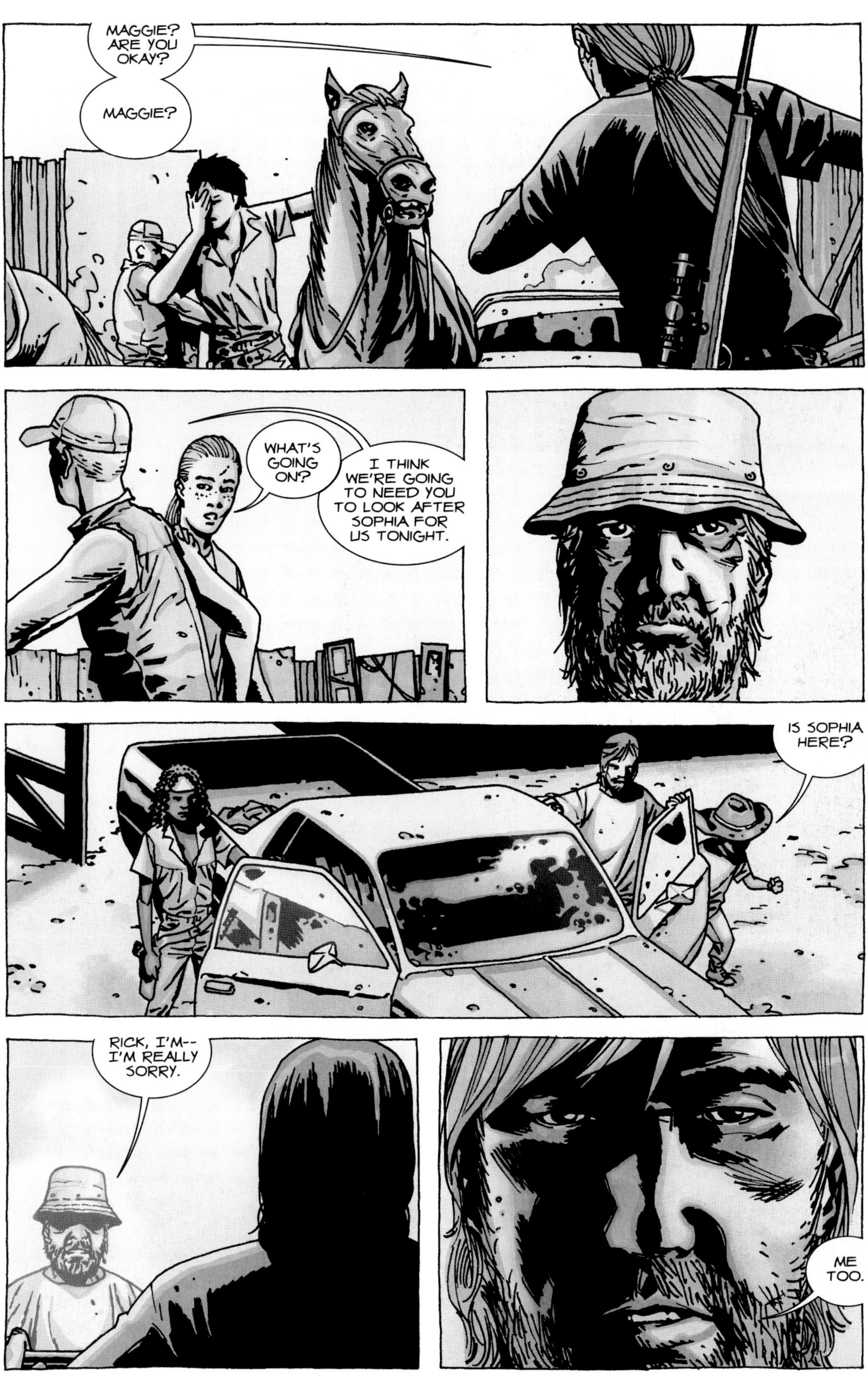
MAGGIE? ARE YOU OKAY?
MAGGIE?
WHAT'S GOING ON?
I THINK WE'RE GOING TO NEED YOU TO LOOK AFTER SOPHIA FOR US TONIGHT.
IS SOPHIA HERE?
RICK, I'M-- I'M REALLY SORRY.
ME TOO.

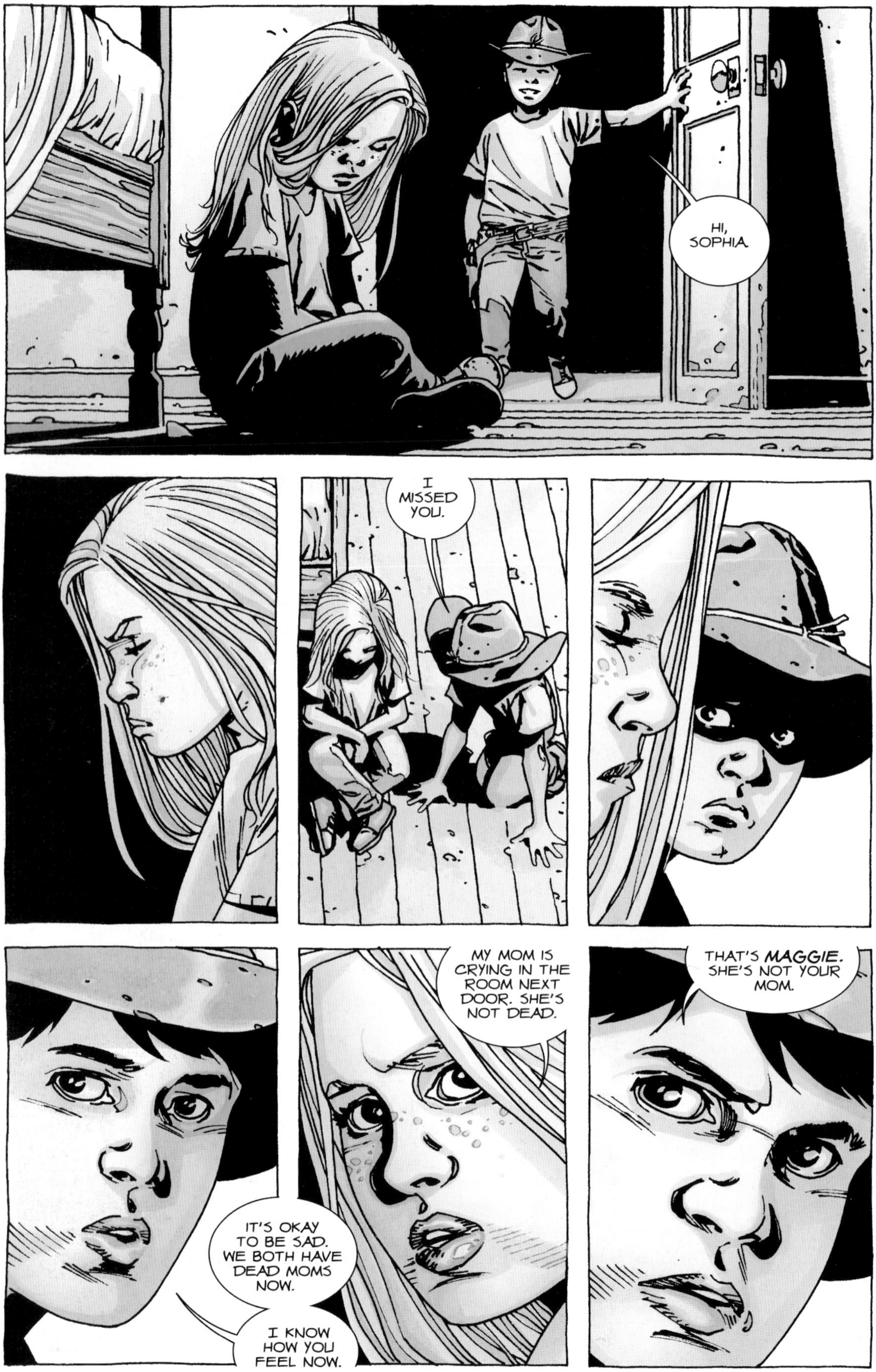

HI, SOPHIA.
I MISSED YOU.
IT'S OKAY TO BE SAD. WE BOTH HAVE DEAD MOMS NOW.
I KNOW HOW YOU FEEL NOW.
MY MOM IS CRYING IN THE ROOM NEXT DOOR. SHE'S NOT DEAD.
THAT'S MAGGIE. SHE'S NOT YOUR MOM.

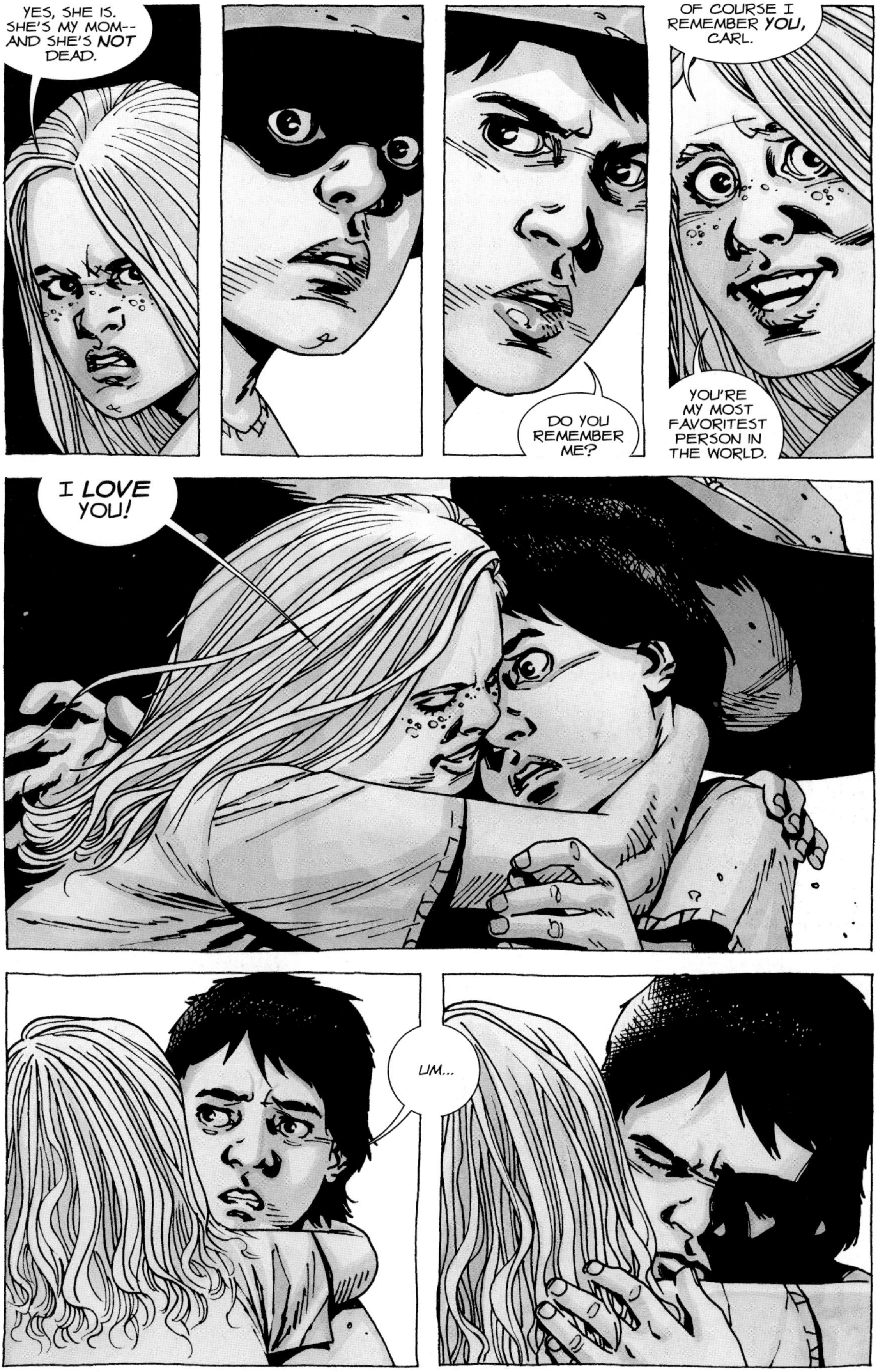
YES, SHE IS. SHE'S MY MOM-- AND SHE'S **NOT** DEAD.
DO YOU REMEMBER ME?
OF COURSE I REMEMBER ***YOU***, CARL.
YOU'RE MY MOST FAVORITEST PERSON IN THE WORLD.
I ***LOVE*** YOU!
UM...

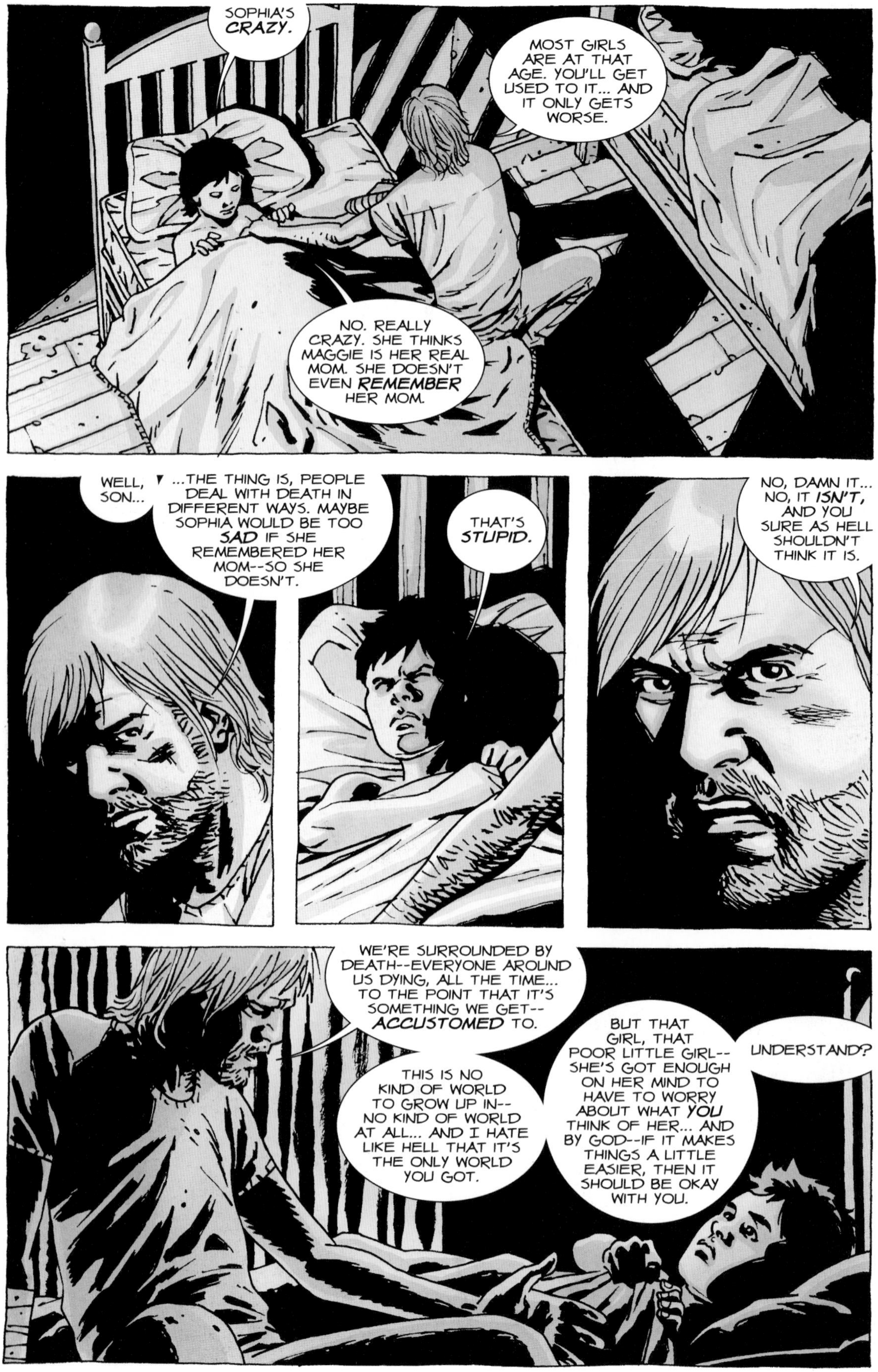

SOPHIA'S CRAZY.
MOST GIRLS ARE AT THAT AGE. YOU'LL GET USED TO IT... AND IT ONLY GETS WORSE.
NO. REALLY CRAZY. SHE THINKS MAGGIE IS HER REAL MOM. SHE DOESN'T EVEN REMEMBER HER MOM.
WELL, SON...
...THE THING IS, PEOPLE DEAL WITH DEATH IN DIFFERENT WAYS. MAYBE SOPHIA WOULD BE TOO SAD IF SHE REMEMBERED HER MOM--SO SHE DOESN'T.
THAT'S STUPID.
NO, DAMN IT... NO, IT ISN'T, AND YOU SURE AS HELL SHOULDN'T THINK IT IS.
WE'RE SURROUNDED BY DEATH--EVERYONE AROUND US DYING, ALL THE TIME... TO THE POINT THAT IT'S SOMETHING WE GET--ACCUSTOMED TO.
THIS IS NO KIND OF WORLD TO GROW UP IN--NO KIND OF WORLD AT ALL... AND I HATE LIKE HELL THAT IT'S THE ONLY WORLD YOU GOT.
BUT THAT GIRL, THAT POOR LITTLE GIRL--SHE'S GOT ENOUGH ON HER MIND TO HAVE TO WORRY ABOUT WHAT YOU THINK OF HER... AND BY GOD--IF IT MAKES THINGS A LITTLE EASIER, THEN IT SHOULD BE OKAY WITH YOU.
UNDERSTAND?

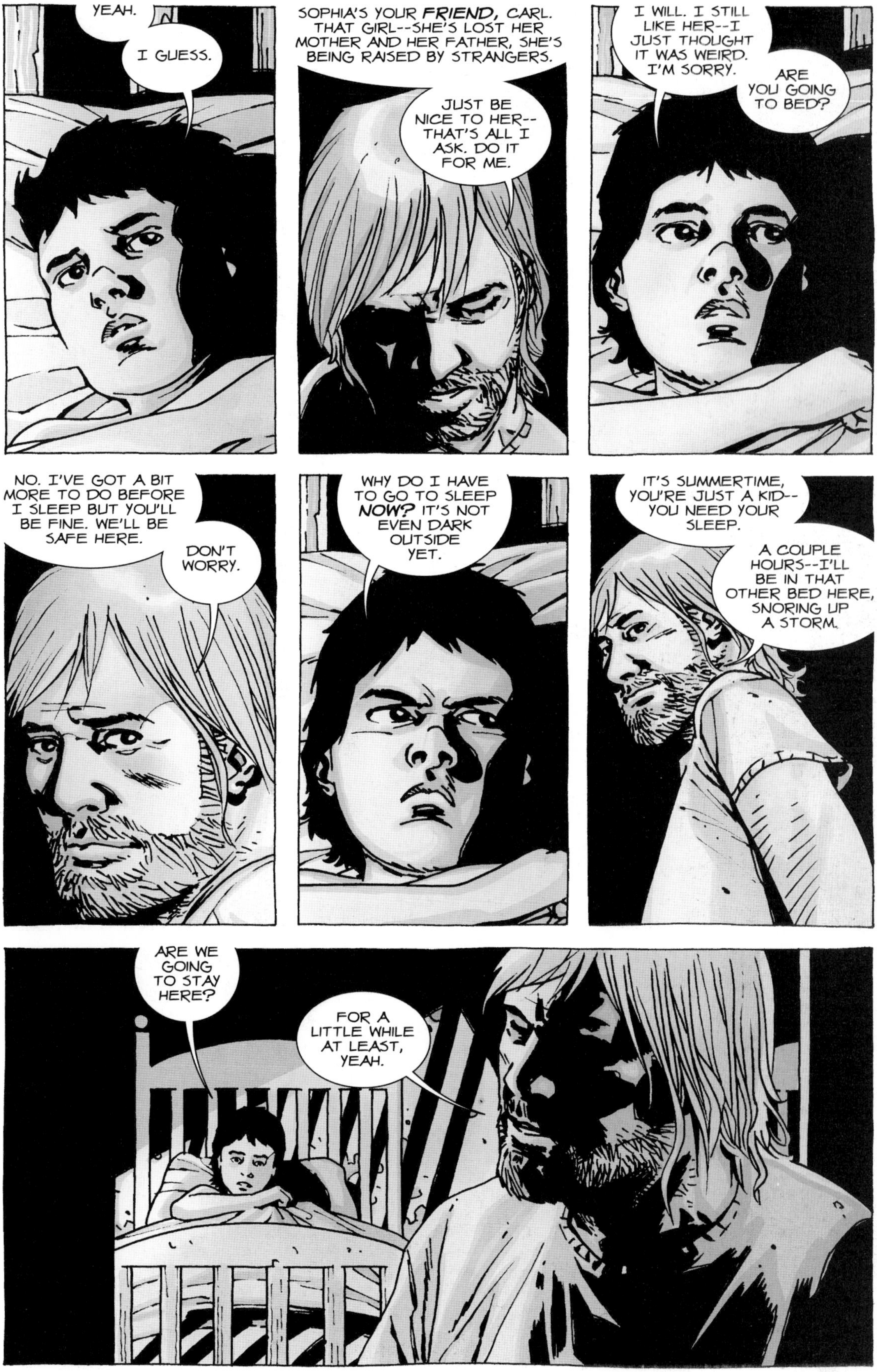
YEAH.
I GUESS.
SOPHIA'S YOUR **FRIEND,** CARL. THAT GIRL--SHE'S LOST HER MOTHER AND HER FATHER, SHE'S BEING RAISED BY STRANGERS.
JUST BE NICE TO HER--THAT'S ALL I ASK. DO IT FOR ME.
I WILL. I STILL LIKE HER--I JUST THOUGHT IT WAS WEIRD. I'M SORRY.
ARE YOU GOING TO BED?
NO. I'VE GOT A BIT MORE TO DO BEFORE I SLEEP BUT YOU'LL BE FINE. WE'LL BE SAFE HERE.
DON'T WORRY.
WHY DO I HAVE TO GO TO SLEEP ***NOW?*** IT'S NOT EVEN DARK OUTSIDE YET.
IT'S SUMMERTIME, YOU'RE JUST A KID--YOU NEED YOUR SLEEP.
A COUPLE HOURS--I'LL BE IN THAT OTHER BED HERE, SNORING UP A STORM.
ARE WE GOING TO STAY HERE?
FOR A LITTLE WHILE AT LEAST, YEAH.

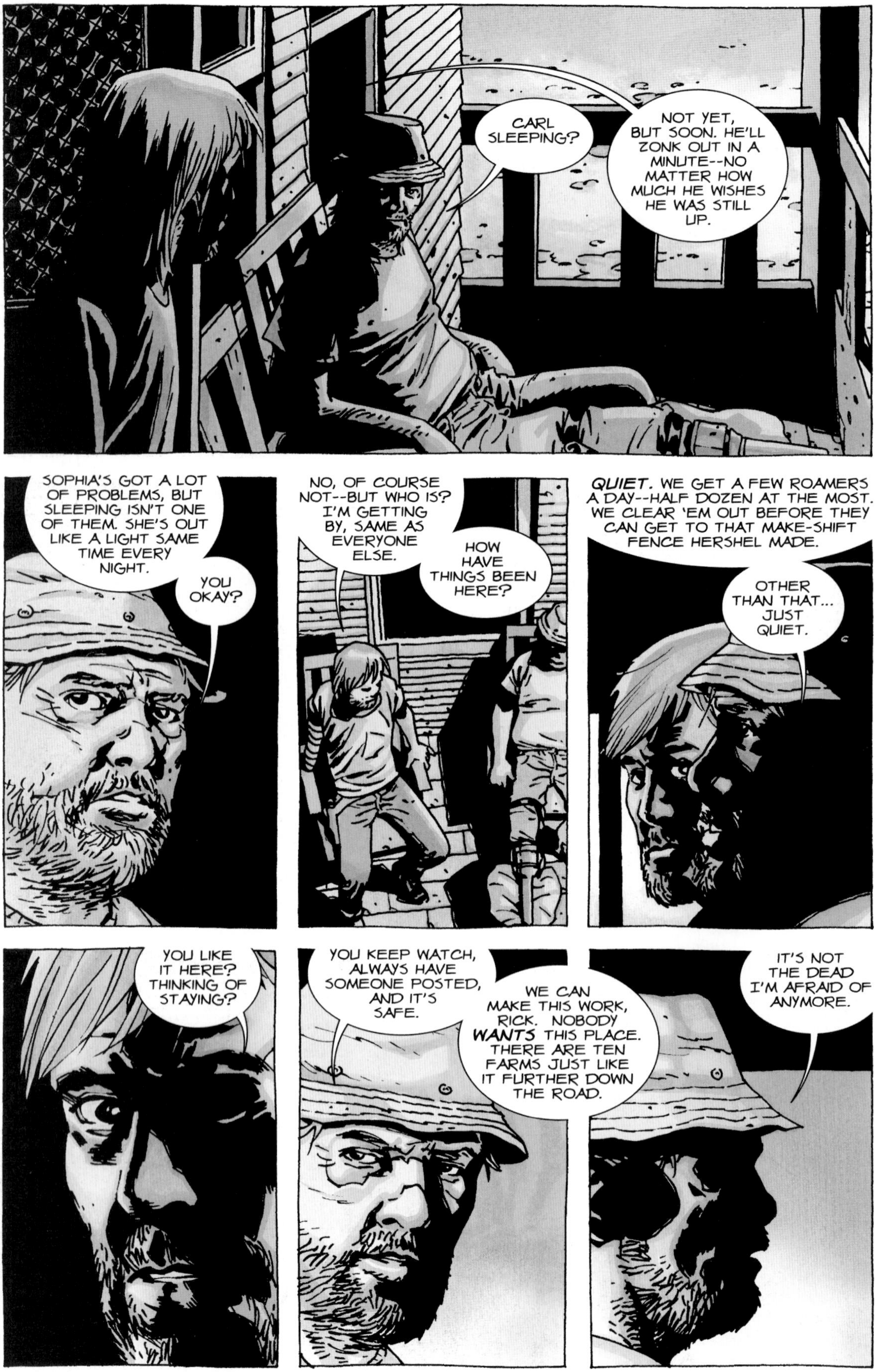
CARL SLEEPING?
NOT YET, BUT SOON. HE'LL ZONK OUT IN A MINUTE--NO MATTER HOW MUCH HE WISHES HE WAS STILL UP.
SOPHIA'S GOT A LOT OF PROBLEMS, BUT SLEEPING ISN'T ONE OF THEM. SHE'S OUT LIKE A LIGHT SAME TIME EVERY NIGHT.
YOU OKAY?
NO, OF COURSE NOT--BUT WHO IS? I'M GETTING BY, SAME AS EVERYONE ELSE.
HOW HAVE THINGS BEEN HERE?
QUIET. WE GET A FEW ROAMERS A DAY--HALF DOZEN AT THE MOST. WE CLEAR 'EM OUT BEFORE THEY CAN GET TO THAT MAKE-SHIFT FENCE HERSHEL MADE.
OTHER THAN THAT... JUST QUIET.
YOU LIKE IT HERE? THINKING OF STAYING?
YOU KEEP WATCH, ALWAYS HAVE SOMEONE POSTED, AND IT'S SAFE.
WE CAN MAKE THIS WORK, RICK. NOBODY WANTS THIS PLACE. THERE ARE TEN FARMS JUST LIKE IT FURTHER DOWN THE ROAD.
IT'S NOT THE DEAD I'M AFRAID OF ANYMORE.

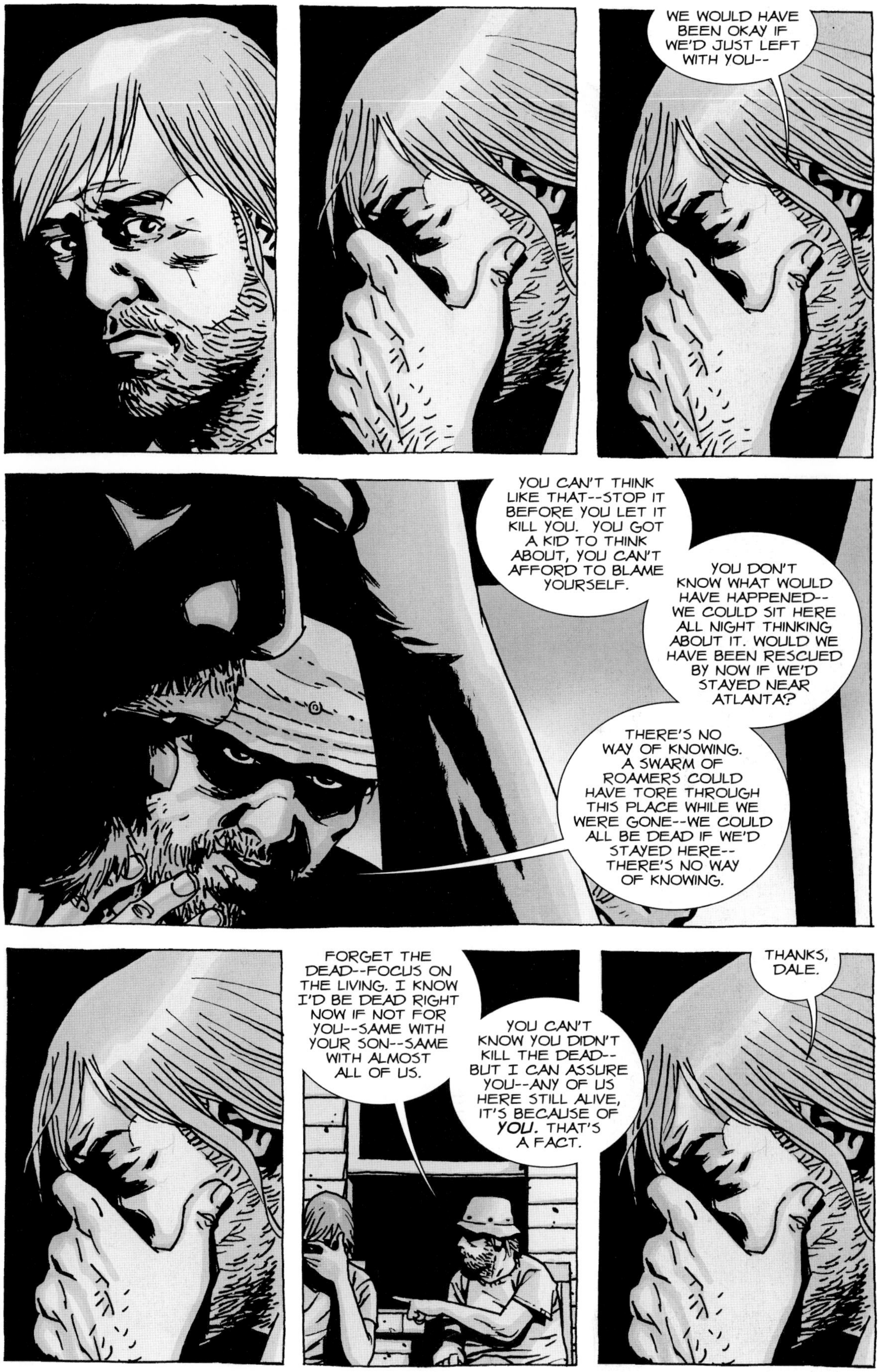
WE WOULD HAVE BEEN OKAY IF WE'D JUST LEFT WITH YOU--
YOU CAN'T THINK LIKE THAT--STOP IT BEFORE YOU LET IT KILL YOU. YOU GOT A KID TO THINK ABOUT, YOU CAN'T AFFORD TO BLAME YOURSELF.
YOU DON'T KNOW WHAT WOULD HAVE HAPPENED-- WE COULD SIT HERE ALL NIGHT THINKING ABOUT IT. WOULD WE HAVE BEEN RESCUED BY NOW IF WE'D STAYED NEAR ATLANTA?
THERE'S NO WAY OF KNOWING. A SWARM OF ROAMERS COULD HAVE TORE THROUGH THIS PLACE WHILE WE WERE GONE--WE COULD ALL BE DEAD IF WE'D STAYED HERE-- THERE'S NO WAY OF KNOWING.
FORGET THE DEAD--FOCUS ON THE LIVING. I KNOW I'D BE DEAD RIGHT NOW IF NOT FOR YOU--SAME WITH YOUR SON--SAME WITH ALMOST ALL OF US.
YOU CAN'T KNOW YOU DIDN'T KILL THE DEAD-- BUT I CAN ASSURE YOU--ANY OF US HERE STILL ALIVE, IT'S BECAUSE OF *YOU*. THAT'S A FACT.
THANKS, DALE.

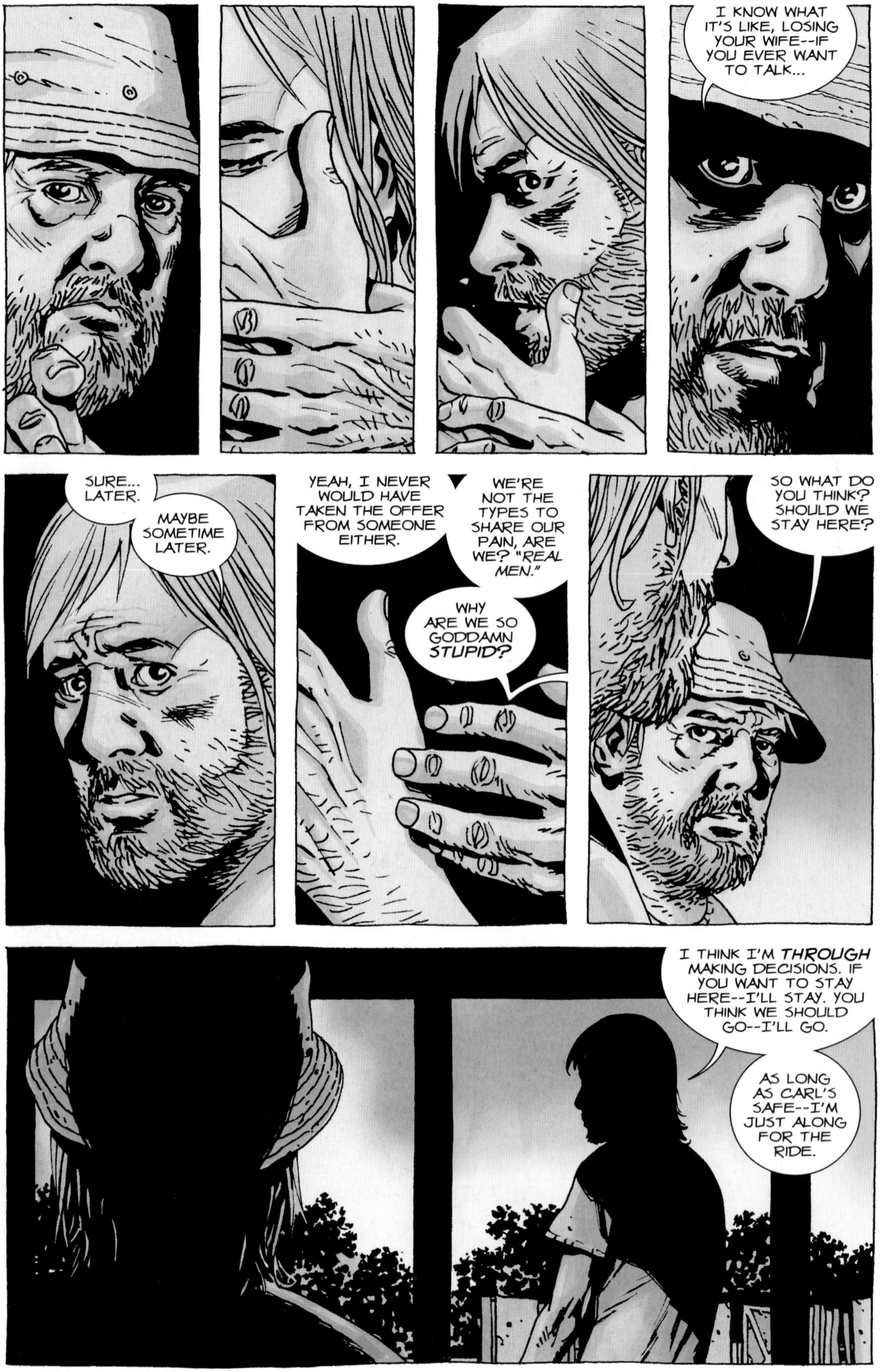
I KNOW WHAT IT'S LIKE, LOSING YOUR WIFE--IF YOU EVER WANT TO TALK...
SURE... LATER.
MAYBE SOMETIME LATER.
YEAH, I NEVER WOULD HAVE TAKEN THE OFFER FROM SOMEONE EITHER.
WE'RE NOT THE TYPES TO SHARE OUR PAIN, ARE WE? "REAL MEN."
WHY ARE WE SO GODDAMN STUPID?
SO WHAT DO YOU THINK? SHOULD WE STAY HERE?
I THINK I'M THROUGH MAKING DECISIONS. IF YOU WANT TO STAY HERE--I'LL STAY. YOU THINK WE SHOULD GO--I'LL GO.
AS LONG AS CARL'S SAFE--I'M JUST ALONG FOR THE RIDE.

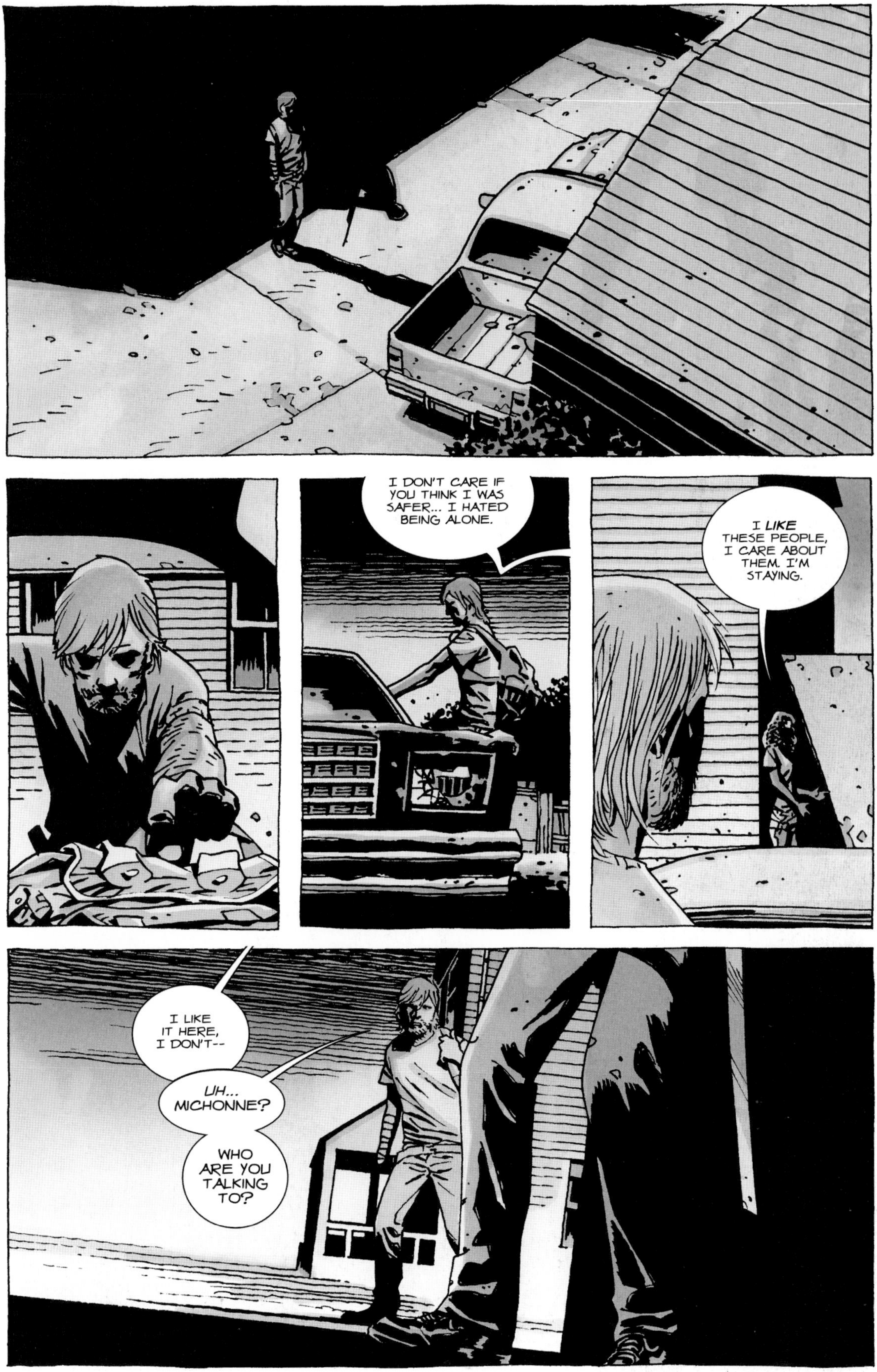
I DON'T CARE IF YOU THINK I WAS SAFER... I HATED BEING ALONE.
I *LIKE* THESE PEOPLE, I CARE ABOUT THEM. I'M STAYING.
I LIKE IT HERE, I DON'T--
UH... MICHONNE?
WHO ARE YOU TALKING TO?

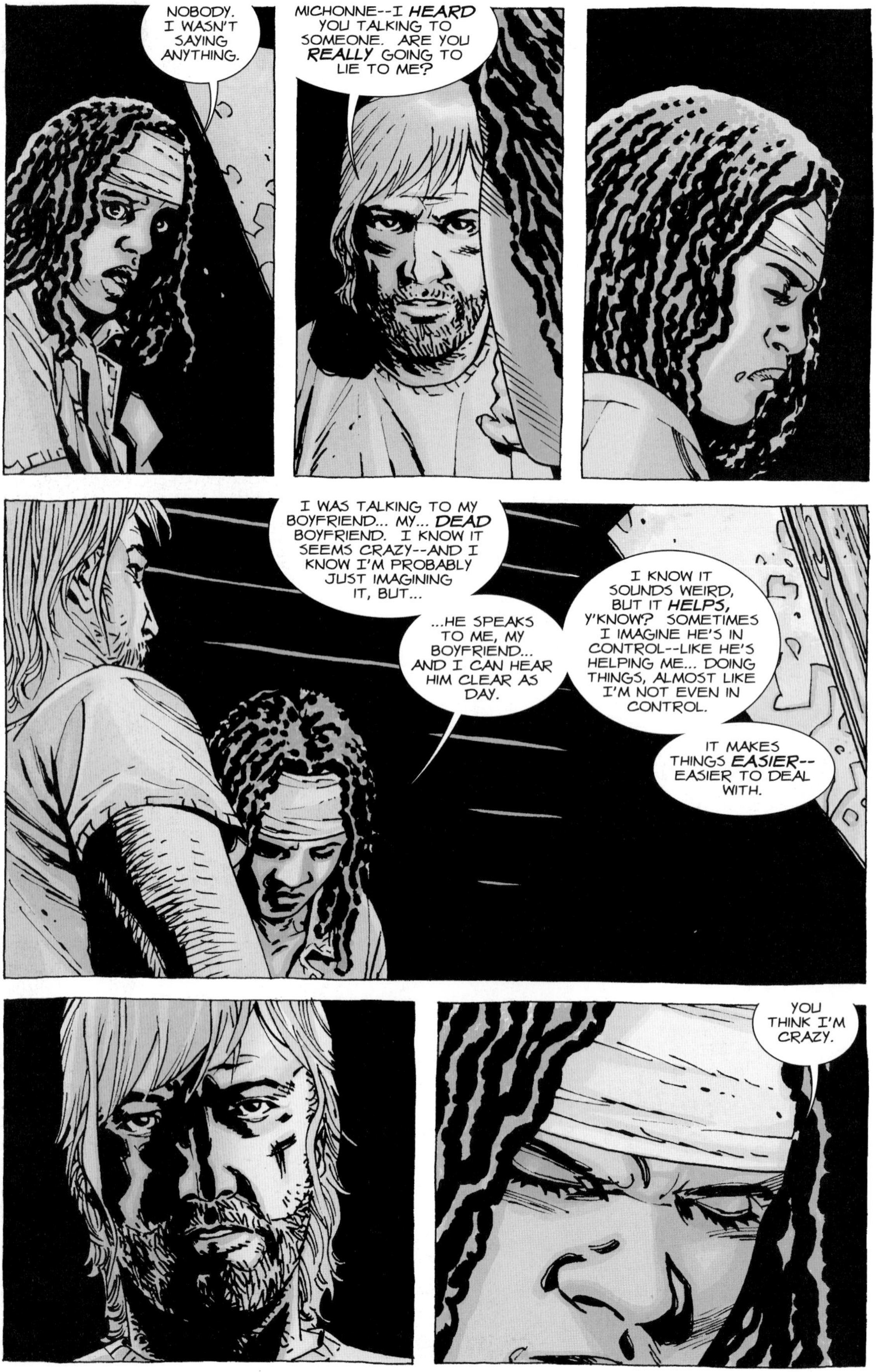
NOBODY. I WASN'T SAYING ANYTHING.
MICHONNE--I HEARD YOU TALKING TO SOMEONE. ARE YOU REALLY GOING TO LIE TO ME?
I WAS TALKING TO MY BOYFRIEND... MY... DEAD BOYFRIEND. I KNOW IT SEEMS CRAZY--AND I KNOW I'M PROBABLY JUST IMAGINING IT, BUT...
...HE SPEAKS TO ME, MY BOYFRIEND... AND I CAN HEAR HIM CLEAR AS DAY.
I KNOW IT SOUNDS WEIRD, BUT IT HELPS, Y'KNOW? SOMETIMES I IMAGINE HE'S IN CONTROL--LIKE HE'S HELPING ME... DOING THINGS, ALMOST LIKE I'M NOT EVEN IN CONTROL.
IT MAKES THINGS EASIER--EASIER TO DEAL WITH.
YOU THINK I'M CRAZY.

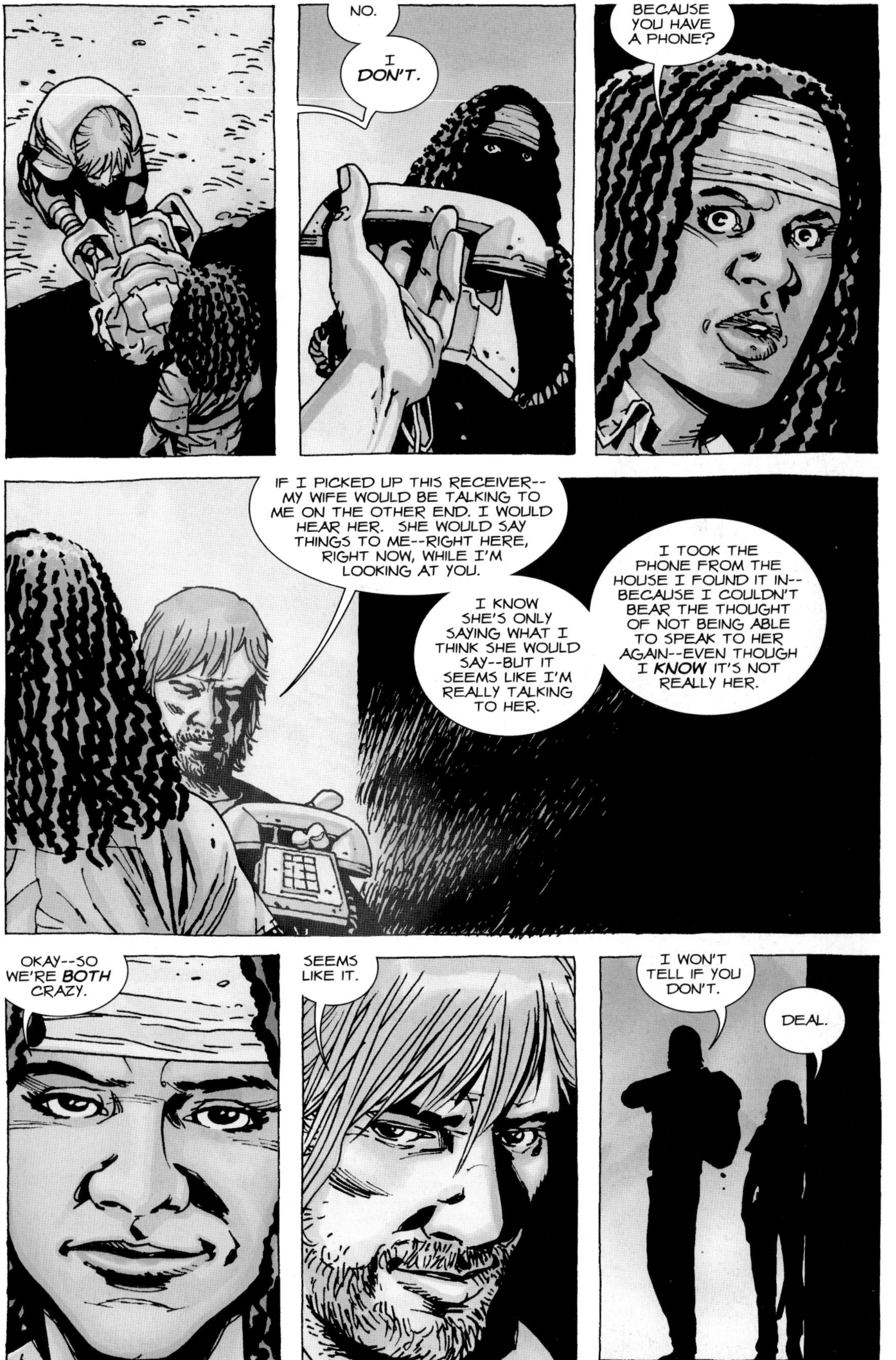
NO.
I DON'T.
BECAUSE YOU HAVE A PHONE?
IF I PICKED UP THIS RECEIVER-- MY WIFE WOULD BE TALKING TO ME ON THE OTHER END. I WOULD HEAR HER. SHE WOULD SAY THINGS TO ME--RIGHT HERE, RIGHT NOW, WHILE I'M LOOKING AT YOU.
I KNOW SHE'S ONLY SAYING WHAT I THINK SHE WOULD SAY--BUT IT SEEMS LIKE I'M REALLY TALKING TO HER.
I TOOK THE PHONE FROM THE HOUSE I FOUND IT IN-- BECAUSE I COULDN'T BEAR THE THOUGHT OF NOT BEING ABLE TO SPEAK TO HER AGAIN--EVEN THOUGH I KNOW IT'S NOT REALLY HER.
OKAY--SO WE'RE BOTH CRAZY.
SEEMS LIKE IT.
I WON'T TELL IF YOU DON'T.
DEAL.

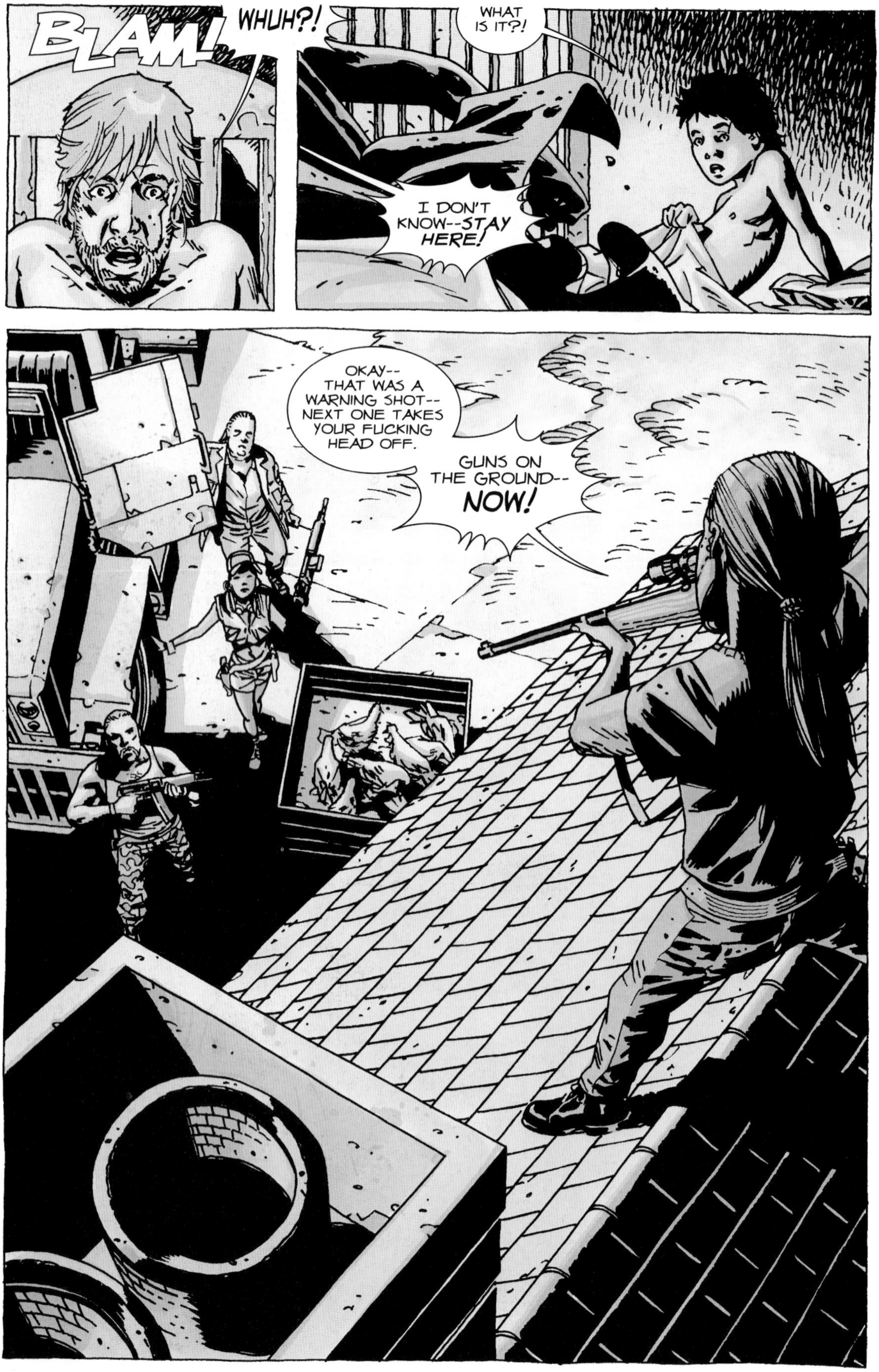
BLAM!
WHUH?!
WHAT IS IT?!
I DON'T KNOW--STAY HERE!
OKAY-- THAT WAS A WARNING SHOT-- NEXT ONE TAKES YOUR FUCKING HEAD OFF.
GUNS ON THE GROUND-- NOW!

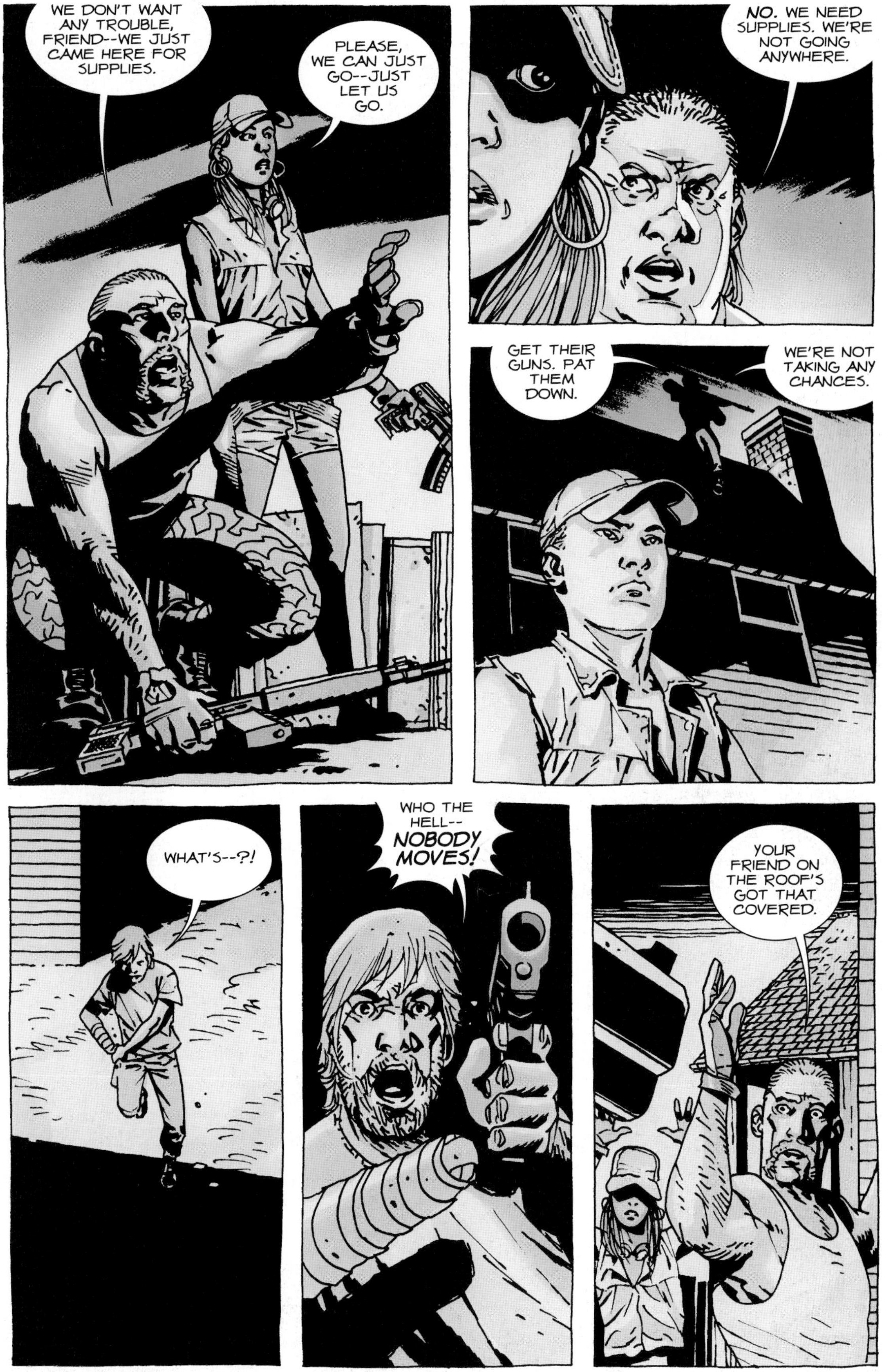
WE DON'T WANT ANY TROUBLE, FRIEND--WE JUST CAME HERE FOR SUPPLIES.
PLEASE, WE CAN JUST GO--JUST LET US GO.
NO. WE NEED SUPPLIES. WE'RE NOT GOING ANYWHERE.
GET THEIR GUNS. PAT THEM DOWN.
WE'RE NOT TAKING ANY CHANCES.
WHAT'S--?!
WHO THE HELL--
NOBODY MOVES!
YOUR FRIEND ON THE ROOF'S GOT THAT COVERED.

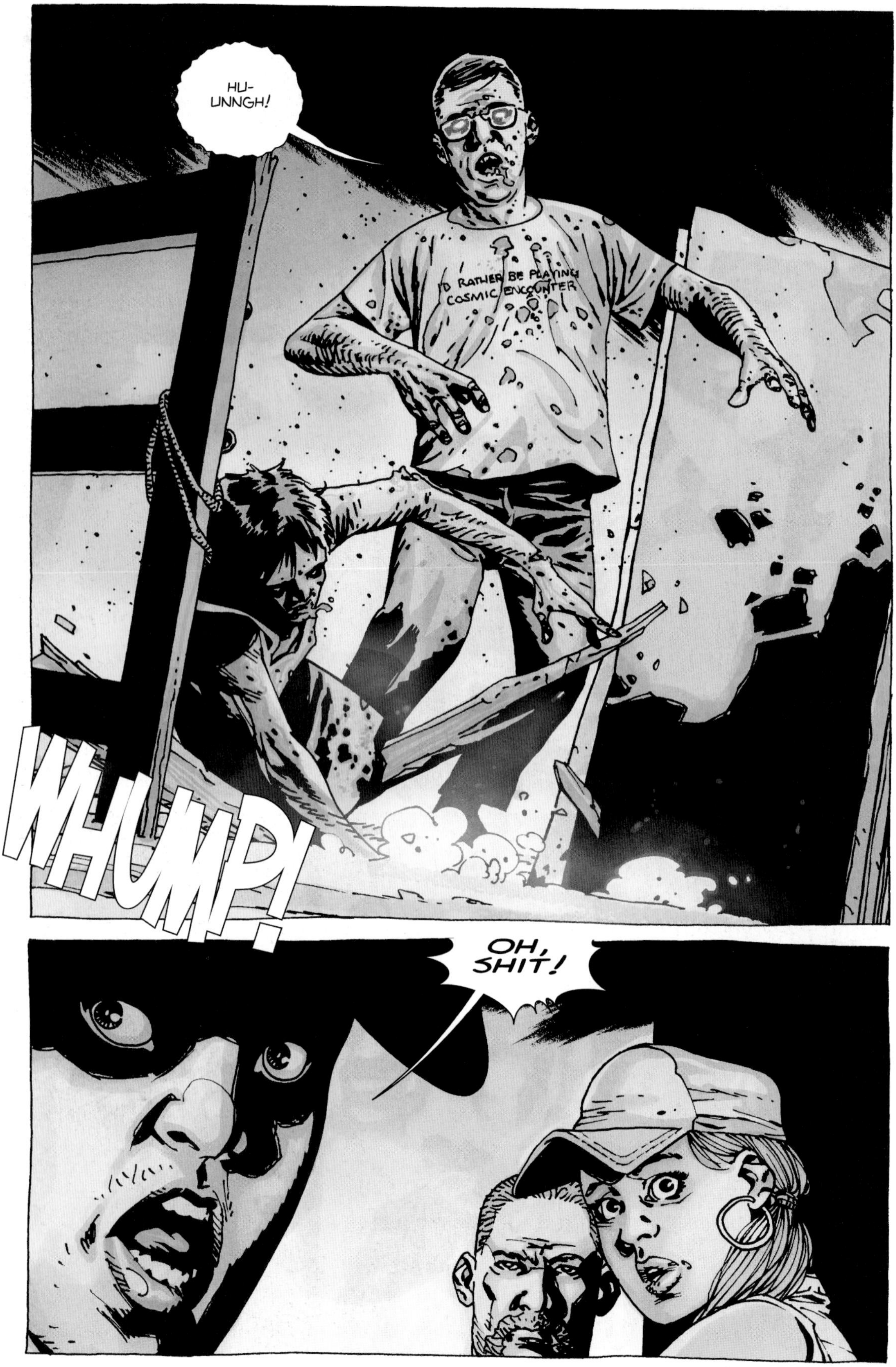
HU-
UNNGH!
I'D RATHER BE PLAYING
COSMIC ENCOUNTER
WHUMP!
OH,
SHIT!

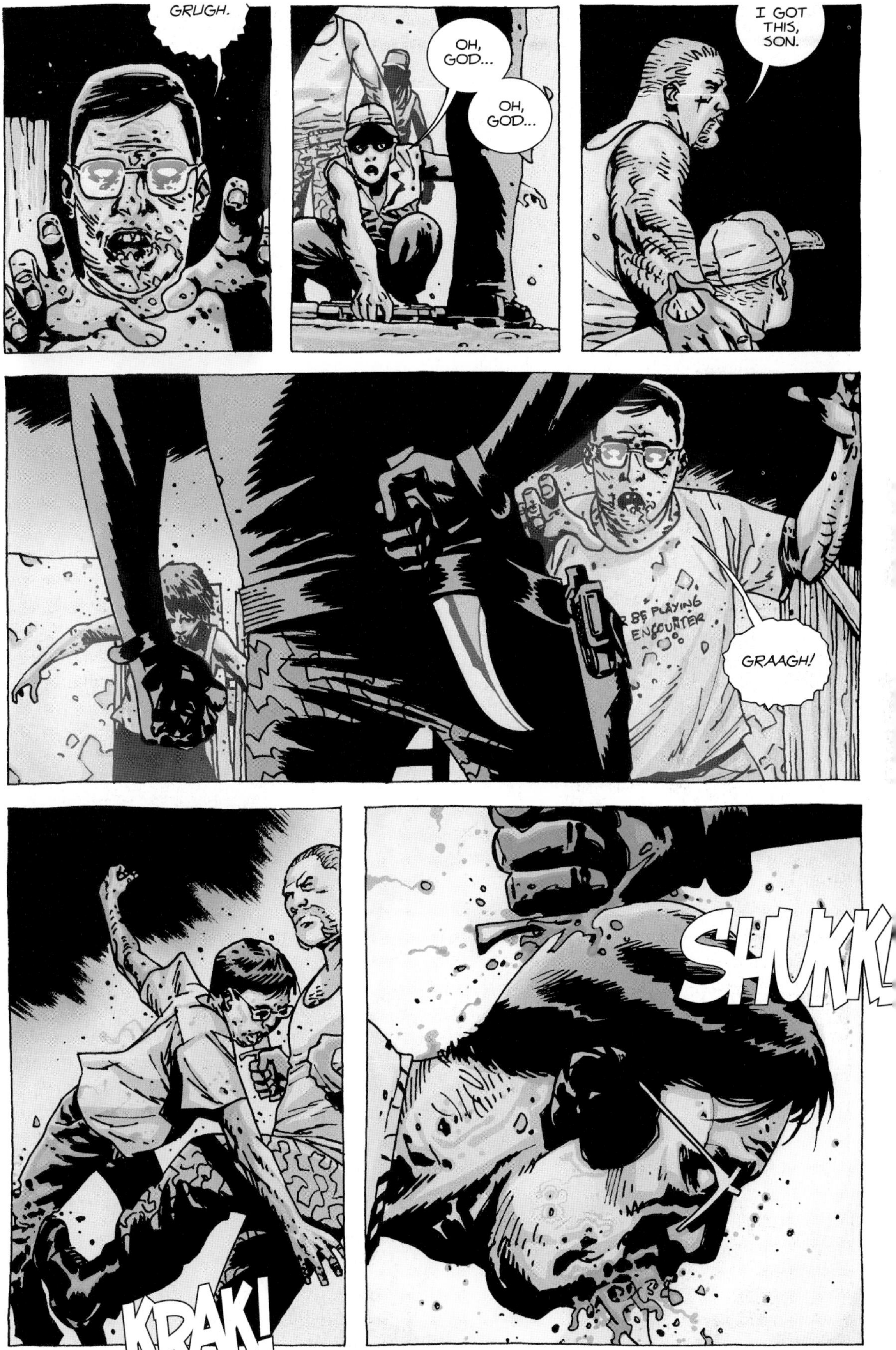
GRUGH.
OH, GOD...
OH, GOD...
I GOT THIS, SON.
GRAAGH!
KRAK!
SHUKK

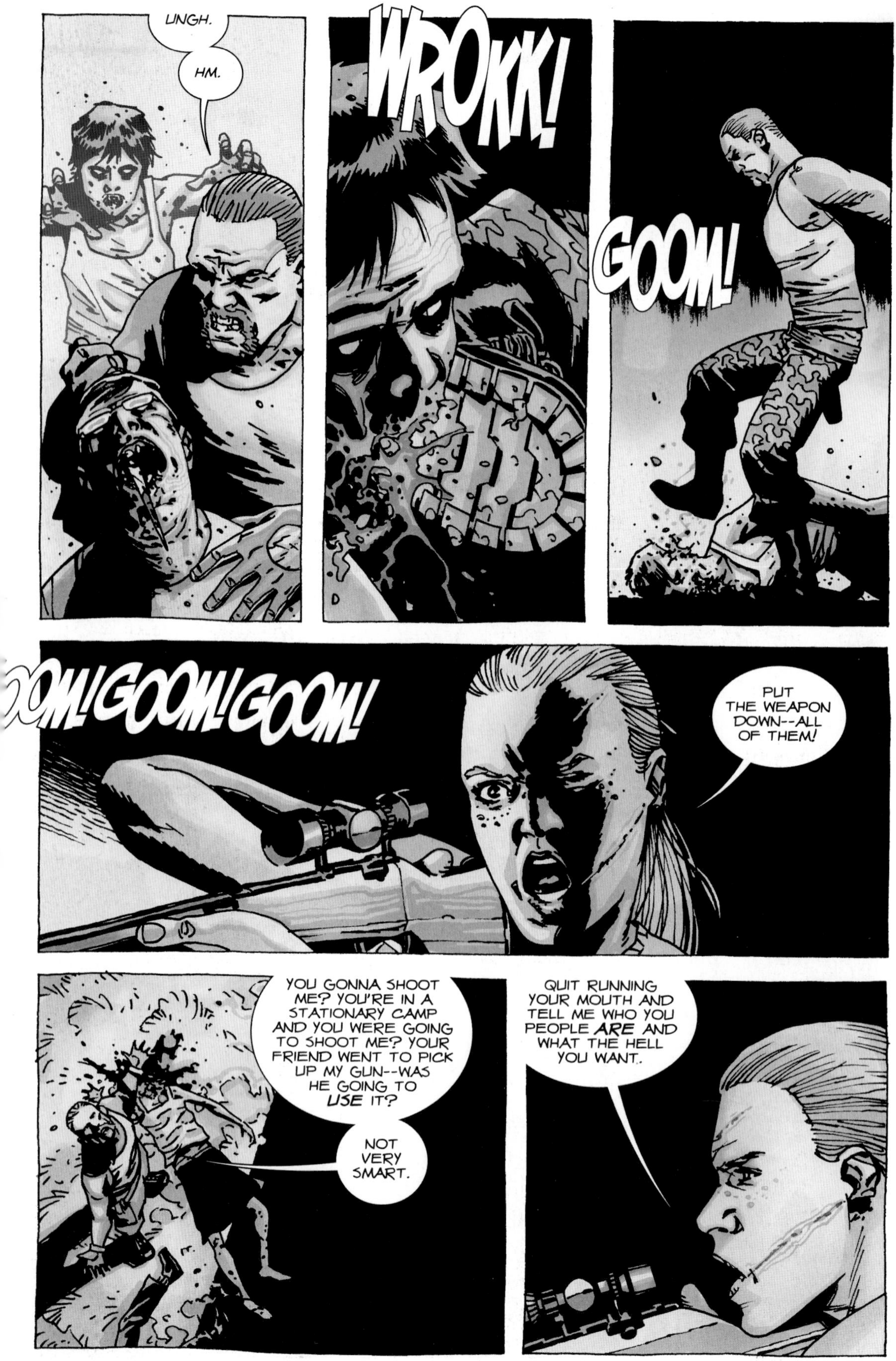
UNGH.
HM.
WROKK!
GOOM!
GOOM! GOOM! GOOM!
PUT THE WEAPON DOWN--ALL OF THEM!
YOU GONNA SHOOT ME? YOU'RE IN A STATIONARY CAMP AND YOU WERE GOING TO SHOOT ME? YOUR FRIEND WENT TO PICK UP MY GUN--WAS HE GOING TO USE IT?
NOT VERY SMART.
QUIT RUNNING YOUR MOUTH AND TELL ME WHO YOU PEOPLE ARE AND WHAT THE HELL YOU WANT.

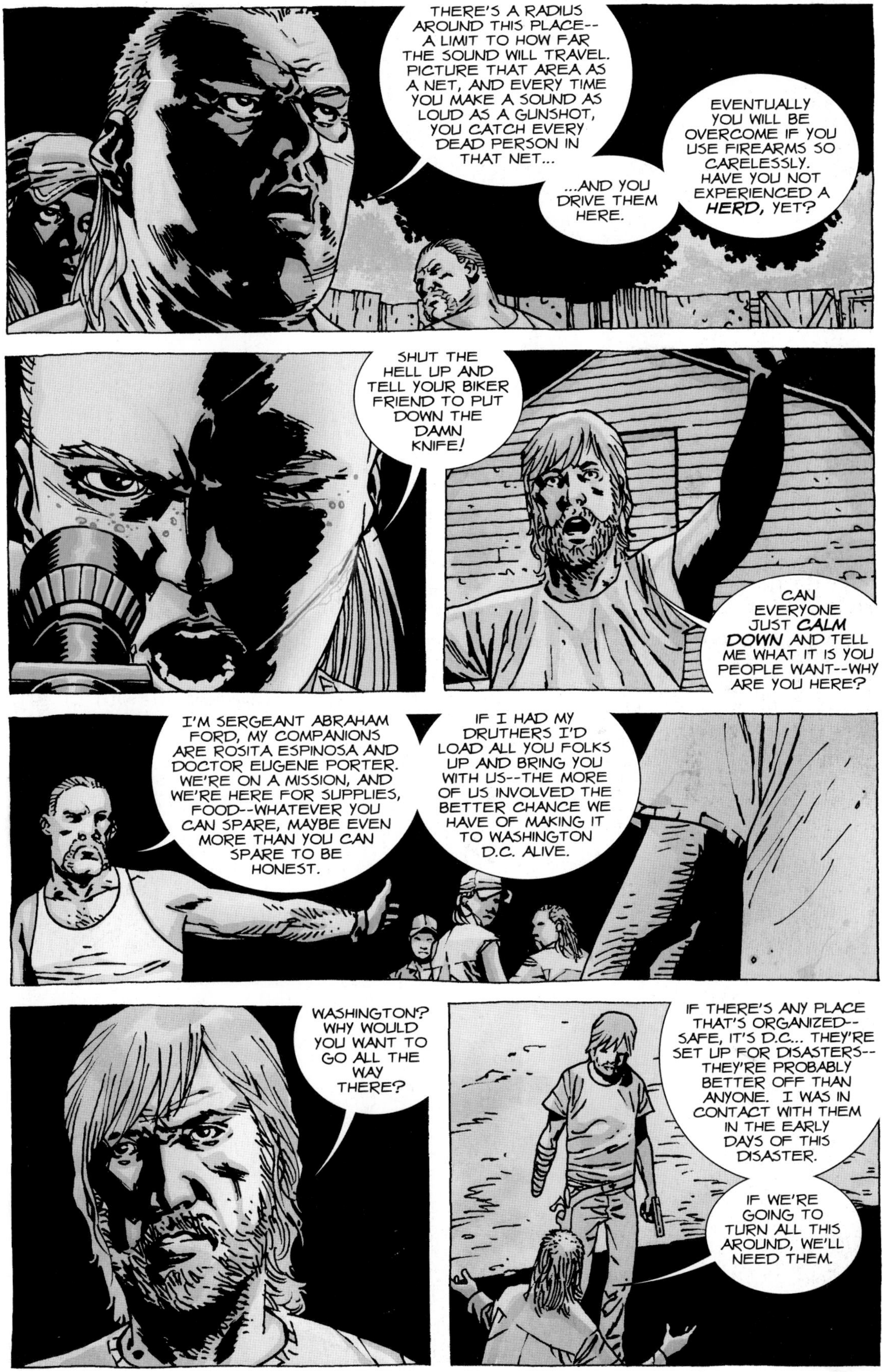
THERE'S A RADIUS AROUND THIS PLACE-- A LIMIT TO HOW FAR THE SOUND WILL TRAVEL. PICTURE THAT AREA AS A NET, AND EVERY TIME YOU MAKE A SOUND AS LOUD AS A GUNSHOT, YOU CATCH EVERY DEAD PERSON IN THAT NET...
...AND YOU DRIVE THEM HERE.
EVENTUALLY YOU WILL BE OVERCOME IF YOU USE FIREARMS SO CARELESSLY. HAVE YOU NOT EXPERIENCED A HERD, YET?
SHUT THE HELL UP AND TELL YOUR BIKER FRIEND TO PUT DOWN THE DAMN KNIFE!
CAN EVERYONE JUST CALM DOWN AND TELL ME WHAT IT IS YOU PEOPLE WANT--WHY ARE YOU HERE?
I'M SERGEANT ABRAHAM FORD, MY COMPANIONS ARE ROSITA ESPINOSA AND DOCTOR EUGENE PORTER. WE'RE ON A MISSION, AND WE'RE HERE FOR SUPPLIES, FOOD--WHATEVER YOU CAN SPARE, MAYBE EVEN MORE THAN YOU CAN SPARE TO BE HONEST.
IF I HAD MY DRUTHERS I'D LOAD ALL YOU FOLKS UP AND BRING YOU WITH US--THE MORE OF US INVOLVED THE BETTER CHANCE WE HAVE OF MAKING IT TO WASHINGTON D.C. ALIVE.
WASHINGTON? WHY WOULD YOU WANT TO GO ALL THE WAY THERE?
IF THERE'S ANY PLACE THAT'S ORGANIZED-- SAFE, IT'S D.C... THEY'RE SET UP FOR DISASTERS-- THEY'RE PROBABLY BETTER OFF THAN ANYONE. I WAS IN CONTACT WITH THEM IN THE EARLY DAYS OF THIS DISASTER.
IF WE'RE GOING TO TURN ALL THIS AROUND, WE'LL NEED THEM.

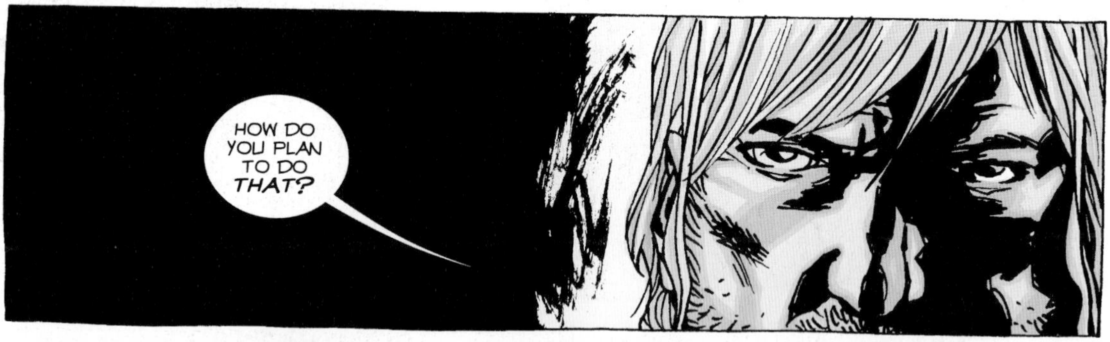
HOW DO YOU PLAN TO DO *THAT?*

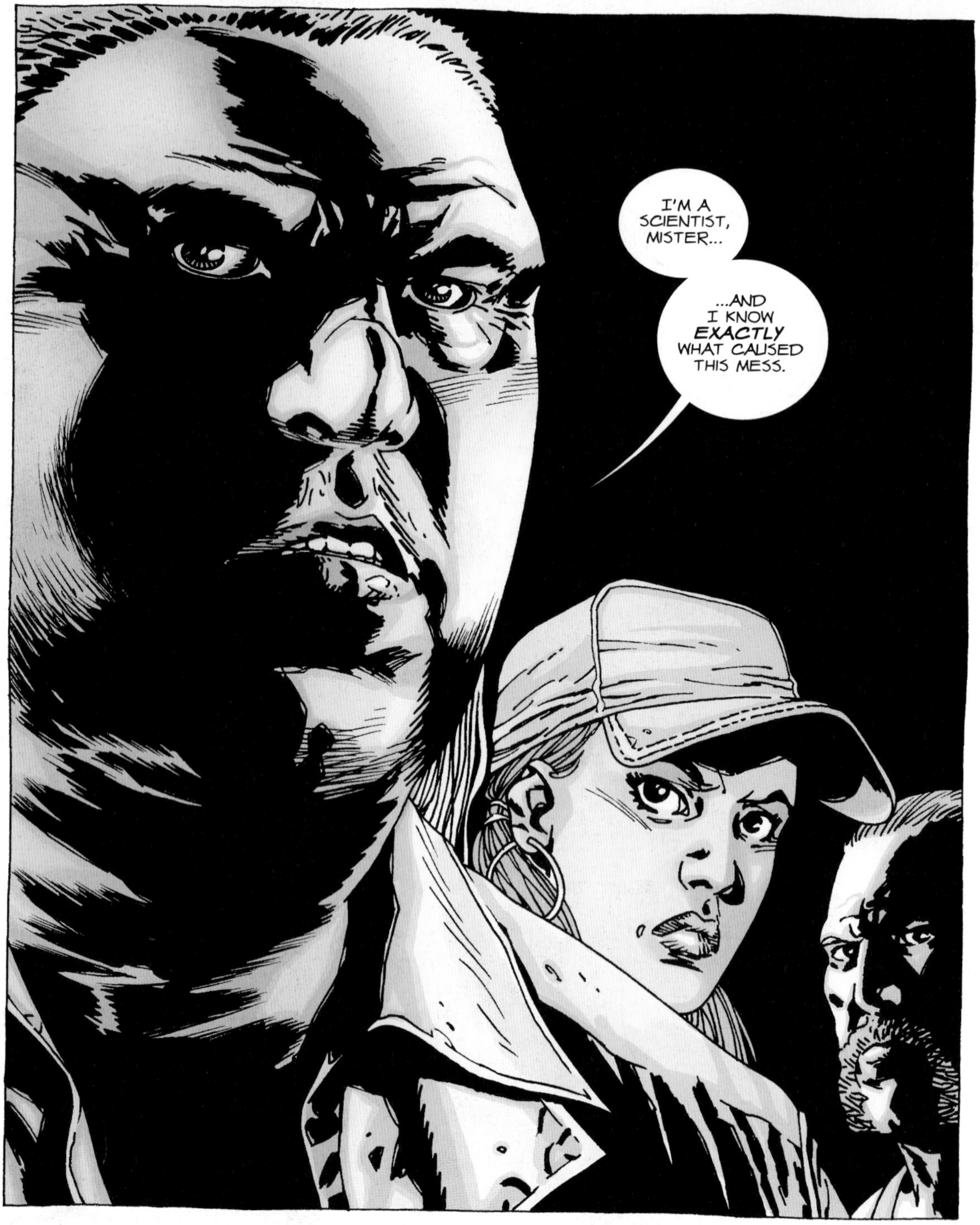
I'M A SCIENTIST, MISTER...
...AND I KNOW *EXACTLY* WHAT CAUSED THIS MESS.

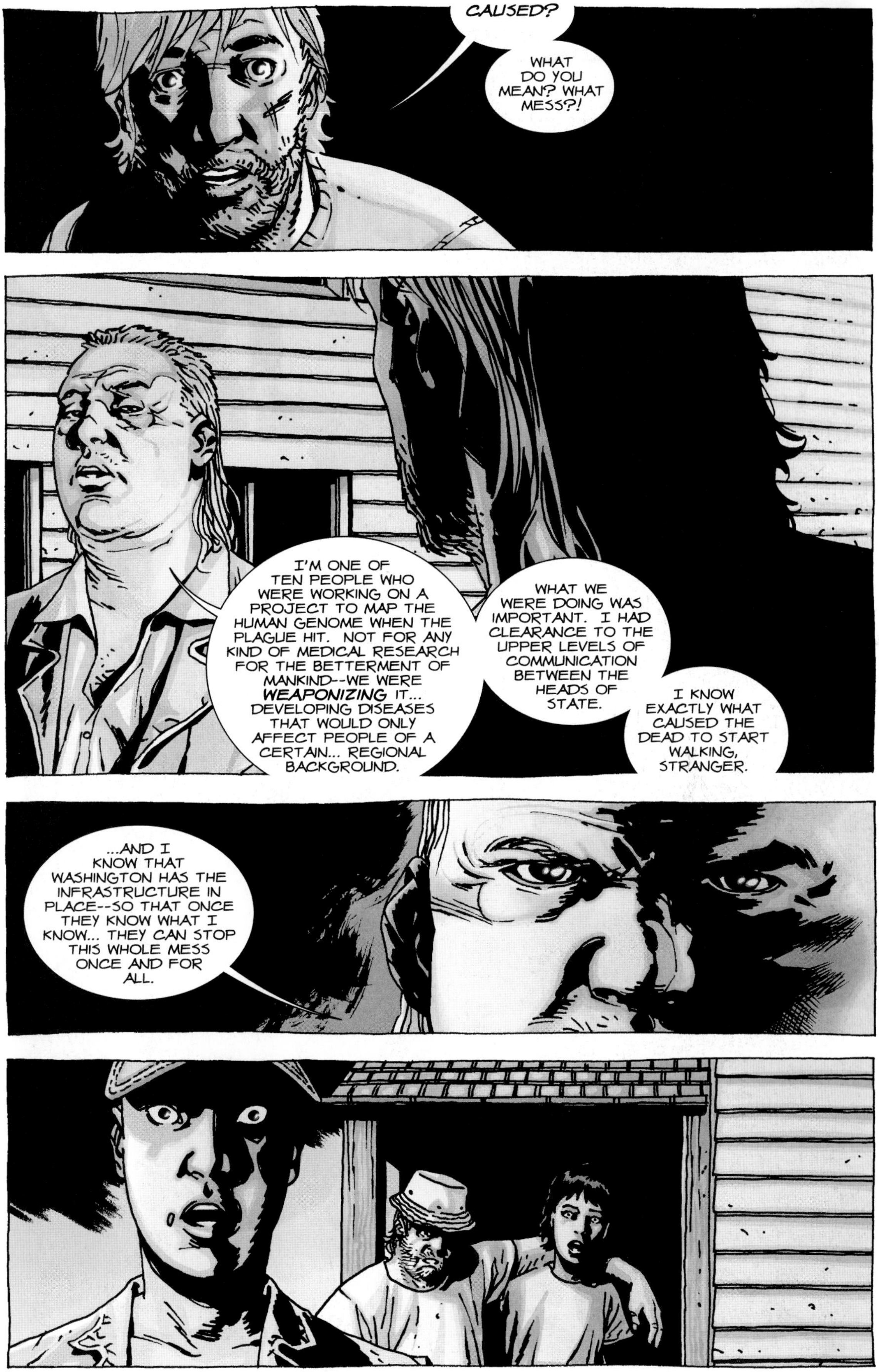
CAUSED?
WHAT DO YOU MEAN? WHAT MESS?!
I'M ONE OF TEN PEOPLE WHO WERE WORKING ON A PROJECT TO MAP THE HUMAN GENOME WHEN THE PLAGUE HIT. NOT FOR ANY KIND OF MEDICAL RESEARCH FOR THE BETTERMENT OF MANKIND--WE WERE **WEAPONIZING** IT... DEVELOPING DISEASES THAT WOULD ONLY AFFECT PEOPLE OF A CERTAIN... REGIONAL BACKGROUND.
WHAT WE WERE DOING WAS IMPORTANT. I HAD CLEARANCE TO THE UPPER LEVELS OF COMMUNICATION BETWEEN THE HEADS OF STATE.
I KNOW EXACTLY WHAT CAUSED THE DEAD TO START WALKING, STRANGER.
...AND I KNOW THAT WASHINGTON HAS THE INFRASTRUCTURE IN PLACE--SO THAT ONCE THEY KNOW WHAT I KNOW... THEY CAN STOP THIS WHOLE MESS ONCE AND FOR ALL.

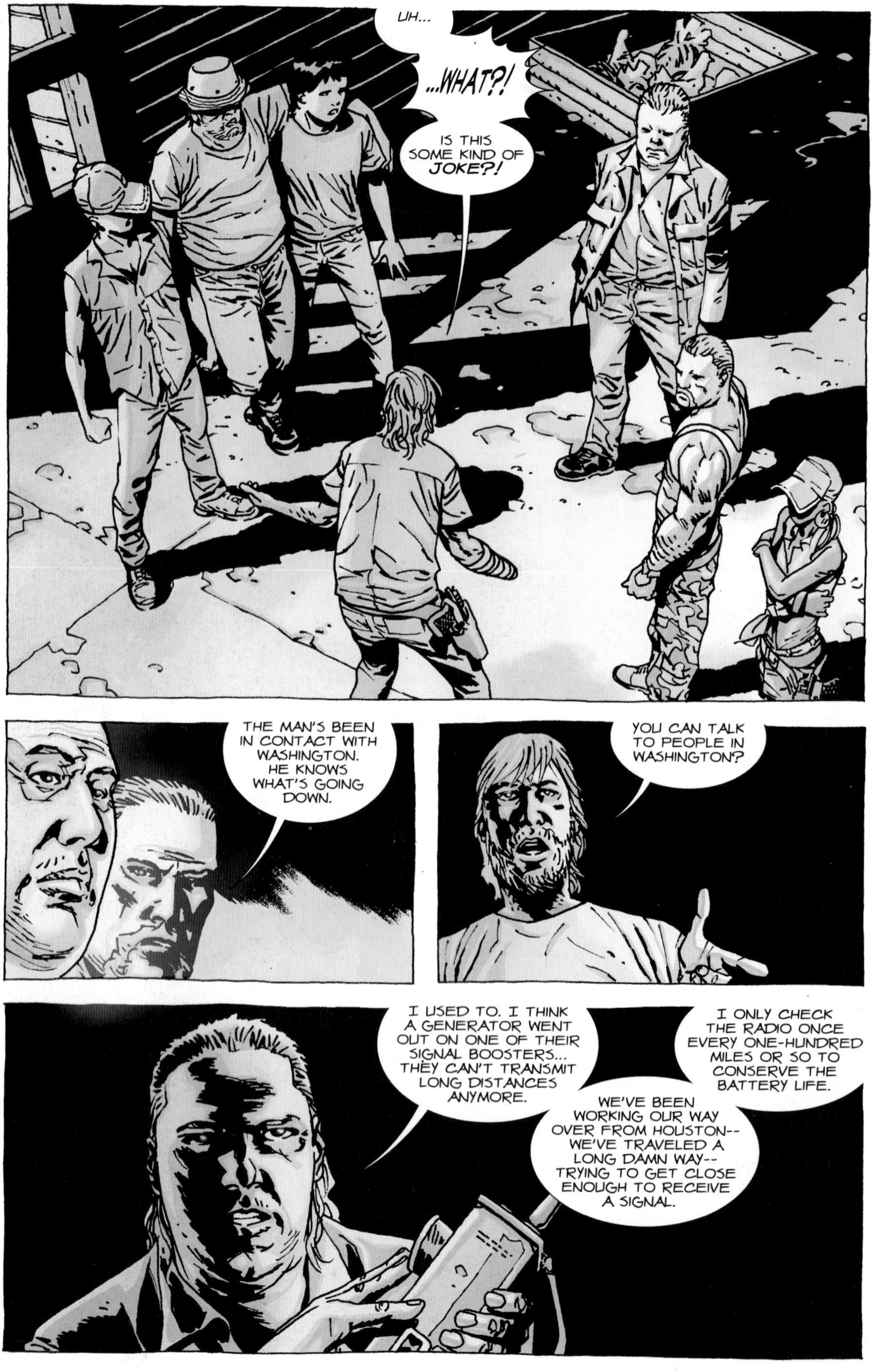
UH...
...WHAT?!
IS THIS SOME KIND OF JOKE?!
THE MAN'S BEEN IN CONTACT WITH WASHINGTON. HE KNOWS WHAT'S GOING DOWN.
YOU CAN TALK TO PEOPLE IN WASHINGTON?
I USED TO. I THINK A GENERATOR WENT OUT ON ONE OF THEIR SIGNAL BOOSTERS... THEY CAN'T TRANSMIT LONG DISTANCES ANYMORE.
I ONLY CHECK THE RADIO ONCE EVERY ONE-HUNDRED MILES OR SO TO CONSERVE THE BATTERY LIFE.
WE'VE BEEN WORKING OUR WAY OVER FROM HOUSTON-- WE'VE TRAVELED A LONG DAMN WAY-- TRYING TO GET CLOSE ENOUGH TO RECEIVE A SIGNAL.

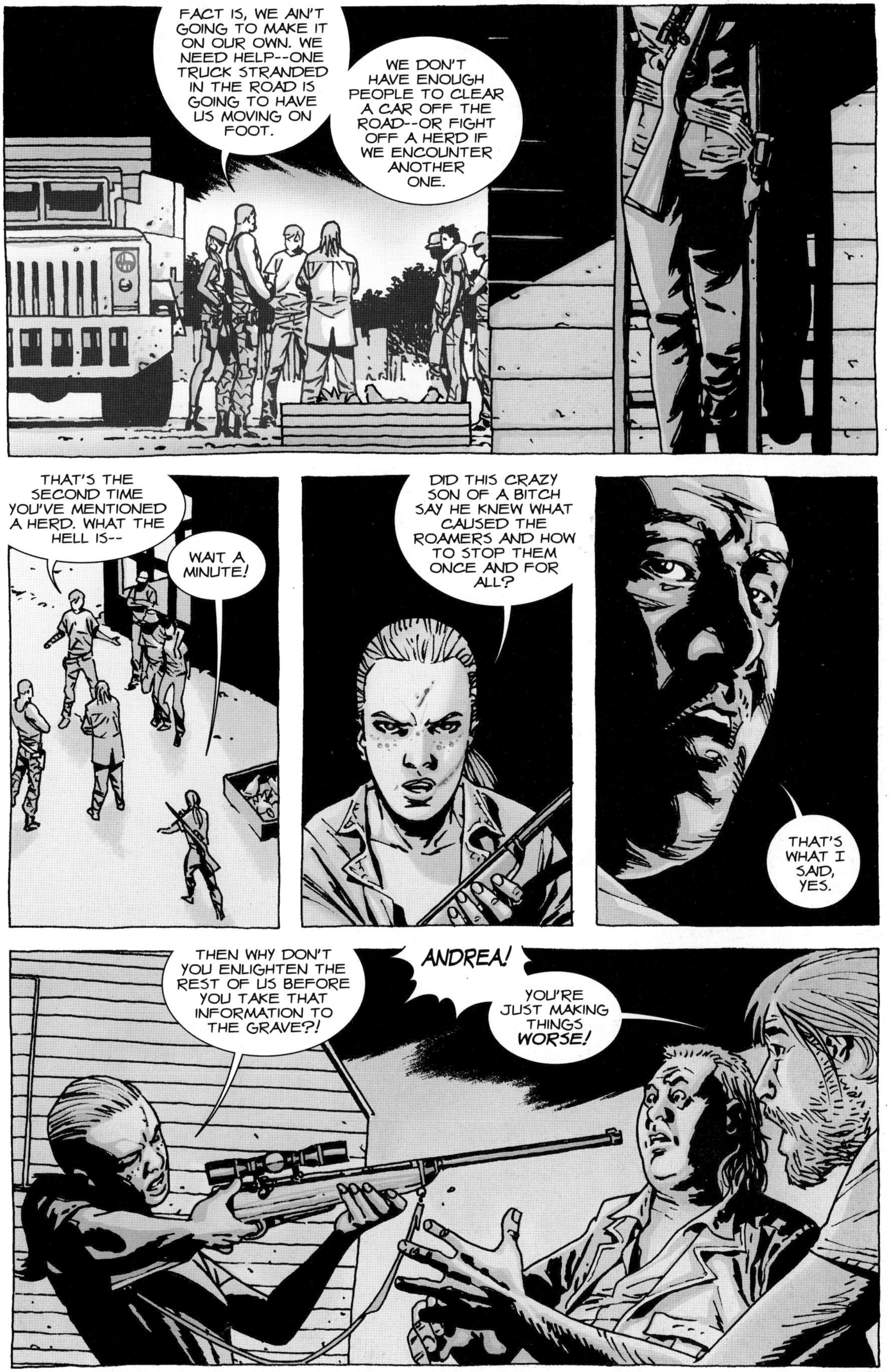
FACT IS, WE AIN'T GOING TO MAKE IT ON OUR OWN. WE NEED HELP--ONE TRUCK STRANDED IN THE ROAD IS GOING TO HAVE US MOVING ON FOOT.
WE DON'T HAVE ENOUGH PEOPLE TO CLEAR A CAR OFF THE ROAD--OR FIGHT OFF A HERD IF WE ENCOUNTER ANOTHER ONE.
THAT'S THE SECOND TIME YOU'VE MENTIONED A HERD. WHAT THE HELL IS--
WAIT A MINUTE!
DID THIS CRAZY SON OF A BITCH SAY HE KNEW WHAT CAUSED THE ROAMERS AND HOW TO STOP THEM ONCE AND FOR ALL?
THAT'S WHAT I SAID, YES.
THEN WHY DON'T YOU ENLIGHTEN THE REST OF US BEFORE YOU TAKE THAT INFORMATION TO THE GRAVE?!
ANDREA!
YOU'RE JUST MAKING THINGS WORSE!

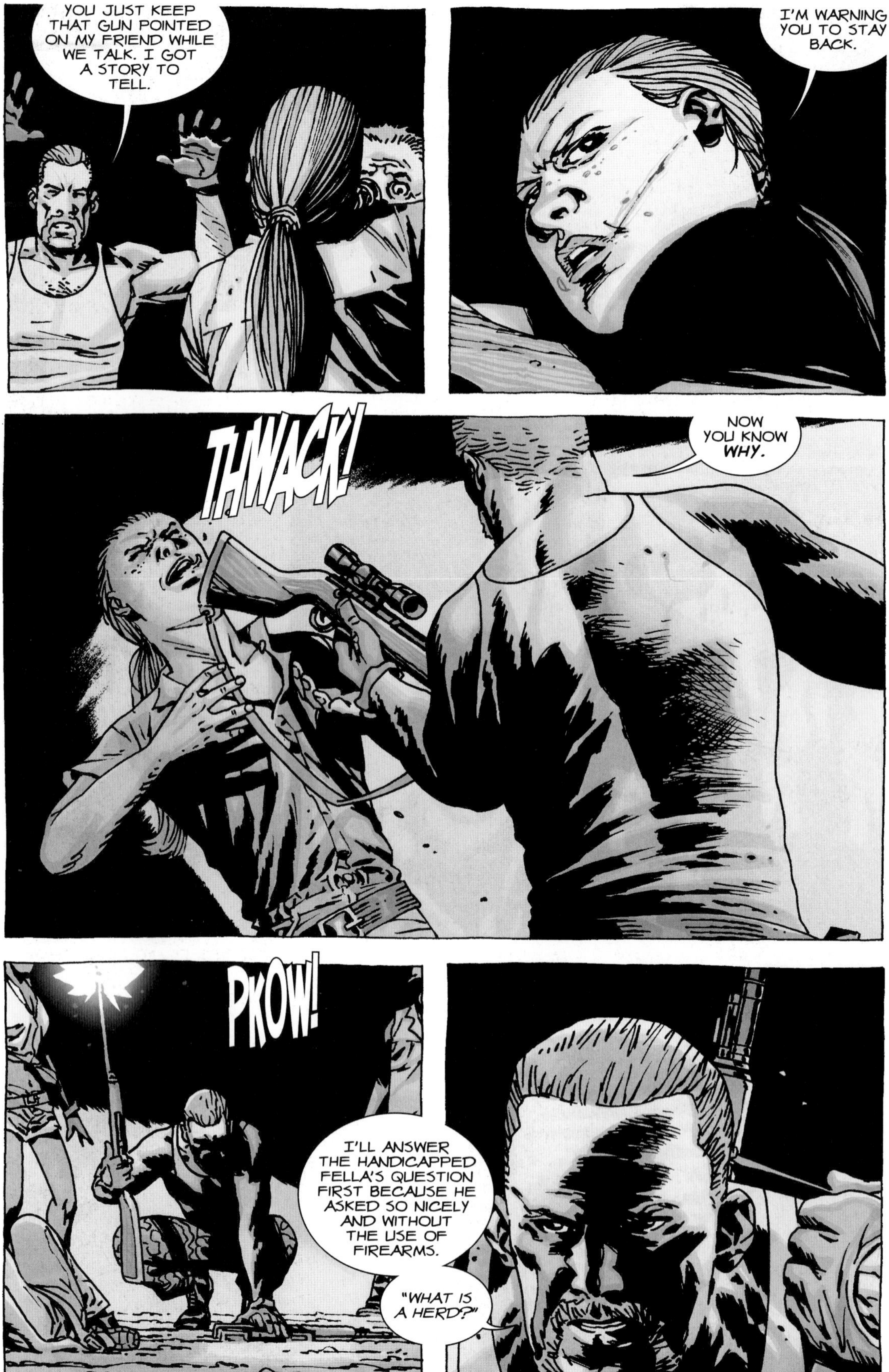
YOU JUST KEEP THAT GUN POINTED ON MY FRIEND WHILE WE TALK. I GOT A STORY TO TELL.
I'M WARNING YOU TO STAY BACK.
THWACK!
NOW YOU KNOW WHY.
PKOW!
I'LL ANSWER THE HANDICAPPED FELLA'S QUESTION FIRST BECAUSE HE ASKED SO NICELY AND WITHOUT THE USE OF FIREARMS.
"WHAT IS A HERD?"

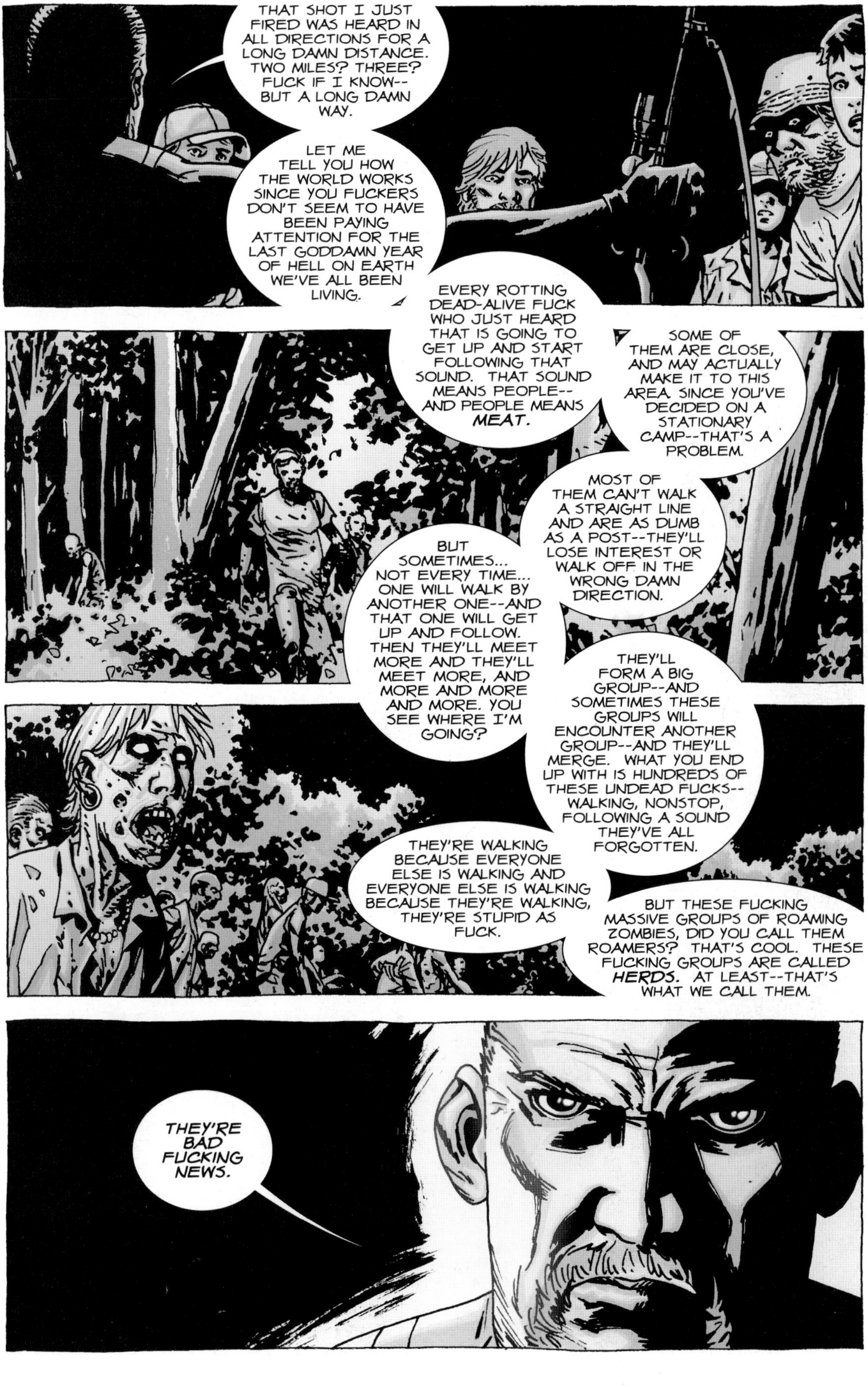
THAT SHOT I JUST FIRED WAS HEARD IN ALL DIRECTIONS FOR A LONG DAMN DISTANCE. TWO MILES? THREE? FUCK IF I KNOW-- BUT A LONG DAMN WAY.
LET ME TELL YOU HOW THE WORLD WORKS SINCE YOU FUCKERS DON'T SEEM TO HAVE BEEN PAYING ATTENTION FOR THE LAST GODDAMN YEAR OF HELL ON EARTH WE'VE ALL BEEN LIVING.
EVERY ROTTING DEAD-ALIVE FUCK WHO JUST HEARD THAT IS GOING TO GET UP AND START FOLLOWING THAT SOUND. THAT SOUND MEANS PEOPLE-- AND PEOPLE MEANS *MEAT.*
SOME OF THEM ARE CLOSE, AND MAY ACTUALLY MAKE IT TO THIS AREA SINCE YOU'VE DECIDED ON A STATIONARY CAMP--THAT'S A PROBLEM.
MOST OF THEM CAN'T WALK A STRAIGHT LINE AND ARE AS DUMB AS A POST--THEY'LL LOSE INTEREST OR WALK OFF IN THE WRONG DAMN DIRECTION.
BUT SOMETIMES... NOT EVERY TIME... ONE WILL WALK BY ANOTHER ONE--AND THAT ONE WILL GET UP AND FOLLOW. THEN THEY'LL MEET MORE AND THEY'LL MEET MORE, AND MORE AND MORE AND MORE. YOU SEE WHERE I'M GOING?
THEY'LL FORM A BIG GROUP--AND SOMETIMES THESE GROUPS WILL ENCOUNTER ANOTHER GROUP--AND THEY'LL MERGE. WHAT YOU END UP WITH IS HUNDREDS OF THESE UNDEAD FUCKS-- WALKING, NONSTOP, FOLLOWING A SOUND THEY'VE ALL FORGOTTEN.
THEY'RE WALKING BECAUSE EVERYONE ELSE IS WALKING AND EVERYONE ELSE IS WALKING BECAUSE THEY'RE WALKING, THEY'RE STUPID AS FUCK.
BUT THESE FUCKING MASSIVE GROUPS OF ROAMING ZOMBIES, DID YOU CALL THEM ROAMERS? THAT'S COOL. THESE FUCKING GROUPS ARE CALLED *HERDS.* AT LEAST--THAT'S WHAT WE CALL THEM.
THEY'RE BAD FUCKING NEWS.

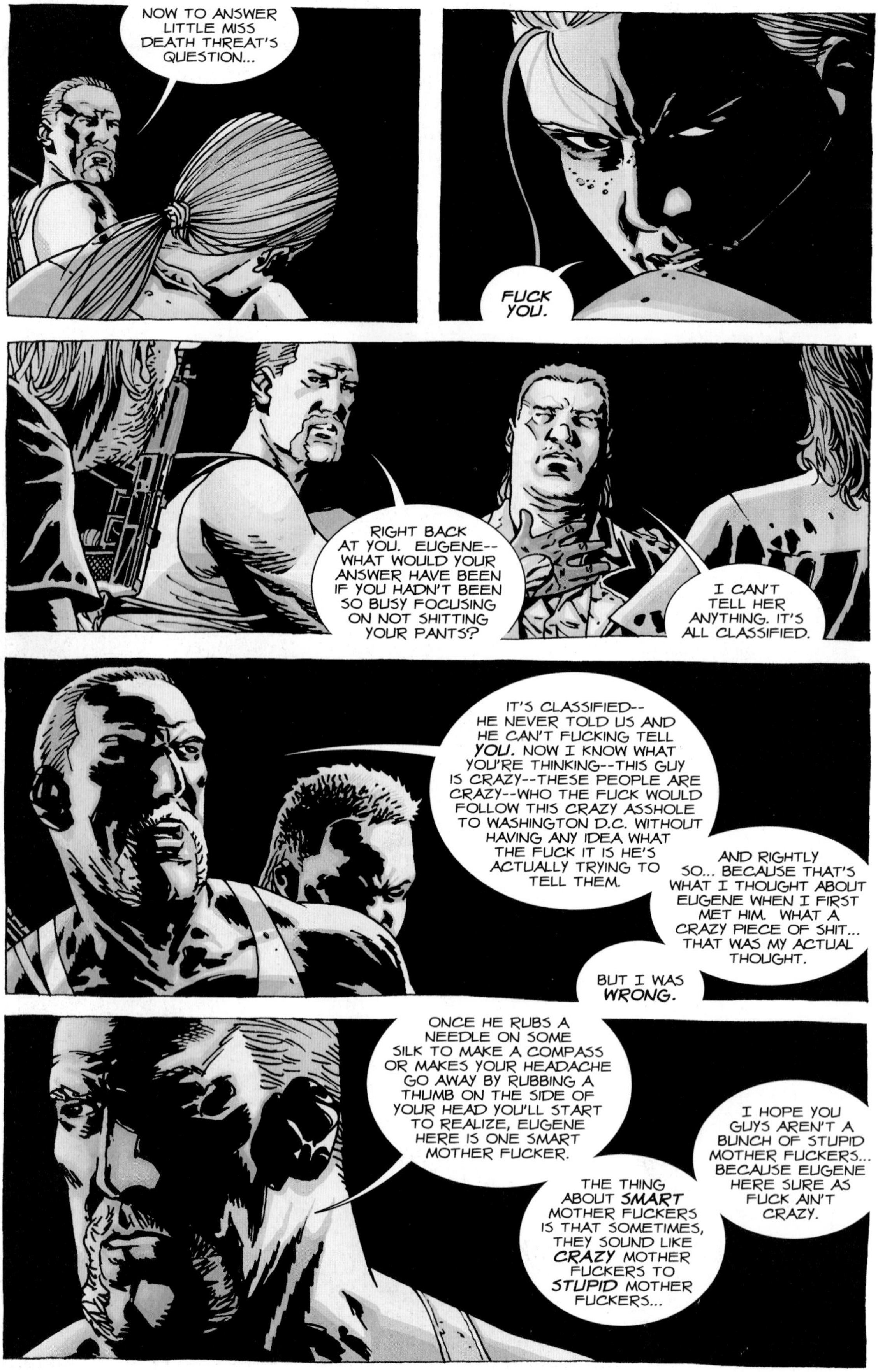
NOW TO ANSWER LITTLE MISS DEATH THREAT'S QUESTION...
FUCK YOU.
RIGHT BACK AT YOU. EUGENE-- WHAT WOULD YOUR ANSWER HAVE BEEN IF YOU HADN'T BEEN SO BUSY FOCUSING ON NOT SHITTING YOUR PANTS?
I CAN'T TELL HER ANYTHING. IT'S ALL CLASSIFIED.
IT'S CLASSIFIED-- HE NEVER TOLD US AND HE CAN'T FUCKING TELL YOU. NOW I KNOW WHAT YOU'RE THINKING--THIS GUY IS CRAZY--THESE PEOPLE ARE CRAZY--WHO THE FUCK WOULD FOLLOW THIS CRAZY ASSHOLE TO WASHINGTON D.C. WITHOUT HAVING ANY IDEA WHAT THE FUCK IT IS HE'S ACTUALLY TRYING TO TELL THEM.
AND RIGHTLY SO... BECAUSE THAT'S WHAT I THOUGHT ABOUT EUGENE WHEN I FIRST MET HIM. WHAT A CRAZY PIECE OF SHIT... THAT WAS MY ACTUAL THOUGHT.
BUT I WAS WRONG.
ONCE HE RUBS A NEEDLE ON SOME SILK TO MAKE A COMPASS OR MAKES YOUR HEADACHE GO AWAY BY RUBBING A THUMB ON THE SIDE OF YOUR HEAD YOU'LL START TO REALIZE, EUGENE HERE IS ONE SMART MOTHER FUCKER.
THE THING ABOUT SMART MOTHER FUCKERS IS THAT SOMETIMES, THEY SOUND LIKE CRAZY MOTHER FUCKERS TO STUPID MOTHER FUCKERS...
I HOPE YOU GUYS AREN'T A BUNCH OF STUPID MOTHER FUCKERS... BECAUSE EUGENE HERE SURE AS FUCK AIN'T CRAZY.

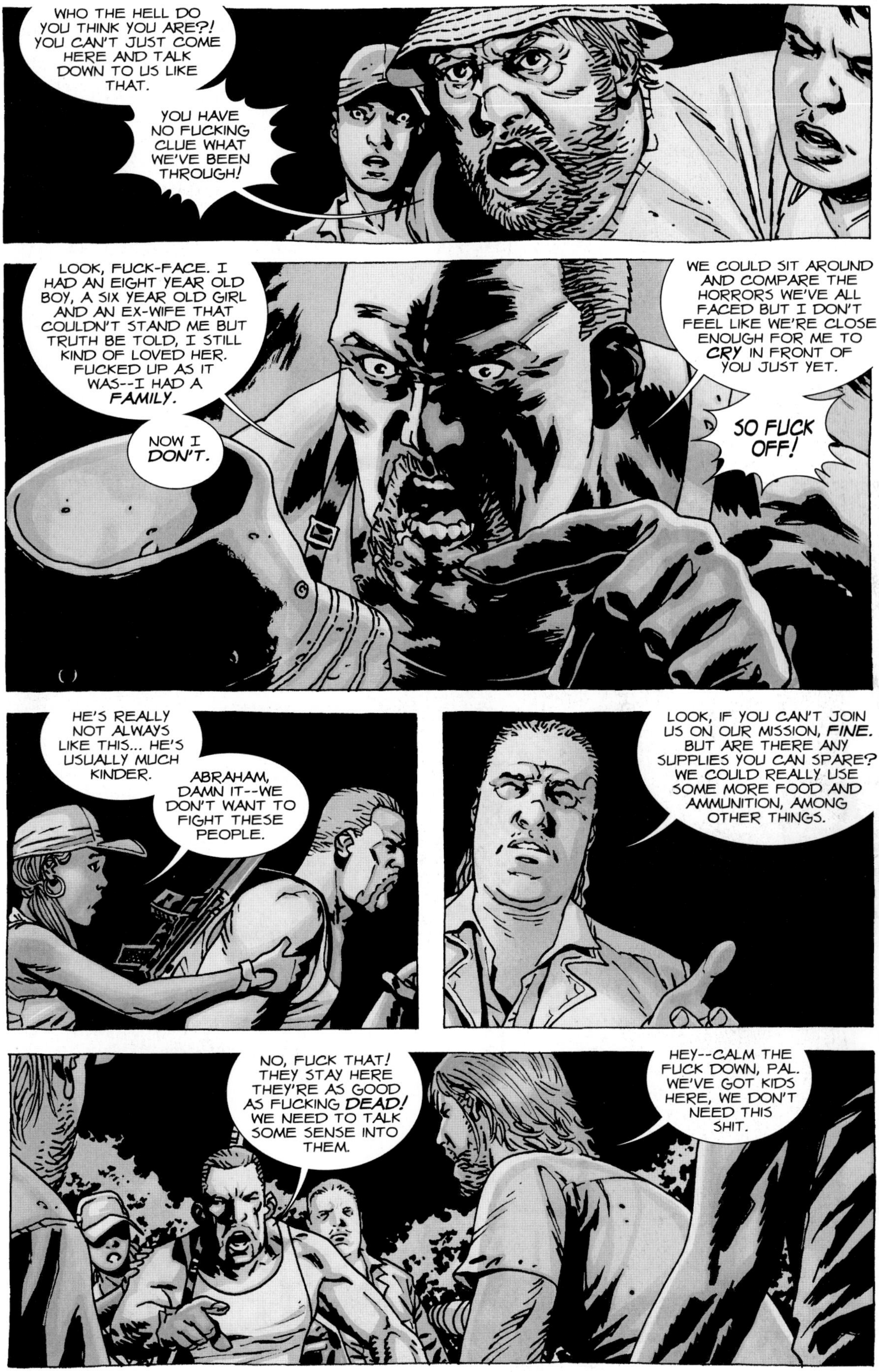
WHO THE HELL DO YOU THINK YOU ARE?! YOU CAN'T JUST COME HERE AND TALK DOWN TO US LIKE THAT.
YOU HAVE NO FUCKING CLUE WHAT WE'VE BEEN THROUGH!
LOOK, FUCK-FACE. I HAD AN EIGHT YEAR OLD BOY, A SIX YEAR OLD GIRL AND AN EX-WIFE THAT COULDN'T STAND ME BUT TRUTH BE TOLD, I STILL KIND OF LOVED HER. FUCKED UP AS IT WAS--I HAD A FAMILY.
NOW I DON'T.
WE COULD SIT AROUND AND COMPARE THE HORRORS WE'VE ALL FACED BUT I DON'T FEEL LIKE WE'RE CLOSE ENOUGH FOR ME TO CRY IN FRONT OF YOU JUST YET.
SO FUCK OFF!
HE'S REALLY NOT ALWAYS LIKE THIS... HE'S USUALLY MUCH KINDER.
ABRAHAM, DAMN IT--WE DON'T WANT TO FIGHT THESE PEOPLE.
LOOK, IF YOU CAN'T JOIN US ON OUR MISSION, FINE. BUT ARE THERE ANY SUPPLIES YOU CAN SPARE? WE COULD REALLY USE SOME MORE FOOD AND AMMUNITION, AMONG OTHER THINGS.
NO, FUCK THAT! THEY STAY HERE THEY'RE AS GOOD AS FUCKING DEAD! WE NEED TO TALK SOME SENSE INTO THEM.
HEY--CALM THE FUCK DOWN, PAL. WE'VE GOT KIDS HERE, WE DON'T NEED THIS SHIT.

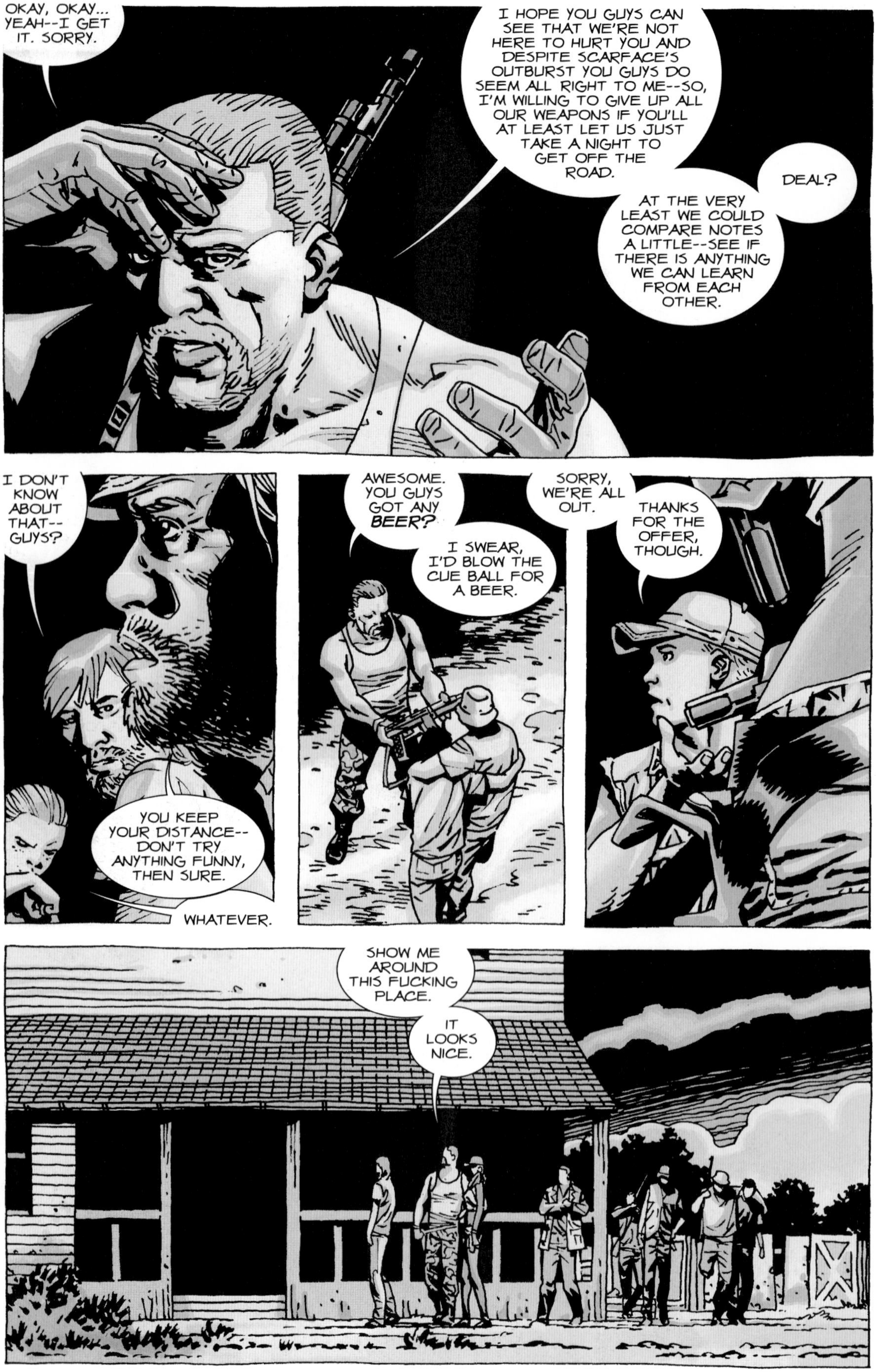
OKAY, OKAY... YEAH--I GET IT. SORRY.
I HOPE YOU GUYS CAN SEE THAT WE'RE NOT HERE TO HURT YOU AND DESPITE SCARFACE'S OUTBURST YOU GUYS DO SEEM ALL RIGHT TO ME--SO, I'M WILLING TO GIVE UP ALL OUR WEAPONS IF YOU'LL AT LEAST LET US JUST TAKE A NIGHT TO GET OFF THE ROAD.
AT THE VERY LEAST WE COULD COMPARE NOTES A LITTLE--SEE IF THERE IS ANYTHING WE CAN LEARN FROM EACH OTHER.
DEAL?
I DON'T KNOW ABOUT THAT-- GUYS?
YOU KEEP YOUR DISTANCE-- DON'T TRY ANYTHING FUNNY, THEN SURE.
WHATEVER.
AWESOME. YOU GUYS GOT ANY BEER?
I SWEAR, I'D BLOW THE CUE BALL FOR A BEER.
SORRY, WE'RE ALL OUT.
THANKS FOR THE OFFER, THOUGH.
SHOW ME AROUND THIS FUCKING PLACE.
IT LOOKS NICE.

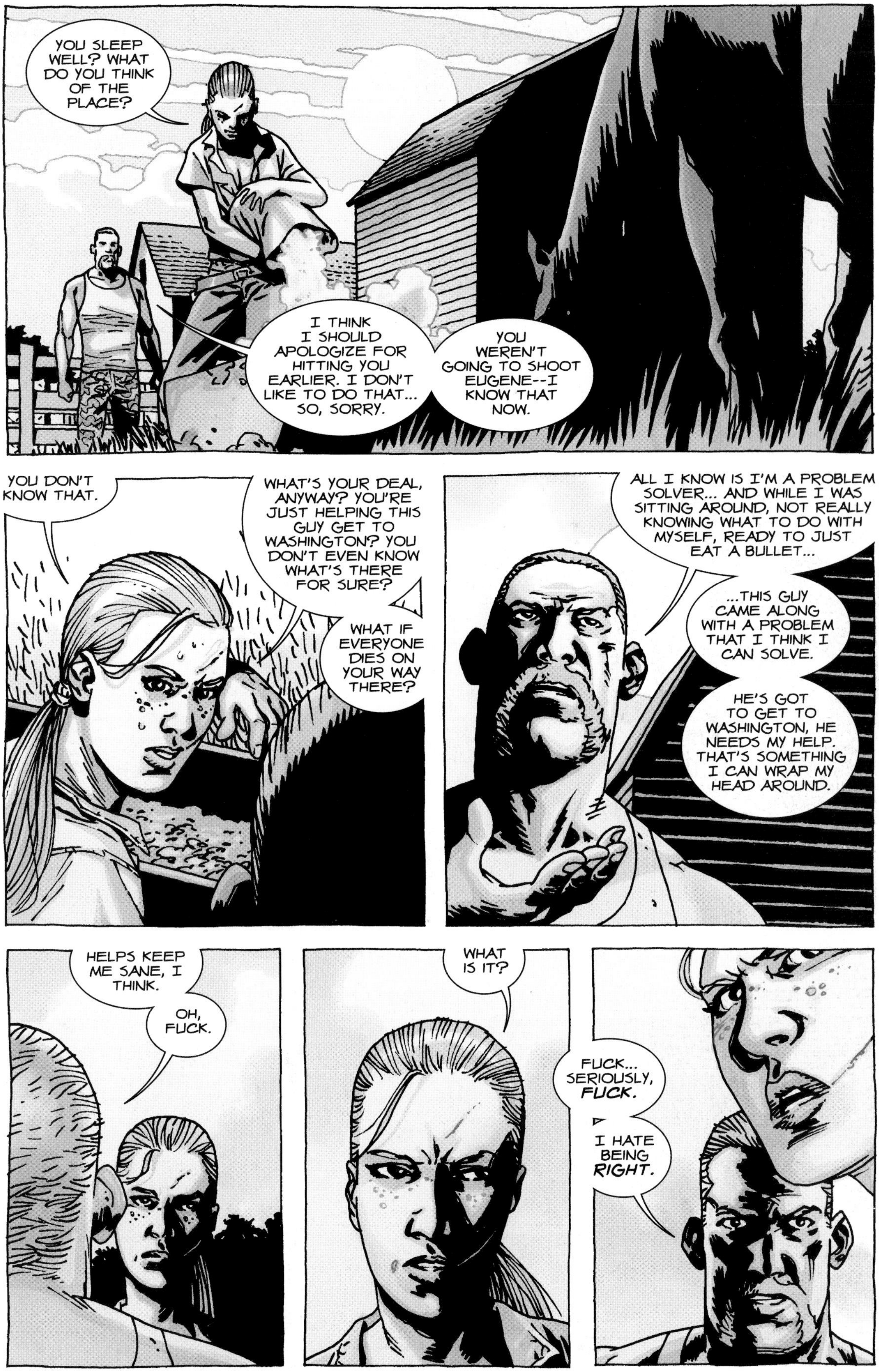
YOU SLEEP WELL? WHAT DO YOU THINK OF THE PLACE?
I THINK I SHOULD APOLOGIZE FOR HITTING YOU EARLIER. I DON'T LIKE TO DO THAT... SO, SORRY.
YOU WEREN'T GOING TO SHOOT EUGENE--I KNOW THAT NOW.
YOU DON'T KNOW THAT.
WHAT'S YOUR DEAL, ANYWAY? YOU'RE JUST HELPING THIS GUY GET TO WASHINGTON? YOU DON'T EVEN KNOW WHAT'S THERE FOR SURE?
WHAT IF EVERYONE DIES ON YOUR WAY THERE?
ALL I KNOW IS I'M A PROBLEM SOLVER... AND WHILE I WAS SITTING AROUND, NOT REALLY KNOWING WHAT TO DO WITH MYSELF, READY TO JUST EAT A BULLET...
...THIS GUY CAME ALONG WITH A PROBLEM THAT I THINK I CAN SOLVE.
HE'S GOT TO GET TO WASHINGTON, HE NEEDS MY HELP. THAT'S SOMETHING I CAN WRAP MY HEAD AROUND.
HELPS KEEP ME SANE, I THINK.
OH, FUCK.
WHAT IS IT?
FUCK... SERIOUSLY, *FUCK.*
I HATE BEING *RIGHT.*

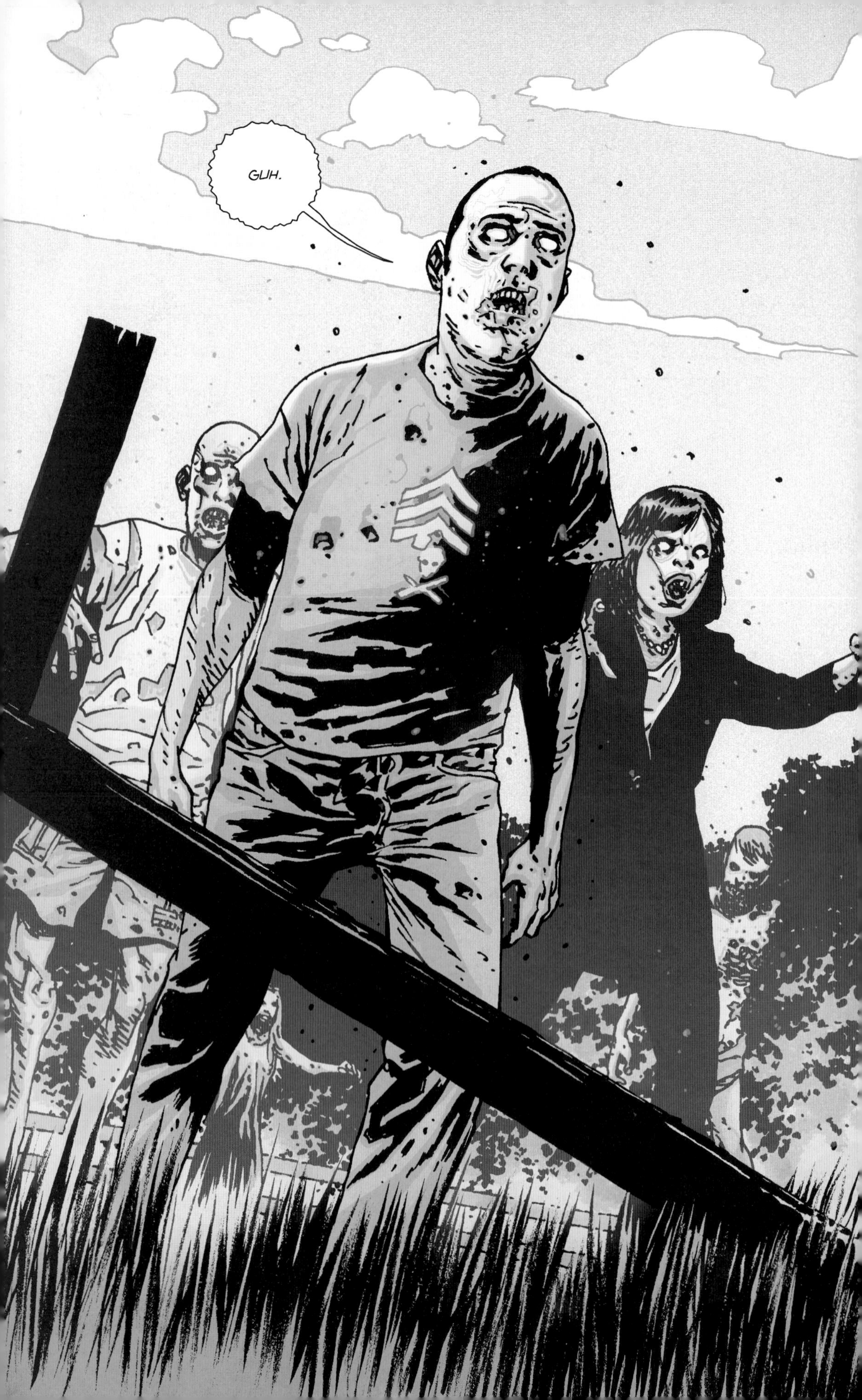
GUH.

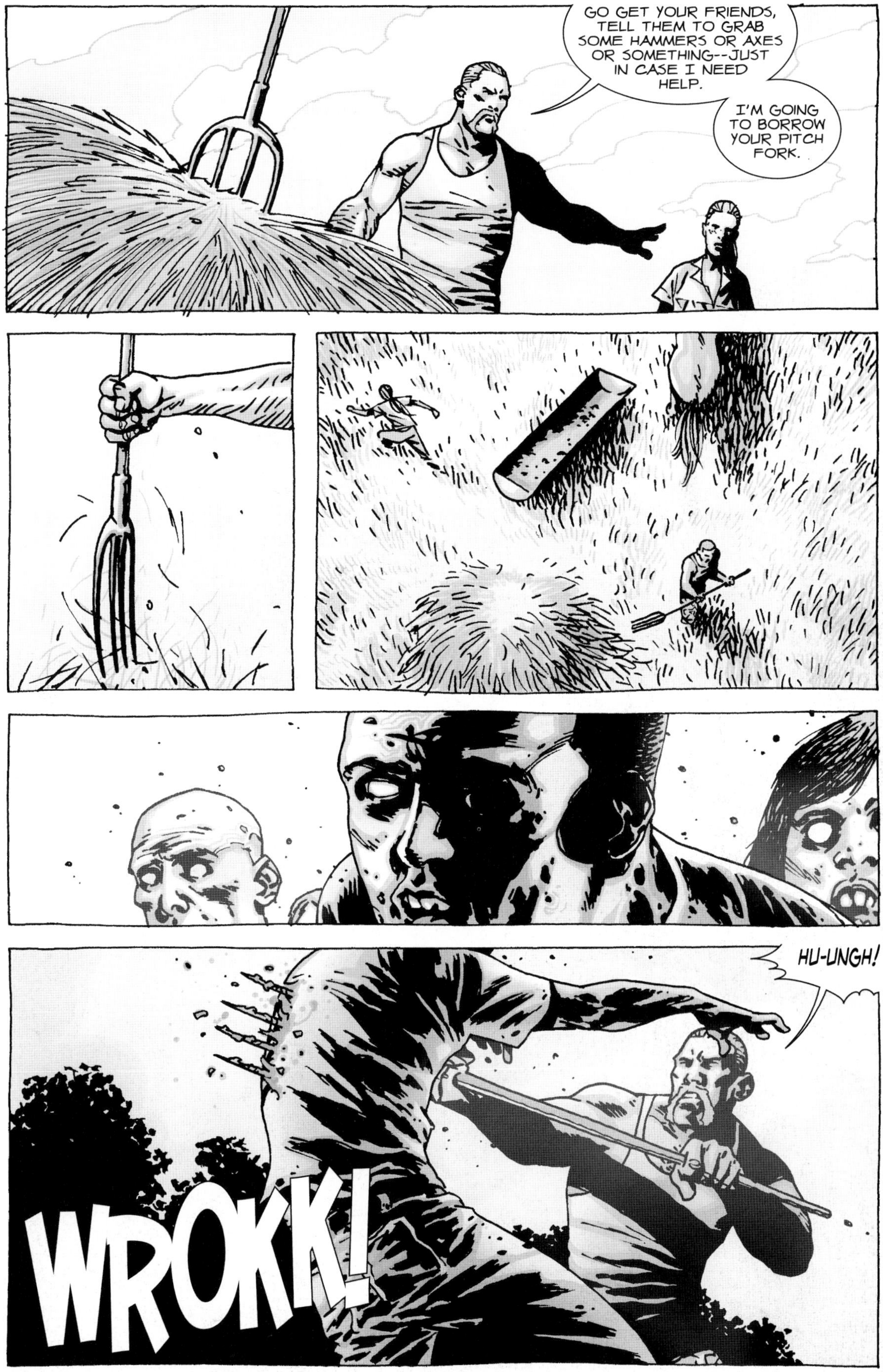
GO GET YOUR FRIENDS, TELL THEM TO GRAB SOME HAMMERS OR AXES OR SOMETHING--JUST IN CASE I NEED HELP.
I'M GOING TO BORROW YOUR PITCH FORK.
HU-UNGH!
WROKK!

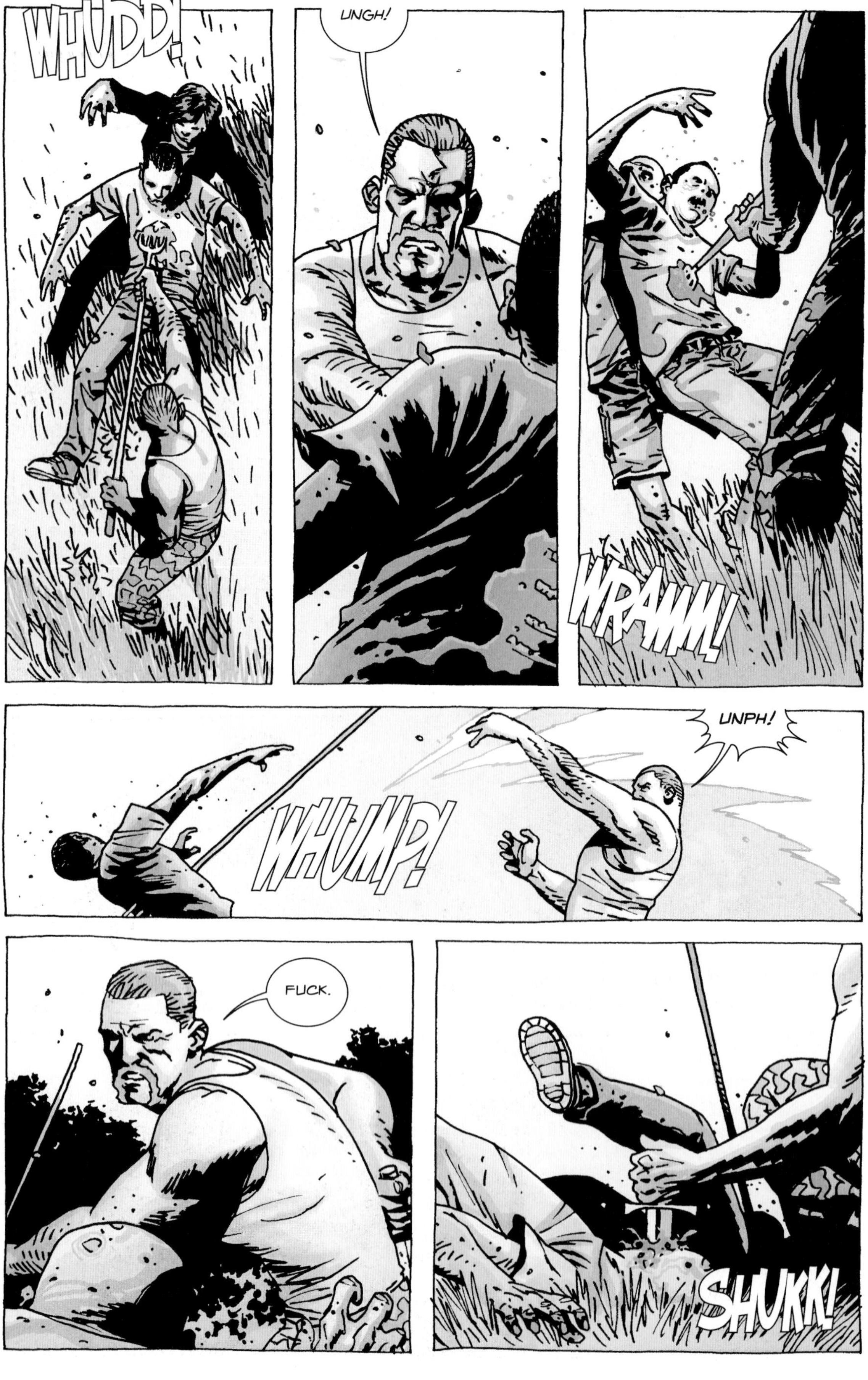
WHUDD!
UNGH!
WRAMM!
WHUMP!
UNPH!
FUCK.
SHUKK!

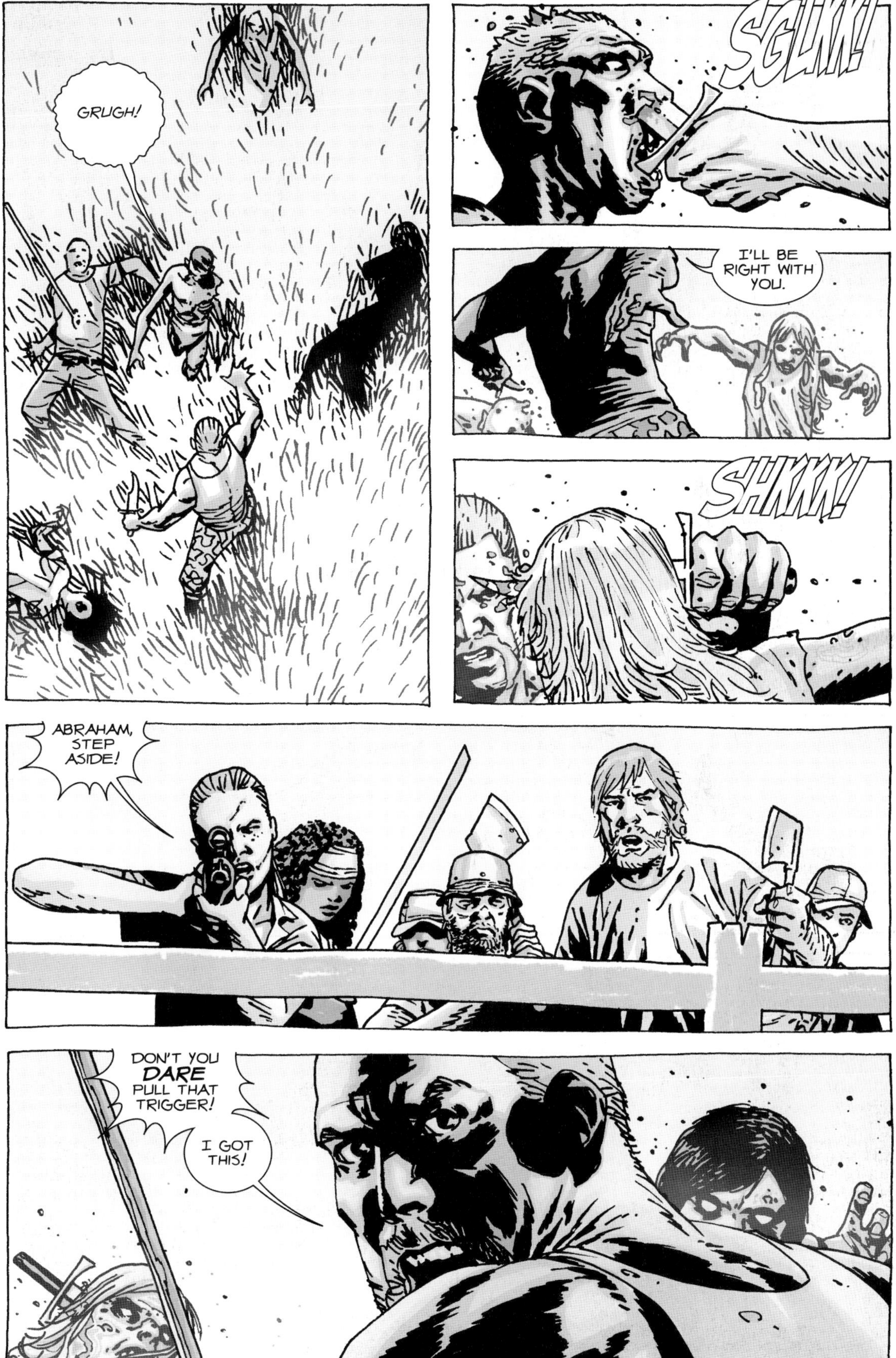
GRUGH!
SGLKK!
I'LL BE RIGHT WITH YOU.
SHKKK!
ABRAHAM, STEP ASIDE!
DON'T YOU DARE PULL THAT TRIGGER!
I GOT THIS!

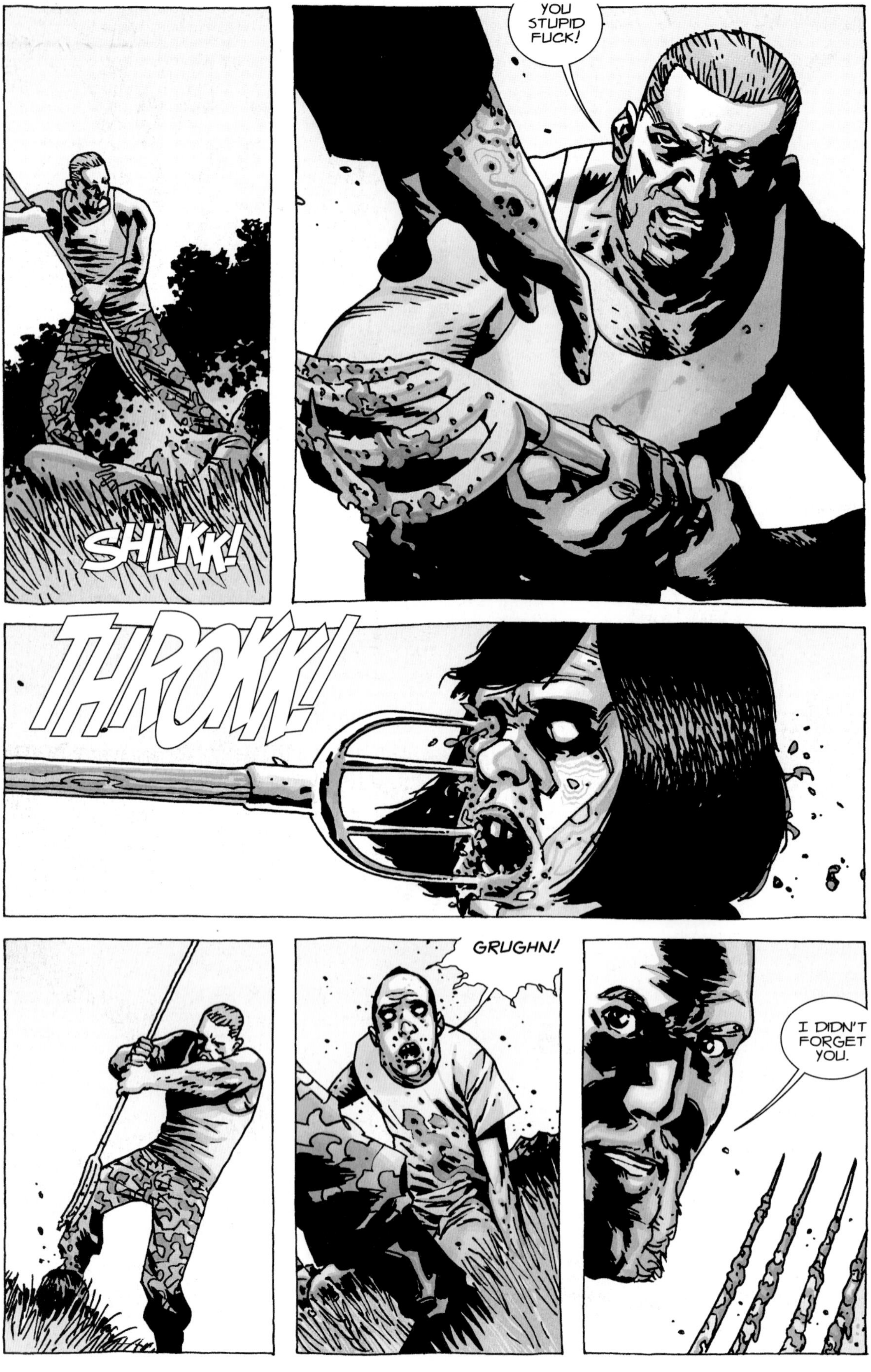
SHLKK!
YOU STUPID FUCK!
THROKK!
GRUGHN!
I DIDN'T FORGET YOU.

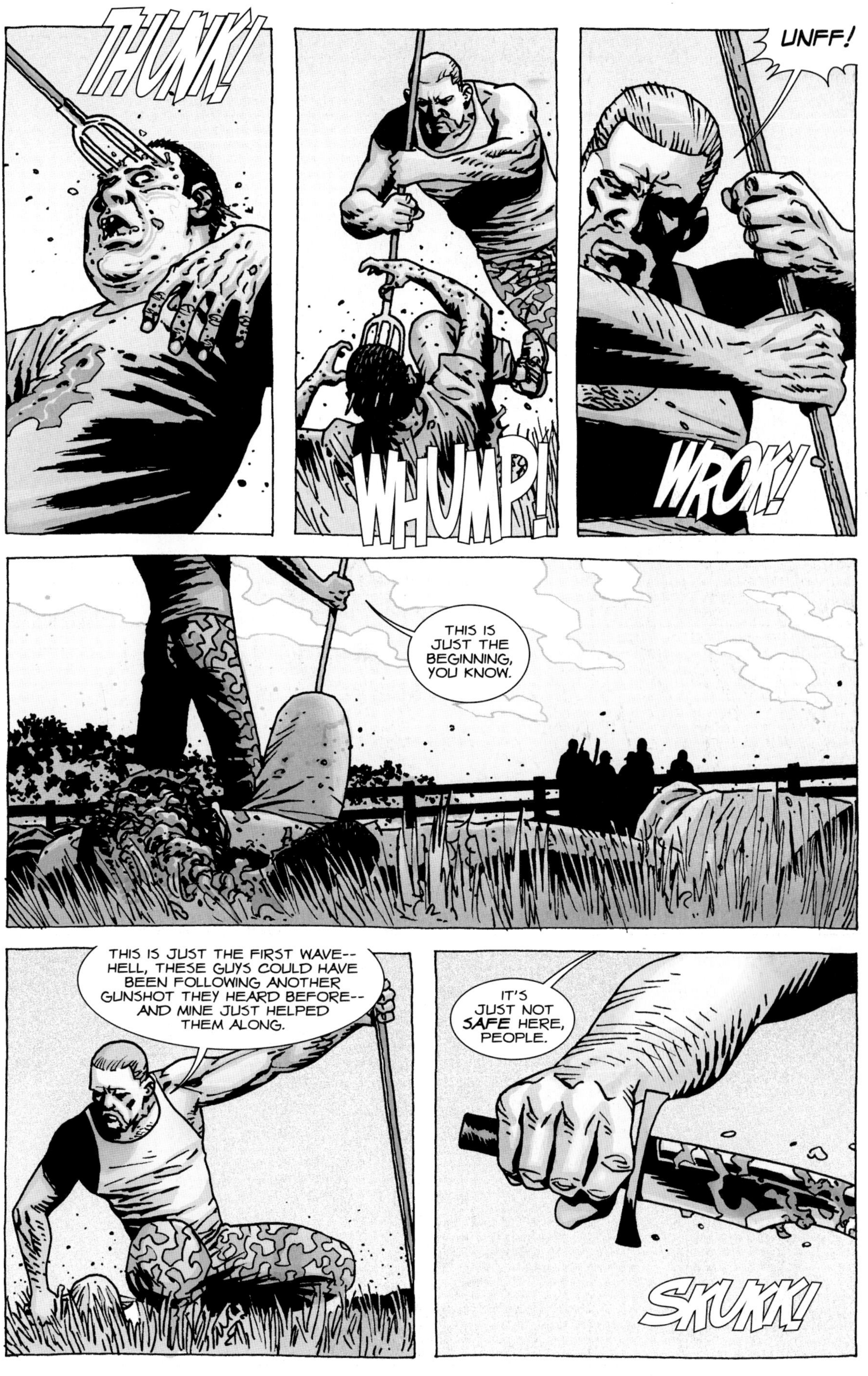
THUNK!
WHUMP!
UNFF!
WROK!
THIS IS JUST THE BEGINNING, YOU KNOW.
THIS IS JUST THE FIRST WAVE-- HELL, THESE GUYS COULD HAVE BEEN FOLLOWING ANOTHER GUNSHOT THEY HEARD BEFORE-- AND MINE JUST HELPED THEM ALONG.
IT'S JUST NOT SAFE HERE, PEOPLE.
SKUKK!

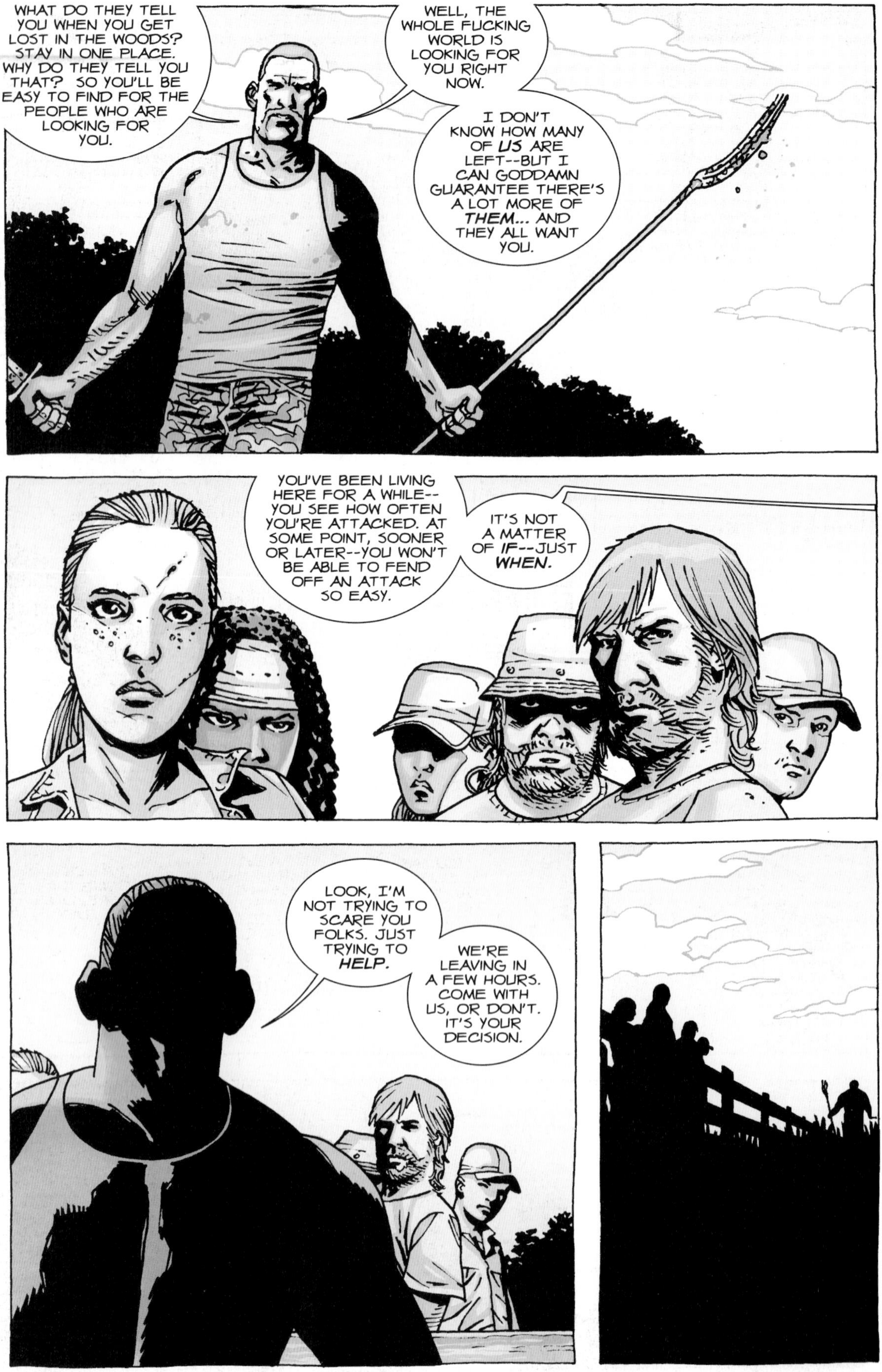
WHAT DO THEY TELL YOU WHEN YOU GET LOST IN THE WOODS? STAY IN ONE PLACE. WHY DO THEY TELL YOU THAT? SO YOU'LL BE EASY TO FIND FOR THE PEOPLE WHO ARE LOOKING FOR YOU.
WELL, THE WHOLE FUCKING WORLD IS LOOKING FOR YOU RIGHT NOW.
I DON'T KNOW HOW MANY OF *US* ARE LEFT--BUT I CAN GODDAMN GUARANTEE THERE'S A LOT MORE OF *THEM*... AND THEY ALL WANT YOU.
YOU'VE BEEN LIVING HERE FOR A WHILE--YOU SEE HOW OFTEN YOU'RE ATTACKED. AT SOME POINT, SOONER OR LATER--YOU WON'T BE ABLE TO FEND OFF AN ATTACK SO EASY.
IT'S NOT A MATTER OF *IF*--JUST *WHEN.*
LOOK, I'M NOT TRYING TO SCARE YOU FOLKS. JUST TRYING TO *HELP.*
WE'RE LEAVING IN A FEW HOURS. COME WITH US, OR DON'T. IT'S YOUR DECISION.

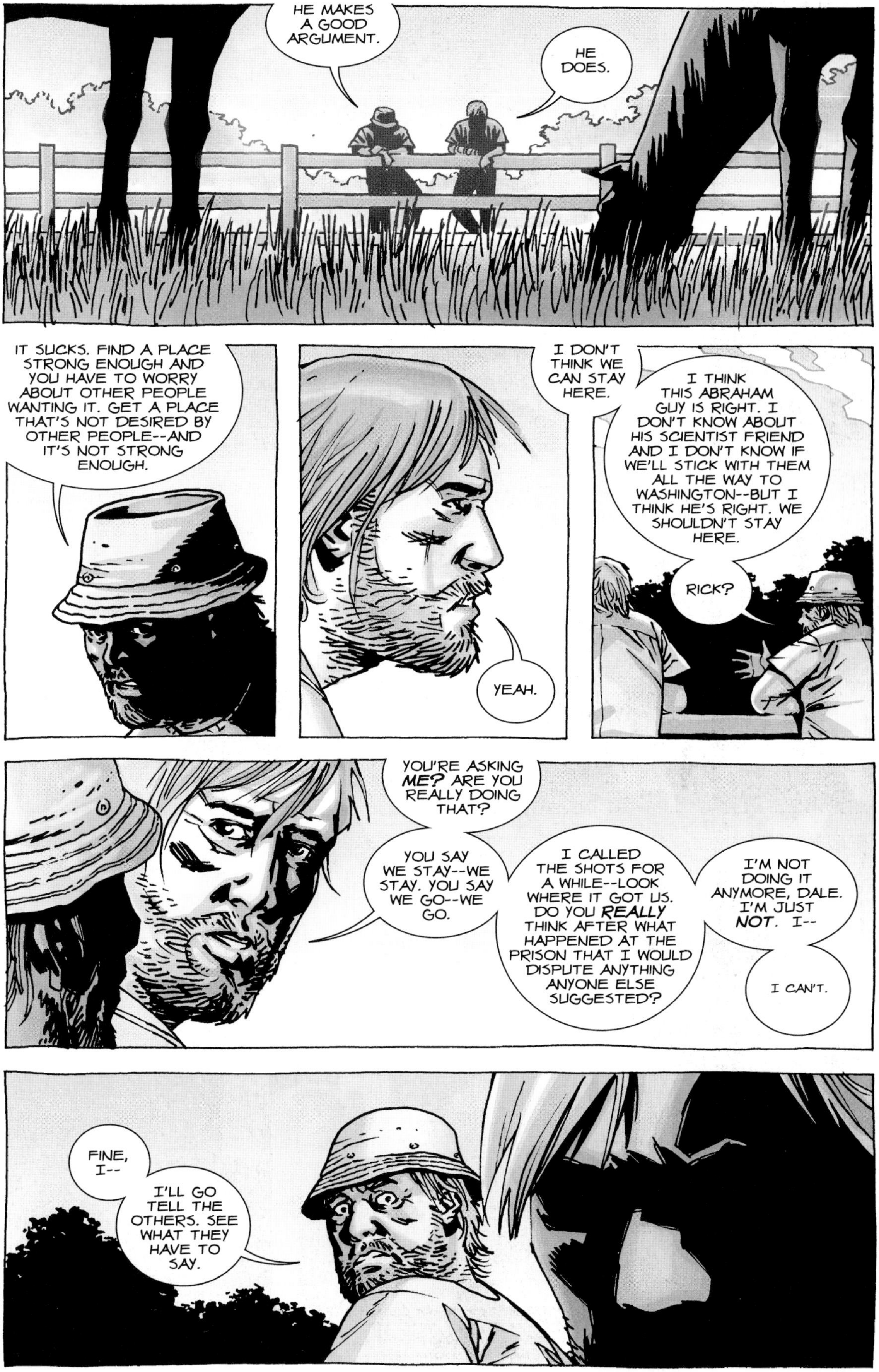
HE MAKES A GOOD ARGUMENT.
HE DOES.
IT SUCKS. FIND A PLACE STRONG ENOUGH AND YOU HAVE TO WORRY ABOUT OTHER PEOPLE WANTING IT. GET A PLACE THAT'S NOT DESIRED BY OTHER PEOPLE--AND IT'S NOT STRONG ENOUGH.
YEAH.
I DON'T THINK WE CAN STAY HERE.
I THINK THIS ABRAHAM GUY IS RIGHT. I DON'T KNOW ABOUT HIS SCIENTIST FRIEND AND I DON'T KNOW IF WE'LL STICK WITH THEM ALL THE WAY TO WASHINGTON--BUT I THINK HE'S RIGHT. WE SHOULDN'T STAY HERE.
RICK?
YOU'RE ASKING *ME?* ARE YOU REALLY DOING THAT?
YOU SAY WE STAY--WE STAY. YOU SAY WE GO--WE GO.
I CALLED THE SHOTS FOR A WHILE--LOOK WHERE IT GOT US. DO YOU *REALLY* THINK AFTER WHAT HAPPENED AT THE PRISON THAT I WOULD DISPUTE ANYTHING ANYONE ELSE SUGGESTED?
I'M NOT DOING IT ANYMORE, DALE. I'M JUST *NOT*. I--
I CAN'T.
FINE, I--
I'LL GO TELL THE OTHERS. SEE WHAT THEY HAVE TO SAY.

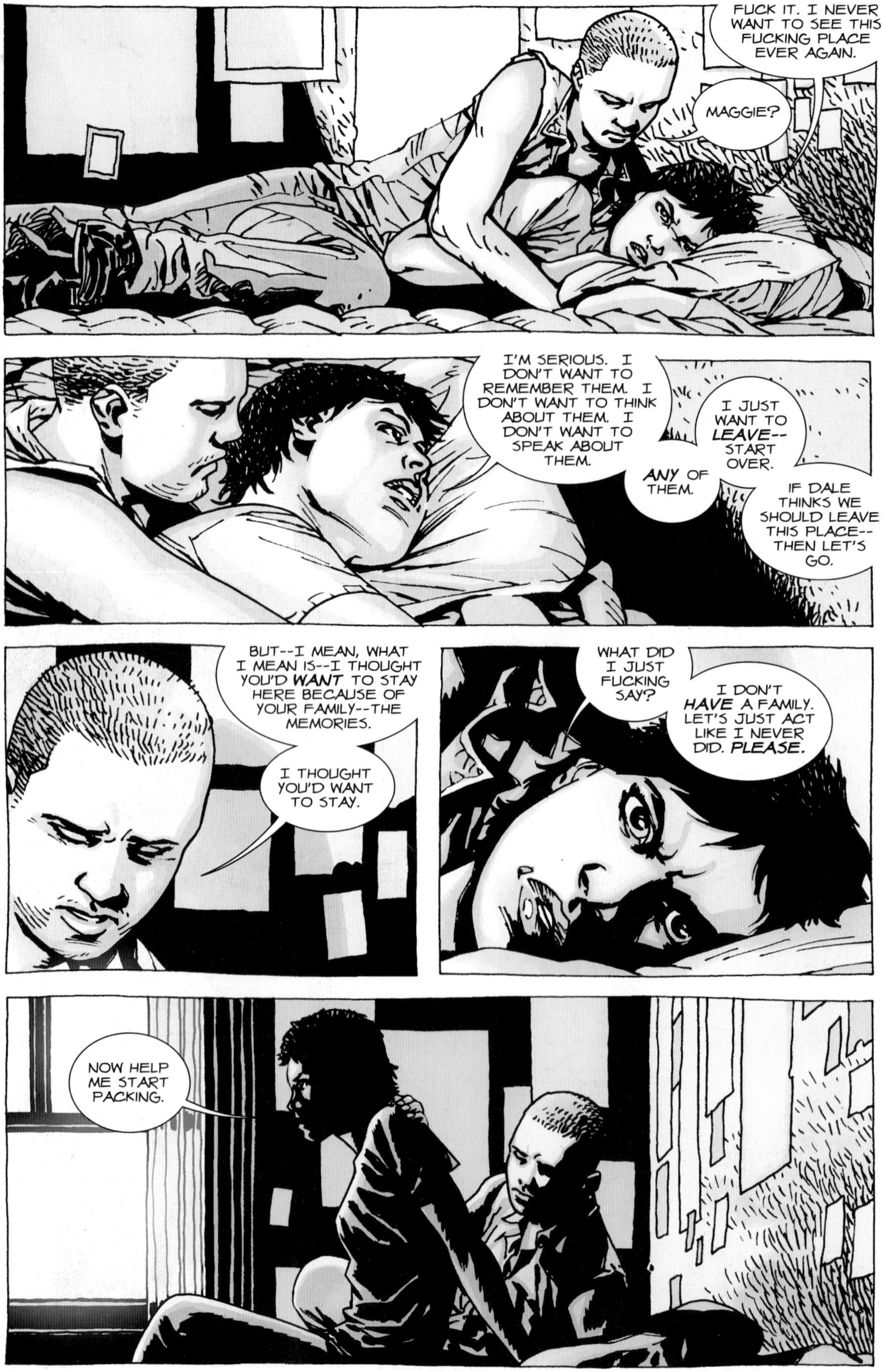
FUCK IT. I NEVER WANT TO SEE THIS FUCKING PLACE EVER AGAIN.
MAGGIE?
I'M SERIOUS. I DON'T WANT TO REMEMBER THEM. I DON'T WANT TO THINK ABOUT THEM. I DON'T WANT TO SPEAK ABOUT THEM.
ANY OF THEM.
I JUST WANT TO LEAVE--START OVER.
IF DALE THINKS WE SHOULD LEAVE THIS PLACE--THEN LET'S GO.
BUT--I MEAN, WHAT I MEAN IS--I THOUGHT YOU'D WANT TO STAY HERE BECAUSE OF YOUR FAMILY--THE MEMORIES.
I THOUGHT YOU'D WANT TO STAY.
WHAT DID I JUST FUCKING SAY?
I DON'T HAVE A FAMILY. LET'S JUST ACT LIKE I NEVER DID. PLEASE.
NOW HELP ME START PACKING.

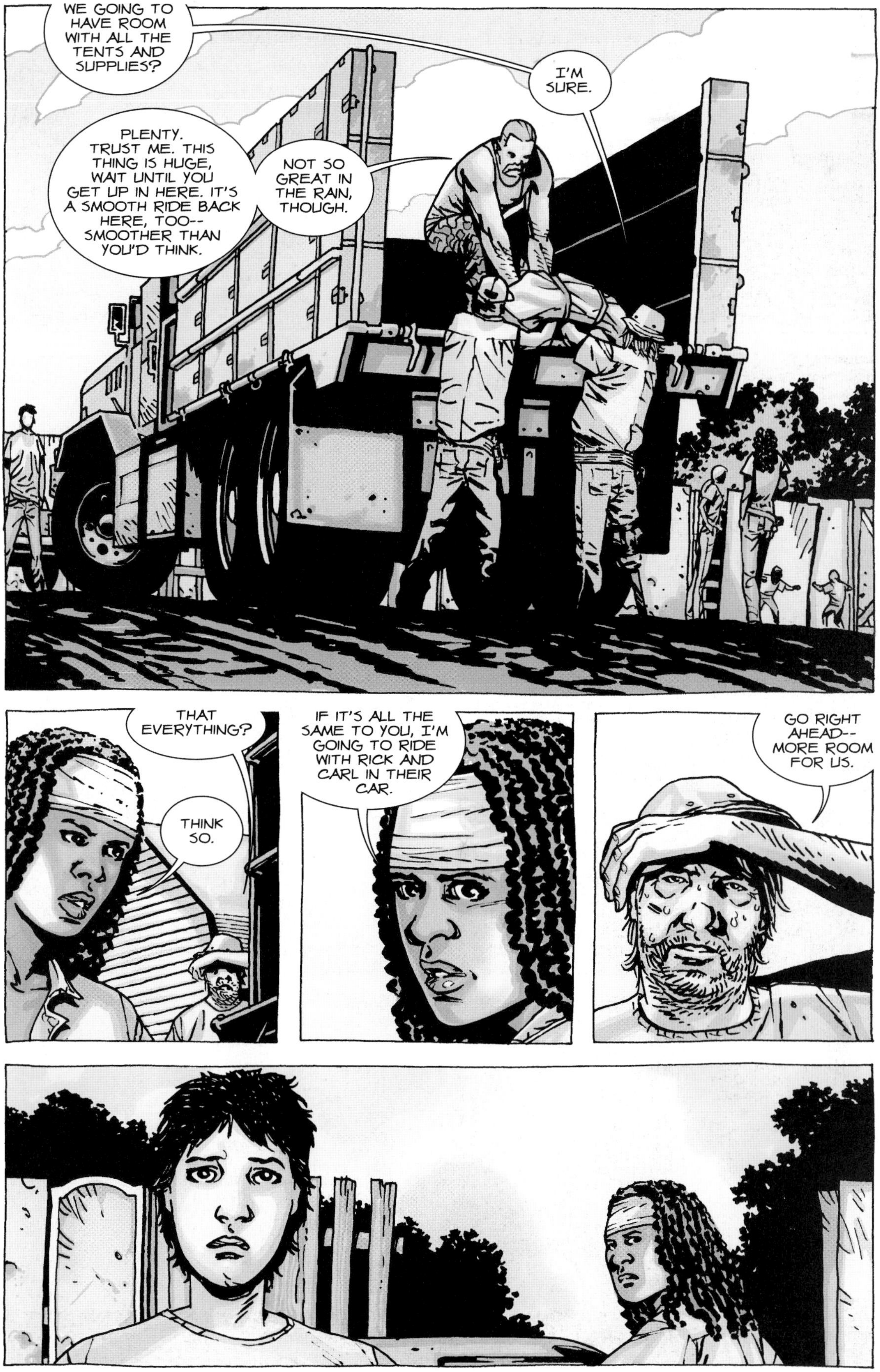

WE GOING TO HAVE ROOM WITH ALL THE TENTS AND SUPPLIES?
I'M SURE.
PLENTY. TRUST ME. THIS THING IS HUGE, WAIT UNTIL YOU GET UP IN HERE. IT'S A SMOOTH RIDE BACK HERE, TOO-- SMOOTHER THAN YOU'D THINK.
NOT SO GREAT IN THE RAIN, THOUGH.
THAT EVERYTHING?
THINK SO.
IF IT'S ALL THE SAME TO YOU, I'M GOING TO RIDE WITH RICK AND CARL IN THEIR CAR.
GO RIGHT AHEAD-- MORE ROOM FOR US.

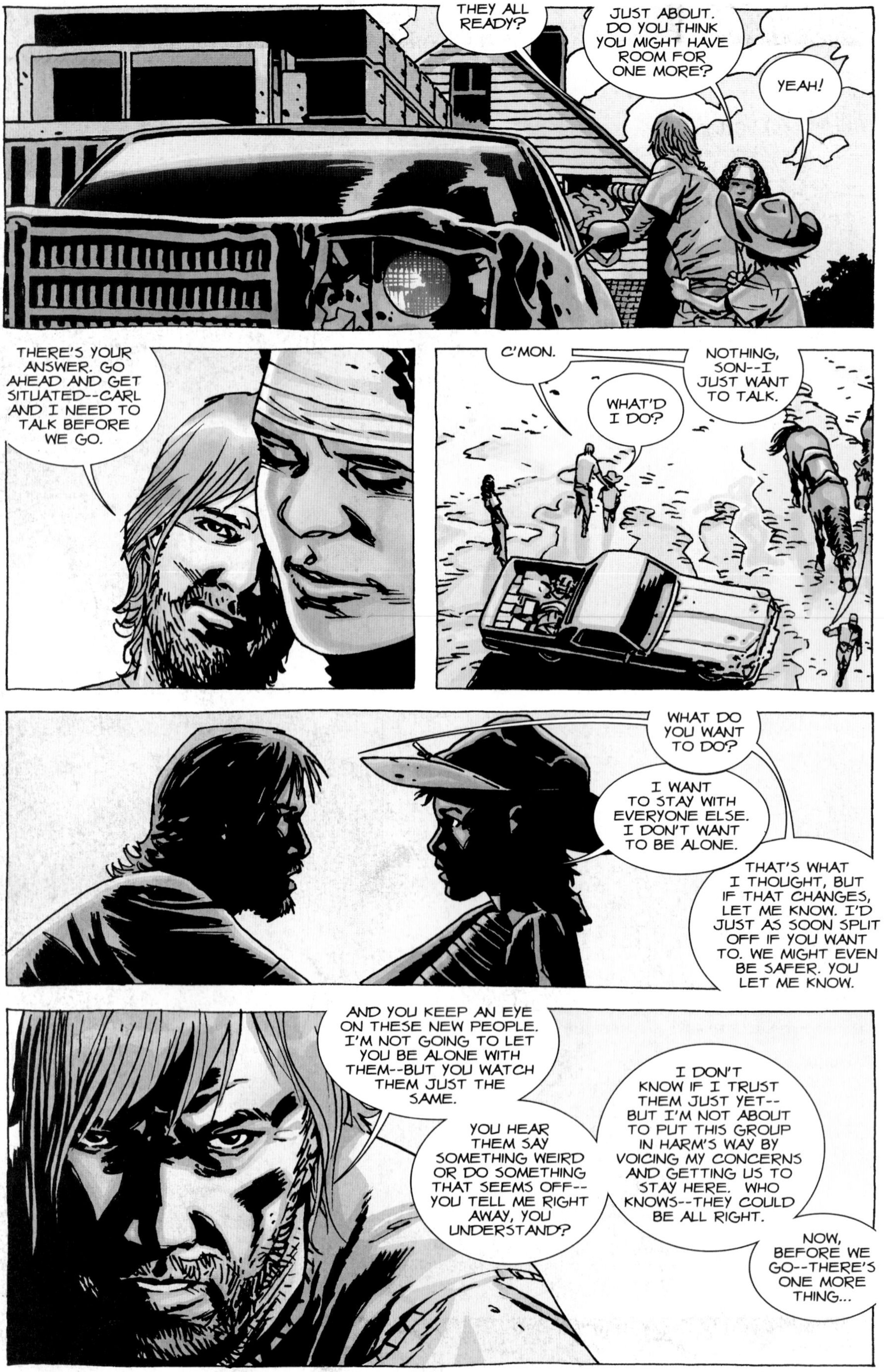
THEY ALL READY?
JUST ABOUT. DO YOU THINK YOU MIGHT HAVE ROOM FOR ONE MORE?
YEAH!
THERE'S YOUR ANSWER. GO AHEAD AND GET SITUATED--CARL AND I NEED TO TALK BEFORE WE GO.
C'MON.
WHAT'D I DO?
NOTHING, SON--I JUST WANT TO TALK.
WHAT DO YOU WANT TO DO?
I WANT TO STAY WITH EVERYONE ELSE. I DON'T WANT TO BE ALONE.
THAT'S WHAT I THOUGHT, BUT IF THAT CHANGES, LET ME KNOW. I'D JUST AS SOON SPLIT OFF IF YOU WANT TO. WE MIGHT EVEN BE SAFER. YOU LET ME KNOW.
AND YOU KEEP AN EYE ON THESE NEW PEOPLE. I'M NOT GOING TO LET YOU BE ALONE WITH THEM--BUT YOU WATCH THEM JUST THE SAME.
YOU HEAR THEM SAY SOMETHING WEIRD OR DO SOMETHING THAT SEEMS OFF--YOU TELL ME RIGHT AWAY, YOU UNDERSTAND?
I DON'T KNOW IF I TRUST THEM JUST YET--BUT I'M NOT ABOUT TO PUT THIS GROUP IN HARM'S WAY BY VOICING MY CONCERNS AND GETTING US TO STAY HERE. WHO KNOWS--THEY COULD BE ALL RIGHT.
NOW, BEFORE WE GO--THERE'S ONE MORE THING...

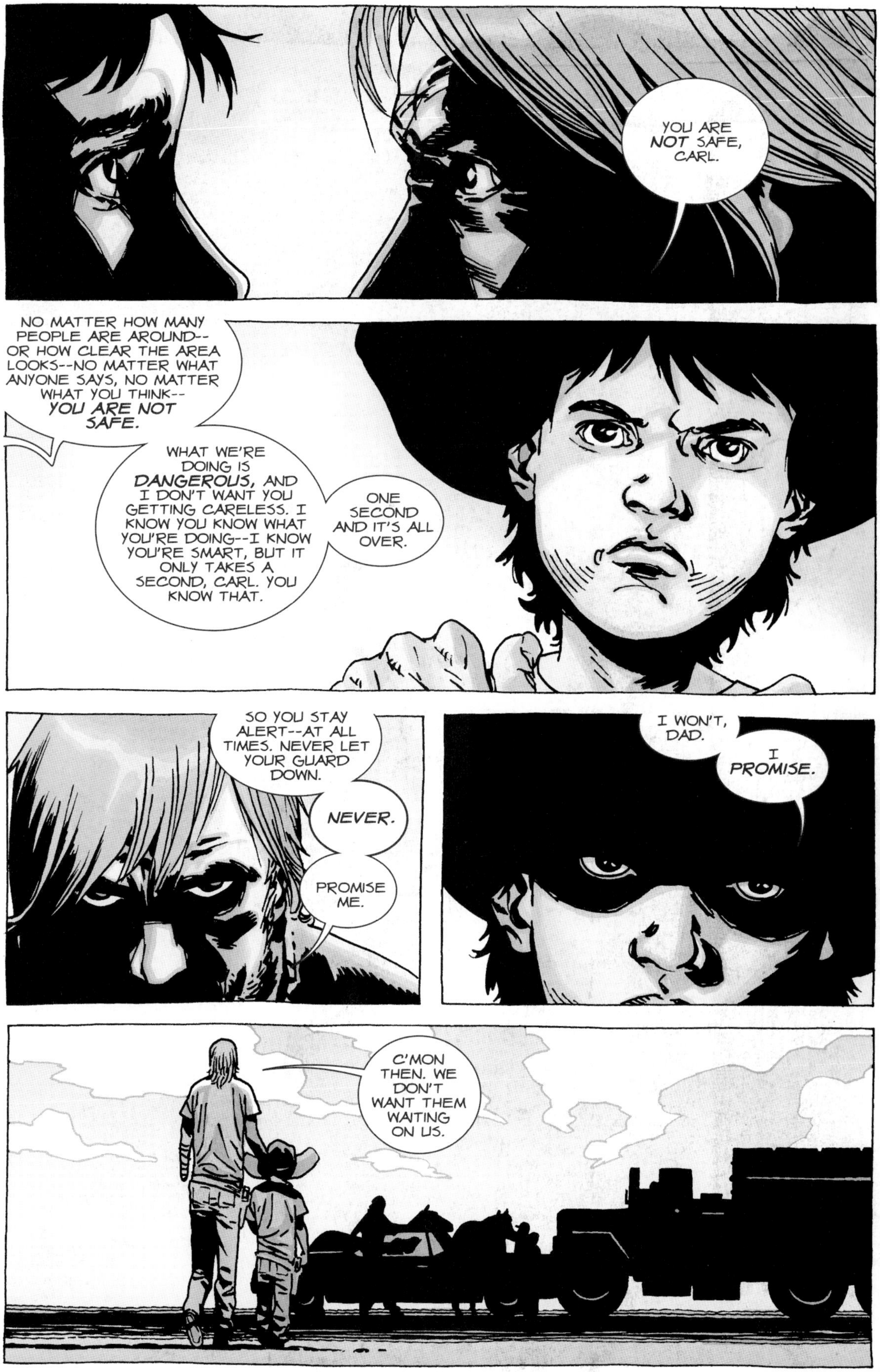
YOU ARE NOT SAFE, CARL.
NO MATTER HOW MANY PEOPLE ARE AROUND-- OR HOW CLEAR THE AREA LOOKS--NO MATTER WHAT ANYONE SAYS, NO MATTER WHAT YOU THINK-- YOU ARE NOT SAFE.
WHAT WE'RE DOING IS DANGEROUS, AND I DON'T WANT YOU GETTING CARELESS. I KNOW YOU KNOW WHAT YOU'RE DOING--I KNOW YOU'RE SMART, BUT IT ONLY TAKES A SECOND, CARL. YOU KNOW THAT.
ONE SECOND AND IT'S ALL OVER.
SO YOU STAY ALERT--AT ALL TIMES. NEVER LET YOUR GUARD DOWN.
NEVER.
PROMISE ME.
I WON'T, DAD.
I PROMISE.
C'MON THEN. WE DON'T WANT THEM WAITING ON US.

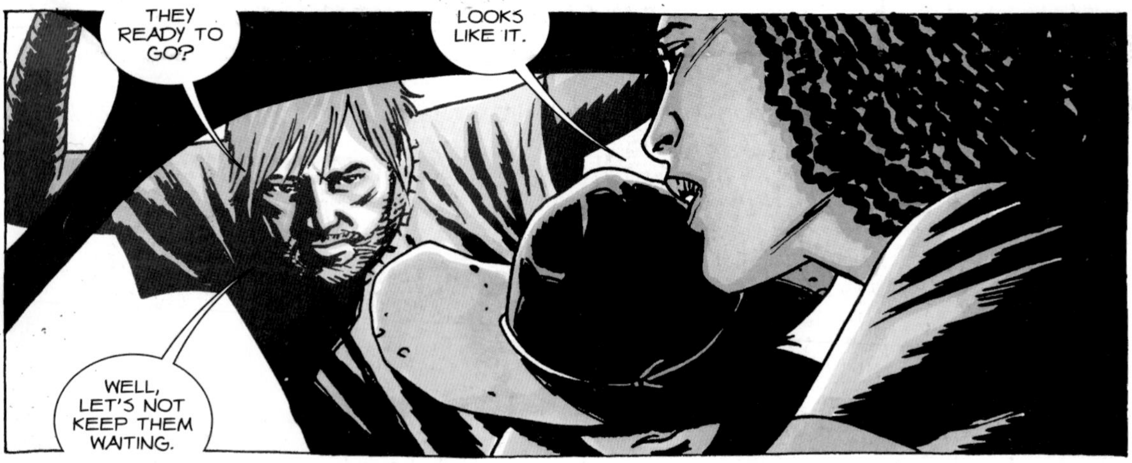
THEY READY TO GO?
LOOKS LIKE IT.
WELL, LET'S NOT KEEP THEM WAITING.

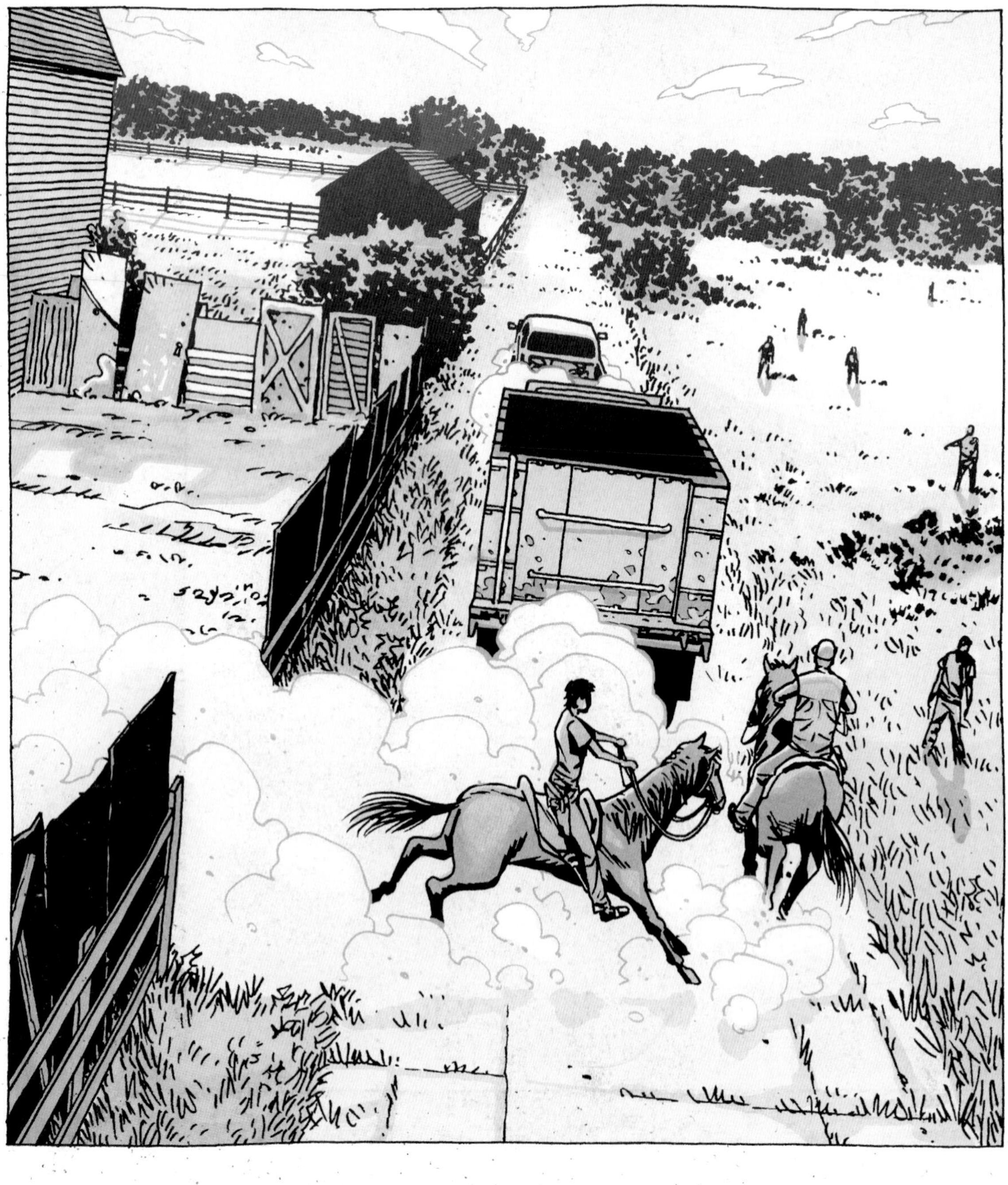